THE DUST OF WONDERLAND

OTHER BOOKS BY LEE THOMAS

Stained

Parish Damned

Damage

The Dust of
WONDERLAND

LEE THOMAS

NEW YORK

Manufactured in the United States of America.

Published by Alyson Books,
245 W. 17th St., New York, New York 10115.
Distribution in the United Kingdom by Turnaround Publisher Services Ltd.,
Unit 3, Olympia Trading Estate, Coburg Road, Wood Green,
London N22 6TZ England.

First edition: August 2007

07 08 09 00 01 a 10 9 8 7 6 5 4 3 2 1

ISBN 1-59350-011-4
ISBN-13 978-1-59350-011-5

Cataloging-in-Publication Data for this book is available
from the Library of Congress.

This book is dedicated to
Donald L. Ferguson for the beginning,
and John C. Perry for the rest.

The face of a lover is an unknown, precisely because it is invested with so much of oneself. It is a mystery, containing, like all mysteries, the possibility of torment.

—JAMES BALDWIN

PROLOGUE:
REMEMBER TOMORROW

ell me a story.

He threw his few belongings into the paper grocery sack. His hands shook, and his ragged breath grated in his ears. A long lock of hair fell into his eyes, and he pushed it away. He shoved two tattered shirts into the bag and then slowed himself. Though hurried, he understood the importance of delicacy and took care not to rip the makeshift luggage. If the sack tore he would have only the clothes on his back.

Upon brief consideration, he realized this prospect worried him little. To be away, filthy but away, would suffice.

Sweat dripped into his eye. The paper grocery sack could hold nothing more. He moved quickly to the rusted basin in his bathroom, splashed his face, and dried it with the frayed towel on the nail. A reflex inspection of himself in the clouded mirror above the sink shocked him. His face seemed to have withered; his skin had turned the color of dust; deep lines traced the contours of his eyes. Only the image was older, he thought. Something was wrong with his mirror. So much damage could not have occurred in the handful of hours since he'd last seen his reflection.

Leaving the bathroom, he made a last inspection of the tiny apartment. Anything that he had forgotten would be left behind. It was time to escape this place. Time to leave the Quarter. Time to get the fuck out of this city before some other nightmare befell him.

His fingers sought out the charm at his neck. He grasped it, then released it.

He left the lights burning in the room as he stepped onto the ratty hall carpet. The dimly lit corridor reeked of mold and urine. Musky odors, filthy odors, all remained trapped within an eternal slick of moisture. The paint on the walls bubbled with the dampness, which grew like a parasite beneath the ugly yellow pigment. In the apartment at the end of the hall, a man coughed in spasms.

Heavy hot air wrapped around him as he stepped onto the apartment stoop. Well past midnight, the day's heat remained a prisoner. Fog had come up over the river. The air, still holding the spice from the many restaurants of the Quarter, was motionless. The streets in this part of the city were silenced by the advanced hour. Far away, crowds would still wander the brightly lit walks of Bourbon Street, but this part of the Quarter rested in somber darkness. His heart tripping, he estimated the direction of the freeway and set off.

Esplanade Street lay two blocks ahead of him. The river flowed like a dark wound on his right. He hurried on.

As always, the low homes and shops of the Vieux Carré looked like a movie set—the buildings were so unreal and spectral in appearance—but on this night in particular they wore a mask of illusion. The stucco exterior of a Creole cottage beside his own apartment moved beneath the dancing glow of two gas lamps like the skin of Leviathan. The fog that whispered over the rushing water might have been pumped from a machine on a Hollywood sound stage. Nothing looked real here. Maybe nothing was.

Across the street, two young men smoked cigarettes.

Vassals.

His already moist hands ran with sweat. His fingernails dug into the palm of his right hand and cut small tears in the bag he held in his left. They *had* come for him. And though he'd played this possibility over in his mind a hundred times, he felt no more prepared seeing them. Like the surroundings, they seemed unreal; they posed like arrogant characters from a film, possessing only attitude and beauty without any true substance.

Only two, he thought.

The Vassals stood slouched like toughs on the far corner, their young faces covered by vapid beauty. Leather jackets and cuffed Levi's defined their costumes. Their thin chests lay bare beneath the heavy black hide. One combed his hair like Kookie Burns. The other played with the knife in his hand as if it were a toy. The blade clicked open, then closed. Again and again it appeared. *Click, click. Click, click.* The sound broke the silence like a metronome. Neither of them even seemed to notice him, so occupied they were with their performance. But he recognized them from The Parlor. They were *his.*

The one boy with the comb casually thumped his friend's chest with the back of his hand. The Vassal with the knife looked up, smiled. His blade clicked open.

He backed away from the boys. Distantly, he recognized physical threat, but he doubted they would kill him. If anything, the weapon was only a prop meant to assure his cooperation as they escorted him through the long blocks that separated them from their master. *Click, click.*

The sound filled his ears as he turned to run. The fragile material of the bag, now damp with sweat, parted. The contents of his life trailed behind him and spilled onto the sidewalk. In the morning they would be gathered up by a curious traveler; a homeless spirit might consider himself blessed to stumble across the discarded garments. Perhaps his clothing would simply be tossed in the garbage with the other refuse that lined the street. He hesitated only a moment to lament his loss.

Again, he ran. For blocks, his feet slapped the sidewalk. The sound of the blade remained in his head, keeping time with his heart. After six blocks, the sound of the knife left his head and moved in front of him. *Click, click. Click, click.* The sound came from somewhere ahead. A perfect image of the knife filled his head. It snapped open with impossible volume, the blade glinting in the dim light cast from one of the dull street lamps. *Click, click.* He stopped running and nearly tripped in his haste. He threw his arms back for balance. The sound came again, more loudly. It grew. Panic sent cold fingers up his spine. He scanned the street for sanctuary, but the quaint façades offered no refuge. Now dark and lifeless, the buildings would be locked and the tenants sleeping. *Click, click.* The sound was too loud. No spring-loaded blade could boast such volume. And when the mule drawing its white carriage and black-clad driver broke across the intersection, he thought the sound would burst his heart.

Desperation grew hard edged in his belly. With it came a certainty: He'd never make it to the freeway. They would catch him. He needed to head in a different direction, needed to be among people.

Ten minutes later he ran onto Rue Bourbon. The lights drew him; the vast numbers of people comforted him. Even at this time of the morning, witnesses abounded on the famous street. His pursuers had not appeared, but he knew they would not relinquish him so easily.

A pack of boys jostled onto the sidewalk. He leapt back. But these faces were not familiar. College students. Not *his*. He hurried into the establishment.

Purple and blue lights bruised the walls. A single neon tube at the back spelled *N'awlins*. Drunks lined the bar, their postures a measure of the alcohol they had consumed. Giant Mardi Gras masks reflected in the mirror over the bar. Smoke rolled in the ceiling fans. He checked his pockets for money as he ordered a pop from the bartender. Counting through the wad of bills and change, totaling little more than fifteen dollars, he considered himself fortunate. He dropped some coins on the counter and moved to the far side of the bar, hiding himself behind a drunken couple who giggled and wrestled lightly on their stools.

The man wore a brightly colored Hawaiian print shirt with white shorts and brown deck shoes with chocolate-colored socks. The sweat on the crown of his head glistened as if his scalp were frosted with Vaseline. The woman, a pretty young blonde with dreamy eyes and bright red lips, kissed her date's ear. Her arm moved rhythmically under the bar. The man's cock glowed lightly under the blue illumination as the woman masturbated his semi-hard sex.

The boy stepped back and leaned on the bar so that his voyeurism would be less obvious, though he suspected the couple would neither notice nor care in their advanced state of dislocation. The row of French doors along the street stood open. People walked or stumbled by loudly, quietly, indifferent to what lay beyond. Others were curious about the interior of the establishment, and they stopped to gaze in as if it were in some way different from the dozens of other bars they had seen while strolling along Bourbon Street. No malevolent servants appeared in the opening.

But they would come, he thought. Keeping his eyes on the doorway, he sipped his pop out of reflex, not thirst. The doorway held the promise of a magician's booth from which something horrible might burst forth. Any moment he might see the Vassals.

He had regained his breath and had almost found himself calming. Plans formed in his head. All he needed to do was wait it out until he felt certain they'd given up for the night. He could take the streetcar out of the Quarter in the morning and then hitch a ride north. He had devised the plan in seconds. It seemed simple.

Before him the man turned his face into the dazed woman's body and worked his mouth over one of the nipples straining against the white fabric of her blouse.

Hitch a ride north, he told himself. *Anywhere but here.* He needed to be away from the filth and the heat and the moisture that insinuated themselves into every pore and crease of his body like some unwanted lover's caress.

He checked the door, looked through the windows flanking them, and his heart tripped. They had arrived. Vassals.

Three of the beautiful boys walked along the sidewalk. His two pursuers had gained an accomplice, but this was not what disturbed him most. No. What stabbed him with unease was the fact that they'd known he was here. There was no casual glance through the opening to scope out the scene; the three took the turn into the bar and began walking quickly to the back, where he stood in anxious resolution.

Are you really surprised he found you?

The three walked to his back. One dropped a hand on his shoulder, but he did not turn. They surrounded him. He was trapped. Why panic now? And though he did not feel nearly this cool, he refused to give the Vassals any further pleasure by crying or pleading with them for his release.

"Come on, Princess," one of the boys said. "He wants to see you."

He looked back at the open doorway. Again he thought of a magician's booth, and he wondered what waited beyond. Though not present, the magician's powers surrounded him, emanating like heat from the boys at his back. Beyond the door of the bar was *his* world. *Just step right in, and he'll make you disappear.* His escorts pushed forward. Their heat pulsed through his shirt and burned his back. The mad magician's lovely assistants were taking him to that box, that chamber from which he might not return.

But he had no choice. The blade clicked behind him, nearly lost in the sound of the music from the jukebox. He stood and shoved his way through the Vassals, bumping the lascivious drunks before him. Quickly, the Vassals fell in around him as they left the bar, surrounding him as the four stepped into the wet heat of the early morning and walked away from reality into the void of the magician's booth.

⚜

They led him to the wrought-iron gate and unlocked it swiftly. They pushed him savagely into the corridor that ran along the outside of the small building where guests were entertained. Tonight, however, no one reveled at The Parlor. No loud voices, no singing. The piano was silent. A terrible odor like the scent of rotting meat filled the alley.

Further shoves ran him toward the courtyard. He spun on his captors, and his stare froze them. "I know the way," he growled. Running a palm through his hair, a nervous reaction, he turned and walked into the courtyard. As always it startled him. No matter how many times he entered the square between the monstrous house and The Parlor, it never failed to take his breath away. Blossoms smiled from the balconies and from rectangular plots on the ground. Day lilies, roses, and hibiscus joined more exotic plants in a colorful display. The reek of the alley gave way to the sweet perfume of rose, sweet olive, and jasmine. A large fountain occupied the center of the flagstone patio. It sprayed the night with more moisture as droplets of water danced in the colored rays of light shooting from the fixtures at the fountain's base. The water shimmered like diamonds or crystals in that light. Ivy blanketed the brick walls to his left and right, and before him, the house stood like an impassable mountain. So beautiful he had always found this place, but he experienced no pleasure at seeing it again. Now it looked funereal. The perfume, sweet and cloying, reminded him of a freshly fed crypt.

"Thank you for coming," the familiar voice called. "I have something special for you this evening."

Seeking the source of the voice, he caught the dark shape on the balcony above him. The fountain light could not reach so high; the master of this place stood beyond its touch. He waited above, an image cast in shadow against a pale screen. In such a setting, the man's movements took on the grandiosity of theater.

His feelings for this man had run from awe to love, from fear to hatred, in a handful of months. Yet despite his varied emotions, the strongest feeling he had toward this man was one of pity.

Power and position had failed him, leaving him unbearably desolate. One unattainable possession had teased the man's mind to insanity, making him at times tragically despondent and at other times wholly fearsome.

"Come on up," he called. The man threw one shadowed arm high in the air. "You'll have a better view."

To his surprise, there was no threat in the tone. The command sounded like a sincere invitation to some unimaginable entertainment.

Over his shoulder, the three Vassals moved forward. "I know the way," he repeated, but his legs struggled against moving him toward the home.

It had been over a week since his departure. Life had regained some of its normalcy. He would have begun a new job in the morning, would have found a new apartment that didn't reek of moist filth. Then, they had come for him, following him through the streets, watching him like spies. Now he was back, and he stepped into the foyer of the grand mansion.

On a couch in the living room one of the Vassals writhed and moaned, pleasuring himself in some unseen way. He watched the ecstatic act briefly and then took to the stairs. He reached the landing, made a right, and followed the hall toward an ornate door. *His* bedroom.

The door opened with a light squeak as it always had. From here, he saw the man's back, a dark form against a glowing backdrop of light, which rose from the courtyard below. His host had turned on the floodlights. He took the first steps toward the French doors and the balcony beyond. He was already tired of the theatrics. Whatever he was meant to see, he hoped The Magician would perform his feat quickly. Moreover, he hoped this trick did not include him. He came onto the balcony, the stench of the man coiled in his nose. The odor, like a viscous syrup, filled his sinuses and his throat.

For several minutes, the man whispered secrets to him. Throughout, threads of hope and longing laced with those of accusation and rage. It was madness. It was another story.

When it was completed, the boy stepped away, shaking his head.

"This isn't what I want."

The man's face slackened with resignation. He even nodded his head as if agreeing with the boy.

It was far from over, though.

"I think," The Magician began, gazing down to the courtyard, "even you will appreciate this."

The three Vassals had been joined by a fourth, perhaps the youth from the couch. The toughs had removed their leather jackets. Their jeans and shoes rested in neat piles along the ivy-covered wall behind them. Their naked skin radiated slightly under the wash of lights from the fountain. Two beautiful children faced two more beautiful children mirrorlike. Shiny things glimmered in their hands. Then The Magician clapped his hands twice. And the show began.

THE QUARTER
OF DREAMS:
WELCOME HOME

1

Kenneth Nicholson stood at the window of his home and watched the sky darken as he struggled with the news that his son might not live through the night. Like the evening light, his son's life was fading and perhaps would soon flicker out. It didn't seem possible. When he'd received the phone call from his ex-wife, Ken had felt a pronounced dislocation as if the news were about someone he didn't know. Moments later, when this particular denial faded, he hung up the phone and tried to lose himself in action: calling his travel agent to book a flight, packing clothes, turning certain lights off and turning others on. He found a dozen meaningless tasks throughout the house to occupy his mind briefly, telling himself with each new chore that this thing had to be done before he left. Then he'd walked into the kitchen to check the lock on the sliding glass door. Through the pane, he noticed the sun setting behind the stand of trees at the back of his property. The vista engaged him. His nerves continued to thrum with the need for distracting motion, but he didn't leave the window. Staring out at the sky, bright with bands of mauve and pink, he thought of flowers displayed at a funeral.

Ken dropped his gaze, following the pine trunks to the ground where woodland gave way to a great run of brown earth. Between this band of soil and his redwood deck, an immaculate sea of grass blanketed the ground. He loved the smell of the lawn on the days Mickey Gorman came by to mow; it was one of the few pleasures the yard gave him. He imagined that if he'd owned this house years ago, his children would have enjoyed it. Bobby might have chased Jennifer through the grass, wrestling and tickling her until she cried for Daddy to make her big, mean brother stop the torture. Bobby might have gone out for football passes along the shallow grade. Jennifer might have marched her dolls into adventure beneath the deck, and in the evening they could have eaten hamburgers from the grill as they sat on a blanket, pretending that they were picnicking in a great park.

Now, Ken's children were too old for such entertainment. They had been too old for them when Ken had left New Orleans the year before. These days, Jennifer's interests ran toward the melancholy and rebellious, dissatisfaction as much a part of her face as her nose, mouth, and eyes.

And Bobby, his son, his star…Bobby was…*in a coma*. He had been taking courses at Tulane—prelaw. The kid was going to go far…if he ever woke up.

Ken needed to keep moving. He left the view and wandered down the cold corridor toward the foyer. Unlike his house in New Orleans, which was adorned with antiques and a warmer aesthetic, his home in Austin was furnished with sleek modern fixtures. Shiny marble tile covered the floors; the walls were coated in ice-gray paint; and sharp lines ran throughout the cavernous house. His decorator had accessorized with crystal and bronze. Walls carried the weight of bright abstracts in lacquered frames. Everything in this place was new and clean and completely void of sentimental attachment.

His luggage met him at the door. He paused, wondering what he had forgotten but could not think of anything, though the certainty he was leaving something behind gnawed at him. He opened the door and carried his luggage to the porch. After locking the place up, he crossed to the white board railing and sat down to wait for the cab. The street was quiet. It was always quiet. No traffic ran along the block, and even the trees stood motionless, refusing to disturb the peace.

Here in Austin he had a gentle existence, spotless neighborhoods inhabited by the June and Ward Cleavers of the DVD generation. In New Orleans he had restless memories, a family, friends, and folks like Old Miss Alice, with hair like plucked cotton and a wrinkled leathery face, who had lived nearly one hundred years and rarely moved from the stoop of the dilapidated shotgun cottage in which she had been born. Here people regarded neighbors as strangers; there the opposite was true.

And this is what you wanted?

It's what I needed, he corrected.

New Orleans. There was no way to avoid memories there; they permeated the place. And to Ken, memory was a disease, a chronic illness that could lay dormant for months, even years, before it woke to virulently infect its hosts.

The cab arrived. Ken stubbed out his cigarette. He rose from the railing and threw the garment bag over his shoulder, lifting the suitcase with his free hand. The driver, a short Hispanic gentleman with a considerable belly, helped Ken toss the bags into the trunk, and Ken stared at the luggage as the man slammed the compartment closed.

Once they were in the car, the driver asked, "Airport?"

"Yes."

With the cab in motion a fraction of Ken's distress was relieved. He was doing something—not enough, he knew—but something. He was moving, making progress. Slow, too slow, but he was going in the right direction. Bobby would be okay; he was a tough kid.

"Where you headed?" the driver asked, attempting conversation. Reflected in the rearview mirror, his face was an incomplete mask, mostly brow and eyes.

"New Orleans," Ken answered, hoping his gaze would indicate he wasn't in the mood for chitchat.

"Business or pleasure?"

"Neither," Ken replied sharply. This shut the driver up.

Business or pleasure? The question was a joke.

&

Full dark settled before the plane left the ground. Ken ordered two vodkas from the first-class cabin attendant. She eyed him appreciatively, and he forced a smile.

Almost half a century of life had done nothing but improve Ken Nicholson's appearance. Thick blond hair shot with strands of gray framed a deeply tanned face with features that had progressed from handsome to striking. His mustache was almost white. His eyes, translucent and the color of ash, startled with their clarity. Men and women both responded powerfully to his appearance, as if he were a big-screen legend dropped down in their midst. Once he had been flattered by the attention and the advantages his appearance conferred, but those days were long behind him. Now, he could not imagine what anyone found pleasing in his face.

Even so, he remained social. Dated. But none of the men he'd met over the past year had stayed around long. Usually Ken ended things, either with a simple conversation over drinks or an even simpler note via e-mail. There was nothing wrong with the men, per se; he just didn't see the point in leading them down a path that had no happy destination.

Last night, he'd broken things off with a kid named Kyle but not because Ken felt frustrated or dissatisfied with the relationship. The fact was, he felt nothing about the relationship. Ken figured the kid deserved a lot more than indifference, and at this point in his life, Ken wasn't sure he had anything else to offer.

The plane seemed to have just reached cruising altitude when the captain announced that they were on their final descent. Only two hours had passed since the cab had pulled in front of his house, and now he was in another state; he was home.

Bobby's going to die.

The thought caught him off guard; it hit Ken so quickly a stranger might have whispered the terrible certainty into his ear. The words held conviction, seemed filled with it, but he refused to give the thought energy. His son was in the hospital, the victim of an unprovoked attack. Comatose and unresponsive, Robert William Nicholson had spent the day in surgery after his body had been delivered to an emergency room. He would not die; Ken held to that. Bobby lay hurt, not dying. The kid was strong. He'd lettered in varsity football and baseball in his sophomore year and every year that followed until he'd graduated from high school. Only once since Bobby had been an infant had Ken seen his boy cry.

Ken closed his eyes and tried to think of something else, but the disease of memory had already settled on him like fever.

They'd been in Audubon Park. Bobby was six years old. He'd wanted to learn to ride a bike like the big kids, so Ken had bought a bright red Huffy and had spent a summer's afternoon fighting a miserable head cold and the oppressive heat while instructing Bobby on the important points of bicycle responsibility. His son had refused the training wheels, saying they were for babies, so Ken ran behind the bike, holding the seat with his hand and gasping for breath to fill his heavy lungs.

On a straight section of path, Ken felt his son gaining control over the bicycle. He tested this theory by releasing the seat for brief intervals, taking the seat in his palm again for his own peace of mind. Finally, he let go. He thought his son would be surprised and happy to see that he could ride the bike on his own, but Bobby's balance was uncertain. The bike began to wobble, and Bobby called out for his father. Seconds later, both boy and bike were sprawled beneath the heavy limbs of an oak.

Bobby cried then, staring at his father, pointing a trembling finger in accusation. *You betrayed me*, his son's red expression said. *I needed you, and you weren't there.*

Ken choked down the bitter memory.

The plane was landing.

*

A blast of cold air froze the sweat on his neck as he entered the lobby of Ochsner Hospital. He carried his luggage to a small desk where he faced a sour, pinched old man sitting like a bridge troll with the power to deny him passage. Ken asked for Bobby's room number, and the old man looked up from his magazine and snuffled.

"It's late," the troll told him. "Visiting hours are..."

From behind him, a woman said, "Oh, Ken. Thank God."

He turned. Even before he could acknowledge his ex-wife's presence, Paula's arms snaked around his neck, drawing him in for a tight embrace. The heat of her body warmed his chest, and he lowered his face to the cradle between her neck and shoulder. When he pulled away, he carried the powdery scent of her with him.

Still beautiful, he thought.

Though Paula Nicholson had never been a slender woman, her extra pounds hung well on her frame. Her hair—long and black, thick and curled—was pulled back from her true source of beauty: her radiant face. Firm skin, free of freckle or imperfection, stretched over fine bones. Enormous violet eyes, now cast in a field of red veins, glittered, and her lips quivered with suppressed emotion. Though her body was thick, even thicker than the last time Ken had seen her, Paula's face defied time.

"You got here so fast," Paula said, her voice husky from a day of crying. "That's good. It's good to see you."

"Where is he?" he asked.

"This way," she said, setting off across the lobby.

"Wait a minute," he said. Ken turned to the information clerk. "Can I leave my bags here?"

The troll, who was again staring at his magazine, shrugged.

Ken left his bags where they sat and joined Paula. They crossed the lobby. With a shaking voice, Paula filled him in. She spoke quickly, as if needing to have the words out and away from her.

"He's in a room now, but it's in intensive care, so it's not really a room so much as a space. The surgery went well, really well. The doctors were pleased with the procedure. That's what they said anyway, but what are they supposed to say?"

"What happened exactly?" he asked as they approached the elevators.

"Nobody knows," Paula told him. She jabbed the button once, twice, and a third time to call the car. "It happened early this morning, but they had to rush him into surgery and nobody could find me, so I didn't know what was going on. You'd think his fiancée would have known to have the hospital call me at the campus, but she was probably so shaken up, she couldn't remember her own name. All they know for sure is that some kid jumped Robert while he was walking to class. They think he used a pipe or a bar of some kind, and he..." Paula's voice faded as the elevator door opened. He followed her into the car. "Anyway, some kids found him and fortunately they had their cell phones, so they called nine-one-one."

"When did you hear?" Ken asked.

"A couple of hours before I called you," Paula told him. He was hurt that she had waited so long, but she was quick to explain. "I had to be here. I couldn't think of anything else. He was already in surgery because of the damage, and I had to be here. They gave me all of these forms, and I kind of got lost in them, which I guess was a good thing. I don't know. Only when they told me that he was out of surgery did I think enough to call Jen. Then I called you at your office, but Donna said you weren't in, and I started to panic."

"I'd already taken the week off," Ken said. They didn't need him at the office; they rarely needed him anymore.

In the early eighties, Ken had gone into partnership with two friends to start a software company specializing in geographical survey programs for the oil industry. Ken had little interest in the technology, but his acumen in business development brought in and maintained a solid client roster. In only a few years, the company earned a reputation throughout the country. International interest followed. He'd built something great with that company, but he'd built it so well that his participation had become superfluous.

The elevator doors opened, and they stepped into a circular ward. Paula led him with determined steps across the fourth floor toward a desk at its center. Three nurses occupied the station. One nurse, a large African-American woman with corn-rowed hair and a softball-sized silk orchid pinned to her uniform, stopped a cup of coffee halfway to her lips. Her nametag read *Stella*.

Paula waved to the woman but said nothing. Behind her, Ken felt the intrinsic morbidity of the ward weighting his steps. His body trembled as if connected to a low-voltage wire, and sweat trickled from his hairline to soak the starched white collar of his shirt. The concern that had been with him since Paula's panicked call only a few hours before sprouted sharp-edged vines that raked through his stomach and chest. In a moment, they would be in Bobby's room, and Ken would have to deal with whatever he saw there.

His pace slowed, letting the distance grow between himself and his ex-wife. On the other sides of the glass walls of the rooms, immobile patients lay hooked by wire and tube to banks of machines. White curtains hung to shade the glass panels, but broad, open doors left patients and their loved ones exposed to observation.

Given his current state of concern, Ken's anger only exacerbated his agitation. These damaged bodies were set up like exhibits for display. It infuriated him that people should be made to lose all privacy and dignity in this manner, and though he knew these cubicles were designed for the patient's well being, Ken could not keep his outrage in check. Furious, wanting to punch one of the glass panels until it shattered, Ken caught his reflection in a window. His hair appeared platinum in the dark glass. Though he knew that the weathered face was his own, he found it difficult to recognize himself in the heavy jowls and clouded eyes.

As he regarded his reflection, wondering where his face had gone, something moved along his cheek. He almost touched the place before he realized that the reflection of his face fell over the reality of another. A woman, her eyes tired and lost, gazed through the glass at him. She had been reading to the motionless form on the bed. Her hands shook, the pages of the book in her hands fluttered, and she lost her place in the story.

Ken moved on.

He met Paula at the threshold of a room that seemed remarkably dark for having nothing but a window separating it from the brightly lit ward. He almost relaxed for a moment when he saw the form on the bed. There had been a mistake; this bandaged *thing* was not his son. This wasn't Bobby, he thought. Bobby was a strong kid with his father's build and his mother's hair. The kid in the bed was some other child, weak and beaten, wrapped in bandages and sprouting innumerable tubes. A mistake. But the tears came before he could muster his conviction, and Ken sobbed quietly, stumbling toward the bed.

⚜

The cab pulled to the curb outside of Ken's house on Dumaine Street. He hesitated before getting out. He didn't want to be here, he realized. Maybe if he had arrived during daylight hours, the unsettling fear might not have been so thick on him, but with the memory of his son's damaged condition so fresh in his mind and with night covering the place, Ken found that he didn't want to enter the house.

Before his move to Austin, his love of the house had waned and ultimately died. Quite simply, the Creole cottage had turned bad. Memories and nightmares grew and found life beneath its tiled roof. Even now, he felt its haunted quality like a shawl of snow on his neck and shoulders. Ken nearly told the driver to take him to a hotel, to drive him back to Paula's in the Garden District, to drive him anywhere but *this* part of *this* street.

Though Ken's anxiety was real— it weighed in his belly like concrete—he knew his projection of emotion upon the house was wholly wrong. If anything was haunted, it was Ken. His son's life was suddenly in question, and he felt somehow responsible. Nothing waited beyond the shuttered doors but rooms, furnishings, and memories.

He paid the driver and stepped out of the cab.

Ken climbed the stoop. The Creole cottage in which he'd lived for seven years before moving to Austin looked very unimposing from the street. The pale yellow façade, with deep green shutters covering both doors and windows, seemed sparse and inelegant.

A picture of Bobby, his shattered head bound in a cap of thick white gauze, unfolded behind Ken's eyes, and he turned back to the street. The cab driver had not pulled away. He sat in his car, staring up at the strange, handsome man who didn't seem to want to enter his house.

Ken dug in his pants for the keys to the padlocked shutters. Once he freed the ring, Ken opened the shutters and the French doors and stepped into the house. It smelled clean, with a slight hint of vanilla and wax in the air. Once a month, Carla, the woman who kept house for Paula, came by to tidy things inside. The exceptionally thorough woman dusted the antiques and vacuumed the carpets; she frequently washed the linens, whether they'd been used or not, if only to keep them from getting musty. Apparently, she'd been by recently.

He dropped his luggage in the bedroom. On his way through the house he turned on several lights.

The restoration of this place had cost Ken a small fortune. Over generations, the building had been chopped into four separate apartments and allowed to fall into disrepair. He'd almost put his foot through the longleaf pine floor where he now had his dining room, because termites had chewed them through. The home had been fumigated repeatedly, gutted, and, based on the original design and the expertise of an old friend, returned to its former simple elegance.

In the kitchen, Ken lifted the phone and checked his voice mail.

The first message came from an old friend. Sam Martin, a professor at the college where Paula worked and one of Ken's dearest friends, sent his regards and regrets about Bobby. Hearing the man's voice comforted Ken. They had gone through a lot together over the years. Apparently Paula had called Sam with news earlier in the day. Ken was grateful for it.

After Sam signed off with "Please call if you need anything," Ken erased the message. The next call was from Paula. It was recent, placed sometime after they'd parted in the hospital parking lot.

"I'm home," she said. "We didn't have much time to talk tonight, and there are some things we should discuss. I can fill you in over breakfast." She told him the time and the place, then said, "Good night."

Ken erased the message and passed through his dining room, with its burnished mahogany table and the embroidered, straight-backed chairs sitting regally along its sides. After a thorough in-spection of the house, during which he found no agitated spirits, he returned to the kitchen to inventory his supplies. Not surpris-ingly, the cupboards and refrigerator were all but bare. He opened the freezer and found a bottle of Level vodka and a tray of ice cubes next to it. He fixed himself a drink and carried it to the liv-ing room, where he dropped onto the plush cushions of the sofa.

He hadn't even finished his first swallow before the phone rang.

Under other circumstances, he would have ignored it. He was exhausted, drained. But one of the doctors from the hospital could be calling, or Paula might need something.

Ken lifted the phone. "Hello?"

"Welcome home, Baby," a woman whispered.

He didn't recognize the voice. "Who is this?" he asked, irri-tated by the woman's attempt at familiarity.

He took a slow draw from his glass as he waited for the re-sponse. "Hello?" he said. He could hear the caller's breath scratch-ing over the line. Maybe the woman realized she had dialed wrong and was too embarrassed to say anything else. Whatever the case, he was too tired to entertain a stranger's mistake. "Can I help you?" he asked, his voice now harsh.

"Tell me a story," the woman whispered.

The line went dead.

With a trembling hand, Ken set his drink on the table. He looked over his shoulder into the darkened room. Then, he looked back at the phone.

2

ell me a story.

The words followed him through his dreams, clinging to his mind as the thick sheen of sweat clung to his body. Images, transparent and faded by the passing of years, returned and fought for their place in his consciousness. The sickening sweetness of rose and azalea filled his nose. He was young again. The warmth of the late evening swaddled him like a child, though the visions of his dreaming mind would not suit the delicate psyche of a babe.

He stood in a courtyard. A fountain spat gem-bright plumes of water into the air: sapphire, emerald, and ruby. The flagstones beneath his feet fitted like a jigsaw puzzle. Voices rose and fell in jovial waves. A piano whispered a solemn rag to accompany the cries of delight, the laughter, and the deeper, animal sounds emanating from the building before him.

And on the stones at his feet...

The soft, seductive fragrance of blossoms pulled away, leaving the scent of sweat and faded cologne. The scene snapped in on itself like a sheet yanked from its drying line, and he was left a forty-eight-year-old man sitting up on the comfortable mattress of his bed.

Despite the dream's retreat, Ken felt the presence of history all around him, wrapping his torso in a hot, scratchy embrace. The courtyard in his dream was as much a part of his history's topography as his place in Austin or the Victorian house he had bought for Paula when they'd married; it was as much a part of his being as his skin, his lust, and his guilt. The dream house was thick with the past's souvenirs, and Ken wished to be anywhere but under its roof. So, he kept his eyes open, refusing to let sleep pull him back into it.

He rose from the bed and walked to the window. To his surprise, his courtyard glowed with electric light. He looked at the switch on the wall; the toggle was up. Though he did not remember turning on the floods, he could not say with any certainty that he had not done it. Most of the previous evening was a blur to him, an out-of-focus slide show. He'd flown from Austin and raced to the hospital to see his boy, resting motionless and silent. Paula had been there. Then, at home, a woman had called and made a simple yet disturbing request. She'd asked for a story.

Tell me a story, Baby.

He hadn't heard that appeal in years, decades. The request, like so much about this city, belonged to the past. But the past was what New Orleans was famous for. The residents of this city could tell you a hundred stories about a single neighborhood and trace the owners of a home back to the day that the first shovelful of dirt made way for its foundation. On Rue Royal, locals couldn't help but point out the former home of Dr. Louis and Madame Delphine LaLaurie. It was reported that the LaLauries' cook set fire to the home in the hopes of ending the master's torture. Just a couple of blocks off Bourbon Street, neighbors might draw attention to the dark structure that once belonged to Travis Brugier. Respected and reviled for his power and influence, Brugier ran a private club for men in a converted space once used as the slave quarters of his house. The story was often told that one night Brugier went mad and hanged himself from his balcony with a cord of piano wire. Tennessee Williams lived in this house on Dumaine, and Frances Keyes leased a bit of this house on Chartres, and did you know that Faulkner wrote his first novel right over there across from St. Anthony's Garden?

Always there, history, like dust, frosted the present. It could be wiped away, scrubbed, and for a time forgotten, but it always returned, settling on life's ornamentation. If left unchecked it grew thick and opaque, covering all that might be with the filth of what had already come to pass.

Clutching for the present, Ken looked out at his courtyard. Garden lights, secured in small black canisters, pointed upward to illuminate the foliage, casting long, creeping shadows over the brick walls. His flower beds, once thriving and beautifully landscaped, were overrun with lush, rampant vines and jutting branches. The cherry trees in the distant corners looked ragged. His cruel imagination put Bobby in there, lying on a bed, head wrapped in cotton, but instead of rubber tubes and monitoring wires, the plants served as his boy's life support. Tendrils from the overrun garden wrapped and punctured his body.

Ken blinked the image away.

Over the years, Ken had imagined for his son a life filled with friends and accomplishments, prosperity, and a family of his own. Bobby had proposed to his fiancée only a month ago. He was too young, Ken thought, but he trusted his boy to be level headed enough to make it work. So, Ken saw himself at the marriage ceremony, pictured the young couple fawning over the Lexus sedan he'd chosen for their wedding present. He could picture his grandchildren, Bobby's children, playing in his yard in Austin while he and his son drank beers on the deck. He imagined holidays they would share, playing Santa to the kids, carving the bird on Thanksgiving. He struggled with these images, this future. His son might never walk again. Might never even wake up.

"Christ," Ken whispered, wiping at his wet eyes.

He opened the French doors and stepped into the loggia. Cool night air greeted him and chilled his exposed skin. The distant sounds of Bourbon Street, still alive and throbbing in the middle of the night, pulsed in his ears. A gentle breeze ruffled his hair. He smelled spices, hot and savory on the wind, mixing with the foul stench of waste.

And somewhere, not very far away, his son slept.

It's my fault. It was an irrational thought, but Ken couldn't shake it. The guilt of the absent parent, the estranged husband, was a constant companion; it had been so even before he separated from Paula and moved out of the house. Every man he met on a business trip or whose home he visited for sex after work added to Ken's culpability. Each indiscretion weighed on him like stones, accumulating over the course of twenty years to become a suffocating burden. So, he'd left.

His children hadn't understood, not at first, but Paula had.

Ken had made his attraction to men clear long before straying from his marriage to indulge it. Paula could never claim surprise or deceit; she had known. With the grudging and miserable determination of the truly pragmatic, she even tried to accommodate Ken's needs, had let him experiment in the hopes he'd quench his curiosity. But her permission did nothing to relieve the guilt. Seven years ago, almost eight now, Ken had moved out. He visited his family often, doing his best to assuage the damage his departure had caused.

Early on, the visits had been a misery, painful and awkward. He suffered the kids' tearful requests that he move home. He endured Paula's anger. But he fought to remain a part of the family. Over the years, particularly the last few, he had grown distant, though he couldn't explain why even to himself.

Halfway across the courtyard, lost in thought, Ken struck his toe on the raised edge of a stone. Pain flashed to his ankle, and he stumbled forward. The world tipped for a heart-stopping second but then righted.

In the street behind his house a drunk kicked an empty bottle, shattering it against the brick façade of the neighboring building.

Across the way, in a neighboring house, a television blared. It was the middle of the night, and the city carried on.

Ken walked back through the loggia to the threshold of his bedroom. Inside, he closed the doors, muting the sounds of the city, but it was not quiet in the bedroom. His heart thundered an uncomfortable rhythm in his chest, and from the next room, music played.

It took him a moment to make out the dragging beat of a solemn rag, played with sensitivity on an upright piano. And just as he identified this as the music that had accompanied his dream, it faded.

A moment later, walking through the rooms of his house, Ken couldn't be certain that he'd heard the music at all.

3

Ken opened his eyes and stared at the slowly revolving blades of the ceiling fan. Sunlight crept into the room, painting a wedge on the pine floorboards. Ken's weary eyes closed for the chore of lifting himself from bed. He showered under hot water, his nerves and muscles waking under the peppering spray. A red blotch at the end of his toe reminded him of the trip into his courtyard. He also remembered music, but of this memory he was less certain. Likely, the piano's notes had played nowhere but in his dream.

Ken dried himself, dressed, and found his keys on the kitchen counter. Eager to leave the house, he had already locked the front door when he remembered his cell phone and Blackberry. He retrieved the devices from his bedroom nightstand and was finally able to escape the house.

He walked under foliage-choked balconies, passed by restaurants that already filled the morning with their teasing scents, and continued toward Jackson Square. Only a few weeks ago the schoolchildren would have made Mardi Gras floats out of old shoe boxes, pasting plastic flowers and Styrofoam sculptures on the surfaces before sprinkling them with glitter and designating Barbie dolls or Jedi action figures as their grand marshals. Two weeks before, these same children would have been on their father's shoulders staring over the throngs of people gathered along the green belt bisecting St. Charles Avenue, catching beads offered up by the various krewes. For years, Ken had been the observation tower for his children. He took turns lifting Bobby and then Jennifer to his shoulders to see the passing celebration. The last time he'd done this, five years ago, Jen had been eleven. Bobby had begged off, because he was going to watch the parade from a friend's house, so Ken had taken just his daughter.

She'd laughed then, reaching out to snatch the soaring beads, and when the parade was done, and Ken saw that Jen was disappointed with the number of necklaces she'd caught, he took her to a little shop and bought her a dozen ornate strands, which she'd worn proudly for the remainder of the morning.

She never seemed to smile anymore.

He stopped in Jackson Square and watched face painters, caricature artists, and palm readers fuss with their tables before the impressive structure of the St. Louis Cathedral.

Bobby was to have been married inside the cathedral with the prestige of a bishop presiding. The bride's father had made the arrangements for his daughter's wedding, and though Ken could not remember the young woman's name (strange how it always slipped out of his mind) he assumed she came from a good family; it takes considerable resources and stature to arrange such a ceremony.

The entire affair had come up so quickly. Bobby had told him that the girl was several years older than himself but also a student. Paula had met Bobby's fiancée on a handful of occasions, and she'd spoken highly of the bright if somewhat cool young woman their son intended to marry. Ken had been looking forward to meeting her. In just over a month both families were scheduled to gather for a "family-to-be" dinner at Galatoire's, Ken's only chance to meet the woman before the wedding. Now, the dinner wouldn't happen, and the ceremony wasn't likely; at best, it would have to be postponed. Ken couldn't even imagine what the girl must be going through now.

He stepped into the shadowed chill of the cathedral. Velvet cords hung to keep visitors from ransacking the place. A small weathered woman stood beside a sign that insisted that people go no further without a guide.

After several minutes of uncertainty, looking into the vast and ornate temple, Ken left the church. He was being foolish, ridiculous, and desperate. He felt weak and hated himself for it. How many of his friends had he watched in their last moments of life, friends who had despised the intolerant religions of their birth, turn back to inefficient faiths? People needed their gods, he knew, and Ken wished he had found one to believe in so his prayers wouldn't feel like the ramblings of a hypocrite, but he wasn't going to indulge in foxhole Christianity. Not yet. Such a turn would mean all other hope was lost.

When he returned to the square, the day's heat was already forming. The sky was bleached. No clouds above, just a silver atmosphere promising discomfort for the afternoon ahead.

Feeling lost, Ken returned to Dumaine Street. People on the sidewalk moved by him like ghosts as he walked toward his breakfast date with Paula. His mind drifted and became tangled with his early memories of the city now surrounding him.

His parents had brought him to New Orleans when he was fifteen years old. They'd come down from Chicago, chasing yet another of his father's easy-money schemes. Living in a small house in the neighborhoods surrounding Tulane University, Ken lived an uneventful life. He'd graduated from high school the same year that his father decided more money could be made in the airline plants in Seattle. His family moved to the Northwest, but Ken stayed. The city appealed to him; it was comfortable and offered innumerable distractions. He had a decent job bussing tables for tourists at the Molière Café, and a friend from high school, Puritan Crowley, needed a roommate at his apartment in the French

Quarter. So, without hesitation, Ken announced that he was going to remain among the freaks and the fabulous of the South.

With Crow, the nickname he had given his best friend, he frequented the bars on Bourbon Street. His friend, a devout hedonist, felt that flesh, like money, was for spending, so they traveled along a path cast in the shadow of morality, trying various drugs when available and relying on alcohol when not. Knowledge blossomed quickly in the moist, heated air. Anything proved possible, particularly for two handsome young men eschewing the burden of responsibility.

Ken never talked about those days, not with anyone. The time he'd spent living in the French Quarter, that first time, was a year-long blank in his personal history. As far as anyone knew, he'd moved to Texas to attend school when his parents relocated to Seattle.

For Ken it had been fun and games, nothing more. He knew the template of a normal life: college, career, marriage, children. This simple path to happiness had been etched into him since childhood. He'd had no intention of giving all of that up, just because he was having a good time.

Later, when it wasn't fun anymore, when the bacchanal turned dark and unreal, he wouldn't speak of that either. Sometimes, he was able to tell himself it had never happened, though the moments of this comforting amnesia were brief. Even now, so many years later, Ken could not fathom what had happened to him then, and he refused to accept what he'd done.

⚜

Ken checked his watch. He crossed the street and entered the Quarter Scene restaurant. Paula sat at a table by the window already well into her second cigarette.

"How are you holding up?" he asked, taking a chair with his back to the sun.

Paula didn't answer at first. Instead she seemed to be reading the expression on his face, digging into his soul as she had so often done in the past. The investigation had always unnerved him, made him feel vulnerable.

"You look tired," Paula said, stubbing her cigarette out in the ashtray. Her large eyes caught his. "And to answer your question, I'm fine."

"Have you spoken with the hospital?"

"No change."

He nodded and withdrew a cigarette from his shirt pocket.

They sat in silence. A waiter appeared and took their order. Ken wasn't hungry, so he requested coffee and gazed out the window at Dumaine Street. The smoke from his cigarette wafted over the glass and clouded the scene.

"How's Jennifer?"

"Scared," Paula replied. "Of course, she doesn't want to talk about it."

Of course not, Ken thought. Jennifer would rather die than give her parents the satisfaction of turning to them. We're the bad guys, he reminded himself. We separated, divorced, and wrecked her life with a premeditated glee.

"How's Bobby's fiancée holding up?" Ken asked, still gazing at the street.

"You mean Vicki?"

And, of course, that was her name: Vicki. Vicki Bach. It came back to him now. He remembered his son's e-mails and excited phone calls. For months all the boy had spoken of was Vicki. "Yes."

"After her initial report to the police, she vanished."

The tone in Paula's voice concerned him. It had been less than twenty-four hours since the attack, yet she made it sound as if the girl had been missing for weeks. "What about her family? Do they know where she is?"

Paula smiled bitterly. "No one can find *them* either."

"What?"

"Well." His ex-wife shrugged as if to say *beats me*. "The address she gave the police was a phony. Some family named Brugier lives there, and they've never heard of Vicki Bach."

Brugier? Icy fingers pinched at his neck. He drew deeply on the cigarette, hoping the warm smoke would pull away his sense of unease.

"The phone number they found for her in Robert's wallet has been disconnected. They traced it to a burned-out gallery on St. Phillips. The place has been vacant for about nine months."

But Bobby had been seeing Vicki for months, Ken thought. He must have had a working phone number for her, a real address. Surely, the police hadn't looked thoroughly enough. Though perplexed by this mystery, Ken's real concern was with another piece of information. The name *Brugier* gnawed at him. It couldn't be a coincidence. He knew the story of Travis Brugier, knew all too well about the night of his death. Everyone in the city did.

"I don't understand this," Ken said.

"Then you're in the majority." Paula folded her hands in front of her face. She bit on her upper lip and looked out the window, fighting her welling emotions.

"Hey," Ken tried.

Paula waved him away.

"I'm just so angry," she whispered, her voice pinched as she tried to keep her tears under control.

"I know," he said. "I feel like hell because I wasn't here."

Paula smiled. "If you'd have stayed, did you intend on walking him to school?"

"You know what I mean."

"No one could have planned on something like this, Ken. It makes no sense." She took in a deep breath and sighed it out with the remnants of her tears.

"Are the police considering Vicki a suspect at this point?"

"I don't know," Paula said. "They just tell me to wait and not worry. Maybe somebody ought to take a club to one of their kids and see how long they wait, see exactly how little they worry."

"Were Bobby and Vicki having trouble? Did he say anything?"

"No, they seemed fine. But there was something."

"Something?" Ken asked.

"Last week, Bobby told me Vicki was scared. She'd told him a young man was following her. Bobby didn't know what to make of it because he hadn't seen the boy." Paula cleared her throat, sipped from her water. "The police asked me about this, said that Vicki had included a description of the kid in her statement, but she was probably lying."

"Why lying? Maybe this other kid was stalking her or had some kind of grudge. For all we know, Vicki could be another victim."

Paula looked at him like he was an obstinate child. "Then why the fake phone numbers, the nonexistent parents?"

Of course, she was right. Ken was looking for a motive and exploring only the most obvious avenues. They weren't likely to solve this mystery over coffee, but if Vicki had lied and subsequently disappeared, then she was likely involved. This meant that Bobby's attack hadn't been a random street crime; it had been planned and carried out with a purpose, which made it all the more sinister.

But why? he wondered angrily. What could his son have done to deserve such brutality?

"I don't think we're going to know anything until they find her," Paula said. "If they find her."

"They'll find her. People don't just disappear."

"They do if they never existed in the first place."

⚜

Paula parked in the lot outside of the hospital. Sunlight glimmered on the shiny surfaces of the cars around them. To Ken, the building seemed malevolent, like the apparition of a haunted keep looming over the heads of unwelcome guests. Inside the belly of this hostile structure, his son teetered above the void, ensnared by machines.

It's not the building, Ken told himself. The hospital was no more haunted than his house on Dumaine. He knew of only one truly haunted place in the city, despite what the carriage drivers and tour guides told the tourists who were hungry for mystical scandals. All of Ken's fears, the spirits that taunted him, were born in that one place.

His Parlor. Wonderland.

Inside Bobby's room, Ken grasped his son's hand with great delicacy to avoid disturbing the intravenous tube protruding from his wrist. Paula excused herself to make some calls, since any use of electronic devices was prohibited in the ICU. After an hour, Ken excused himself, telling Paula that he had some calls of his own to make. He flipped open the cell phone when he reached the lobby and checked in at his office. Donna, his assistant, assured him all was running smoothly. She asked about Bobby and asked that Ken pass along her concern to Paula and Jennifer. He told her that he would do so. He called Sam Martin and left a message on his machine.

Ken closed his cell phone. He searched the lobby and followed signs to a bank of pay phones. He was considering making one more call, but if he could actually bring himself to dial the number, he didn't want his name to appear on the man's caller ID.

"For God's sake," he muttered to himself, knowing how childish it was to hide at the end of a phone line. He also knew he would not make the call, but he wanted to. He wanted to hear David Lane's voice.

Ken paused in the cool hallway, staring at the pay phone, reading the numbered grid, the reflection of his torso painting the chrome faceplate. He didn't reach for the headset, just stared at the machine.

He hadn't spoken to David in nearly a year, not since he'd left New Orleans and taken up residence in Austin. They'd been lovers—the only real relationship Ken had forged after leaving Paula—but in relocating, Ken had handled things badly with David.

To Ken, the situation made no sense, though he'd fabricated more than enough excuses. He considered David Lane the most honest, deepest love of his life, and yet Ken had walked away from the man, severed all communications as he'd done with no other person in his life.

That's because I've never been so scared in my life, he thought. *That's a lie.*

Late that evening, Paula left Ken outside of his house, but he couldn't bring himself to enter. Instead, he walked down the street to Lafitte's. He ordered a Level on the rocks and observed the crowd. Masks of joviality and hunger and sadness hovered in the dim light cast by the video screens. Light danced from the small flame burning in a brazier near the entrance. He felt out of place, having been removed from this scene for so long.

Like a bicycle, he mused bitterly. It'll come right back.

But he didn't want it back. Not now. He needed comfort, warmth. Undoubtedly, finding an attractive volunteer in the crowd would be easy. If he were daring enough to actually pick someone up, the guy might succeed in taking Ken's mind off of his problems for a few minutes, but in the end he would still be alone; nothing would have changed. In the past, he had settled for this sublimation, convincing himself that it might lead to something more than distraction. The bodies he had found under him, over him, next to him, struggling for pleasure in a bed, on the floor, or in a darkened room as a party raged beyond closed doors, belonged to nameless men whose only important attribute had been their presence. The whole time, he'd believed that something more might come from those sweaty encounters. Often enough, he'd been wrong.

And then he'd met David.

Ken found it impossible to describe the man beyond the most general terms: attractive, intelligent. Frankly, the only way Ken could express his feelings about David Lane was with the simple hyperbole of "perfect," which would have meant nothing to most people and made Ken sound like a love-blind idiot. But he'd never seen a face that could trigger his trust, his respect, and his lust in the way David's could. He'd never felt a body that so ideally contoured to his own, that moved with his in perfect synchronization, that was always the right temperature. With David there had been no emotional power struggle, no complicating insecurities. He neither doted on Ken, as so many others had, nor did he pretend superiority. They had been extremely comfortable with one another, but it was a passionate comfort, alive and exciting. And Ken had walked away.

No, he corrected. I ran.

Across the bar, a door opened, and a young man with a shock of blond hair stepped through. Ken sensed the attention the youngster drew. The boy was attractive, and he knew it. His face, carved with fine features and lightly tanned, wore an expression of superior indifference.

The vodka burned Ken's throat as he finished his drink. He ordered another and walked to the back of the bar to hide in the shadows where he could be at peace with the thoughts of his son.

The doctors had told him that Bobby's chances of survival were fifty-fifty: terrible odds when considering the life of a twenty-year-old boy. Worse than the odds was the fact that in all likelihood, Bobby would spend the rest of his life severely impaired. And, of course, the doctors qualified all of this with statements like "We can't be sure," and "We don't know enough right now." Vague guesses abounded, leaving nothing to comfort Ken, who waited expectantly for even the slightest hope.

Maybe he should have taken Paula up on her offer of dinner. He knew he should see Jennifer, but he needed peace right now, and his daughter offered anything but peace. Tomorrow, there would be time for Jennifer.

Still running?

Ken turned to see who was speaking to him; the voice had been clear and sounded nearby, but he was the sole occupant of the corner. The music blared. The voice had come from his head. He drew from his drink and leaned back on the wall. Already, he thought, history repeating itself.

You didn't pay attention the first time.

This time when Ken surveyed the corner, looking for the source of a voice, he saw the blond kid leaning against the pole in front of him. Hard eyes burned into his. The obvious cruising pose humored Ken. He rolled his head along the wall and returned to his thoughts, but the young man would not be put off. He stepped forward, nearly into Ken, who gazed down on the kid as he might an irritating salesman.

"Hey," the boy said, his voice barely audible over the loud dance music pumping through the bar's speakers. He shifted his drink to his left hand and extended his right. "My name's Chuck."

"Hello," Ken said, withholding his own name. His gaze returned to the video screen, where a man in drag sang about love. Maybe the kid would get the message.

But he didn't.

"How ya' doin'?" Chuck tried.

"Fine," Ken replied. He looked back at the video screen. He did not mean to be rude. In fact, he felt that he should be flattered that the haughty and handsome kid sought him out, but something about the boy was wrong. Ken found the predatory interest disturbing, and he was in no state of mind for it.

"You visiting or something?"

"*Mmm*," Ken said with a nod of his head.

"I'm in from back West," Chuck said. His eyes were as hard and cold as glacier rock even when he said, "I love it here."

Ken didn't answer. The predatory vein he'd sensed in the boy seemed to be surfacing. The kid was getting frustrated. He wasn't used to having to work a trick this hard. Ken imagined most men just gave Chuck what he wanted, if only to spend more time looking at his attractive face and muscled body.

"It's just a big loud party, kind of like Oz," Chuck said coldly. Then a razor thin smirk cut his lips. "Or that other place. What was it called? The story about the big white rabbit and the little girl and the queen who chopped off people's heads?"

The skin on Ken's neck and back shriveled as if he were leaning against a frozen sheet of metal instead of a wooden wall. Forcing his eyes away from Chuck's snakelike grin, he looked down and saw the cup in his hand was shaking.

"What was that called?" Chuck continued. "Oh God, someone just told me that story."

"Excuse me," Ken said. Though he wanted to be away quickly, he forced himself to show none of his disquiet.

He walked toward the door. He put his empty cup on the long bench beside the exit and left. Crossing Dumaine, he checked over his shoulder to make sure that the kid wasn't following him. Three blocks down he stepped into the madness of a crowd, college kids and tourists mingled to drink Hurricanes and beer, sidestepping the barkers of the knocker shops and the men waving menus in their faces. He walked nearly to Canal, then turned around and retraced his steps. He stopped in at a bar and got two shots of vodka on ice in a plastic cup. Neon lights lined the street for blocks, and he wanted to remain under these lights and among this throng. An angry sensation, like the one that had come from the boy, covered him. Old paranoia returned, carried in the arms of ghosts conjured by his teasing mind. At least here, he had the comfort of the crowd.

"Nothing to be afraid of," he whispered to himself.

As if in reply, a girl screamed in his ear. She ran down the sidewalk with two young men in pursuit. All three wore wide grins. The innocence of their actions did little to alleviate the panic that raced through Ken's chest.

4

A constant stream of faces moved along Decatur Street. Even so early in the day, the sidewalks were teeming.

Paula Nicholson sat in a restaurant, gazing through the window at the pedestrian parade, waiting for her best friend, Esther Bowers, to return from the ladies' room. Some of the people walking by blatantly stared at Paula as if she were on exhibit, offered up for their enjoyment. She imagined that if a painting possessed vision, its existence might be similar to this: numerous faces passing, perhaps appreciative, perhaps ignorant, but all ultimately indifferent. None of these gawking wanderers would know about her daughter, none would care about her son. What they read on her face might intrigue them, might raise questions, but in the end, they recognized only distance and pain, and it meant absolutely nothing to them.

Further into this fancy Paula sank, imagining herself as nothing more than pigment and canvas, a two-dimensional image of pain, anger, and confusion.

Esther returned, taking a chair with her customary energy. Though the same age as Paula, Esther looked years younger. Aerobics and dieting, collagen and surgery had gone a long way toward creating the Malibu Beach princess image Esther coveted. Yet despite her perky demeanor and silicone beauty, the woman exhibited a deep sincerity and intelligence that was often overlooked by the people she met.

"So," Esther said, "tell me how Ken is doing."

Paula wondered that very thing. A full day had come and gone since Ken's return. They had sat together at the hospital, but Ken said little. He discussed his concern for their son; he asked after their daughter; he wanted to be sure that his family had everything they needed. But about himself, he said absolutely nothing. And he looked so different. His gaze, mysterious and haunted, was disturbing. When faced with Esther's question, Paula found she could neither say how Ken was nor exactly *who* he was these days.

"Is that a difficult question, dear?" Esther asked.

"Yes," Paula said. "It is a very difficult question."

Esther traded her cheeriness for an earnest expression. "I'm sorry," she said. "I know this is a hard time for you." She sipped from her mineral water. "It's just that I always hate it when I'm upset and everyone around me feels it's their place to be upset too. Frankly, I want to be fiddling while Rome burns, if you know what I mean."

Paula smiled and nodded. "I know what you mean. I just don't really know what to say about Ken. Every time I see him, he seems further removed."

"I'm sure Robert's condition doesn't help."

"Of course," Paula said. "But I'm talking about the last several years. It's like he's evaporating. When he first moved out, we were close, closer than we'd been for a long time. But a few years ago he began fading into…Well, I don't know."

"And you have no idea what it's all about?"

Paula shook her head.

"Maybe it's easier for him this way. You know, the distance? Besides, how much do you really want to know about that other stuff?"

"I'd listen to whatever he wanted to share with me."

"Really?" Esther said, now very interested. "All of the details?"

"Don't be such a republican," Paula said. "He's gay. It's not like he's doing anything perverse. And yes, it used to bother me but only because he was my husband. Finally, I realized that he wasn't going to change, and I wouldn't be sprouting a penis, so I accepted it."

Paula left it at that. There was more, a lot more, including her fascination with Ken's sexual habits outside of their home. Though she could never have told Esther—or anyone else for that matter—she often wondered, or perhaps *fantasized* would be a better word, about Ken and the men he took to bed. At first, she'd been embarrassed by such thoughts. God knew, it wasn't something you brought up in the teacher's lounge or at a cocktail party, but she found herself giving these thoughts a lot of energy. In return, they gave her pangs of conflicted, if wholly lascivious, hunger.

She could only imagine what two men did together, and, for her, the imagining had to be enough.

"You're stronger than I am," Esther said.

"Stronger?"

"Sure. I mean Burt screws around. That's a given. But if I ever caught him or had to think about it too much…Well, he'd be walking sideways for weeks.'

Paula smiled. She was about to ask more about Burt when a face appeared in the window over Esther Bower's right shoulder. Paula knew the face, and its sudden appearance stunned her. Delicate features wrapped in reddish brown hair floated beyond the glass.

She pushed back from the table.

"What?" her friend asked. "Paula!"

But Paula wasn't listening. She stood up and charged toward the front of the restaurant. A waitress said, "Good morning," but Paula pushed the cheery woman aside as she ran to the exit. By the time she reached the heat of Decatur Street, Paula was in a full sprint, bumping one person after another as she focused on the crowd ahead of her, searching for the beautiful face and the shoulder-length auburn hair that framed it. She slowed her pace and then stopped, scanning the street for any sign of the woman, but the crowd was too thick. Paula spun around just in case she'd missed the girl in her haste but found only the gaze of strangers reflecting her own confusion. She saw Esther's face in the restaurant window looking out at her with an expression her friend must have reserved for the insane, but that didn't matter.

Vicki Bach, Paula thought. The face had belonged to Vicki Bach.

5

Sam had asked him to lunch, and though Ken wanted to see his old friend, he felt badly about spending time away from the hospital. He'd convinced himself that Bobby needed him, but the comfort, what little came from the visits, was Ken's.

Sam had suggested Martino's, a comfortable if unexceptional Uptown restaurant less than a mile from Paula's house in the Garden District. Ken arrived first and was seated in a booth in back beneath a great, drooping plastic vine with fat leaves, many of which were sun bleached to a pale olive. From the speakers, a tinny piano played the Muzak version of an Elton John song that Ken couldn't remember the words to.

Sam arrived a few minutes later, pushing through the tightly packed lunch crowd. He waved in a silly exaggerated manner, skirting the tables and chair. The years were not being kind to Sam. Three years Ken's senior, the teacher looked sallow and haggard, a rough etching of the striking man he'd once been. But Ken was glad to see him. Sam's smile, which had not changed, brought back so many good memories that Ken couldn't pick a single favorite: meeting for happy hour, sharing stories about the men they'd fucked, cruising the baths and the bars, being in a constant state of erotic charge as he explored a world his marriage should have forbid him. He had never been proud of his infidelities, and hours, sometimes days, of soul searching often followed them, but in their grasp, with Sam and the adventures he orchestrated, Ken lost himself in the excitement. And Sam was always there to listen, to nod and smile and offer rational advice, even when Ken felt his life had spun far away from reason.

When he'd told Sam about his impending separation from Paula, his friend had hugged him and kissed his neck. "You're both going to be miserable," Sam had whispered in his ear. "Then, you're both going to be happy. I'm congratulating you on the happy part."

Upon reaching the booth, Sam leaned over the table and kissed Ken on the lips. An old trepidation flared in Ken's chest.

"Still uptight about PDAs?" Sam said with a smile.

"Something like that," Ken replied, reflexively looking around the room to see if anyone had taken notice of the affectionate greeting.

"Get past yourself," Sam said. He took his seat and pushed the menu to the side. "So, how are you? All of this shit with Bobby has got to be a nightmare."

"I don't know what to say. It doesn't seem real."

"Yeah," Sam said. "Paula told me a lot about it, especially about that bitch he was seeing. None of it makes much sense, but he's alive and we're going to keep him that way."

Ken wasn't so sure, but he knew that Sam had a tough time seeing the dark side of anything. His friend accepted the blows the world gave him along with the gifts, and he kept his smile at the ready regardless of what came his way. When his lover, Jersey, had been diagnosed seropositive, Sam refused to be angry or accusing. Instead, he'd gone on about the wonders of the drug cocktails. Still, Ken could see something had been wearing at Sam; the lines around his mouth and eyes were far deeper than they'd been over the holidays when Sam had brought Jersey to Austin. His eyes were circled with dark skin, and the puffy bags Sam called "hang-over tits," hung beneath them.

"How are you?" Ken asked. "How's Jersey?"

"One crisis at a time," Sam said. He flashed his smile, but it lacked its usual light.

The waitress arrived and took their lunch order, including Sam's request for a whiskey, neat. Sam's drink order, hard liquor so early in the day, told Ken things weren't going well for his friend.

Ken waited for the girl to leave before he said, "So, it's getting bad?"

"Getting?" Sam asked, exaggerating the word. "No, things are okay. Really. Jersey just started a new round of meds, and they aren't exactly agreeing with him. As a result, he isn't exactly agree-ing with *me* about anything."

"I'm sorry to hear that. Do you need anything?"

"Not a single thing. We just hit a little bump in the road. That happens when you're on the long haul. We'll find the right combi-nation and shazam! All will be right with the world. Until then, I just keep my head down and make sure his gun is hidden in the laundry room."

Ken smiled. He reached across the table and patted Sam's hand.

"So, have the police found anything?" Sam asked.

"No. Right now, they're looking for some kid Vicki described. Before all of this happened, she told Bobby she was being fol-lowed. Considering she disappeared and is probably involved, the description isn't worth shit."

"Are they even looking for her?"

"They'd better be. She may not have actually attacked Bobby, but no one's going to convince me that she wasn't involved."

"Which brings us back to the bitch," Sam said. "I don't see how anyone can just disappear these days."

"For all we know, nothing Vicki Bach told Bobby was true. We may not know until they find her."

"That address she gave," Sam said, shaking his head slowly.

"That family named Brugier? That is severely fucked up if you think about it."

"I've thought about it," Ken said.

"Maybe, but for us locals it's a different beast," Sam told him.

The girl returned with their drinks. They clinked their glasses, and Sam poured a generous gulp of whiskey.

"You were off in Texas getting edu-ma-cated. I lived here, and I'll tell ya', nothing you picked up later, even the most exaggerated stories, can compare to the shit that went down when the cops discovered those bodies. After they found Travis and those kids, all hell broke loose in this town."

"Really?" Ken said. Though he'd lived in the Quarter while Travis Brugier's Parlor was in operation, he'd been gone before the bodies had been discovered on the property. He knew almost nothing about the aftermath of those killings.

"Considering the kind of folks that frequented Brugier's Parlor, it's not surprising. I mean if he'd pulled a Heidi Fleiss and actually kept records, a lot of important people would have been ruined. Not to mention the fact that early on, no one believed Brugier had done it."

This was news to Ken. As far as he knew, there'd never been any other suspects in the crime. "Who else could have done it?"

Sam laughed. "Irrelevant. We're talking about gossip here. If I remember it right, some woman was walking her dog and saw a guy sneaking out of Brugier's place the night of the murders. The police never followed up on it as far as I know, but a lot of queers were getting nervous, because if Brugier didn't commit the crime, someone else did, and he was still out there. We had us a good dose of paranoia there for a while, thinking some gay-hating psycho was prowling the Quarter."

"I think it's pretty clear Brugier did it," Ken said.

"*Now,* yes," Sam replied. He took another sip from his whiskey. The glass was already half empty. "And good riddance. I never went to The Parlor. My first lover wouldn't let me anywhere near the place, but he said it was the closest thing to evil he'd ever experienced on this earth, and this is a guy who had seen some nastiness in his day."

Ken nodded his head. He had nothing further to say on the subject. Brugier was another chapter in the city's miserable history, and though Vicki Bach had chosen to resurrect this particular nightmare with her perverse charade, Ken didn't see any reason to reward her perfidy by investing himself in its details.

The waitress delivered their lunch, and the conversation returned to the present. Sam asked him about his business, asked about Austin and about Ken's love life, specifically, Kyle.

"I'm not seeing him anymore," Ken said.

"A personal trainer?" Sam asked. "Are you nuts? What was he, brainless?"

"He had a brain. He had a lot of things, but it was just fun and games."

"Why?" Sam asked. The playful edge in his voice was gone.

"Why what?"

"Well, you wrote the guy off as fuck practice awfully quick."

Ken bristled. "How long does it take? Christ, you and Jersey moved in together the night you met. It's either there or it isn't."

"Okay, calm down," Sam said. "Just asking."

But Ken knew his friend wasn't just asking. He was trying to maneuver the conversation to a particular issue, a specific person. Ken couldn't count the number of times Sam had gone down that path over the last year. Late-night phone calls, e-mails, nearly every communication included barely concealed allusions, if not outright discussion, of David Lane. Right now, with everything else happening—Bobby's attack and injury—the last thing Ken needed was that particular pain.

"Sorry," Sam said. "We don't seem to have many happy topics to choose from today."

"It's like that sometimes."

"Well, here's to hoping we have some good news by Friday," Sam said.

"Friday?"

"My birthday," Sam said. "Shit, I told Jersey to make sure you had an invitation. I imagine since he's feeling particularly contentious these days and you live in another state, he decided to save the postage."

"Sounds like fun," Ken said, but it didn't, of course. It sounded wrong. He couldn't imagine himself enjoying a party, not with Bobby in the hospital.

The conversation waned throughout the remainder of their lunch. Ken was feeling guilty about his time away from the hospital and also was discovering that there wasn't a damned thing in his life he felt comfortable talking about, even with Sam.

After Ken paid the bill, they walked outside. He told Sam that he'd see him on Friday, and Sam gave him another kiss on the lips.

"Things can only get better," Sam said.

Ken couldn't remember a phrase that sounded more like a curse in his life.

6

After his lunch with Sam, Ken returned to the hospital. In the lobby, he checked messages at the office, retrieved voice mail, scanned through his Blackberry looking for some distracting bit of business, but things were quiet. His business obligation complete, he went upstairs and looked at his boy. Only a swatch of Bobby's face, gleaming with an unhealthy pallor, peeked through the bandages and tubes: closed eyes, a bit of cheek smaller than Ken's palm. Nothing more. Bobby's chest rose and fell in barely visible waves. Still, every sound on the ward, in the room, needled Ken with unlikely hope. The whispered conversations, padding footsteps, the sound of a pen clacking to the floor behind the nurse's station made him alert, made him search Bobby's face for some sign of waking.

Sitting in the chair, Ken drifted into a doze. The familiar tune of an old upright piano played in his head. Despite the unhappy history Ken associated with this song, the tune lulled him, and he rode its notes into a shallow sleep.

Then, he was back in a night-cloaked courtyard, bathed in the cloying sweet scent of rose and jasmine and azalea. Beside him, the concrete fountain was silent, water pooled in its basin, motionless. Bobby stood on the flagstones ahead. He was whole and awake but naked. Behind his son stood a two-story structure. Along the lower level, windows and French doors revealed rooms full of men surrounded by thick clouds of smoke. The men were laughing, toasting one another, kissing one another, but as Ken looked on, the revelry ceased. The ragtime lullaby ended midmeasure, and all of the men turned to gaze out on father and son.

Ken couldn't move. He felt he should say something, do something. But even when Bobby turned his back and walked toward the building and the dead blank faces of the men behind the glass, Ken remained paralyzed. A door opened as Bobby approached. The men framed by the jamb pushed forward. They had gray skin, gray clothing. Where they should have had eyes and mouths, there were open pits of endless black, and Ken saw that these men were not standing in clouds of smoke; they were carved from it.

Arms trailing wisps of fog reached for Bobby. Ghostly hands grasped him, holding his shoulders, caressing his back, cupping his buttocks. The faces of the groping men did not change; they remained emotionless and empty, even as their exploration of his son's skin grew frantic.

"Bobby?" Ken called.

His son turned around. All about him, the smoke grew thick. The bodies of his admirers lost definition. Fingers, hands, and arms spread and thickened. Shoulders and legs bled out into the hazy material that had made them. Only the faces remained, hovering over Bobby's shoulders, at his sides, and between his legs.

"Why did you bring me here?" Bobby asked.

A hand fell on Ken's shoulder. He came awake with a start.

"Sorry," Paula whispered.

He blinked several times to get the sleep from his eyes and to recalibrate his mind to the real. Once the dream was wholly gone, Ken looked up at his ex-wife and searched the door behind her.

"Where's Jen?" he asked.

"She's meeting us at the house." Paula walked around the side of their son's bed and rubbed his cheek, carefully avoiding the plastic tube that fed him oxygen. "Have you been here all day?"

"Uh-huh. I had lunch with Sam."

"And how'd that go?"

"Fine," he said.

Ken wasn't in the mood for conversation, not just now. Even without the unsettling dream so fresh in his mind, Ken would have preferred silence. His chat with Sam over lunch had proven that Ken could trust no topic of conversation to comfort him.

Finally, after thirty minutes of stilted chitchat, Paula suggested they leave.

As they drove away from the hospital, Ken tried several times to speak, but the words weighed too much. Instead, he watched the lights burning in the houses and marveled at the rainbows exploding from the bevels of crystal imbedded in the heavy doors of the Garden District homes.

Their home, now Paula's, was a large Victorian with a single turret to the left of the porch. Standing on a stone foundation, the house was painted in the Queen Anne style, with rich green, brick-red, salmon, and cream in the gingerbread trim. The ceiling of the porch was painted sky blue, which Ken had heard kept bees from building hives. Though the exterior was considered authentic to the style, Paula had wanted something more modern for the interior, so much of the wallpaper had been stripped away and the walls resurfaced and painted.

It was a nice house, but it belonged to Paula, always had. Ken found the place, despite its colorful façade, somber and claustrophobic.

With the house looming over him, apprehension crept into Ken's chest. He followed Paula up the back stairs to the porch and caught a glimpse of Jennifer talking on the phone in the kitchen. His heart raced, and he braced himself for whatever was to come.

Seeing his daughter saddened him. Jennifer had inherited her mother's battle against weight but unfortunately not her beautiful bones. She had her father's face, square and pleasant, but hardly the striking features of Paula Nicholson. Makeup did little to hide the masculine bent of her nose and cheeks. Her mouth had lips too thin to be considered lovely. When she smiled, it seemed to hurt her. Pinched and crooked, her happiness showed through a look of bitter uncertainty, though, admittedly, Ken had not seen her smile in a long time.

Paula pushed open the door. A cold swathe of air conditioning wrapped itself around Ken's neck, and he took his first step into the house.

Jennifer looked up. In one hand she held the headset of a cordless phone; with the fingers of her other hand she absently twirled a lock of thin, stringy hair. Even her mother's hair had been denied the girl. For that matter, so too her father's. Ken remembered his mother's hair—all unmanageable twine—and unfortunately Jennifer had been its unhappy recipient. He ached for her to be beautiful, but she wasn't. Even with a father's bias, Ken couldn't convince himself she was anything but plain.

Ken said, "Hello," and Jennifer waved, holding up a palm to let her parents know that the call was very important. She stood and left the kitchen.

"Nice to see you too," he whispered.

"She's at that age," Paula replied, immediately moving to the refrigerator to begin dinner.

"She's been at that age for years," Ken said sadly. He took a step forward, then another. Finally, he reached Paula and wrapped his arms around her, pulling her tightly to his chest. Paula returned the embrace momentarily, and then she patted his back, the universal symbol that an embrace had come to an end. He didn't let go, though, not at first.

"I have to fix supper," Paula whispered, again patting his back.

He dropped his arms hesitantly and stepped away. Ken crossed the kitchen and leaned against the counter. Paula removed four bowls from the refrigerator and placed them gently on the countertop.

"Can I help?" he asked.

"I just have to heat the veal," she said. "The vegetables are chopped, so I think I have things under control." She pulled plastic off of the bowls' lips. "Do you want to talk…"

Jennifer returned to the kitchen, wearing a pair of jeans, a T-shirt, and a heavy cotton shirt that accentuated her weight. The girl hugged her mother quickly from behind and then moved to her father. The embrace was brief: Jennifer turned her head to the side, her cheek barely skimming his before she pulled away.

"Welcome home," she said lightly. After the lackluster greeting, she turned and pulled a carrot stick out of the closest bowl. Noisily she crunched on the vegetable.

"How have you been?" Ken asked.

"Fine."

"Still fighting the boys off with a stick?"

Jennifer shrugged, crunching her carrot. She smacked loudly as she ate. Having finished the first, she fished another out of the bowl and stepped backward, leaning on the counter opposite Ken.

"How's Robert?" she asked her mother.

But Ken replied, "No change. Have you been out to see him?"

His daughter shot him an angry glance. Of course I have, the look told him. How dare you?

"Couple of times," she said.

He fell silent and scanned the kitchen. The house, once *his* house, felt alien. He knew its layout, knew how to find everything from the bathrooms to the corkscrew buried in the third drawer to the left of the oven. But now he was an intruder.

"You want a drink?" Paula asked.

"I'll get it," he said, pushing away from the counter.

Half of the drink was gone before he spoke again, the warmth from the vodka limbering his throat. "How's school going?" he asked his daughter.

"Fine," she said.

Dinner went little better. His attempts at conversation were shot down by his daughter with monosyllabic replies that made it clear that no more information would be given on any of the respective topics. Ken couldn't help but remember how his daughter had been as a little girl. In fact, up until only a few years ago, she had been talkative and animated; everything had been interesting and engaging to her. He saw none of that winsome child over dinner, hadn't seen her in a very long time, so he focused on his meal when the burden of conversation grew too heavy. He finished three glasses of wine, making his stomach rumble and his head feel light.

As Paula cleared the dishes, Ken leaned back with a cigarette and eyed his daughter. So much lost there. Not like Bobby. He had no inkling of what to say to the young woman.

"You know," Jennifer finally said, "Bobby used to talk about his girlfriend, Vicki, a lot."

"I know."

"He told me," Jennifer said, "that she knew you."

The cigarette stopped in front of Ken's lips as he looked at his daughter. A match strike of anxiety lit in his gut, and if this conversation continued in the direction that he thought it might, that tiny flame would soon be raging. "Really?"

Jennifer nodded, saying nothing more as her mother came into the room with two cups of coffee.

"You still take a disgusting amount of sugar don't you?" Paula asked. After accepting the slight movement of Ken's head as a yes, she excused herself. "I'll only be a minute with the dishes."

Around a sly smile Jennifer appraised her father and the effect her words had had on him. "Very interesting stuff," Jennifer baited.

"Why don't you just say what's on your mind?"

"You used to live in the Quarter," Jennifer told him.

"I'd think my house there would have cleared that up," Ken said.

"Before you met Mom," Jennifer added.

He said nothing.

"Bobby used to laugh about it. He said that Vicki made all of this stuff up, just like the stories she told him about the Civil War and colonial times. She was always joking about historical stuff. Anyway, she had this great story about a man who used to keep slaves in his house in the Quarter. They weren't real slaves, just little boys who did whatever he told them. And there was this one boy…"

"For God's sake," Ken interrupted. He chuckled and tried to pass it off as a joke. Ice flowed and cut his veins; sweat popped out on his neck and brow; the smile on his lips was heavy, false. Jennifer's eyes told him that she recognized the charade.

"It's a good story," she taunted.

"I'm sure it must be." He heard the tremble in his voice, knew his hands shook. "I thought you meant she really knew me."

"Oh, Daddy," Jennifer laughed. Ken caught himself staring. He tried to bring the smile back to his lips, but the attempt died when Jennifer's frigid eyes locked on his. "How could anybody know *you?*"

7

Chuck peered through the window the family gathered around the dining table. That Nicholson jerk looked scared. Chuck liked that. His daughter, the ugly little cow, looked pleased. Yeah, things were going good. Vicki really knew how to pull strings, but then it didn't take a genius to figure that out. From the first moment he'd seen her barreling down the highway in the red convertible, he knew that they would have good times together.

Three months ago, he'd left home, left the fucked-up couple he called his parents back in Houston. There was a whole big world out there, and the last thing he wanted was to be stuck with those two. They were a pair all right. Either one of them would have guzzled drain cleaner if they'd thought it would get them high. His mother expressed affection by screaming like a crazy-ass bitch, and his father expressed it with his cock late at night in the darkness of Chuck's bedroom. His father: the prick of the universe, the master of all he laid.

Yeah, that guy was about as stable as nitro on a pogo stick.

Once, on his thirteenth birthday, Chuck had been playing in

the garage. Though he had been warned away from his father's lame collection of beat-up old tools, he'd managed to get his hands on the electric drill. He had collected some eggs from a nest in the backyard and was attempting to punch tiny holes in the shells. He wanted to see the babies sleeping. Two of the shells had burst apart in the vice, depositing their wet, ugly contents onto the floor. Damp feathers had looked like shredded meat; the babies' tiny wings slapped the concrete for a heartbeat or two and then collapsed. Huge lidded eyes like yellow blisters rested on heads too large for their tiny, weak bodies. They had been disgusting. And with only one egg left he was being extra careful.

Now, so many years later, he could not fathom what curiosity had driven him to locate and destroy those eggs, but at the time, it had seemed the most important project known to man. It had so thoroughly engrossed him that he hadn't heard the garage door opening or his father's approach. But when he saw the shadow fall over him, painting his shoulders, the vice, and its delicate contents, he knew he was in for a hurt. Even though Chuck's dad was as calm and deliberate as his mother was bat-shit nuts, his father's preacher-cool voice was ice on a river. His father ran deep and dark, like that river, and the fucker knew how to dispense a hurt.

Chuck had kept his back to his father, afraid to turn around. He released the drill trigger and put the tool down on the bench, already voicing apologies and excuses. His father pushed into Chuck's back. One fist locked around Chuck's wrist to slam his palm against the workbench.

"You gotta feel your mistakes," his father had said evenly, reaching over Chuck's shoulder for the drill. "Otherwise you'll never learn."

The drill whirred into life. Chuck cried and struggled, never able to break his father's grasp. The cacophony of his pleas got lost beneath the drill's high-pitched whine. The bit hummed, poised above the meat between Chuck's thumb and index finger.

"You gotta feel 'em."

Chuck rubbed the web of skin between his thumb and forefinger as he gazed in at the Nicholson family. The scar there, nearly perfectly round, looked kind of cool to him now.

The drill was by no means the last of his father's lessons. After five more years of that shit, Chuck had *felt* and *learned* more than enough. So, he took off, leaving his father behind, unconscious from the farewell beating Chuck had given him with a wrench.

He'd left home with a simple plan. He would hitch to Key West or Palm Beach, someplace where men paid for the right to fuck someone like him. Maybe he'd find a nice old woman who wanted a pretty escort and a name to put in her will. It didn't matter to him. Gay or straight were irrelevant titles; they suggested that he gave a shit about whom he was fucking. Chuck couldn't care less. As his father's apprentice, he had learned that a cock operated for reasons extending far beyond the ridiculous concept of love. Money, power, hatred—all seemed equally effective aphrodisiacs.

Men were easier though. He knew that. Lessons in the alleys behind dark bars, lessons in the quiet park only a few blocks from his house—they taught him men were easier, more willing to part with a bill to get their rocks off.

On that day three months ago, with his throat dry and his belly just starting to kick for food, the red convertible pulled to the side of the road and waited for him. Behind the wheel, a woman with dark glasses that hid her eyes and accentuated the pale skin of her face leaned back against the seat and introduced herself as Vicki. In those first moments, he understood that Vicki was very comfortable in her skin. In the hours that followed, she made promises to him, and he believed every word. Despite a life built on cynical ground, he knew Vicki could give him the things she promised. And more.

Money was only the beginning. She'd shown him plenty of that. Already he had a closet full of new clothes, a cell phone, and three hundred bucks in his pocket. A decent enough start, considering he wasn't paying rent or bills or buying his own meals. It was a good gig, and it was just going to get better. Hell, he figured she'd give him just about anything he asked for. And it all had something to do with this guy on the other side of the window.

Ken Nicholson stood from the dining table and lit a cigarette, watching his ugly daughter run up the stairs. The boy liked the guy's look. Nicholson looked classy, but he was in for a world of hurt.

Sometimes Chuck wondered what Nicholson might have done to piss Vicki off. Knocked her up, maybe. But no, after so many months that would show. Besides, she'd told him that the guy was a fag (though he hadn't shown the least bit of interest in Chuck). So maybe the old guy cheated her out of some cash. Chuck's imagination went no further. But that was cool. It didn't need to. Vicki had more than enough imagination for the both of them.

8

Following the disastrous dinner with his family, Ken knew he'd keep his distance from the Victorian in the Garden District. Maybe just a day or two, but he couldn't manage his own grief while under attack. Paula had been uncharacteristically distant throughout the evening, and his daughter had deemed him unworthy of conversation, save for sharing an odd bit of history she'd picked up from Vicki Bach.

She knew you.

Ken didn't believe that. Even if her name was a lie, Ken socialized with few, if any, women of that age. Hadn't in years. Even his office staff, though predominantly women, were mostly career veterans who were well into their forties. Vicki might have been the daughter of a business associate, maybe even a competitor, but to the best of Ken's knowledge, he had made no enemies in his small corner of the business world.

That night, back in his house on Dumaine, Ken had run the possibilities over in his head a dozen times, and discounting any association proved simple enough. These days, his sphere of interaction was severely limited.

But that's not what really worried him. Looking for a connection in the present was just a distraction, a mental exercise, keeping him from the truly disturbing prospect of looking at the past.

...she had this great story about a man who used to keep slaves in his house in the Quarter. They weren't real slaves, just little boys who did whatever he told them....

Jennifer had never finished telling him the story about the man in the Quarter and his boy-servants. She hadn't needed to. His daughter was alluding to Travis Brugier. The boys she'd mentioned weren't slaves, not even by the broadest definition of the word. Brugier had owned a private club and filled the establishment with attractive young men for the amusement of his clientele. Many of those kids, from what Ken understood, did quite well for themselves. Though Ken had heard some people call Brugier's lounge The Parlor, most referred to it as Wonderland.

The place hadn't existed for over thirty years. Wonderland died with its owner. But this was the second time Vicki Bach had attempted to weave herself into the mythology of a long-dead psychopath: the address she'd given the police and now this bizarre tale. He didn't understand how Vicki might have discovered this hidden fragment of his past.

History is dust, he reminded himself. No matter how thoroughly you wipe it away, it always returns to settle. Since his first night home—the phone caller requesting a story (Vicki? he wondered), the piano's rag, Travis Brugier, Wonderland—the dust had been gathering.

Later, as he lay in bed, dreaming, the past and present came together. Like vicious birds, the memories swooped in to peck and break apart his emotional integrity. David Lane, the man he had dated and had wanted to build a life with, figured prominently in his nightmares, but he wasn't alone. Bobby was there, and Jennifer and Paula, and a woman he'd never met named Vicki Bach.

Throughout the night, fragments of history jolted him from sleep and into the sweat-drenched bed of his home, his breath halted by the images, his body quaking before their power. Early the following morning, he wasted no time in deserting his house to free himself from its isolation and its memories.

He had been back in New Orleans for two days.

❧

As this third day began, Ken waited until he was certain that neither his ex-wife nor his daughter would be at the hospital before having a cab drop him off. He bought a *Times Picayune* in the gift shop and stopped at the cafeteria for some coffee. Upstairs, he entered the ward, saw Stella behind the counter, and raised his hand in greeting.

"Mornin'," Stella said, meeting his wave with a bright smile. "You two have a nice time."

Ken nodded and continued across the floor to the threshold of his son's room. They'd turned a light on in the corner to go with the dim bulb glowing from the headboard of Bobby's bed. The extra light did little to brighten the place.

Ken went to Bobby and kissed his cheek. Familiar pain greeted him as he looked down on his son, motionless, eyes closed.

He sat in the room for nearly an hour, trying to read the newspaper, but his cluttered mind batted the words out of his head the moment he'd read them. In addition to his scattered thoughts, he was again aware of the sounds of the ward, of the room. He would no sooner read a paragraph when a noise would interrupt him, make him look at his son, hoping, always hoping, that the sound—a sign of waking—had come from his boy.

The decision to read aloud, to read to Bobby, emerged when Ken's frustrations had escalated to the point of nearly driving him from the room, the ward, and the hospital.

On his first night visiting Bobby, he'd seen a woman reading to a patient. He'd thought it sad, then somewhat desperate, but he understood its value now. Even if Bobby didn't hear him, if he was incapable of knowing that his father was in the room, speaking to the boy reminded Ken that his son was alive.

At first, talking to the motionless form and hearing his voice floating in the room unnerved him, a premature elegy. Then he relaxed and just read, hoping his words could somehow dismantle the blockade behind which his son slept.

He read the sports page—Bobby's favorite—first, then the world news, local stories, and the entertainment section. Ken kept his voice low, speaking just loud enough to reach his son.

After finishing the paper, Ken stood and stretched. The machines around him, twisted technological sculptures, hissed and whined. Ken folded the paper and replaced it on the chair before leaving the room and walking into the ward.

Behind the circular desk Stella sat, sawing at a long red fingernail. Another nurse was speaking quietly into the telephone, assuring the caller that "When we know something more, we'll let you know."

In the cafeteria, Ken poured his second coffee, paid for it, then made his way to the lobby and the spring day beyond the electronic doors. Heat filled the air, and above him the sky threatened to rain. Beneath the overcast sky, Ken found himself feeling better. He couldn't say why exactly. Reading to Bobby was part of it; somehow, even if his words never found their way into Bobby's head, Ken felt like he was participating in his son's recovery. He had issues of his own to be sure, but they didn't seem as important just now.

Despite his dreams and the disease of memory, Ken realized that history had one particular quality that made it a benign if disturbing entity: The people who survived wrote the history. Ken had survived. Perhaps dreams and memory were vicious attempts to reinforce the lessons of the past, but they held no real power.

An ambulance passed slowly in front of him, kicking up a cloud of dust and pollen. The red and white paint on the vehicle seemed particularly stark even with the dark sky above. When it passed, Ken saw the handsome young man who had spoken to him in Lafitte's the day after his arrival.

His name was Chuck, wasn't it?

Chuck stood across the drive, between two cars. Leaning

against a red BMW roadster, the boy had a hard expression. He sported a tank top to show off his muscles and wore sunglasses. He waved a hand in the air as he tried to explain something to a young woman in a robin's egg–blue dress. She had short, reddish-brown hair cinched in back with an elastic band and stood in partial profile as she listened to Chuck's animated speech. From where Ken stood, only the rise of her cheekbone showed.

Ken checked his watch. It was just after noon.

When he looked up again, both the young man and the woman were staring at him. A smile cut along Chuck's mouth, but it was the woman who truly caught Ken's attention. She had an amazing face, round and youthful like a porcelain doll's and a tight, slender figure. She seemed startled, and then something else crossed her face, something wholly unexpected. Her features softened for a moment as if she were seeing a lost child. Only for a moment did Ken notice this. Then her expression grew rigid.

The weight of her stare pushed at him, forced him backward. He turned and hurried into the hospital lobby, back to the elevator and up to his son's ward.

❧

Tonight the torments of history remained locked away, giving him a few hours of peaceful rest. In a dream, Paula had been teaching him to dance; patiently, she was showing him the waltz in the living room of the tiny apartment he'd rented while still attending the university in Austin. Candlelight followed them around the room as they spun on their toes and came back into the simple box step she had shown him. He pressed his face into her neck. Then, he was holding someone else—a stronger grasp around his waist, a sturdy body contoured perfectly to his own. *David?* But a demanding tone woke him and canceled his joy. The phone's cry startled him. His first pleasant dream since his return to the city faded to light as he opened his eyes.

Ken cleared his throat and lifted the phone. "Hello?"

"He's awake, Ken," Paula said, all but gushing. Tears filled her throat, making her voice crack. "Bobby's awake. The hospital just called. He's going to be okay. Bobby's going to be okay."

Awake? Bobby was awake, and he was going to be fine. No not fine. Not yet. But awake.

"Yes," he said. "Yes I'll meet you." Heart racing, Ken felt exalted. He hurried out of bed and into his clothes.

The night embraced New Orleans as he rode through the outskirts of the city toward Ocshner Hospital. The residents were sleeping. History slept too. No disturbing echoes from the shadows of youth pushed their way into his excited thoughts. Memory lay where it belonged—quiet, restful, harmless in its slumber—but not his son. Bobby was awake.

The cab stopped at the hospital. He paid and rushed out. Ken ran through the lobby, ignoring the imploring voice of the information desk attendant. The elevator opened, and he held his breath waiting for the door to close. He jabbed the plastic disk with the number four on it, and it lit. He pressed the glowing button half a dozen times hoping to speed the elevator to the fourth floor.

Come on. Come on.

In painful slow motion, the door opened. A young man with bad skin and thick wavy hair regarded him from behind the nurse's station. His mouth was opening to say something, but Ken didn't wait to hear. The obstruction of the desk passed beside him as he raced forward, his eyes locked on the little glass room. Paula had not yet arrived, but that didn't matter.

Still, he thought, each step seeming to take him no closer to his son, shouldn't there have been attendants? Doctors? He slowed his pace, gazing over his shoulder at the young man coming from around the desk.

"My son?" he asked, as if that explained everything.

"Sir, you can't be here…" Ken didn't hear the nurse. He spun on his heels and walked into the room, his heart shrinking with every step.

No change. His son lay in the same position with the same

machines making the same noises doing the same things to keep him alive. No change. Perhaps they were letting him rest. Perhaps the doctors, having succeeded in his son's revival, had gone down to the cafeteria to celebrate their life-giving power. But no, he knew, he could see there was no change in his boy.

A firm hand grabbed his arm, and Ken spun quickly, expecting to see the blemished nurse. Instead of the pimply face, he encountered a sturdy young woman with short, dark hair and thick, pouting lips.

"Mr. Nicholson?" she asked.

"Yes," he replied. This was the woman who had called Paula; this was the woman who would give him the same wonderful news.

"Is something wrong?" she asked. "Can I help you?"

"Didn't you call?" He heard the plea in his voice. If she hadn't called then…

"Sir, there's still no change in Robert's condition."

But the call?

The doctor seemed confused. She blinked her eyes. "I understand your concern…"

"But the call. My wife…ex-wife, she said that he was awake. She told me that you called her. Goddamn it what's going on here?"

"Sir, I'm not…"

"What's going on?" he demanded. "I know my wife's voice. She called me. And I…" A possibility surfaced, and he discounted it immediately. "…did not dream this."

"There's obviously been a mistake."

No mistake, he thought. Paula's voice was too clear. He had been awake, leaping from the bed even as she told him to meet her at the hospital. No dream. It had been her voice.

The silence of the ward crashed in on him. His thoughts became too loud, his voice shrill and demanding. Even the subdued condolences of the doctor struck his eardrums like thunder. Before him, the nurse, his pimply face harboring pity, gazed at the exchange. Nothing else moved, there were no other sounds, and the only odor was the horrible cleanliness of the place, his sweat, and a thin waft of men's cologne. He hated the ward, hated its pretensions. They cured nothing here, merely monitored the dying until a new piece of meat came in. Then the whole festival of impotency began again.

No change. We'll let you know. I'm afraid there's been a mistake.

"Damn it," Ken whispered. He put a fist to his throbbing head. "Damn it," he cursed, and again and again.

"Mr. Nicholson," the doctor said, "maybe you should sit down."

Maybe you should go fuck yourself, he thought. But he said nothing. He shook his head and held up his arm. Calm settled slowly, easing into his system, edging out the frustration and disappointment.

He had been awake. It had been Paula's voice. But why? he wondered. Had *she* imagined the call? Were her dreams corrupted by wishful thinking? Had she dreamed about this happiness and then woken to call him to share the bounty of her fiction? Though possible, he doubted it. Paula was too logical, too precise. And hadn't the call sounded emotional? Too emotional?

A joke? he wondered. A cruel, inhuman joke?

"Mr. Nicholson…"

"Fine," he grunted. "I'm fine. Just…give me a minute okay?"

The doctor and nurse withdrew from the room, leaving him alone with his son. Ken took the chair and pulled it to the side of the bed where he had spent that afternoon reading Bobby the newspaper. The desolate expression on his boy's face made him ache as it always did, but particularly now with the veil of night over Bobby's features. He looked dead.

This shouldn't be happening. He's just a kid. *You were younger than him when you…*

Ken shook the voice out of his head. This wasn't about him; it was about his son. A boy. An innocent. Someone had viciously attacked Bobby, and the police had come up with nothing. Vicki

Bach, the boy's fiancée, vanished after the assault, leaving nothing of herself behind but a mystery.

The address belonged to a family named Brugier.

Stop it, Ken scolded himself silently. This isn't about you or about that place.

He needed to focus, needed to keep his wits. He couldn't go through another breakdown. Not now. Not when Bobby needed him.

"God," Ken whispered to his son's motionless form, "what am I supposed to do?"

Ken didn't expect a response. He received one nonetheless.

When Bobby spoke, filling the room with a ghastly moan that barely resembled human language, Ken froze. Joy and relief were kept at bay by a familiar command put forth by a voice that could not belong to a living soul. Though Bobby Nicholson moaned a series of nonsensical sounds that could hardly be called speech, "Tell me a story," were the words Ken Nicholson heard.

9

Exhaustion. Exhilaration. Ken felt both as he sat at the cafeteria table with Paula. Staff and visitors wandered through the room. Last night had passed in a blur of anticipation and endless movement. Numerous voices had come and gone. Paula arrived sometime after three thirty, with no tears or panic, just her calm presence as she entered the room and moved directly to Ken, accepting his embrace and whispering "Thank God" in his ear. Jennifer had followed her mother into the ward, taking in the quiet commotion behind a veil of indifference. She'd hugged her father lightly and pushed up against Paula's side. Both women listened as Ken repeated what the doctors had told him.

Jennifer stayed until it was time to leave for school. She accepted the money Ken gave her for a cab, shoving the bills into the pocket of her jeans without a thank-you, and left her parents in the cafeteria.

The relief was so great that Ken hadn't felt like talking. He wanted to enjoy the step Bobby had taken without the burden of analyzing it. He was also exhausted, and his mind was winding down, making conversation difficult.

Paula wanted to chat, of course. She was happy and hopeful, so Ken remained, listening to her but offering little in the way of insights of his own. During lapses in the conversation, he was more than pleased to remain silent.

"What were you doing here?" Paula asked. "I mean, you were here when he woke up. What brought you here so late?"

You called me, he thought, but he settled for "Premonition."

This answer didn't satisfy Paula, he could see, but it was all he was willing to say.

After a minute of silence, she said, "Now I guess we just have to wait, see how much damage was done."

Ken knew that this was going to be the worst part. The doctors had prepared them only slightly for their son's future, if he indeed had one. Bobby might have regressed to childhood. Walking, eating, toilet training, and learning the world all over again might be awaiting him. Even worse, his mind might not accommodate this learning, and the boy could be impaired for the rest of his life.

"Will I see you tonight?" Paula asked.

"We could have dinner," Ken said, sounding wholly uninterested in the prospect, though the indifference in his tone was not mean spirited. He was just so tired that all he wanted to think about was getting home to bed for some rest.

"I meant at Sam's party."

"Oh, yeah," he said. His friend's birthday celebration. "I forgot about that. It's at their place?"

"Yes."

"I suppose so," Ken said.

"Are you going back soon?" Paula asked.

"To Austin?" Ken said. "No. They don't need me there."

"It's nice to have you home for a while," she said. "You usually just pop into town for a couple of days and then disappear."

"I'm sorry," Ken said, wondering if that was what she wanted to hear. "I suppose it wasn't really fair to you, my leaving so suddenly."

"Do you want to talk about it?"

"What?"

"Why you left. I knew it wasn't business."

Ken stared down at his coffee as if the answer floated on the oily surface of the black liquid. "It was personal," he said. "At the time, I thought it was best."

"Did you meet someone out there?" Paula asked.

"No." He shook his head slowly, not looking up from the coffee. "I was…I was involved with someone here. It didn't work out."

"It must have been serious."

"I suppose it was," Ken lied. He knew damned well it had been serious with David. It had been serious and wonderful. "But when it fell apart, I needed some distance."

"Do you stay in touch?"

God, I wish we did, Ken thought. Especially now. How many times had he fought against calling David's number even in the last few days? A dozen? Two dozen? But he wouldn't do it. Over was over. Ken had made the decision, and it had caused enough suffering. He shook his head.

Paula leaned forward on the table. Her movement forced Ken to look up. "Are you seeing anyone now?"

"No."

"No one at all?"

"For God's sake," Ken whispered, returning his eyes to the slick on his coffee.

"I'm serious, Ken. I'm worried about you."

"I'm fine."

"You are anything but fine," Paula said.

"Our son is lying upstairs with very little chance of leading any kind of normal life," Ken snapped. The anger came out of nowhere, startling him as it fueled his voice. "All I can think about is Bobby never getting out of that bed, living like an invalid, and being treated like an infant by attendants who pat his head. I see him eating baby food. I see him shitting his diapers and lying in it waiting for changing time. I see him spending the next forty or fifty years in an institution. So I really don't think you need to know what I'm doing with my dick. It's none of your fucking business, and it is certainly inappropriate. So lay off."

Paula said nothing. She looked neither angry nor hurt. She merely looked thoughtful as she regarded the people, or the room, or nothing at all over Ken's shoulder.

Despite the peripheral noises of the cafeteria, the jangling of flatware and hush of conversations, Ken found the room terribly quiet. It seemed that silence, like atmosphere, engulfed him. He saw people's lips moving but heard no sounds. And then he realized that noise, raging and static, not silence, had seized him. His heart pulsed in his ears, and the sound of a tortured ocean filled his head.

His temper subsided, and, as he regained control, his hearing was restored.

"I'm sorry," he said. "I just…" his voice faded. He wanted her to say something. He wanted her to accept his apology. Maybe, he even wanted the argument that he felt certain he had started, but she gave him nothing.

Instead she stood from the chair. "I'm going to be late for work," she said. "Do you want a ride back to the Quarter?"

"It's out of your way," he said.

"Fine," Paula said before leaving him alone in the cafeteria.

⚜

For the second day in a row, heavy clouds covered the city, but today they were going to work. The rain began just as the cab passed into the Quarter. At first the drops came down timidly, hitting the windshield in sporadic splashes as if testing the world below. By the time the cab came to a stop in front of Ken's house, a noisy downpour had begun, casting a veil of gray over the street and buildings.

The scene with Paula ate at Ken, but there was nothing he could do about it now. She'd always taken an undue amount of interest in his personal life. Always probing for more information.

Usually, he could successfully steer the conversation to a different topic, but this morning, his frayed nerves had forgone logic, leaving only defensiveness.

He'd often thought Paula's interest was unhealthy. She'd spent far too much time examining his life and seemed to be doing little to move forward with her own. For all Ken knew, she hadn't even dated anyone since their divorce. If she had, she certainly didn't volunteer the information. Furthermore, he found this morning's inquisition particularly distasteful. Her insistence on information, knowing what he'd gone through the night before, smacked of manipulation, as if hoping to catch Ken in a weak moment to extract whatever tidbits her ego needed. But no, he thought. He was just tired and frustrated and angry. Paula wasn't the enemy here.

He paid the driver, walked to his stoop, and fumbled the keys out of his pocket as he pressed under the eaves of his house to avoid the rain. He yawned widely.

Once the door was opened, Ken's knees went weak. A wave of dizziness hit him like a blow to the side of his head. He barely caught himself from falling over the threshold. His hands sprang out to grasp the shutters, and he threw a leg forward to catch his weight. He had no time to understand what was happening; all of his energies and thoughts were focused on trying to keep himself upright as he stumbled forward, barely able to maintain his footing. He breathed deeply, hoping fresh air would cool his delirious brain.

Ken stabilized himself by using the couch and then the wall for balance as he passed around into the second row of rooms. He ran a hand along the mahogany dining table David Lane had suggested he buy. The surface felt velvety under his trembling fingers. He stopped for a moment, leaning on it for support.

He needed a phone to call an ambulance. There was a phone in the living room behind him, another in the kitchen ahead. He chose to go forward.

Icy sweat covered his neck and brow. His brain began swimming again. His stomach threatened to relieve itself on the floor.

No longer did the table beneath his palm feel stable. Rather it seemed made of gelatin or some other malleable material that promised to entrap him. Ken moved his hand to a chair, but it too gave under his grasp, and he nearly fell to the floor.

Ken stepped forward, exchanging one chair back for another. His legs wobbled beneath him, but he maintained his footing for another three steps, enough to reach the door and prop himself against the jamb.

He pushed the kitchen door open. He could neither speak nor scream when he saw the contents of his kitchen. A watery gurgle, like the cry of the drowning, rose in his throat. He wanted to step back, away from the horrors of this room, but he couldn't move. Images flashed. Thoughts raced. But he could make sense of nothing except for a single statement that repeated horribly in his head: *Not again. Not again.*

David Lane, hanged by a thread of metal wire, dangled over Ken's kitchen floor, His body swung slowly, silently. The wire noose, connected at one end to the ceiling and looped at the other, cut through David's throat. Skin the color of paste stretched over the once-handsome face. Beautiful green eyes, pale and cold, stared into Ken's, and his tongue, stained purple, pressed against sagging lips. Below this, his chin rested against a broad bib of crimson, his blood still cascading down the front of David's shirt while a swarm of flies flitted and dove for a meal.

David's swollen tongue moved and his lips parted.

"Welcome home, Baby," David said, his voice a dry wind quickly vanishing beneath the hum of the flies' beating wings.

10

He was often told that he looked like a young Sean Connery. At forty-three, David Lane could not imagine looking like a "young" anybody.

He drove in circles through the French Quarter neighborhood, searching for parking, as his frustration grew. The rain had come on only a few minutes before, and now it was getting serious. But why not? Already, his morning had become a comedy of errors. His coffeepot lay shattered in the sink. He had left the house twice without his briefcase, having to return both times for it. The pile of unmailed letters he'd set out on the desk in his home office still sat on the desk in his home office. And now he was driving around the Quarter, looking for parking so he could pick up a piece of art he'd had framed.

But someone had decided to film another movie in the grubby elegance of New Orleans's French Quarter. Two blocks were taken up with trucks and lighting rigs, and no parking was to be found anywhere near the frame shop. This kind of annoyance had been one of the reasons that David had moved out of the Quarter. Though he'd enjoyed the variety of entertainment that the neighborhoods offered, the area had lost its magic for him.

David turned right and cruised along Dumaine Street.

Ken's house was on this block, David noted with an uncomfortable mixture of fondness and pain. He slowed the car as he approached the familiar stoop. His heart crept into his throat.

You're not over him yet. Wonderful.

The shutters were open, he noticed. David wondered if Ken was back in town?

And you want to see him.

David brushed the thought aside as he approached the end of the block, his eyes captured by the reflection of Ken's place in the rearview mirror. He cast a glance at the road ahead of him and slammed on the brakes to avoid hitting a figure standing in the crosswalk.

A beautiful woman stood in the intersection only a few feet from the grill of his Mercedes. She wore a yellow dress, darkened by the rain. The droplets also pasted her brown hair to her scalp and made her dress cling to her well-formed body. Adrenaline raced through David's system, carrying self-reproach and a bit of fear with it.

What an idiot. He'd almost run this woman down because of a ludicrous romantic distraction. Embarrassed, he looked at the woman. He mouthed, "I'm sorry," through the windshield, wondering if the apology would be seen through the rain and the sweep of his wipers.

The woman smiled and continued walking to the far curb.

David crept into the intersection and turned. He cast a final glance into the rearview and saw a taxi pulling to the curb. Had it stopped in front of Ken's house? Did Ken even own that house anymore?

And you want to see him. You want answers. You should pull around the block and park. It might be good to see him after all of this time. You might even be able to convince yourself that it would close that chapter of your life completely.

He discounted the voice in his head, telling himself that he already had closure. Ken had been gone for a year, and he hadn't bothered to stay in touch. That pretty much said "closed" to David.Not that he understood what had happened between them. Ken's flight from the city, from him, had been so abrupt, so damned odd, that he doubted he'd ever really know what happened. What he did know was that Ken had changed, and not for the better. In the weeks leading up to his move, Ken had been sullen, humorless, and constantly distracted—a man very different from the one he'd known, certainly different from the man he'd met over three years ago.

They'd met in what David considered the least romantic place imaginable: in a men's room. It hadn't been a tawdry porno scene, filled with heated cruising and culminating in a fast slam against a stall partition, though in the months to follow, they'd managed that a couple of times. No. It had been far less tawdry.

David was out for dinner with friends at NOLA, a funky restaurant in the Quarter. He'd had a couple of martinis in him, and throughout the meal, he and his friends had laughed and gotten a bit loud but were having such a good time that David, normally more reserved, barely noticed the annoyance of the diners at neighboring tables. When the waiter came by, suggesting that his party "turn it down a notch," David apologized, but his friend Greg copped an attitude and started berating the poor waiter.

In an attempt to avoid the unfolding drama, David excused himself to the restroom, though he doubted anyone at the table noticed. They were all quite engrossed in Greg's performance.

David had been washing his hands when the door opened and Ken stepped in. Catching the man's reflection in the mirror, David's first thought was that the handsome guy looked vaguely familiar. This was a common enough response. New Orleans was a smallish town, so David often saw the same faces but rarely remembered the context. He might have seen Ken at a hundred different functions or simply walking down the street; the guy certainly had a face he'd take note of.

Instead of going to one of the urinals or stalls, Ken walked toward David at the bank of sinks.

"Hi," Ken said.

Simple as that. There had been no awkward eye hockey, no casual assessment tempered by a façade of indifferent cool. He'd just followed David into the restroom and said, "Hi."

"Hey," David said, uncertain about what was happening but more than willing to find out.

"I'm hiding," Ken said.

"Really? From what?"

"My date. I think he's a little crazy."

"How do you know it isn't you?"

As Ken laughed at this question, David took the time to really look at him, to absorb the lines of his face, the color of his eyes.

"Good question," Ken had said. "Maybe it is me. Why don't we have dinner tomorrow night and you can decide?"

"Good setup. I walked right into it."

"I'm serious."

"You're on a date," David reminded. "And you're cruising the restroom for another? Somehow, that doesn't give me a lot of faith in a long-term commitment. Besides, you're assuming I'm single."

"When you and your friends came in, I knew I was at the wrong table, and that was before I suspected my date was crazy. As for whether you're involved or not, I don't care. I don't mean to sound rude or arrogant here, but I honestly don't care."

David had seen the sincerity and intensity in Ken's face. It had been magnetic, and at the time, he wondered if anyone ever said no to the man. He doubted it. Confidence was as well fitted to Ken as his Italian sport coat, and he was arresting to look at. People probably said yes to Ken, if only to feel that they shared common ground with someone exceptional.

"Now, I have to get back," Ken said, "before my date hits a new level of crazy. I'd give you my number, but I'm thinking you might not call. So, I'm going to book a table at Arnaud's for tomorrow night at eight. I hope I'll see you there." And then Ken left without even an exchange of names. Furthermore, David already had plans for the following night, a business dinner he couldn't cancel, but he'd found something charming, even romantic, in Ken's proposition.

Back in the dining room, David searched the tables until he found Ken sitting across the room with a young man wrapped up in typical club-clone drag: short hair, swept up in front; tight shirt made of some shiny material; muscular arms, testing the fabric's limitations. The two men, though both attractive, looked completely wrong together, like someone had parked a Miata next to a Rolls Royce.

Ken looked up, saw David, and stared. The club-clone turned, saw David, and glared.

David returned to his friends. They were still laughing, being too loud, but the waiter had obviously given up trying to tame them. Casually, he asked Greg, "Do you know that guy," and pointed at the mismatched couple across the room.

"Daddy or boy?" Greg asked.

"Daddy."

"That, Dearest, is Ken Nicholson."

So, he had a name. The next morning David had a phone number, and that afternoon he had a date with Ken for cocktails before meeting his clients for dinner. The rest, as they say, is history.

Though he intended to drive further down and search for parking on one of the blocks on the other side of the frame shop, David emerged from his reverie about the time he turned onto Ken's block for the second time.

David was never able to fathom their breakup. Ken's story about relocation for business was bullshit; his corporate offices were in New Orleans, and Ken owned the company, so he could be anywhere he saw fit. The company had a small interest in Austin, a distribution center or something, and nothing more, certainly nothing so important that it required Ken's on-site supervision.

No matter how many times David worked it over in his mind, it always came out the same: The prick had dumped him. But here you are circling the block, hoping to get a glimpse of him. Are you going to go up to that door and knock? *And then what?*

He didn't know. The last time he'd spoken with Ken face to face had been, to say the least, odd. David had been installing a new ceiling fan in his living room. As he teetered on the ladder, stringing a cord through a length of chain, Ken had walked in. Upon seeing David high above the floor, the color had drained from Ken's cheeks; his eyes had grown wide; and he'd fallen against the doorjamb for support. The rest of the day Ken had been quiet and distracted, and then he'd disappeared: a couple of phone calls to tell David about the move, then nothing.

David approached Ken's house. The woman in the yellow dress stood next to the stoop, her back to the wall. She seemed euphoric under the downpour. Her lovely face was slightly upturned to accept the spatter of raindrops, and her eyes were closed. She wore an expression of delight. To David, she looked like a statue, motionless and indifferent to the cascade: a goddess of water frozen by a spell.

David slowed. The front door of Ken's house stood ajar. The woman was forgotten as David nearly stopped the car, searching the open interior for signs of its occupant. But the light fell only along the building's façade. The interior of Ken's house was black as a cave.

This is so damned childish.

But Ken had always had that effect on him. In his forty-three years, he'd fallen in love approximately a dozen times, but once the wide-eyed infatuations of his youth and the icons of his lust were weeded out, only two people remained.

David's first lover, Joe, had died long ago. The man had had a lot of problems with drugs, and in the end, the combination of meth, rum, and a broken-down semi truck in the middle of an off ramp had resulted in a collision, a fire, and a fatality. Closure had been easy to come by on that one. Despite some sweet memories and more than a little guilt for having failed to get Joe clean, David had dealt with and moved on after Joe's death.

So, that left Ken.

Caught in memory, David did not realize that he was being stared at. The water goddess had broken the spell holding her in place and now gazed at David. She seemed to be taking great pleasure in his investigation. Something else might have been amusing her, but David got the impression that he was the source of her good humor.

More than ever, he felt childish and silly for his interest in Ken Nicholson, his house, anything about the man. David nodded at the woman, who just stared. He pressed hard on the gas pedal and drove away.

11

Paula Nicholson held the phone to her ear. The ringing on the other end was faint because of all of the noise of the birthday party. Music pulsed in the living room, and though she was calling from the kitchen, many people had gathered there to converse. Between the music and the chatter, the light sound of Ken's phone might have been her imagination. It mattered little. He wasn't home or wasn't answering. Paula hung up.

She left the kitchen and worked her way through the crowd to the tiny bar set up in Sam Martin's living room, where she had her gin and tonic refreshed. One third of the faces in the vast crowd celebrating Sam's fifty-second birthday were familiar to Paula. Some faculty members and a handful of students roamed about, and she greeted them, spoke briefly, but was unable to remain engaged in any discussion. She recognized a few of Ken's old friends in the crowd and had already fielded numerous questions about her absent ex-husband as well as accepted good wishes for their son.

Paula had arrived early, when only a dozen or so people were present, but now the party was in full swing, and the noise, the crowded rooms, were starting to get to her. Carrying her full drink carefully so as not to spill, she eased through an opening between two groups to find a bit of space next to the wall. Once positioned, she observed the crowd and tried to look interested if not involved.

It was nice to be out of the house, away from the hospital. It was good to hear people laughing and to see smiles. Sam's party was full of young, vibrant people, many closer to the ages of Paula's children than to her own or the party's hosts. Energy poured off of them in waves, but the good feelings and enthusiasm saddened her. Her son would have fit in well with these young folks. They would have welcomed him, would have found Robert charming and attractive. Paula wished he were here, wished he would just get better and stop scaring her.

Jersey Fleagle, Sam's lover, waved to her from across the room. Paula smiled and waved back. Then, Jersey disappeared into the kitchen.

A biology professor she knew, Kurt Lawson, appeared in the hole left by Jersey. He winked and lifted his glass at Paula, who forced the smile back to her lips before looking away.

Paula found Lawson to be a rather tactless little ass and something of a sleaze. During her divorce from Ken, the man had circled her like a vulture, dropping hints and forced compliments at every opportunity in an attempt to win her over. Whether he was actually interested in her or was simply hopeful about the myth of the merry divorcee, Paula didn't know. She didn't care, either. What Lawson tried to pass off as charm amounted to little more than nasty double entendres. When the divorce was finalized, he'd told Paula that "if you ever need anything," she should call him. With the tone in his voice and the look in his eyes, Paula had found it easy to hear "if you ever want to sleep with me" instead. She tried to maintain a civil face for Lawson, but even after seven years, she was still appalled at his behavior, all but celebrating the end of her marriage and masking it as concern.

Other men had asked Paula out over the years, but she invariably declined. She just wasn't interested, might never be again.

Though Esther Bowers loved to tease Paula, saying that Ken had ruined her for other men, Paula found that notion ridiculous. She had children to raise, a job with overwhelming responsibility. Why add the stress of dating, of a new relationship, to that mix?

Are you still waiting for Ken?

The whispered voice took Paula off guard. She even looked around her immediate vicinity to see who had said such a ridiculous thing. *Waiting for Ken.* That would be as foolish as waiting for a yacht in the middle of the desert.

Paula sipped from her drink and searched the crowd for the guest of honor. Other than quick glimpses here and there, she hadn't seen Sam all night.

Then, as if thinking about the man had conjured him, Sam appeared.

"Hey, Sweetness," he called, pushing his way through a tight group of men.

Standing just over six feet with a truly silly Van Dyke, Sam looked heavier and slightly worn down, despite the grin pulling at his lips. Once a marvelous-looking man, now he just looked middle-aged. Happy but middle-aged.

Happens to the best of us, Paula thought.

"Sam," she said. "How are you?"

The pleasant face twisted. "I'm fifty-two," he said through mock sobbing. "How the fuck should I be?"

Paula laughed lightly and gave Sam a hug.

"Where's Ken? I thought he said he'd be here."

She scanned the room as if he might magically appear, then said, "I don't know. I spoke with him earlier. Maybe business."

Already drunk, Sam leaned against the wall and breathed whiskey into her face. Though Paula didn't really mind the odor, she was uncomfortable. Her skin itched all over; the noisy people jostled for space; and the heat in the small house was starting to drive her nuts.

A new song came on the stereo, and the entire room screamed simultaneously. Men's voices rose in falsetto and joined the women's as some thundering rhythm shook the walls of Sam Martin's living room.

"Could we go to the stoop where it's a little saner?" Paula asked.

"Sure. Do you need another drink?"

"I'm fine."

As she turned to be led through the open door onto the stoop, a familiar face caught her attention. A young man stood with his back against the wall by one of the stereo speakers. The boy was a student, or at least she'd seen him on campus several times in the last few weeks. The first time she'd noticed him, he'd been standing alone outside of the administration building, posing like James Dean with one leg kicked back against the brick wall. His eyes had been so intense, his lips drawn into a solemn pout. A beautiful if unhappy young man, she'd thought.

Looking at him now, Paula had to agree with her earlier assessment: beautiful. He reminded her of Ken, the way he had been in the year before they'd married, except Ken had never fabricated such a hard expression.

Sam caught the stare and followed it. "Trouble," he said with a laugh.

"What?"

"That boy's trouble."

"Do you know him?"

"No, I think he's here with one of Jersey's clients. But if I did know him, I'd be in trouble."

Sam pushed his way through the bottleneck near the door, extending his hand behind him to guide Paula through the revelers and out to the relatively cool evening beyond the party. She and Sam moved a little way from the door and stood by the wall. The night air, cleansed after a day of rain, soothed the itching on her skin, and the light breeze refreshed her.

"Thank God," Sam sighed. "I was getting tired of everybody asking me 'Do you feel old now?'"

"You're not old," Paula offered.

"Funny," Sam said, "I never felt old until people started asking me if I felt old. Now I feel older than dirt."

"You're not old," Paula repeated.

Sam nodded. His perpetual smile grew sly. "So, it's good to have Ken back. The city's missed him."

"I didn't know he was so popular," Paula told him with a distance in her voice.

"Sorry," Sam replied soberly. "That didn't come out right."

Paula waved it off. The comment didn't upset her.

"How's Bobby?"

"You know he's awake?" Paula asked, noting that Sam used the same less formal name for her son that Ken did. She'd always preferred Robert, but Ken insisted on calling him Bobby. It had been a minor point of contention between them, but Ken hadn't budged on the issue.

"Wonderful," Sam announced. "Something good for my birthday. And how are you doing with everything? I mean it's easy to get caught up in something like this and forget about yourself."

"I'm fine, Sam. Thank you. Right now, all we can do is wait."

"That's the bitch of it."

"Yes, it is."

"Ken seemed okay over lunch the other day. As well as can be expected."

"I'm glad he's here," Paula said. "Maybe he can stick around for a while this time."

Sam nodded and sipped from his drink. "No reason for him to go back from what I gathered. The business is clicking along just fine."

"Isn't he seeing someone?" Paula asked, immediately feeling guilty about the question. She'd always made it a policy to ask Ken directly about such things, though he never told her anything. Digging for answers from his friend felt wrong, and perhaps it was wrong, but Paula wanted to know.

"Nah," Sam told her. "He broke things off with the guy before coming out here. No big surprise, there."

Paula noted that Sam assumed she knew who this guy was. She took it as a good sign and pressed further. "No," she said. "No surprise."

"So far, David's been the only one to keep his attention for more than a few weeks. But we all know what happened there."

"No," Paula said. "I don't, actually."

"He never told you what happened?"

"He never told me about David."

Concern and embarrassment fell over Sam's face like mingling clouds. "Shit. I don't see how that is even possible. He never said anything?"

"No."

"Well, then I probably shouldn't." Sam looked over Paula's shoulder and whispered, "Trouble."

Paula turned and saw the young man again. He followed a woman out of the house and onto the stoop. Both seemed oblivious to the crowd around them as they walked down the stairs and into the street. She could not see the girl's face as her head was turned over the opposite shoulder while she spoke with her companion. For a moment she thought of Vicki Bach, though why she couldn't say. The woman's hair was blonde, and the cut was different. Still, a strong needling in her stomach arose. Vicki could have bleached her hair easily. She could be wearing a wig.

The young couple walked away from her up the street toward Rampart. Uncertain, but agitated and curious, Paula wanted to bolt after them; she wanted to turn the woman around and see if she had once been engaged to her son. But that was ridiculous. How many women in the Quarter alone had that build? And what if it was the young Miss Bach? What then?

Calm down, girl, Paula counseled. She'd been at the party for nearly two hours. If Vicki Bach had been in those rooms, she would have seen her.

"He is pretty," Sam said.

"What? Oh yes," she said, not sure she had heard her host correctly. "About Ken…You were saying?"

"I was saying that I probably shouldn't be saying anything."

"I don't see the harm," Paula said. "It's over isn't it?"

"*Over* is such a strong word," Sam replied with a laugh. "Look, Ken was seeing David before he left town. I guess they'd been together for a couple of years."

A couple of years?

"I'll tell you, it surprised the hell out of me. I mean, here's Ken, what was he then? Forty-five? Forty-six?"

She nodded.

"That's like a thousand and fifty in gay years, but the guy was fighting them off left and right. The most beautiful men in the city wanted him. He'd go out with a guy a few times and then move on to the next. A real player, you know? Then, he starts showing up at parties with this guy, and they're seen everywhere together." Sam shrugged. "Anyway, the guy's named David Lane. I hope you don't mind me saying this, but they made a really great couple."

"I asked," she said.

Paula checked the street. The young man and woman stood before a wrought-iron gate several houses down the block. She could see his white pants and her legs, but the rest of them were cast in shadows.

"Jersey and I had dinner with them every now and then, but David and Ken were mostly into each other. As I said, they'd show up at parties and functions all the time, but they never stayed long. You could tell they just wanted their time together."

"What's David like?" Paula asked.

Sam shrugged. "He's a good guy, kind of quiet unless you really work him. A few of my friends dated him over the years, and every one of them fell pretty hard. He is intensely hot," Sam said with a chuckle, "but I never knew him all that well, just a social acquaintance. What I do know is that there isn't an ounce of bullshit about him. No games. That's what my friends said anyway. They always knew exactly where they stood with him. You can't imagine how refreshing that can be."

"And Ken broke it off when he left?" Ken had told her as much at the hospital. He'd been involved with someone here, and when it ended, he'd needed some distance.

"That's the part that I can't figure," Sam said. "Just before he left, I had dinner with Ken, and I asked him what the hell was going on. He and David seemed to be getting along really well, and then Ken up and decides to move. Alone."

"And you don't know why?"

"No," Sam said. "But I'll tell you, Ken was in pretty bad shape. I've never seen him look that scared before. He was desperate, practically rambling. Apparently, the move and the therapy helped."

"Ken was in therapy?" Paula couldn't believe this.

"Oh hell," Sam said. "That's it, I am done talking. My feet just don't taste good anymore."

"He never said anything."

Paula was in shock, still reeling from the news that Ken had been involved with a man for two years and had never said a word about it, only to be hit with the news that he'd found something in his life so overwhelming that it had driven him to seek help.

What else had Ken left out?

Jersey Fleagle poked his head through the door. "Hon', it's time for the cake."

Sam held up a hand. "One minute. You know," he said, turning back to Paula, "I'm kind of surprised we haven't talked about this before."

"I wasn't sure it was any of my business."

"What changed your mind?"

"I'm not sure that I have changed my mind. Look, you better get inside or you'll miss your cake."

"Okay. You comin'?" Sam asked, already starting for the door.

"I think I should be getting home."

⚜

As Paula walked away from the stoop the celebrants inside Sam's house began singing "Happy Birthday." The song followed her to the corner, where she paused and glanced over her shoulder at the young couple standing in the darkness. The familiar young man and his female friend remained where they had been, still barely visible against the dark fence.

Were they watching her? Did they wonder what this crazy old woman was looking at? Or, had they already begun planning their evening together?

Paula walked the two blocks to her car, which was parked just past St. Ann Street. She pulled the keys from her purse but did not press the button to disengage the lock. Ken's house was on the next block, and the urge to see him needled at her.

Of course, if she did stop by for a visit he'd see it as an intrusion. He might ask her in, might even seem pleased to see her, but it wouldn't be long before she saw that he was merely enduring her company, and then she'd feel awkward and foolish. But in light of what Sam had just told her, she found herself at a loss. David Lane? A therapist? These were only two clues to a greater mystery, and their gravity exasperated her, made her feel betrayed.

Paula walked past her car to the next corner.

She told herself that it was none of her business, yet she kept walking. She and Ken were divorced. He owed her neither explanations nor excuses. They had both moved on with their lives. The children joined them, but was this their only connection? Paula hoped not. She wanted to believe they were friends, but friends didn't keep such secrets from one another.

She turned the corner onto Dumaine Street and made it three steps past the Quarter Scene restaurant before stopping.

The street ahead of her was quiet. Across the road a plant-choked balcony hovered above the walk, and a single candle flickered high up in a hurricane lantern. Wet yet motionless the air brought neither scent nor cooling breeze. Two blocks down she saw cars racing along Rampart Street, but the blocks in between were lifeless, creating a disturbing sense of dislocation after the thundering mob of Sam's party. Ornate ironwork and shredded siding, visible even in the dim light, made her think of a ghost town. And wasn't it? she wondered. In the truest sense of the term, this part of this city belonged to spirits. The dead held sway here but allowed the living to exist among them. In return, the living sustained the dead with their memories, their photo albums, and their stories. The living spoke often of ghosts, of family and friends, the famous and the notorious, the elegant and the perverse.

The street ahead of her, where Ken had chosen his home, certainly appeared haunted, but in many ways that was appropriate; he seemed little more than a ghost to her these days.

She tried to work up the nerve to continue to his door, but found the conviction that had driven her this far waning.

What if he's not alone? she asked herself. Ken would be furious at the interruption. Paula rubbed her cheek lightly and looked back over her shoulder as a picture unfolded in her mind.

Ken's sweaty body rolled with another. Legs and arms coiled around thick torsos as two men played out their passion on the floor of Ken's cottage. Paula's body went hot in a breathtaking flush. The two bodies rocked in the darkness, only the vague glow of candlelight illuminating flesh made wet with perspiration. A leg rose slowly into the air to wrap tightly around the back of Ken's thighs. His body rocked insistently as a strong hand traced down his spine and cupped his buttocks. A masculine face, indistinct and unfamiliar, rose up to kiss Ken passionately on the lips. The coupling became a furious struggle and then a blur.

Paula turned away from the house and hurried the way she had come, returning to her car. The intensity of the vision had excited her initially, but its clarity and detail soon became frightening. For a moment it had felt like she was actually standing in a room with the two men, terrified that they might look up and see her.

Inside of her car, feeling secure behind its locked doors, she wiped her brow and laid her hands on the steering wheel.

"You've got problems lady," she told herself.

Then she smiled nervously and started the car.

12

David?

Ken shot up on the bed, suddenly struck by the strange room. Not his house. Not his bedroom. Where was he? The remnants of terrible dreams confused him further: Bobby's capture in the mechanical web of medicine; Paula's brutal assault by an unseen assailant; and David Lane stepping off of a chair, dropping, a metal wire tearing into his throat. Ken rubbed his eyes, then shook his head.

The room was small and crowded. An armoire stood open against the wall facing him, revealing a television's dark screen. A hotel room?

Of course, that's exactly where he was. He had found David Lane's hanged corpse in his kitchen, or, rather, he had imagined it. Even then, seeing the grotesque detail of David's lifeless face and the swarming flies, Ken had doubted the integrity of what he was witnessing, because he'd seen it before. This exact image, just one of many waking nightmares, had appeared to him half a dozen times before he'd left New Orleans for Austin. And though he knew that what he saw was at worst a sick delusion,

Ken's exhausted mind had not been able to manage the sight, so he'd fled the house.

Late in the morning, he'd checked into the Bourbon Orleans Hotel, where he now sat on the edge of a queen-sized bed. He looked at his watch and saw that he'd slept the entire day away. Ken walked to the window, peered out at the squat buildings of the Quarter now covered in night, and found the sight depressing. Returning to the bed, he grabbed his cell phone and Blackberry from the bed table. He checked both devices for messages but found nothing of importance. Using his cell phone, he called the hospital, hoping for more encouraging news about his son, but the nurses gave him the familiar refrain, "no change." In this case, Ken took the phrase as good news. Bobby was awake. That was good enough for one day.

Ken turned off the cell phone and rolled across the bed. He lifted the headset from the hotel phone and stared at the keypad with some misgivings about what he was about to do. His trepidation lasted only a few seconds before Ken began dialing a number.

When a thick male voice answered, "David Lane," Ken hung up the phone.

⚜

Ken left the Bourbon Orleans early the next morning. He'd showered at the hotel, but he needed a change of clothes from the house on Dumaine. He walked through the Creole cottage, his nerves jangling as the rooms closed in around him. After changing clothes, he went out to the stoop where he could be seen, hoping he wouldn't feel as isolated as he did in the house. He returned several messages, typing short lines of text into his Blackberry, speaking briefly with associates and at greater length with his assistant, Donna. She was thrilled to hear the news about Bobby and wished Ken well, and she assured him that everything was just fine at the office. After completing these tasks, he stood and turned to face the open door of the cottage.

In Austin, even before the paint had dried on his house there,

Ken had gotten the name of a respected therapist from a business colleague. The doctor, a burly and bearded man named Forester, was solemn and intense, with no discernible sense of humor. During his first session, after he'd made reference to hallucinations, Dr. Forester insisted that they not proceed until Ken underwent specific tests to rule out the possibility of chemical imbalances and other physiological pathologies that might cause such delusions. Ken had agreed, almost grateful to think that the dreadful sights he'd left in New Orleans were the product of a real and manageable disease, but the tests had come back negative. His chemistries were fine, which meant that there would be no magic pill to keep the waking nightmares at bay.

Dr. Forester did start Ken on a round of antidepressants, saying they had a better chance of managing Ken's problems if they started from a level playing field. Ken had taken the pills dutifully, but after weeks they'd had no apparent affect.

All in all, Ken's sessions with Dr. Forester lasted less than two months. He went in, spoke, and listened to the therapist throw out words like guilt and stress and abandonment as if Ken hadn't considered all of these things hundreds of times. Though he found the sessions unhelpful and more than a bit predictable, Ken hadn't used these as his excuses to stop seeing Dr. Forester. He ended his sessions because the hallucinations had stopped. It was more than that, though. In Austin, he didn't experience the cloying sensation of dread that held to him in New Orleans. He had no past in Austin, no diseased memories. There, the dust of history had no place to settle.

Ken gazed into his house. He stepped over the threshold. At the kitchen door, he paused. Needling fear erupted in his stomach. David was fine; he was alive and well. Why Ken projected David's face onto that hanging corpse, he didn't know, but it was not a portent of doom or spirits playing cruel tricks with him; it was in his head, and he had to face it.

He pushed open the door, looked around the clean and empty kitchen. He cocked his head and listened, almost certain that he heard the first three notes of a song, played on an old piano, but the music was distant and without substance and had probably never played at all.

Ken let the kitchen door close.

❧

In Bobby's room, Ken sat in the uncomfortable plastic chair, reading the sports section of the paper to his son. The boy was awake though showed little sign of it. Still, Ken had begun to enjoy his part in Bobby's recovery. He read, and it helped alleviate his sense of helplessness.

Ken started on a story about a football player who had been called up on drug charges. He read it like he might a fairy tale, lifting his voice in the exciting parts and doing his best to keep the piece interesting. Halfway through the column, Ken stopped. He looked at his son, who blinked and gazed at Ken with what seemed to be recognition. Before, with his eyes open, Bobby had appeared distant and lost, but now, looking at his father, it seemed some understanding of his location had crept back.

Folding the paper, Ken leaned forward, heartened by what he took as Bobby's acknowledgement of him. He cupped his son's hand and smiled.

Bobby blinked.

"Can you hear me?"

Again, his son closed his eyes. When they opened, Ken lost any doubt that his son was conscious and aware and answering his father the only way he could. Elation filled him like a gasp of air after having been held underwater for far too long.

"I'm so proud of you. You know that, don't you?" Ken waited for his son to respond. When this didn't happen, he continued speaking, determined to maintain the communication. "Maybe you don't. I probably didn't say it enough, but I am."

Bobby's eyelids batted down, fluttered, and opened wide.

"You and your sister deserved a lot better. I know that. When you're up and around, I'll try to explain it to you. Then you can tell me to shut up when you get bored."

Bobby closed his eyes, but didn't open them. Ken grasped tighter on his son's hand. He leaned over and kissed Bobby's forehead.

"Get some rest," he said. "I'll be here when you wake up. I love you, son."

Ken sat silently, following the lines of his son's face and the contour of the bandages wrapping his head.

Everything was a mess right now, he knew. He'd let his family slip away by bits and pieces. Looking at his son, he realized he knew very little about the boy. Bobby was an athlete, a good student. He was good looking and responsible, and he was going to be a lawyer. Ken knew these things, but little more. Watching his wounded son sleeping, Ken berated himself for not knowing more. He'd created a divide, keeping his children at a distance, so they could not see the details of his life. That was going to end, he thought. Things were going to get better. Things were going to change.

From the ward, the elevator bell rang, announcing a car had arrived on the fourth floor. It broke Ken's reverie. A second after its sound faded, a woman screamed from the opposite side of the ward. It was so startling that Ken leapt from his chair. He went to the door of Bobby's room and looked out. Attendants and nurses ran toward a room on the other side of the ward; a security guard, one hand on the butt of his gun, pushed his way through announcing his authority. The frantic woman screamed again from amid the gathering crowd of inquisitive and concerned. Ken checked Bobby one more time before stepping into the reception area of the ward.

The panic continued. Nurses shouted for everyone to "calm down." Curious, Ken walked across to the edge of the aggregation. Only nine people stood before the glass-faced room, but it might have been three times as many for all of the noise and movement. They jostled for space like fans at a rock concert.

At first he saw nothing through the crowd except the bank of sputtering machines with their flashing lights on the other side of the bed. Then a face with two blank eyes appeared as the patient sprang forward. The white-clad man with tubes coming from his nose and mouth burst into view so quickly, that Ken pulled back, startled. The patient was trying to scream or speak. No words emerged though he seemed desperate to be heard. A thin blossom of blood soaked the bandage around his head. His hands slapped madly at the plastic tubes in his arms. His skin went the color of bacon fat. The security guard tackled the patient and, with the help of the nurses, pinned him to the bed. An intravenous tube buckled, tore free and whipped through the air. Attendants secured straps around the patient's ankles and his wrists.

"Grand mal," one of the nurses called, pushing the crowd back as two doctors shoved in from the side.

Something large moved at Ken's back, displacing the air as if with the passing of a car or carriage. A wave of nausea ran down his throat to his belly, and his vision grew fuzzy. The dizziness settled on him quickly, then dissipated. He turned from the commotion and looked back at his son's room, where a young blond man emerged. In his hand he held a length of metal pipe that dripped red onto the floor as he hurried away.

This was the same young man Ken had met at a bar, had seen in front of the hospital, chatting with a beautiful, cold woman.

Chuck ran across the ward away from Bobby's room toward the elevator. Ken started after him, and then stopped. *Bobby? What was...?* He looked at his son's room, suddenly understanding what he was witnessing. He resumed his cancelled stride. That kid had no business, *no right*, near his boy.

Ken raced toward the glass-faced cell. Tears filled his eyes. His thoughts erupted in a cacophony like a screeching, chaotic choir. He flew over the threshold of Bobby's room, and what he saw inside sent him back to the wall.

The wall over his son's bed wore a fan of crimson stipple. Similar patterns covered the sheets, the machines, the floor. At their center, a hood of blood covered Bobby's head and face. The shape of the head was wrong now, not the smooth oval it had been. Instead, it was dented and ragged, like an apple with a bite taken from it.

Ken didn't want to see this; he could *not* be seeing this. Stepping forward, his mind flooded. His leg went out from under him, sending him to one knee beside his son's bed. He reached out for Bobby's hand, draping from the edge of the bed, and he held it firm.

He cried for help. His voice entered his ears as if coming from very far away, and he held his son's hand, gripped it with all of his strength. He had to hold on.

Please, hold on.

II

THE DISEASE
OF MEMORY

13

Ken sat dazed in the visitors' lounge faced by two detectives. He could barely breathe, hadn't been able to catch his breath in the hour since his son's murder. He was in shock. On some level he knew that. That's why he felt so numb, so empty.

Bobby was dead. He hadn't protected him, hadn't done anything.

And the two detectives wanted their answers, though Ken could hardly keep a cogent thought amid the noise and shoving of his emotions. They kept asking Ken about enemies he might have had and enemies his son might have had. They already knew about Vicki, but he reminded them anyway. He told them about the man he had seen that morning, Chuck.

A knowing look passed between the two detectives, then his interrogators resumed the questioning. Their names were Ogilvie and Reilly. Ogilvie, the taller of the two had a thin mustache and a gaunt face that tightened in stern regard as he made notes on a palm device. His gray blazer went well enough with his black slacks, but overall Ken found the man's entire appearance void of color. His partner, Reilly, was a pleasant, even attractive, shorter man with a burly frame, full cheeks, and kind eyes.

"And you say you saw your son's attacker?"

"Yes," Ken said in frustration, "I've told you twenty times."

How long were they going to grill him like this? They should have been out looking for the little bastard, not asking him what he looked like over and over. "I told you, I've seen him before."

"Outside the hospital?"

"Yes and at the bar," he said.

"You've seen him socially?"

"No. He was just there. I told you this. It was about a week ago. We spoke briefly."

"What bar?"

"Lafitte's. It's on Bourbon and…"

"We know it," the detective interrupted. "What did you talk about?"

"Nothing really," Ken said. "I think he was coming on to me. Look, is this necessary? He's about five-foot-ten…"

"We have the description, and the security tapes have him entering and exiting the building."

"So what are you doing about it?" Ken asked. His voice was even and surprisingly calm. They had been over the same ground three times. And where the hell was Paula? It didn't take that long to get from the campus to the hospital. Distantly, he heard Ogilvie say, "All that we can," but his mind was drifting. Anger pulled him away, left him floating in a dead-calm sea. And though he felt extremely lucid, considering the circumstance, he found it increasingly difficult to keep his mind on the detectives or their questions.

"What?"

"You said his name was Chuck?"

"Yes," Ken said. "He told me his name was Chuck. He didn't give me a last name. Did I mention the woman?"

"The woman with the man outside of the hospital?"

Good, he thought, he hadn't forgotten.

"Was she with the man at the bar?"

"No," Ken said. "I just want to make sure that I didn't forget anything. I think she was my son's fiancée. I think she was Vicki Bach."

"But you can't be certain?"

"I've never met her."

Paula appeared in the lounge, brushing past the detectives and stopping when she spotted Ken out of the corner of her eye. Her eyes were puffed red from crying. She fell into his arms. The sound of her weeping was sufficient to dismiss the two detectives.

❧

Ken drove Paula home, where they sat on the sofa. Wrapped in each other's arms, they stared through the large plate window into the street beyond. Neither Ken nor Paula had been able to shed a tear since leaving the hospital. The pain was too great for such a simple release; it pierced Ken with sharp gouging barbs. He sat with Paula for over an hour. They said nothing. They stared. Memories came and went in slow succession: Bobby playing Little League, then posing by his first car, then graduating high school, then crying at the base of an old oak in Audubon Park. Things that Ken had not given thought to in years became vivid. Forgotten conversations rewound and played back at excruciatingly slow speed. And though anger—at his son's killers and the seemingly useless police force—kept him from sinking into absolute sorrow, he found himself unable to move. Ken could not let go of the woman next to him anymore than he could let go of the face of his son.

But eventually he had to let go of her. Ken stood. His body screamed with the motion as if he had been beaten. He made a phone call to the police, assuring them he would remain in town for another week. He thought about making dinner, but knew neither of them could eat.

When Jennifer came home, he told her about Bobby's death. His daughter's disinterested expression slowly blossomed with misery. Her condemning eyes grew wide and moist, and she ran to her mother on the couch, replacing him as Paula's source of security. They cried together. The sound of their sorrow worked through his chest like a serrated blade, slicing and tearing at him with furious strokes.

Ken left the two women alone to mourn. In the kitchen, he sat at the dinette, lit a cigarette, and watched the smoke whorl. Arrangements would have to be made. Ken had never organized a funeral before; he didn't have a clue where to begin. He'd have to contact a funeral home, he knew that, but what else? Flowers? Did he have to call a florist or did the funeral home manage those kinds of details? How long would the police hold Bobby's body? They'd said an autopsy would be performed. How long did that take, and how did they get the body to the funeral home?

Slowly, he stood from the chair and crossed the kitchen to the phone, but he didn't know whom to call. He didn't know what to do.

⚜

The next morning, reporters tried to make contact, but Ken told them he had nothing for them and to leave his family alone. The assholes still camped on his wife's lawn and made every attempt they could to shove cameras in their faces, but Ken had instructed both Paula and Jennifer to say nothing. Even "No comment" was too much of a comment. Give them nothing, and like hungry dogs, they'll go away. The home had become a fortress, and despite his long absence, Ken had returned to rule it. He wandered through the rooms, refusing to leave his family alone. Until the authorities had some answers, he didn't feel right about leaving them.

Paula's face had gone pale when he'd described Chuck to her. She too had seen him before; he'd been at Sam Martin's birthday party, and she'd noticed him around the campus. Both of them felt certain they had seen him with Bobby's fiancée. More than ever, they were convinced that Vicki Bach was involved with Robert's attack and murder though neither could fathom why. He'd written no will. What twenty-year-old had? So if Vicki expected no financial gain, then what was her motive? What could Bobby have done to her, or to Chuck for that matter, to warrant such violence?

An officer arrived midmorning to take Paula's statement. Once his questions were answered, Ken and Paula drove to the funeral home. Jen refused to go, wouldn't leave her bedroom. Together, Ken and Paula picked a casket. He carefully examined each polished coffin, picturing Bobby locked inside. With trembling hands, he indicated the casket he would buy and then, unable to look at the damned box again, ushered Paula out of the room. In a small office they went over the specifics of the services with a young woman in a black suit. After dropping Paula at the house, Ken drove to Rubenstein Brothers on St. Charles to buy a black suit.

Once the specifics of the funeral were taken care of, Ken found himself losing his ability to concentrate. He paced through the Victorian, never able to settle in one spot for long. He tried speaking with friends. Sam Martin kept him on the phone for nearly twenty minutes, but between them, the two men spoke hardly two-dozen words. With his mind racing between events long past and those still fresh, Ken could find nothing of substance to hold on to.

As a result, the three days before the funeral became an extended blur for Ken, like a movie running out of focus. He took calls and read condolence cards from friends and business associates and from family members as far away as Germany, where Paula's sister lived with her husband. He picked through meals and looked at the television unable to find anything that didn't strike him as insipid. Mostly he walked through the house, through the Garden District, but he could find nothing to distract him.

Then the day of the funeral came. Paula's parents arrived early that morning, and Ken did what he could to avoid them. A church service, then a service at the cemetery where Bobby's body was slipped into a marble vault that Ken had purchased nearly twenty years before, never imagining at the time that his son's name would appear on the granite tablet before his own.

During the services, Paula stood silently, supporting a teary Jennifer. The church was filled with the same aggregation of people who had sent cards. In addition to these people was a cluster of Bobby's friends, most of whom looked shocked as if they could not comprehend one of their immortal brothers' passing.

At the vault, Ken watched as the mahogany coffin was rolled into place amid words of prayer and incomprehensible fate. The press had shown up at both services. Ken's disdain for them intensified with every camera that flashed and every hushed voice that suggested a family's sorrow was newsworthy.

That night he would be back at the house in the Quarter. Paula's parents would be staying for a couple of days, and though there was more than enough room in the large Victorian, he knew that Bill and Margaret Jones would not approve of his presence. They had been less than friendly since the divorce (as any good Catholic parents would be having heard that their son-in-law was living a life of unrepentant sin). He felt their disapproval of him, could see it in their eyes and the heavy corners of their mouths. Still, the thought of wandering around the rooms of the Dumaine Street house alone frightened him. Even broad daylight could not keep the dread from him.

⚜

So many hands to shake, so many condolences to accept and to say "thank you" for. It felt unreal. Carla set out the food, and her husband, J.D. fixed drinks for the guests. The inevitable casseroles were placed on the kitchen counter. Bobby's friends spoke quietly in a corner by the back door. Paula's parents had her trapped by the stairs off of the living room. Black suits and dresses filled the lower floor of the Victorian. Drinks were consumed rapidly. Voices spoke in hushed tones, and Ken meandered through, tired, lost, and angry.

Playing the host seemed completely inappropriate, yet he tried his best to make his guests feel comfortable. However, it took only thirty minutes in the house, feeling Bill Jones's eyes on his back, shaking hands with people he had never met, and offering his cheek for lipstick-moist kisses from women friends, before he'd had enough socializing.

Ken walked onto the front porch, where he found Sam whispering to his lover, Jersey Fleagle. Sam wiped cream cheese from his beard with a small paper napkin. When he stepped onto the porch, the two men regarded Ken with warm and consoling expressions.

"We're so sorry," Jersey said, hugging Ken tightly and kissing his neck. "I can't imagine what you must be going through."

"Thanks," Ken said, surprised to see the illness on Jersey's face. He'd looked tired over the holidays, only three months ago, but now he looked sick. Ken tried to smile to put the men at ease. It was too much effort. "How have you been?"

"Fine," both said in unison.

"Is there anything we can do?" This from Sam.

"No." he said. "Thank you for being here."

The awkward silence that followed was only awkward for Jersey and Sam. Ken felt perfectly content not to speak. So much talk at these affairs. So much polite conversation. Too many pleasantries exchanged. What people needed after a funeral was complete isolation so they could pray to whatever gods they had created for themselves. They could ponder the redundant questions that always surfaced during times of crisis—Why me? Why him? Why us?—and try to sort through their fucking heads without the intrusion of a pack of well-wishers who only served to remind them that their lives were irreparably broken.

"Call us," Jersey said, moving toward the house. Sam, who grasped Ken's shoulder tightly as he passed, followed.

Alone now, Ken looked in the window at the crowded living room. He wondered if standing on the porch away from his guests was appropriate funeral etiquette. Not that he cared. He just wondered if such a thing existed. Paula glanced up from her parents' fussing, and Margaret Jones turned to see what had attracted her daughter's attention. The old woman's face soured upon seeing Ken. She immediately turned her back.

Fuck you, Ken thought. He was my son.

Ken spun slowly on his heels and nearly dropped his cocktail. A man stood on the porch not ten feet from him. At first, fear caught the breath in Ken's throat. When recognition set in and his stomach tightened to an intolerable ache, his breath hissed out.

So little had changed in the man's appearance. Though, his handsome face seemed uncharacteristically uncertain. Salt-and-pepper hair, now longer in the back, still hugged the head neatly. Ken had to see every line and every shade of green in the eyes before he would be able to move.

Then the guest stepped forward with arms spread wide.

"David," Ken said.

⚜

"I didn't know if I should come," David Lane said.

"I'm glad you're here but ..." Ken was still too shocked by David's presence to know what to make of it. "I figured you'd..."

"Think you were an asshole?" David finished.

Ken smiled. "Yes."

"I do." David backed up a step but continued smiling. "A whole year, Kenny. You never called, never wrote. I was about to start dating other people."

David was trying to make light of their situation, and Ken was grateful for it. He knew an apology wouldn't say a fraction of what he needed to say to the man, but "I'm sorry" is what he said.

"So am I," David replied, looking serious now.

"I've missed you."

"You didn't have to."

Yes, Ken thought, I did...for both of us.

"I don't think," he said, "that this is the time."

David looked at his feet. "I know, I know." He tried to say something else and faltered, so he threw his hands out and shrugged. "I don't know what to say to you. You're going through something I can't even imagine right now, and I know I'm intruding on it. But I wanted you to know that you're in my thoughts."

"You're not intruding, David." A pulse of emotion ran through Ken. He breathed deeply and choked back the sob rising in his throat. "Look, I know I handled things between us badly."

"As you said, this isn't the time," David told him, reaching out to pat Ken's shoulder. "You should be inside with your family. If you want to talk later, you know my number."

"Actually," Ken said, looking over his shoulder at the house and thinking about the somber group inside, particularly Paula's unforgiving parents, "I'm not staying much longer."

The news, or what it implied, seemed to trouble David. Concern veiled his face, and David said, "Ken, I just came by to pay my respects and see how you were doing. That's all. Believe me, this was hard enough."

But Ken wouldn't let it go. "I'm going to get a table at Gillian's at four o'clock." He'd used a similar line on the night they'd met, and only after he'd uttered it did Ken realize it was a mistake.

"Don't," David warned, his voice sharp with anger.

"Okay, you're right," Ken said. "That wasn't fair. But I want us to talk, so I'm going to ask you to meet me anyhow."

"I don't think that's a good idea. Not right now." David walked to the stairs. "Maybe in a few days. I don't know."

"I'm going to be there at four," Ken said. "I'll understand if you can't make it, but I hope I'll see you."

David looked back at him. He shook his head in consternation and turned. "Take it easy," he said, walking away.

14

Ken finally left Paula's a little after three. He walked the two blocks to St. Charles and cursed the streetcar for not getting there faster. By the time he left the car on Canal, it was three thirty. He had wanted to shower and change before going to Gillian's, but he would barely have time to slough off the suit and throw on a comfortable pair of shoes.

At home, he discarded the black suit and put on a pair of khaki Dockers, a white shirt, and a comfortable pair of deck shoes. Fifteen minutes later, he sat in the cool air and warm décor of Gillian's Nest, a restaurant that offered the heavy paneling and dark atmosphere of a gentleman's club. A large square bar filled the center of the room, and a young man with a muscular build stood in its center, looking bored. It was four o'clock.

Ken wasn't expecting David to show; the look he'd given Ken before walking back to his car had been damning enough to squash any hope Ken might have had. Granted, he'd handled the request poorly, wrapping it in a bit of romantic memory, which had no doubt soured for David. But he'd felt so much with David standing in front of him that he couldn't think clearly. He didn't want the man to walk away, wanted to know that the words on the porch would not be the last between them.

When he thought about their time together, the two years leading up to his flight from New Orleans, Ken realized that he'd never been happier; his life had never been that good before and certainly hadn't since. Part of that, a large part, was David, but it wasn't just him. Ken had had security in his business, with still enough work to keep him feeling vital. He'd gotten over what he thought were the worst years with his family.

All of that changed, seemingly overnight.

He and David had just returned from two weeks in Italy. Still jet lagged, Ken had not been able to sleep, so he'd gone into the kitchen to fix himself a drink, leaving David snoring in the bedroom. He'd been about to sit on the sofa in the living room when the music started. At first, the tinkling of piano keys had startled him, but since it emanated from the bedroom, he assumed that David had woken and turned on the radio. The song was not familiar, just a slow and solemn rag, played by skilled fingers, but the melody unnerved him.

He'd left the living room and followed the music to the bedroom, where he found David's body hanging from the ceiling. Ken had stumbled back to the wall, spilling half of his drink on the floor. He couldn't comprehend the sight. The detail of the vision was sharp, and the sound of a hundred hungry flies circling the cadaver resonated in the room, but Ken still stared on in disbelief.

"Hey," David had said. Ken looked at the lifeless face, but it had not moved. "I'm getting cold in here."

Ken looked at the bed where David lay, holding the covers back and patting the sheets. He turned back toward the hanged man, but the vision had gone.

That was the first time he'd endured the hallucination but not the last. Things began to fray soon after.

The disruption of his life was not limited to his slipping sanity. In the days following his return from that vacation, Paula began interrogating him, and Jennifer, who had been reserved in his presence, turned absolutely cold. It all seemed to happen within the span of a week, maybe two. Things began unraveling, slowly at first but then rapidly and totally until he felt unsafe and unwelcome anywhere he went in the city.

Now, at Gillian's, he knew that those two happy years would never be repeated. He might find happiness again, and maybe his world would fall back into balance, but Bobby was gone, and David was out of his life, so it would never be the same.

Ken looked at his empty glass. He didn't even remember drinking from it, but only a half-moon of ice remained.

David appeared then. The man walked into Gillian's, looked around until he saw Ken, lifted a hand in a quick wave, and went to the bartender for a drink. Ken was stunned to see him, and fingers of trepidation tickled his stomach. David didn't look glad to see him, nor did he look upset. Ken couldn't read his expression at all.

Drink in hand, David crossed to the table and sat down.

"Thanks for coming."

"Yeah," David said, sounding distant. "Well, I wanted to see you. That's why I went to the house." He stirred his drink. "I really am sorry about Bobby. It's an awful thing, so young. I hope they catch the bastard."

They won't, a tiny voice whispered.

"Yes," Ken said. "How have things been with you?"

"Nothing new. Business is good, keeps me off the streets."

"And personally?" Ken asked.

"I don't think that's any of your business these days."

David looked through his lashes at Ken, and the crystal-green disks at their center flashed cold light.

The air in the bar grew hot, and the paneled walls suddenly felt too close and too low. They should have met somewhere else, Ken thought. Maybe they shouldn't have met at all.

"David, I'm sorry. About the way I left, about a lot of things."

"So, why'd you leave?" David asked. "I know this isn't the right time with everything you're going through, but I don't see how we're supposed to sit here and talk around the subject. You left. You cut me out completely. Do you have anything to say about that?"

Ken didn't know what to say. Of course, he expected David to have questions, and he wanted to answer them, but the truth was too confusing. He'd never be able to explain it. Maybe in time but not now. Still, he knew he couldn't fall back on the lie he'd told a year ago.

"It wasn't business."

"No points for stating the obvious, Ken. Was it me? Was it the relationship? What?"

"I just couldn't live here anymore."

"You're kidding, right?" David asked. He looked into his glass and shook his head. "That's your revelation? You got tired of the zip code and moved west?"

"No. It's not that simple." Ken lit a cigarette, to give himself an extra moment before he had to speak. "If I thought I could have made you understand what was happening or convinced you to come with me, I would have."

"Ken, you never tried. One day, you just didn't show up for dinner. You called me and told me you were in the process of moving. How the hell do you think that made me feel?"

"I know," Ken said.

"I don't think you do." By now, David was fuming. His face wore a flush, and his voice trembled. "When we were together, I accepted your little juggling act. You had the family and the business, and you had me. You managed to keep a couple balls in the air while you had the other in your hand. And, you know, I got it. I understood. But we're not together anymore, so if you expect me to sit here, you better stop juggling and answer my question."

"In simple terms, I was scared."

David looked on expectantly.

Tell me a story.

"I used to live in the Quarter," Ken said. "Before I went to school in Austin. I never told you that, did I?"

"No."

"Fun and games," he continued. "But a friend introduced me to this man."

"A man?" David asked.

"Everyone knew him or knew about him. I was a stupid kid. Kind of starstruck, I guess, but it went bad. I won't get into that. All I can tell you is that I had to get away from him. And I did. But he forced me to come back, and by then it was too late."

"You'd already decided?"

"I think we both had," Ken said. "He died that night. A lot of people died that night."

David nodded. "Brugier," he said.

Ken wasn't shocked that David knew the name. Everyone knew the story of Travis Brugier. No surprise, just discomfort at having the name spoken aloud. "Yes. Travis Brugier," he said.

"I can't believe you knew him," David said. "Jesus, were you there the night he…?"

"Yes," Ken said. "I was there."

David sat quietly. Ken could see him working over the information, trying to digest all that it meant. He hoped it would be enough for the man, because Ken couldn't say any more about it.

When David spoke, the edge on his voice had dulled. "I'm not sure I understand how this applies. To us, I mean."

"I had what I can only call a delayed breakdown as a result of that time in my life. I thought I'd dealt with it, but last year everything just fell apart, and I panicked."

"You never said anything."

"I couldn't," Ken replied.

"And so you left?"

"I thought a different city, fewer mementos of that night…"

"And after you left?"

"What do you mean?"

"Did you recover?"

"Yes. It all stopped. Some semblance of normalcy came back into my life, but I was miserable." Ken paused to stub out his cigarette. Regret and grief were building up in him, mixing into a thick fluid, clotting in his chest. He tried to speak, but the words stuck in his throat. He breathed deeply to clear the viscous emotions. "You don't have any idea how much I missed you."

Ken stood from the table. Too much pain surged in him. He'd been holding it back for days, trying to be strong for his family while he watched them put his baby son in a stone crypt, but the anguish refused to be quelled any longer. Seeing David and layering his grief with all that he felt for the man and with the traumatic memories of a place called Wonderland was just too much. It hit like a fever, making him tremble and sweat. Soon, the tears would come. He had to get home.

"Oh shit," David whispered.

The anger and disappointment were gone from his voice, replaced by concern. Ken was grateful to hear it. His gratitude increased when David stood and wrapped his arm around Ken's shoulders, holding him tightly and leading him out of the lounge.

15

What the hell was happening?

David sat quietly next to Ken on the sofa, wondering how he had ended up in Ken's house, consoling the man over the loss of his son. He'd helped Ken through the door over an hour ago, and every few minutes he told himself he would go, but he couldn't bring himself to leave.

Since reading about Bobby Nicholson's death in the paper earlier in the week, he'd thought about attending one of the services, but he had chosen the repast instead. Considering their history, attending one of the formal ceremonies might have proven more than awkward; it might even have been disruptive, and David didn't want to cause any undue stress. As he'd told Ken, he simply wanted to pass along his condolences.

Things had gone better than David expected. Then, Ken made that stupid remark about reserving a table at Gillian's, trying to bring charm to a seriously uncomfortable situation. David had found that particularly ill-conceived tidbit to be less than enchanting. Furious and dismayed that Ken would even attempt such a ploy, David had vowed he would not show up for the date.

And yet he had. But why? he wondered.

Ever since that rainy morning, driving by the front of this house, peering in for a glimpse of its owner, Ken had been thick in David's thoughts. The desire to see him had reached a point nearing obsession, and for the life of him, David could not understand why. It was almost like he had someone in his head, goading him on, needling him to see the man. He'd never gone through anything like this in his life, and it was maddening.

Ken's body still trembled. His eyes gleamed with pools of moisture, but the racking sobs had passed for the time being. With a quick shift of his hips, Ken moved closer. David responded with a weak smile.

There was a lot about the man to love, David thought, or at least there had been. Now, he couldn't say he knew anything about him. David had spent too long trying to reconcile the Ken he'd known with the man who had vanished from his life to have any clear understanding of him. He was certain of little, except that Ken looked exactly as he had: Same body. Same face. Same eyes.

Though David had studied many men's faces, Ken's eyes were like nothing he had ever seen before. The irises were the color of ashes, nearly transparent in certain light. They were amazing, and just then David felt tremendously uncomfortable looking at them. He had to turn away.

Now was the time for excuses. He would make up some lie and remove himself from this man's life. If he stayed any longer, he'd be issuing a clear invitation to complications he wasn't willing to take on.

"You doing okay?" he asked. He needed a preface to saying good-bye and hoped Ken would say something positive, making his departure easier.

But he should have known that nothing with Ken was easy.

"I can't stop looking at you," Ken said.

David fumbled for something to say, but he had no reply. Then, Ken was kissing him, lightly at first and then more passionately as he adjusted his position on the sofa to secure the embrace.

His mind racing, protests shooting like lightning in his head, David did not pull away. In fact, he pushed in closer.

A moment later, he did pull away. For the first time, though by no means the last, David Lane wondered what he was getting himself into. He saw the need in Ken's eyes and recognized it in himself. The question was, for the time being, forgotten.

❧

Full darkness met David as he let himself into the courtyard of Ken Nicholson's house. Stepping back inside for a moment, David turned on the lights. The courtyard, dismal and unkempt, was the perfect place for him at that moment.

Sleeping with Ken had been a mistake. That much was clear. David could not imagine what Ken was going through. Sure, David knew loss. Friends, family, a lover, even Ken had sort of died to him for a while, but this loss he could not fathom. There was a presumed cycle to death, and parents assumed that they would find it long before their children.

And the violence? Senseless. Random.

It brought back the name Brugier. David's friends had whispered about Brugier's Parlor; they'd called it Wonderland. The place had served as a darker and clandestine counterpart to the bars that now filled the Quarter but was a private club. Men went there to meet boys, and boys went to experiment, to play, and sometimes to get rich.

David himself had never gone. He'd only been fifteen when Wonderland was spoiled, but he remembered the newspaper accounts vaguely. Four boys and Brugier were found in the courtyard that separated The Parlor from Brugier's house. Though the reticent media reported only the most superficial details, word in the Quarter was Brugier had torn the kids apart. He'd used some kind of knife, and when he broke the blade off in one kid's ribcage, he used his bare hands to finish the work. Then, he took a piano wire and hanged himself with it. Rumor had it that when the police tried to take him down from the balcony of his house, the head separated from the body. Though David found the story gruesome and more than likely embellished by the fertile minds of his peers, there could be no question that five people had been found dead on Brugier's property and that his house had remained empty ever since.

Had this been the last night that Ken spoke of? Had he witnessed the fall of Wonderland? Had he been its cause?

David Lane shivered despite the muggy night. The air settled on him in an oppressive film. He walked back into the house and sat on Ken's couch. A few minutes later, Ken entered the living room. He looked in better spirits, though his eyes were puffy and his hair was rumpled. A smile lit his face when he saw David on the couch.

"How are you feeling?" David asked.

"Better," Ken replied. "Is there any coffee left?"

"Should be; we didn't drink any. Sit down. I'll get it."

Ken waved him to sit and walked into the kitchen. David heard him fussing in the room for several minutes, and the microwave buzzed twice. Ken reappeared in the living room with two steaming mugs.

David's stomach rumbled at the smell. A little supper would be welcome about now, but he said nothing as he took the mug and made room for Ken next to him on the couch.

And now, he thought, we come to the moment of truth.

David considered sleeping with Ken a mistake for two very distinct reasons: Either it would put them back on the track they'd been on when Ken had left, or it wouldn't. David found neither of these possibilities comfortable.

Years ago, long before Ken, he had dated a man named Harvey. Harv was a good enough guy though he had more than a few hang-ups about sex. David hadn't been exactly surprised, what with Harv being a Catholic priest and all. The man had made it clear early on that he was devoted to his church and his parishioners, which precluded any romantic notion of a long-term commitment. As with Ken, the man did a lot of juggling. In the course of their relationship Harv made it clear that there would be *no riding off into the sunset*. In fact, he used the term with annoying frequency. By it, he meant that David should enjoy the moment because there was no future for them.

At the time, David had accepted Harv's philosophy. Only now did he begin to see how pointless such a conceit could be, like laboring to sow seeds for plants that would never grow.

Sitting in Ken's living room, David couldn't shake Harv's oft-used phrase; he didn't want to, because while David could admit to himself that when the sun set on this scene there would be no loving silhouettes—it would be just another passing of time, another day gone in preparation for the coming night—accepting this fact was a different story.

"I'm glad you're still here," Ken said. "I kind of panicked when I woke up and didn't see you."

"I didn't want to disturb you," he replied. "You were out cold."

"How long did I sleep?"

"Couple of hours, I guess," David said. "I came out here and read through some of your magazines. Your selection isn't very current: Nick and Jessica are still married. I was about to get out of here when you came in."

"You're leaving?" Ken looked disappointed.

And though he hated to say it, "Yes." David knew he had to leave; proximity made things more complicated. Seeing this man and having him within reach fouled David's perspective. "I have an early meeting," he said. "I'll give a call tomorrow and see how you're holding up."

The awkward departure—Ken's thank-you, the last too-rapid kiss, the good-byes—scratched over David. Through it all, he saw uneasiness in Ken's eyes.

"Are you sure you can't stay?" Ken asked, leaning on the doorjamb, looking down at David, who stood on the stairs.

The question came out softly and brushed over David like a teasing hand. He almost changed his mind and returned to the house, but something about Ken's expression stopped him.

It's not me he wants, David thought. He's just afraid to be alone.

16

The morning after Bobby's funeral, Ken considered his return to Austin, though he was reticent to do so. He knew he had to stay several more days in the city. Paula might need him, and he even tried to convince himself that he and Jennifer might reconnect in the aftermath of Bobby's death. The police would want him to be available in case they had any further questions. These threads of obligation formed a thin veil behind which stood a far more complicated incentive to stay in the city: David Lane.

As for Jennifer, this was hardest for her, Ken thought. She and Bobby had been so close, with rarely an incidence of petty rivalry. Even when she'd needed to exert her rebellious independence against her mother and father, Ken knew she had remained close with her big brother. The tragedy of his death had pushed her deeper into herself. In the days before the funeral she had been a ghost in Ken's presence, flitting through a room, speaking with her mother but refusing his comfort in any way. He took it personally, though in the form of self-reproach not accusation. He couldn't blame Jennifer. She was just a kid, and she was hurting. With Bill and Margaret Jones still in town, he would have preferred to keep his distance from the house in the Garden District, but he couldn't let them and their familiar disdain keep him away. Ken had to reach out to her. They had to talk.

And he wanted to see David again. Despite his mourning for Bobby and the uncertainty of his future plans, he had not been able to stop thinking about the man. His morning was spent in an irrational state, waiting for the call David had promised.

When the call finally came, Ken was dressing to go out.

"Hello."

"Ken," David's unmistakable voice said. "Good morning."

"Hello," he repeated.

"How are you this morning?"

"Better than expected," he replied coolly. David sounded uneasy, but Ken's own voice disturbed him more. Why did it sound so dry and formal? He considered this, realizing that the line between them was quiet.

"Well," David said, "just checking up."

Again, a long silence filled the phone line. Like strangers it seemed, they had nothing to say to one another. What was this? Ken wondered. And how the hell did he get past it?

"I guess I'll let you go," David said. "It was good to see you again."

Let you go? The words sliced into him, but his throat was closed. Ken felt like he was sinking, able to see the saving line but unable to grab it.

"Ken?"

"Why is this so damned awkward?" Ken asked.

The line was quiet for a moment, and then David said, "Maybe because we both realize that we made a mistake last night."

"I don't believe that," Ken said.

"Yeah well, you needed someone."

"Don't," Ken snapped. This was ridiculous; they were both mature men yet he felt like a fumbling adolescent.

"Ken, it's not a problem. For God's sake…"

"David, stop it. The wounded duck crap doesn't suit you."

"And this doesn't sound like a mistake to you?" David asked. "Fifteen seconds and we're on the verge of yelling at one another?"

"It's only a mistake if we keep up this bullshit."

"Isn't that what I just said?"

"No," Ken said. "We're looking at this the wrong way. I'm looking at this the wrong way."

"Is this that 'I just wanna be friends' speech?"

"Fuck, David," Ken said. "I don't know what this is. Last night was wonderful. It felt right. But this doesn't, and I can't figure out why."

"Look, Ken, forgive the cliché, but last night just happened. I don't know what it meant, but you haven't exactly fostered a sense of security in all of this."

"I know that," Ken said. "I'm not asking you to forgive me or to understand, and worse yet, I can't promise a damned thing because, more than likely, I can't stay." Ken forced himself to quit speaking. He was rushing way ahead of himself, and his words were getting jumbled.

"Let's make this easy," David said. "You tell *me* what you want, and I'll tell *you* if you can have it."

This was the easy way? Ken wondered. How the hell was he supposed to know what he wanted? He only knew that he didn't want to lose contact again. But was that true? Was that all he wanted?

"I can't predict the future, but for now, can we have dinner tonight?"

"Yes."

❧

He walked the Quarter, trying to manage his thoughts about Bobby and Jennifer and David Lane. Also, though he hated to admit it to himself, he was trying to build up the courage to face Bill and Margaret Jones, particularly Bill.

Even well into his seventies, Jones was an intimidating man who wore the courage of his convictions like armor. Over the years, they'd argued so often that Ken could scarcely remember a single pleasant moment between them.

Maybe one, Ken thought. The day Bobby had been born both Bill and Margaret Jones had been euphoric. Bill had even hugged Ken on that occasion, perhaps simply caught up in the joy of being a grandparent. It hadn't taken long for Jones to revert to his usual posturing of contempt and disapproval. And that was before Ken had come out and left Jones's daughter.

At Bobby's funeral and after, Jones had shot cruel and accusing looks. It didn't matter that Ken too had been wounded by loss. The man's grandson was dead, and somebody was going to pay. Why not the queer who had wrecked his daughter's life and the lives of her children?

Finally, Ken left the Quarter. If Paula's father wanted to cause a scene, there was nothing Ken could do about it. He needed to see Jen.

He walked uptown toward the Garden District, worms of trepidation writhing in the pail of his stomach. It would have been far easier to take Jennifer out, find some neutral ground on which they could both stand while Ken made the initial steps to rebuild their relationship. He imagined that Jennifer would become instantly defensive and withdrawn in such a situation, if she even agreed to meet him. Her home, someplace familiar and comfortable would be better, so Ken walked, running what he might say to his daughter through his head.

Standing on the porch of Paula's house, Ken breathed deeply. He braced himself and reached for the doorknob. He walked in after a short series of knocks and caught Bill and Margaret Jones by surprise. They had been sitting in the living room, clasping hands on the sofa. Margaret, her hair a perfect white helmet, was just rising from the couch to answer the door as he entered the foyer. The familiar "Oh, it's you" look fell over her face, and she returned to her seat. Bill, however, got to his feet and wedged his fists to his hips, a fighting cock ready for a scrap.

Ken walked to the arch of the living room but did not enter. He said, "Good morning."

Margaret Jones replied with a clipped "Morning," never taking her eyes off of her husband. Jones just nodded sharply, pecking at the air.

"Are Paula and Jennifer home?"

"Upstairs," Jones said, "but you'd better come back later. Jennifer is upset and needs her mother right now."

And she doesn't need you, Ken added for Jones, who may not have said the words, but certainly wore the denouement in the creases around his eyes.

"Is something wrong?" he asked.

"Yes, Ken," Jones replied coldly. "Her brother was murdered, and she's hurt and confused."

Ken almost shrank before the man's words. He didn't expect civility from Jones, but such blatant cruelty, all but saying that Ken was indifferent to the death of his own son, was simply unfathomable.

"Thank you," he said, in no mood for Jones's emotional slapstick, and started for the stairs.

"Now, wait a minute," Jones crowed.

Ken ignored the bitter old rooster and climbed toward the second floor.

The light in the upstairs corridor was out, giving the hall a gloomy cast. From the room farthest down on the left, he heard muted voices. He passed the first open door barely able to look in: Bobby's room. The next, facing the street, was the master suite. It looked hardly different than it had on the day they'd moved in. He came to the last room and peered in.

"Morning," Ken said.

Both Paula and Jennifer looked up in surprise. "Oh, Ken," Paula said, moving around her daughter to hurry across the room.

Ken had the uncomfortable sensation that they'd been talking about him, and from the looks on their faces, particularly Paula's, he understood that what they'd discussed was not flattering. As for Jennifer, he read little that was new on her face. She remained on the far side of the bed, looking sour and annoyed.

His ex-wife led him into the hall, and he asked, "What's going on?"

"Just girl talk," Paula said, making a visible adjustment to her expression, which now seemed lighter and nonchalant. "This is a surprise. You usually call first."

"Sorry," he said. "How's Jen holding up?"

"As well as can be expected, I suppose," Paula looked over her shoulder at the open door of their daughter's room. "Let's go downstairs and have some coffee."

"Actually, I came to speak with her."

"Oh, Ken, you'd better wait. Really."

"I need to speak to her, Paula."

"I know, and I'm not trying to keep you from her. I just don't think this is a good time."

"There's not going to be a good time," he said. "I've been putting this off for too long, waiting for one."

Paula must have seen the resolve in his face, because she nodded her head, acquiescing. "You do what you have to, but try not to upset her too much."

She walked away, down the gloomy hall to the head of the stairs. She gave Ken a cautious look and then started down.

When Jennifer had been born, Ken had hired a crew to paint the room a pale pink. He'd bought a beautiful white lacquered bedroom suite, including a canopied bed, nightstands, and chest of drawers. Gauzy white curtains with lace edges dipped from the window's top, gathered neatly in pink tiebacks. It had been a lovely room and everything Ken could have imagined for his daughter. That room was gone now. The walls of his daughter's room were now brown, a hue two shades deeper than beige, and covered in posters for rock bands made up of boys with numerous tattoos and piercings. The pretty canopied bed had been traded for a wrought-iron monstrosity that looked industrial. Black drapes pooled on the floor, replacing the lacy curtains. On the desk in the corner, her computer monitor sat amid a litter of papers, pens, and compact disks. An acoustic guitar stood propped against the edge. Ken wondered if she actually played the instrument. He'd paid for seven years of piano lessons but had never heard his daughter play an entire song.

He stood on the threshold of this room, which he found overly dark and depressing. Jennifer sat on the far edge of the bed, staring at the floor. Her mousy brown hair fell to her shoulders in clumps and frays.

"Do you mind if I come in for a minute?"

His daughter shrugged, didn't turn around.

Ken stepped inside and felt the room settle around him like a dismal cloud. He walked to the near edge of the bed and sat.

"How are you holding up?" he asked.

Another shrug. "Fine," Jennifer muttered.

She was not going to make this easy for him; that much was clear. Ken shifted on the bed, and looked at the digital numbers of the alarm clock on the nightstand beside his daughter.

"We're all upset, Honey," he said. "I still can't understand how something like this could happen. I loved Bobby so much, and he's gone now. And I'm angry and hurt, and I don't know what to do about it."

Jennifer made no response, just continued looking at the floor, keeping the curtain of tangled hair between them. Ken cleared his throat lightly, choking back a knot of emotion in his throat.

"But I love you too," Ken said. "And I know you're hurt. I also know that I've played a part in that, and I'm sorry. I haven't always handled things very well, and that's going to change."

"Because of Bobby?" Jennifer asked.

"Partly," Ken said. "But I think we both know that things haven't been right for a long time. I just never knew how to talk about any of this before."

The grim room shrank tighter around him. His daughter's silence pulled uneasy emotion from him like abrasive twine unraveling from a spool threaded through his chest. He hadn't expected to deliver a monologue, didn't know what to say without prompting, but he had to say something.

"You know, when your mother and I got married, there were a lot of problems. We discussed them, and they didn't seem insurmountable. As you've seen, that wasn't the case. I accept a lot of the responsibility for that. I kept telling myself that certain things would change if I had a family…"

"Oh my God," Jennifer said. She finally turned to Ken. "Could we have a little *more* drama?"

"Excuse me?"

Jennifer grimaced. Her voice was filled with mocking when she said, "In the aftermath of family crisis, Jenny discovers her father's darkest secret: Next, on Lifetime. This is so stupid."

"It's not stupid, Jennifer. I'm trying to explain."

"Explain what? That you're gay? It's about ten years too late for that little bit of news."

"I know this can't be easy for you to understand, but I needed something…"

"Just stop it," Jennifer said, interrupting him again. "Spare me your coming-out story. Nobody cares who or what you're fucking."

"Hey," Ken warned.

"Did you really think Bobby or I cared about that? Did you think we were that stupid?"

"No, I never thought that. It had nothing to do with you or your brother."

"It was all about you. Like everything else."

He looked back at the face of the digital alarm clock, tracing the numbers with his gaze. He wouldn't argue with her. Not now. If she needed to believe he'd acted solely from self-interest, he'd let her. All he could do was try to explain.

"The way I left was difficult for all of us," Ken said, "but I honestly believed it was for the best. Now, you say you're not upset about my sexuality, but it's obviously been a problem for you."

"You don't know anything."

"Then, you tell me, Jennifer, because I don't know how to fix this. I don't know what you need."

"Big surprise. You don't know anything about me. If you did, I wouldn't have had to endure a billion lame conversations with you. Do you know what you say every time you come over? You should. You always say the exact same thing. You ask how things are going at school. You say, 'Are you still fighting the boys off with sticks,' even though neither of us believes it. Bullshit like that. I tried talking about it with you, but it wasn't worth it. The small talk wasn't worth it."

Ken saw Paula in his daughter's face then. Intelligence and strength came through just as it always had with her mother. "I'm sorry. I didn't know I was doing that to you."

"You always thought we were so stupid."

"That's not true. I was just..."

"Yeah, you were scared. You didn't think we could handle it."

"Are you going to let me finish?"

"No," Jennifer said. "No. You're just doing this to ease your own conscience. Bobby's dead. You blew it with him, and now you're scared that you're going to be old and alone. Well fine. I hope you are."

"Jennifer." He'd tried to sound forceful, but the word came out as a whisper.

She left the bed and walked to her dresser. From its top, she pulled a necklace and dangled it in the air between them.

A brittle tide of fear ran through his veins. He recognized the trinket far too well.

"Where did you get that?" Ken asked. The charm at the end of the golden chain spun lazily in the sunlight.

"Bobby wanted me to give this to you if anything happened to him. I thought he was crazy, but maybe he knew something we didn't." She threw the chain and its bauble at him.

As a reflex, Ken caught the necklace. Though he didn't want to touch it, Ken tightened his fist around the charm.

Thoughts of his daughter were forgotten. His son's death had never occurred. He was not married. He was eighteen years old, running through the streets of the French Quarter, fearing a man who wanted more than his life.

             ⚜

"You were right about him," Jennifer Nicholson whispered into the phone. "He thought that his great confession would make everything all right. He's such an asshole."

"What did he say?" Jennifer's friend asked.

"Oh he tried to explain how he was confused when he married Mom. How he thought a family would make him normal. Everything you told me he'd say."

"Did you give him the necklace?"

Jennifer laughed. "Yes, and you should have seen his face. He looked like I'd just kicked him in the balls."

"Well, then, this might be the lesson he needed. Given time, he might become the father you wanted."

"Never."

"Jennifer," her friend said soberly, "never is a hopeless commitment. Are you sure you want to write him off completely?"

"I'm not writing him off. He wrote us off. And now he's afraid no one will be there for him. Well, good."

"Yes," Jennifer's friend replied. "Good."

             ⚜

Tell me a story.

The necklace in his pocket told a story. Given him thirty years before by a handsome and terrible man, a man who had died before his eyes, the necklace told a violent, tragic tale. Decades ago, Ken had disposed of the necklace. Who knew enough to find this horrible memento and give it to his son? The possibility terrified him.

He pulled the long golden chain Jennifer had given him from his pocket. A sharp tooth with a crosspiece, like a feral crucifix, glowed in his palm. His mind drifted back to an old storybook. It wandered into the sultry heat of a magnificent courtyard where a man spoke a simple request. How many stories had Ken read from that book? Had he read them all? Amid the heat and the perfume of those long afternoons and nights, had he spoken each word in that volume or had he merely repeated the same handful of tales again and again?

"Tell me a story," a familiar voice whispered.

History had returned to be rewritten, but Kenneth Nicholson battled this notion as he sat in his living room, staring at the necklace. The survivors wrote history. Brugier and his Wonderland were gone. Puritan Crowley was gone. Bobby was gone. The dead only moved in thought. Their only power came from tenacious memory.

At the back of his house, from the courtyard, somber notes began to play. The piano's lament, muffled by distance, crept over Ken's shoulders like a palpable cloth, a shroud. The room grew hot, its air scented with smoke and cologne, cloying in his throat. Footsteps padded in the hall behind him, startling Ken, who turned to find the room empty.

David was coming over soon to pick him up for dinner. If everything went well, Ken would invite himself back to David's house for the night. He didn't have the courage to remain among his memories.

From the kitchen, a shuffling noise rose as if something had slid across the counter. A grinding squeal and a sound like paper tearing followed it. Ken did not leave the sofa to investigate. The sounds were all in his head, he told himself. All in his head.

17

David woke in the middle of the night. The bed next to him was empty, the sheets cool. He wiped the sleep from his eyes and rolled out of bed. He checked the bathroom across the hall, but the door was open, and Ken wasn't there.

Still drowsy, he wandered down the hall to the stairs, blinking away the blur in his vision. Ken might have gone home, but David didn't think so. He'd been upset over dinner, something about his daughter. They weren't getting along these days, but for all David knew, they never had gotten along. Ken kept information about his family close to the vest and vague. It was often maddening, but David didn't press.

Halfway down the stairs, David stopped. He saw Ken, standing in the center of the living room behind the sofa. His head was down, staring into an upturned palm, and his naked body looked ghostly in the dim light. David watched for several moments, expecting Ken to move, to look up, and notice him, but Ken's attention remained on his open hand.

Was he holding something? From his position on the stairs, David couldn't be sure.

"Ken?"

"You're not there," he whispered.

As the bizarre claim rolled through the air, the room below took on an unsettling quality. Dappled in unmoving shadows, the darkened room suddenly struck him as threatening and not the comfortable space where he took his morning coffee, read his newspaper, called friends on the telephone. The prospect of Ken's naked body, strong and smoothed by murky illumination, was stirring, but in this setting it seemed perverse to want him, because Ken, though standing, looked dead.

"Where did it come from?" Ken's empty voice asked.

It occurred to David that Ken was caught in a dream. He'd never known the man to sleepwalk, but nothing else explained the disturbing vacancy in his voice or his odd position in the middle of the room. David had heard that you weren't supposed to wake sleepwalkers because they could hurt themselves. He'd also heard that it was a myth.

Uncertain what to do, David remained on the stairs.

"Ken," he said again.

This time, Ken looked up at him. Though David could not read the expression on his face, he noticed a start of surprise jerking Ken's shoulders back.

"Hey," Ken said, turning to face David. He closed his palm around whatever he held there, perhaps nothing more than a fragment of dream. With the other hand, he smoothed the hair down on his scalp.

"Are you okay?"

"Fine," Ken said. "Did I wake you?"

"No," David said, still unnerved by the deathly cast on Ken's skin, though now relieved to see that whatever spell had held him was over. "I managed that on my own. You coming back up?"

"Sure."

In the bed, David lay on his side. Ken's arm draped over him, his palm resting lightly on the sensitive skin below David's navel. The weight of Ken's chest pressed into his back and the tuft of his pubic hair nestled David's ass. David stared at the wall, fixing his gaze on a small chip in the paint. He'd never noticed the flaw before; it was barely the size of the nail on his pinkie finger, but now, in the dark, it drew his attention. He'd have to sand that down and paint it, he thought.

Ken adjusted his position until his penis rested in the groove of David's buttocks. David lay motionless, staring at the shallow divot in the wall. An overwhelming sense of unease had followed him back to bed. Though Ken's touch did not bother him, quite the opposite actually, David couldn't help but feel trapped—not with Ken but by him—in something that David didn't understand. Which was completely ridiculous. He didn't owe Ken anything. The guy had up and moved, ending their relationship with the subtlety of a gunshot. The guy hadn't bothered to call, to write, or to do one thing to show he gave a damn about David once he'd run off to Austin. Ken had mentioned something about a breakdown, and considering what David had just witnessed in his living room, he imagined that Ken's descent into emotional instability hadn't quite played itself out. And yes, David felt tremendously sorry for Ken, for his losing Bobby, but what exactly—what in the hell—was David doing to himself?

He wasn't a teenager. He didn't carry romantic expectations in his pocket, nor could he overlook the damage that had been done or the implausibility of a future between them. Ken was going back to Austin. David wasn't going with him. So what exactly did all of this say about David that he was so compliant, welcoming Ken back into his life?

Warm breath covered his neck. Ken's cock grew hard against him.

Longing and logic wrestled in his thoughts. I can't get involved in this again, he told himself. Life was too damned short to go on the same ride over and over. No matter how much fun it was, the ride always ended at the same place. More to the point, it always ended.

David dropped Ken off at the house on Dumaine just after eight in the morning. He had a full day of work ahead, preparing for a client meeting. When Ken asked if he was available for lunch, David said, "Not today. Too much work. I'll call you later." Then David pulled away from the curb and made the right on Burgundy. He found himself driving too fast and forced himself to slow until the one-way streets returned him to Canal.

He tried to get his mind into the work waiting at his home office, but his brain wouldn't cooperate. It was still sifting through the maybes and what-ifs of Ken's return.

You're already in love with him again.

"No way," David whispered to the windshield.

There was a mystery in Ken's life that he refused to reveal. Ken insisted that the city itself was the root of this enigma. Even if David could bring himself to believe that the city was responsible, the fact that the torment of this mystery was something that Ken's influence could not subdue and Ken's money could not quell fed David's trepidation. Something of that magnitude did not just vanish because one chose to move to another state. Perhaps location focused Ken's anxiety, but something else fed it.

At home, David pulled the Mercedes into the driveway. He leaned back in his seat and stared through the windshield at the magnolia tree at the back of his property. A black roach ran across his windshield, startling David so badly that his heartbeat jumped into his ears. He followed the progress of the horrible creature across the glass until it came to rest before the passenger seat. David turned on his windshield wipers to annoy or possibly maim the little bastard. The wipers swooshed quickly over the glass, and the bug vanished. David could not see where the roach disappeared to, but for the moment it was gone, and he leaned back again to observe the peaceful tree.

Flesh Eaters, he thought. He hated the damned things.

18

The walls of the Creole cottage whispered. Thirty minutes after David's hurried departure, the house, no longer content to haunt Ken with the past, exploited the present to prickle his insecurities with accusations of ineptitude, apathy, and selfishness. You failed your family, the house told him. Ken hadn't been there. Bobby and Jennifer had looked for him, tried to reach him, but they just couldn't find him, so they went on without his guidance. And David. He'd all but fled after dropping Ken off that morning.

And why wouldn't he? Ken wondered. It wasn't like he'd made any effort to explain the bizarre events that occupied his mind. He was delusional, that much was clear. Maybe David would understand, even help him through his emotional wreckage, but Ken didn't want to take that chance. Of course, more than just his mind betrayed him these days. His haunted memories fed on tangible sustenance. The Thorn, that ugly and haunting piece of jewelry his daughter had given him at Bobby's bequest, was no figment. Bobby's fiancée and the blond thug, Chuck, were real enough.

Ken didn't know what to make of it all. He didn't believe in ghosts or bogeymen. Even if he did, those things didn't explain Vicki Bach or Chuck, the kid who had murdered his son. Both were human and dangerous. All he could know with any certainty was that elements of the past were again weaving with the present.

In Austin, he'd experienced none of the nightmares that befell him here. It was this place, this city. New Orleans was punishing him; for what crime, he didn't know. For Ken, the reason was becoming less and less important. All he had to do was leave. The city that had once excited him with endless possibility was now reduced to a trash heap, piled high with fetid history and rotting emotion. Its reek covered him. Everywhere he turned, refuse clung to refuse, blanketing anything he might have cherished. It would be better for everyone if he just went back to Austin.

Ken crossed his kitchen to the loggia and stepped into the courtyard to let the sun's heat soothe him. A few steps into his yard, he grew dizzy. His knees grew weak, and he nearly crashed to the flagstone path. His vision skewed and grew fuzzy. The courtyard before him and the fence beyond seemed to melt. The dying plants in the wall hangers took on a new life: Their dead, brown tendrils oozed along the brick walls and crept like serpents along the painted siding. The pots at his feet began a slow respiration, growing and shrinking like muddy lungs.

He knew this feeling. He tried fighting it, but it wrapped around him, penetrated him. Ken moved to the ivy-covered brick and leaned against it. He rested on the wall to let the wobbly feeling pass. Bright lights, like the blinding flash of a camera popped before his eyes. Ken blinked. He turned back toward the house and stopped.

Travis Brugier stood in the shadow of the balcony, blocking Ken's path to the house. Naked, then dressed in a crisp linen suit, then in shorts with a brilliant colored shirt, then naked again.

"I'm hurt, Baby. You barely remember what I looked like," the apparition told him. "Perhaps I can be of some help." Brugier took a step forward. His nudity fell beneath the linen suit again. "Shall we go into the house?" he asked. "After you've pulled yourself to-gether, of course."

The dream sensation, and the sickness it brought began to slip away; they receded but left room for the onset of fear. Blinking wildly, he hoped his eyelids would sweep Brugier back into his mind, but Brugier remained.

"Dead," Ken whispered.

"But not forgotten," his guest replied. "Sad thing about Bobby. A handsome boy, much like his father. It was a shame to see his beauty dashed, but I had to get you here, back to the beginning."

Ken stumbled forward, stepping across the flagstones. Still dazed, he fought to control his legs.

"You didn't really think I'd leave you?" Brugier asked, stepping aside to allow Ken's passage into the house. "Not after all that we meant to each other."

"It didn't mean anything," Ken said. His head felt bruised, but he managed to get into the kitchen and through the dining room. He leaned on a chair for support. Brugier spoke at his back.

"Didn't mean one little ol' thing? Is that what you tell yourself? After all I'd done for you?"

"I never asked." Ken pulled on the chair and sat heavily in it. He accepted Travis Brugier's presence but dressed it up as delusion. "I didn't want anything from you."

Brugier stepped around Ken. The linen suit looked impossibly crisp. It only looked that way for a few minutes on a human body, then the wrinkles came. An illusion, Ken decided, a dream and nothing more.

The dream chuckled. "Much more," it said. "I told you I'd see you again, and I never lied to you."

"What do you want?" Ken asked.

"I want you to consider the offer I made."

Offer? Ken's mind raced, trying to remember. The spirit was talking about their last night together, but Brugier had rambled about so many things. Ken thought he remembered something from that night: something about time, something about forever.

And when his mind finally cleared and he had the answer, it repulsed him.

"Never," he said.

"Really," Brugier asked. "After Paula and David follow Bobby? When everything is taken from you by me or by time, when you have nothing except your own miserable, aging body, will you still be so confident in your commitment to never? I know loneliness, Baby. I know desolation. Perhaps, just for fun, I'll leave you Jennifer for a while. I almost like her. Such a bitter child. Perhaps the ugly sow will have children of her own. How will Grandpa feel when he visits the house and finds the babies hanging by their tongues? Will you still say never?"

"I…" Ken gasped. With the threat had come a picture, a perfect picture: two children, still infants, dangling from the eaves of Ken's house with Jennifer, their mother, in a heap on the flagstones beneath rigid pink toes.

"Don't force me to be cruel," Brugier said. "I find it far too easy. Especially when it comes to love."

"This…is not…love!" Ken said.

Brugier stepped forward to grasp Ken's shoulder. "Baby, this is what the poets have written about for centuries: unforgiving, uncompromising, and *undying*. Sounds like love to me. But don't take my word for it. Ask anyone. Better yet, just ask Sam."

"Sam?" Ken asked. "What does Sam have to do with this?"

"No more or less than anyone else in your life."

Brugier released his grip on Ken's shoulder, turned toward the kitchen, and walked away.

"Travis," Ken called. He stood from the chair and followed the apparition, the delusion, the damnable ghost—whatever Travis was—into the kitchen, but the man was gone. He continued through to the courtyard, but it too was empty. Back inside, Ken returned to the chair and leaned forward on the table.

Travis had taken credit for Bobby's murder. Was that possible? Had it been Brugier's influence that had driven Chuck to kill Bobby? And what had Travis meant about Sam?

Then, Ken caught himself. Travis wasn't real; he was nothing more than a figment of Ken's damaged imagination. He was no more genuine than the piano dirge or the frightening vision of David Lane's dead body. Ken's guilt over his son's death had brought Travis back as a tormenting spirit that spoke nonsense, a memory given life by decaying sanity.

"I need some help," Ken whispered.

The moment the word *help* left his lips, a flurry of knocks landed on his front door, startling him up and out of his chair.

❧

Sam Martin stood on Ken's stoop looking frantically from one side to the next. His narrow face was written in panic; a thin film of sweat covered his brow; his upper lip twitched nervously. When Ken opened the door, Sam rushed in.

"Lock it," Sam commanded as he spun into the living room.

"Sam, what's…"

"Lock the door," Sam insisted, spinning quickly to look around the interior of Ken's house. "You've got to help me. I don't know what I'm going to do if you don't help me. I can't believe this. I…"

"Sam, what the hell is going on?"

Martin scanned the room one final time. "Not here; he might see us. Let's go to the back."

"Okay, just calm down," Ken agreed. "We'll go to the kitchen. Who might see us?"

"Jersey," Sam said before retreating to the back of the house.

In the kitchen, Sam resumed his pacing. "It's my fault," he said. "Let's get that out first. I'm a selfish prick, and none of this would have happened if I hadn't been such an ass. But Jesus Christ!"

"Sam, tell me what happened."

"Give me one of those," he said, indicating the cigarette in Ken's hand. He fumbled the slender tube in his fingers before he managed to get it pinched firmly between his lips. "Have you got any coffee?" Martin asked.

"It doesn't look like you need any coffee," Ken said.

"I haven't slept all night. I was afraid to."

"Sam, you need to settle down."

"Damn it!" Sam cried. "Just make the fucking coffee!" He immediately realized his irrational tone. In a second he went from raving to complacent as if every ounce of strength had drained from his body. He put a hand on Ken's shoulder. "Please. I'm sorry."

Ken nodded slowly and turned for the coffeepot. "Why don't you want Jersey seeing us together?" he asked.

"I'm not worried about him seeing us together," Sam corrected. "I'm worried about him finding me."

"Are you going to explain this?" Ken asked. He pulled the coffee beans from the freezer and filled his grinder.

"The night of my party," Sam began, "there was this kid. I went outside to have a smoke while the stragglers were still carrying on. Jersey had already gone to bed," Sam turned away. His hands ran quickly over his scalp and then rested on the back of his neck. "I told you that Jersey and I were having some trouble. Things haven't been all that good between us lately, particularly in bed. All of his medications have made it kind of tough. His stomach is always upset, and he doesn't have any energy. We haven't made love in months. And I know that's no excuse for what I did."

Ken took this silence as an opportunity to grind the coffee beans.

As he poured the powder into the filter, Sam resumed speaking. "The kid was beautiful. He was interesting to talk to, or I was so drunk I thought he was. We sat outside for about an hour, and I finally told him that I had to go to bed. He asked if he could join me. Well, I wasn't that drunk. I told him that Jersey was inside, and he asked if he could stop by sometime when Jersey wasn't home. I figured he was just flirting and told him that he could stop by anytime he wanted.

"Well, he took me up on it. I got home from school yesterday about three. Jersey was on his way out to show a client a few properties uptown. I sat down and started grading papers when the doorbell rings. It's this kid. I don't know what I was thinking when I asked him in," Sam said. Then he chuckled bitterly, "That's a lie; of course I knew what I was thinking. Ten minutes later we were doing exactly what I was thinking. I don't think I've ever been through anything so intense in my life. Maybe it was the guilt. Maybe it was the fear of getting caught. I don't know. I was so lost in it all that I didn't hear Jersey come in."

"Oh shit, Sam," Ken whispered. The coffee was brewed, and he poured them both a cup. "So he left you?"

"He tried to kill me, Ken." Sam drank from the hot coffee and leaned on the kitchen island. "At first, he was incredibly cold about the whole thing. He told the kid to get dressed and get out, and the little fucker was gone in about two minutes. I'd gotten dressed myself, and I apologized. I was sorry. I am sorry. And Jersey just nodded his head and walked out of the bedroom. I broke down completely. The look on his face killed me. I was crying and trying to figure out anything I could say or do to make this not have happened. When Jersey came back into the room he was holding a knife."

"What?"

Sam nodded. "He had gotten the carving knife from the kitchen. He stood in the doorway for a minute, completely blocking it with his body. He started talking quietly, almost whispering. I couldn't understand a word of it. My attention was focused on that blade. Then, he charged me. He dove at me with the knife, and I dodged him and ran out of the house.

"Fortunately, I'd hidden his gun, because he would have used it. I know he would have. Anyway, I got in the car and started driving. Eventually, I stopped at a motel in Metairie. I waited a couple of hours for Jersey to cool off, but when I called, I found that he hadn't cooled any. He told me that he was going to kill me,

Ken. He said he'd wait as long as he had to, but wherever I went he was going to find me.

"When I drove to school this morning, I saw him sitting in his car on the street outside of the lot, and I high-tailed it out of there."

"Maybe he wanted to talk to you," Ken suggested. "He's had the whole night to think about it and calm down. He probably just wanted to work things out."

Sam shook his head. "I'm scared to see him, Ken. I don't know what he's thinking."

...unforgiving, uncompromising, and undying—sounds like love to me.

Ken searched for something rational to say but found himself at a loss. Less than an hour ago, Brugier had told him to ask Sam about the ramifications of love, but if Travis's ghost was simply an extension of Ken's own fragile sanity, then how had Ken come across this information? He couldn't have created it for himself. Which left the possibility that the apparition of Travis Brugier had a source outside of Ken's own mind, but that was impossible.

"Ken, what am I going to do?"

"I'm not sure, Sam," he said, struggling to put away his ridiculous speculations. "Jersey overreacted last night, but it's not like you made this easy for him. Maybe he's calmed down enough to listen to you. We could go back over to your place and wait for him. If he's still upset, you can come stay here for a few days until you guys get this thing worked out."

"You'll come with me?" Sam asked pathetically.

"Yes," Ken told him, "but don't expect this to be easy."

"I know." Sam suddenly looked incredibly small as he hunched over his coffee. "But he's got to forgive me," Sam whispered. "He's got to."

"Let's hope he does," Ken said. "Just finish your coffee."

Once the mugs were in the sink, Ken led Sam to the door and locked the house behind them. The wet heat of the day settled on them instantly, and Ken wished he had worn a lighter shirt instead of the cotton sweater he had thrown on. They wandered slowly up Dumaine. Sam stared at the ground like a punished child. They took the left on Burgundy Street.

"Maybe if you talked to him first," Sam suggested.

Ken had been thinking the exact same thing. He could get a reading on Jersey's temperature before the two men were forced to face one another. Maybe he could talk Jersey down a little. "We'll see," Ken said.

"Thanks," Sam muttered.

"So, was this guy a friend of Jersey's?" Ken asked as they neared the next corner. "You said he was at your party."

"No. Some woman, a client of Jersey's, had brought him. I thought he was her date. God knows they looked like they belonged together. I figured he was straight until we started talking. Then he dropped a few familiar names, and I knew he was family."

"You guys know the same people?"

"I guess," Sam mumbled. "He said he knew Lance and Pug. He knew a lot about David Lane, and he even mentioned you."

Ken stopped walking. "Sam, what did this kid look like?"

"He was blond..." Sam began.

A gun's report interrupted Sam's description. Ken would have thought the explosion nothing more than a car's backfiring if it weren't for the divot the bullet tore from the sidewalk ahead. He spun around, saw Jersey Fleagle aiming down the barrel of a small handgun and stumbled back.

At his side, Sam had already weighed his options and chosen flight. "Run, Ken," he cried, not waiting to see if his friend took the advice or not.

Another shot fired, and Ken leapt back, pressing himself against the building, a pointless reflex that provided no cover from Jersey at all. Sam had already reached a full sprint by the time he left the sidewalk, crossing into the street.

Ken heard the rumble of the truck barreling down Burgundy, traveling too fast for the neighborhood. Sam bolted out in front of the vehicle. The truck's brakes squealed the second before it hit Sam Martin, knocking him off of his feet. Sam spun through the air like a discarded doll back toward Ken and the lover he was trying to flee. Then he crashed to the ground, his face cracking on the edge of the curb only a dozen feet from Ken.

"Sam!" he cried.

Face down, his friend's body convulsed, legs kicking the ground in a spastic syncopation. Blood drooled down the curb and pooled in the street, mingling with dirt and litter.

Ken stumbled forward, already in shock, but knowing he had to help his friend. He only finished that one step before a strong hand threw him back to the wall, where he crashed into the wooden siding.

That same hand encircled his throat, and Jersey Fleagle's lunatic features rose before him. The barrel of the small pistol pressed deeply into Ken's cheek. Jersey's gaunt face was pulled into a mask of pure hate. Saliva foamed at the corner of his mouth. Nothing sane existed behind the wild eyes.

"Thought I'd just let you fuck him?"

"Jersey," Ken said, trying to placate but sounding panicked, "he was going home to find you. He wanted to apologize."

The barrel of the gun ground into Ken's cheek. "Lies!" Jersey said. "All lies. You wanted him, and anything you want you take. You don't care who gets hurt. The great Ken Nicholson and all of his admirers. Such a charmed world."

The grip on Ken's throat tightened; fingers gouged his neck. The gun muzzle at his cheek pushed in painfully.

"But you'll see," Jersey growled. "When everything's taken from you, everything you love, everything that loves you. Gone. Then, you'll see."

People had begun to gather on the far sidewalk; they stared and pointed at the dead man and the man who would soon be dead, but nobody said a word. The gun traced over Ken's cheek; it drew from his eye down to his jaw.

"Jersey," he said. "Don't do this."

The man shuddered violently. He bellowed a cry into Ken's face, spraying his chin with saliva. Jersey released his grip and leapt back. Ken gasped in hot air.

"Your charmed world is behind you, Baby," Jersey said, his voice high and raving.

In the next moment, Jersey's eyes flared anger. He brought the gun up and pointed it at Ken's chest, then he moved quickly from one foot to the next in a lunatic jig. The crowd across the street gasped and muttered. A calm sense of resignation filled Ken. He could not hope to outrun or outmaneuver a bullet, and the rage on Jersey's face made it clear there would be no bargaining. Ken closed his eyes tightly waiting for the explosion and the pain. The street remained silent.

"The charmed world is behind all of us," Jersey said,

The tone of the voice struck Ken as different, no longer manic. Ken opened his eyes. Jersey Fleagle's countenance had changed. The insanity had drained from his face, leaving him looking hollow and afraid. He gazed at the body of Sam Martin, and tears slid down his cheeks.

"So, Alice," Jersey said, dropping his gun on the sidewalk, "welcome to Wonderland." Then Jersey ran off, leaving his lover's body on the street.

⚜

Across the street, witnesses pointed. A slender man in white shorts had a cell phone cupped to his face, and he babbled rapidly into the device.

Ken pushed away from the building. Dazed and stumbling, he walked toward Sam's body, already certain his friend was dead. He leaned down and grasped Sam's wrist, probing with his fingers to find a pulse, but his fingertips were met with nothing but cooling skin.

Sam's legs kicked in spasm. Ken leapt back, a low groan rolling from his throat. He backed up a step and then another, repulsed by the postmortem throes. At the corner he turned, and not knowing where he intended to go but knowing what he was escaping, Ken walked away.

Rational thought was gone for a time, knocked out by the impact of a small paneled truck. Distantly, he knew he should stay at the scene. The police would want to speak to him, more so because Sam was the second victim from Ken's life in under a week. Regardless of this consideration, with his thoughts and emotions in tumult, he kept walking.

So strained was his thinking that he began to seriously consider Brugier's involvement in the recent tragedies. It made no difference that the man had been dead for the last thirty years. Everything that had happened tied back to Brugier and that time in Ken's life, and Vicki Bach was the connection, he knew. But why? And how?

Ken was so lost in his thoughts that he walked right into two young women.

"Hey, man," a tall blonde with straight hair said. "Be cool."

Ken looked at the girls. Their bellbottom jeans and floral print blouses made them look like extras from a remake of *Easy Rider*, but there was something else. The street seemed to have changed. Ken couldn't put his finger on exactly what had changed, but it all felt different, out of place, and wrong.

"Papa Square is trippin'," the brunette said.

Ken walked around the women, ignoring their jeers and laughter. A 1972 Camaro raced by, and Ken gave it a cursory glance, noting the classic vehicle. Behind it, another old car, a powder-blue Plymouth Duster, rolled down the street. And behind that, a white VW Beetle from 1969. More cars came and went, and not one of them was less than thirty years old; some, like a black Cadillac, its shark fins cutting a wake through the morning air, were even older. Ken searched the far sidewalk and saw three men dressed in seersucker suits and proper white plantation hats who were smoking cigars and laughing. Behind this trio of gentleman, a kid of twelve or thirteen bopped along to a tune pouring into his ear from a transistor radio.

Travis Brugier had told Ken that he'd needed to get him back. *Back to the beginning.*

Around him, New Orleans, as it was thirty years ago, thrummed with life. In the distance drums and horns announced a makeshift parade, and the scent of boiled shrimp, all pepper and ocean filled his nose.On the corner, a young man stood with his back propped against the building, which should have been a restaurant but wasn't. It wouldn't be a restaurant for another ten years. As he approached, Ken's stomach leapt into his throat because he recognized the young man, despite the damage that had been done to him.

Puritan Crowley, his old friend, the one he called Crow, the one who had died so similarly to Sam Martin, leaned against the wall. The right side of his face was torn away, exposing dangling muscle and bone. Blood soaked the front of his A-shirt and the thighs of his ripped jeans. His right shoulder was a froth of meaty pulp surrounding a club of white bone where his missing arm had once attached.

The newspaper said that Crow had gotten hooked up on the rear bumper of the car that ran him down and dragged a good distance before the driver finally stopped. A lot of him was left on the street.

"You been bought and sold," Crow said, drooling teeth and spit and blood over the mush of his lower lip. "He ain't never letting you go."

"I have to leave, have to get out," Ken said, the words a hushed and desperate babble in his ears.

"If you leave," Crow said, "who's gonna protect them? Not one of 'em knows what's comin'. Not David. Not Paula. Not Jennnifer. But you know, don't you, Sweetie? You know good and well what's comin' down the road."

Ken looked at the remains of his old friend, still leaned up against the building, a smile cutting his destroyed face.

"I suppose you could always come back for the bone parties."

Whether sane or not, Ken refused to engage the apparition in conversation, feeling that even a simple acceptance of the chimera would pull him deeper into the madness. Instead, he ran. He could not tell which props—people, cars, and carriages—were real and which were part of the delusion playing around him, so he ignored all of them, running headlong through intersections and down blocks traveled by pedestrians wearing retro fashions and silly hairstyles. Horns blared and passersby shouted their annoyance at his rudeness, but Ken couldn't stop running, not until he was back in the present.

A sound like thunder exploded in his ears. Ken stumbled. Around him, walls and street lamps melted and dribbled as if they'd been coated in watercolor camouflage, now being washed away by an invisible downpour. Some of the houses changed colors; others simply faded or brightened in subtle degrees. The odors of the street grew more pungent. The sky brightened. In cascading waves, the façades fell away until Ken found himself gasping for breath, heart thundering in his chest, amid modern vehicles and familiar buildings.

Movement ahead caught his eye, and Ken, struggling to sate his lungs with air, bent forward to rest his hands on his knees, never taking his eyes off of the form. Dressed in white, the boy hurried toward him, a messenger with yet another dreadful communication. Recognition settled in slowly; it scraped and gnawed its way into Ken's already aching mind.

On the sidewalk, Bobby Nicholson, his white hospital gown flapping behind him, ran forward, his arms wide as if to greet his father with an embrace.

19

I suppose, you could always come back for the bone parties.

Ken sat in the living room of his home, brushing off remnants of dread. In his left hand he clasped the Thorn, whose chain snaked from his palm along the rough material of his sofa.

You go ahead and leave, Baby. You go live in this fantasy of yours. You'll never know what life could be because you're too caught up in what it should be. But that will pass, and when it does, and when you think you're happy, that's when you'll see me again. That's when I'll show you exactly how fragile all of this is. No one can give you what I can. No one!

He could attribute his hallucination to numerous factors—exhaustion, guilt, grief—but there was just too much that Ken could not have created for himself. Sam. The Thorn. Vicki Bach and a boy named Chuck.

Tell me a story.

History wanted to be recognized, and in the light of that memorable command, Ken Nicholson told himself this story:

⚜

Late one July evening when the sunset did nothing to alleviate the sticky heat in the air, Puritan Crowley led Ken deeper into the French Quarter along an unlit alley and through a black-mouthed doorway. They had been having an argument over good and evil. In Puritan's mind, there were no such distinctions, and Ken took exception to his friend's frivolous attitude. This was a regular argument they often engaged in late at night when pills kept them up long after exhaustion would have closed their eyes.

Crow led Ken into a dark hallway scented heavily with incense and marijuana. Alcohol had blurred his vision, and Ken felt certain he would never be able to make his way out of the building, let alone back to his apartment. So, he had no choice but to follow his friend deeper. The hallway might have been fifty yards or five feet—Ken was too intoxicated to tell—but it seemed a great trek from the time that the dark mouth accepted them. Eventually, they came to a doorway. Puritan rapped lightly with his knuckle. *Shave and a haircut.* The two bits never came. Instead, a small window opened, and a stubbled face appeared asking them what they wanted.

"Travis invited us," Crow whispered.

The odor of spice and smoke wafted heavily through the window, and Ken felt dizzy under its oppressive cloud. He leaned against the wall, trying not to stare at the gruff face framed in the window that was observing the two boys like they might have shat on the doorstep.

"Never heard of him," the doorman replied.

"Look, Sweetie," Puritan said. "Travis owns this place, probably owns you, so be a pal and open the door."

Ken felt uneasy. His stomach rolled from the immense amounts of scotch and the hideous reek of the chamber beyond the gruff face. He didn't care if they got in or not. He'd be just as happy to slink back to the apartment and climb into bed and hope he could find sleep before the spinning world made him vomit. And now, Crow was threatening a guy who might easily kill them both. A bad scene. A very bad scene.

The door opened. Another wave of stench passed into the hall, and Ken choked down his stomach. He followed Crow into a small room blocked from the rest of the place by a long red velvet curtain. The distant tinkle of a piano mingled with voices and other noises that sounded animalistic. The doorman stood to the side, clutching the open door in a meaty fist. Standing at Ken's height, the doorman weighed a good thirty pounds more, and his muscled body, covered with only a pair of swimming trunks, seemed tensed as if to pounce. Ken tried to smile as he passed, but the doorman's face ate the expression.

"Alice," Crow whispered. "Welcome to Wonderland." With a dramatic gesture, the curtain was pulled aside.

The memory came so clearly that Ken found himself startled out of it. He scanned the living room around himself. Jersey Fleagle had said nearly those same words to him before running away from the scene of his lover's death. Perhaps the fresh memory had mingled with ancient history, but Ken could not convince himself. Past and present were coming together. That which had passed, that which should have been dead and dust had returned.

Welcome to Wonderland.

⚜

Travis Brugier's Parlor was little more than a three-roomed hovel dressed up like a lounge, a whore painted to imitate beauty though it had never genuinely touched her features. The walls were covered in thick red wallpaper. Dirty mirrors suspended over raw pine flooring reflected back the withered appearance of the chamber. Furniture—ornate chaise lounges, armchairs with detailed needlework, and velveteen benches—ran along the walls. A dim light glowed from the yellowed crystal of a small chandelier. The smoke-filled air swirled among the patrons and filled the room like a vision of the heavy perfume that choked the small space.

The patrons lounged, spoke, and laughed. Many held martini glasses in one hand, using the other to pincer cigarettes or cigars or joints. Some wore suits; others were in costume, pretending to be women, pretending to be rough trade, pretending to be anything but the respected businessmen that many of them were. Young men mingled in this crowd. Some looked confident and others appeared frightened, but whether predatory or pretty, the boys were constantly engaged by their older counterparts. Two doorways led out of the room on the far side. Their pitch-black invitation to enter seemed wholly correct. Again, a whore, inviting yet unclean.

Crow moved into the crowd easily. Ken lingered behind, still trying to understand what purpose this place served. He gazed at the heavily made-up men and their clean-cut counterparts. Something moved in him, something that was made equally of fear and sick anticipation. His head refused to stop spinning. He felt certain that his weak knees would give out on him in moments, sending him to the filthy, stained boards at his feet.

Up ahead, Crow turned with a wide grin. He moved back to Ken's side and grasped his elbow. The action was not one of support but rather one of impatience. He guided Ken through the crowd, saying hello to the various admiring eyes that fell upon them.

The room was wall to wall with bodies reeking of cologne and French perfume. Sweat gathered at Ken's neck and traced along his back. He regained some control of his feet and shook free of Crow's insistent grasp, righting himself for a moment before he was nearly toppled by a small round man shaking his hips for his friends' amusement. The fat man called an apology after him, but Ken was lost. He knew that Crow was up ahead somewhere in the thick wall of bodies. He hurried through, excusing himself at every step. The last thing he wanted was to be alone in this place.

He found his friend standing by one of the doorways, speaking with a slender, mature man wearing a summery yellow dress. The man wore no makeup, no wig. His thin features, drawn with sharp lines, exploded when he smiled: a sunrise on flesh, a blossom of good cheer unfurled in less than a second.

"Is this the one?" the man asked.

"This is Ken," Crow announced proudly. "Ken, this is Gordon."

Ken listened to the exchange. Suddenly, he realized that he had been expected. Somehow, his presence was not only welcomed but required. Familiar unease coiled in his throat. He took the offered hand and shook it lightly, unable to greet the man with words.

"Well, Travis will love him," Gordon said. "Go on out. He's holding court."

Crow's face sparkled. The man's praise, though directed not at him, had hit the mark.

The hallway was short, and the air in it was clearer than that in the stifling room. They passed an open door, and Ken looked in. A single row of candles running along the back wall lit the room, and between their flickering cast and the open doorway, numerous shadows moved. The noises from this room, the grunts and gasps, and the thick musk of sex, defined its purpose. As he walked, Ken saw two men against the near wall. A man with white hair, dressed in a business suit, pinned a younger man to the wall. His suit trousers gathered at his knees, and his front shirt tails draped over the young man's ass, hiding the point of their union. The mature man's palm wrapped over the boy's mouth, covering the lower half of the kid's face. Ken caught a glimpse of the young man's eyes—wide and staring and blank—before turning away.

Ken felt along the wall, supporting himself on the rough, black painted surface. Up ahead, candles flickered, and he realized that they were not going deeper into the building, but rather they were leaving it behind them.

They stepped into the courtyard, and Ken barely stifled a gasp. Everything moved here. A handful of people meandered about, pointing at the flora, commenting on its beauty. Candles in large hurricane lamps flickered, dancing over the beautifully diverse array of blossoms pushing from the ground and dangling from ornate pots hung from the wrought-iron balconies above. A fountain spat its plume through electric illumination. It seemed the entire courtyard was alive. Even the flagstones at their feet seemed to move, trembling with some unknown energy. A spray of leaves covered the ground like lacy carpet. Hibiscus blossoms speckled the courtyard floor. And their host sat in a chair at the far end of the yard.

Crow hurried them along, past the fountain with its amazing colored fluid twinkling along the dull gray concrete basin.

As Ken drew closer to their host he felt the sobering effects of anticipation creep into his head. Obviously, the handsome man with the broad toothy smile was the master of this place. Everyone in attendance was so at his tolerance, and they would be removed at his request. As the face became clearer, the eyes beamed out at him, so alive yet with no discernible expression. Power, he thought. Those were the eyes of a man who worried about nothing because nothing was beyond his control. So many impressions settled on him then—the amazing face and strong neck, the broad grin that spoke to pleasure not frivolity, the deep skin color, and the thick wavy hair—but the most mesmerizing aspect of his host were those ice-blue eyes telling the world that he would forgive no trespass. Not only did Ken read all of this in a matter of seconds, but he felt the certainty of his impression as if the man himself were verifying the information by speaking directly into Ken's mind.

"Welcome," the man said warmly, lifting himself from the chair. He stood several inches taller than Ken, casting his shadow over both of the boys as he rose.

"Hi," Crow said. "This is the friend I was telling you about. Ken, this is Travis Brugier, our host."

Ken took the hand and felt a strange shock at the touch of the man's cool, dry palm. No longer was he standing in an amazing courtyard somewhere in New Orleans's French Quarter with his friend at his side. Instead he was in a void where no other human being could see him, save for the man whose hand held his.

The void whorled around them, and Ken fought to keep his footing. Lost in the man before him, Ken saw himself in fields, in battles. He found himself sitting quietly on a tree limb as he shook apples free of branches, laughing as they rained down on some form below then disappeared into the night which replaced the ground. Rivers and oceans and lakes, valleys and mountains and cities, places he'd never been filled him. Seconds passed, the amount of time it took to recall the name of an acquaintance, and he was back in the courtyard.

Now, however, it was his host's turn to flinch. Travis stepped back, releasing Ken's hand. Some alien emotion clouded the strong eyes.

"Mr. Crowley," Brugier said with a smile. "Go inside and entertain my guests."

Now they were alone, Ken and the man named Travis, in a courtyard miles from any other living soul.

Travis Brugier's presence sobered him. Twilight engulfed them, dancing like the flames in the many glass lanterns, and the blossoms offered up their perfume into the humid air so that it fell in a baptism of scent. The piano, harbored in the parlor, played a melancholy rag. He barely heard the tune as his mind sought to recapture the flashes of scenery that had accompanied his introduction to Travis Brugier. And the man gazed down on him, unmoving since his dismissal of Puritan Crowley minutes before. Arrogance never touched the features; the man was far too refined for such a petty façade. Indeed, he looked little more than content within himself and with all around him. But the power Ken had felt upon first laying eyes on the man remained, even grew the longer he looked at him. Standing there in his fine linen suit with the tightly knotted tie at his throat, the man effused confidence.

"Well," Brugier said, breaking the silence, "your friend speaks highly of you."

"He's a good guy."

"I think he was accurate in his assessment." Brugier smiled, turning his back on Ken for a moment. "You're a very handsome young man; he was right about that."

Ken felt the flush cover his face, and while he'd never considered himself naïve—books had provided him with an education in matters that he had not yet had the time to cultivate in his short life—he realized exactly what was expected of him. Crow had offered him up as a gift to this great man. He felt embarrassed, felt ashamed. Something else too: a feeling he could only later describe as longing.

"Don't be embarrassed," the man said. "There's no shame here."

As Brugier took his seat, Ken wondered if the man could read so much from his face. Obviously, Brugier weighed people day after day for their strengths and weaknesses. Surely he could pick up on the blatant flush of a young man's cheeks.

"Please," Brugier said, "have a chair." He indicated a wicker stool next to him, and Ken moved toward it. His belly twisted into a knot of indiscernible emotions. The weight of the air settled on him and filled his lungs like a gelatinous fluid, growing firm and suffocating in his chest. "He tells me that you're something more than an idiot as well. That's good. It's rare and therefore precious."

Brugier smiled, his brilliant white teeth showing against the deep color of his skin. The expression cut deep wrinkles around the man's eyes and created creases at his mouth. He looked thoroughly amused at Ken's silence. "I feel the same way," he whispered, leaning forward as if to share a secret. "Awkward isn't it?"

"What's that?" Ken asked. His nerves were jangled, but he tried to regain some composure.

"All of this."

"Exactly what is this?" Ken said.

Again Brugier laughed. "I believe your parents would call it courting."

⚜

In Brugier's Wonderland, there was a hierarchy, a pecking order that became obvious with every day that passed. Like a family, with firstborns and babies, so was Travis's world. The firstborns, the older acolytes (*older* being a relative term as most were generally in their late teens and early twenties), ran the place. They kept the parlor and house clean and moved through the home with great care, cleansing the crystal and china as if these ornaments might bite should the boys be indelicate. They were spoiled but not lazy. Haughty stares fell upon the newborns, the children who came to Travis's domain with their youth wrapped about them like ermine. Pampered and cajoled, the newborns held the older children in disdain as they were forced to perform the menial tasks of the house. The middle children, those who no longer pleased by their mere presence, were taught the maintenance of the grounds, how to keep the bugs off of the garden and the proper way to serve guests cocktails. Every youth who stayed on went through these stages, living the role of baby, middle child and firstborn. Not all stayed. Some left early on, but there were never less than a dozen young men living in the house. As time passed and the firstborns were replaced, leaving the house and the parlor behind to experiment with the real world, new faces appeared.

Travis called these children *Vassals*. He used the term affectionately like a parent, like a lover, but Ken sensed that the word camouflaged a less kind feeling.

Ken was never the baby, never the middle child, and he certainly could not have been a first child. He was something wholly different, and the young men in Travis's employ treated him as such. Though it was clear that he belonged with them, the others regarded him angrily, suspiciously. He seemed to be a new creature in their community. They gave him space but made their displeasure known with glances of ice and razor-sharp words.

Only a week had passed since Ken first wandered bleary eyed into Travis's presence, but they were inseparable in this time. Nights were filled with embraces and stories, magical stories of other times and other places.

"Tell me a story," Brugier would request, handing Ken a thick leather-bound book. Ken read from the book, finding many of the stories tragic. Both genders and a number of races were represented in the tales. Some were humorous and some outright frightening, but nearly all were laced with tragedy and loneliness.

Throughout those first few evenings an anxiety weighed on Ken as he wondered when this relationship would be consummated, but his mentor kept their passion to embraces and kisses. Even in the bed, late into the morning, Travis kept Ken at a distance as the young boy felt the heat radiating from his mentor's body. Ken's thoughts, clouded by expectation, ran through the exotic possibilities, but release was found with his hand as he showered in the morning or lay alone in the warm bed after his companion rose.

Ten days into his stay, Ken left the compound and wandered through the Quarter, back to the flat he and Crow shared. His roommate was sleeping, arm across his eyes to shield them from the daylight penetrating the thin curtains. Weary and disheveled, his friend looked up in surprise.

"What are you doing?" Crow asked, his voice concerned.

"I thought I'd see how you were."

Then the familiar smile returned to the face. "Things're fine," he croaked. "I thought you'd forgotten about me."

Ken laughed, uneasy from the rapidly changing emotions displayed in his friend's eyes.

"The restaurant called," Crow said. "I told them you had a new job."

The restaurant? Jesus, Ken thought. Ten days without a call. How would he pay his bills? Panic came and went quickly. It didn't seem to matter any more. Travis would not let him starve. God knew he didn't really even need the flat anymore. But Crow? How could he afford the place on his own?

"I guess you're kind of mad," Ken said. "I mean I just left like that."

"It's fine," his friend said, but something about his eyes gave him away.

It wasn't fine. Something was bothering Crow. Was it the money? If not, what else could it be?

The conversation, less intimate than some they had shared, went on for a couple of hours as Ken told Crow about the strange order of things at Travis's and his own place among the Vassals. Crow didn't seem curious in the least. He didn't ask a single question about Brugier, his home, or The Parlor. Instead he let Ken divulge those things he felt comfortable divulging, and left the rest to imagination. Crow never left the bed through the entire dialogue. He remained propped against his pillow, nodding and fitting exclamations of his own into the conversation while not really saying anything.

After a while, Ken sensed a difference in the room. New furniture stood in place of the ratty wicker pieces they had scavenged from behind an apartment building, and the two mattresses they had slept on were gone, now replaced by a small but intricate brass bed. He had not noticed any of these things when he'd first come in, and now they screamed at him.

"Are you sure you're all right?" Crow asked.

The tone of the question bit at him. Ken tried to read his friend's thoughts, tried to understand why he should be concerned. The question had scared him, made his skin crawl.

How many times had he heard that term and not realized exactly what it meant? Before, he could not imagine the sensation of skin crawling, but now, as his flesh pimpled and the meat on his back seemed to creep up his spine, he understood the term far too well. "What's going on?"

"Nothing."

"Crow what is this shit? Where'd you get the money for all of this? You doin' something illegal?" He knew he had changed the subject but feared delving further into his friend's personal affairs.

"What difference does it make?" Crow asked. He sounded angry. "You don't live here anymore."

"You throwin' me out?"

His friend burst out laughing. The anger on his face disintegrated as his features blossomed into pure humored delight. "Throwin' you out?" Crow spat amid a flutter of giggles. "Baby, don't you get it? You been bought and sold." His guffaws ceased abruptly, and he wiped the tears from his eyes. "You ain't gotta worry about nothin' no more."

Bought and sold? Like a statue? Like some fucking piece of furniture? Everything Ken had, which was not much, he had gotten honestly, had paid for with sweat and hard work. Yet here was his best friend accusing him of…What? Prostitution? Selling himself for a few bucks?

"Hey," Crow said. "What are you fumin' about?"

Ken didn't answer. He wanted to punch the charming face, wanted to break it open, but he couldn't bring himself to do it. As always, he realized that Crow meant nothing by his comments. Just being flip, complimenting his friend by telling him how easy he had it.

"Sweetie, you're going to have it all," Crow continued, "but be careful."

"Of what?" Ken asked.

"Be careful of forever," his friend advised. Crow's voice quieted. He looked out the window, holding a pillow to his chest. "Forever is just too damned long."

Months passed as he allowed Wonderland and Travis Brugier to intoxicate his senses. Days were spent on long walks, shopping, or just lying in the bed until sunset, and evenings were spent at the theater, at dinner parties, in extravagant restaurants regaling with the best society could provide for companionship. But neither needed this last. They were ample companions for one another.

Ken might have considered Travis more than sufficient had it not been for the limitations of their intimacy. Most of the time, Ken felt perfectly content working out his passion with his hand, but there was so much he wanted to know, wanted to feel, and Travis refused any such displays.

One evening Ken had asked him about the distance between them. He felt awkward bringing it up, but he could not stop himself. Insecurity played on him.

"I'm saving myself for marriage," Brugier quipped.

But Ken persisted. "If you need me to do something…anything, I'll…"

The man hushed him with a finger on his lips. "In time," Brugier said. "We have plenty of time."

Ken agonized over it. As the weeks passed, a seed of uncertainty took hold in his mind. He spoke with his parents rarely; never saw his friends. He had become, as Crow suggested, a piece of furniture, bought and sold and now in the possession of this man. Perhaps he could have lived with this, had it not been for that piece of his life that he felt was missing.

Some small part of him wanted out of this fairy tale. A little part of his mind ached for normalcy. His notion of normalcy was the life one experienced when watching family television in those days. He wanted to go to college. He wanted to meet a nice woman and have a family. He could put Wonderland behind him, could make something normal of his life.

Out of Wonderland, he thought. All of its pleasures and all of its simplicity were truly addictive, but like a favored yet overindulged drink, the sweetness had grown tedious.

After his fifth month in Travis's presence, he spoke out for the first time. They were in the courtyard in Travis's comfortable chair. Though chill, the day offered sunshine. Neither had said anything for several minutes as they watched two of the babies fussing in the flowerbeds. Ken knew the way they looked at him:

like servants who one day hope to marry the king only to have their hopes dashed by some unexpected suitor. They looked at him bitterly, envied him. Many of them out and out hated him.

"I think I want to go to school," Ken said. A simple statement. So why the fear?

"I know," Travis replied. "I wondered how long it would take you to tell me."

"I can't sit around forever doing nothing."

"Why?" Travis asked. "What do you need? An education? I can give you more knowledge than any university. A career? The only purpose of a career is to make money. You'll never need that with me."

"But what if something happens?"

"Something?"

"With us," Ken said. "I just feel lost in all of this. I'm floating here, and I need an anchor."

"I'm your anchor."

"But you might not always be here," Ken said. His voice had risen. This was not his true concern; his true concern was that his dreams of normalcy would be nothing more than dreams if he remained in the sanctuary. When he looked at Brugier, hoping to glimpse understanding in the eyes, he only saw humor.

"I'll be here forever," his mentor said. "*We'll* be here forever."

And Crow's voice came back to him. *Forever is just too damned long.*

That night, Travis remained downstairs in the library. Ken lay in the bed watching the fan spin above him. His inexperienced mind did not understand Travis's intentions, though he tried to puzzle them out. Sure, they had a good time together, fun and games, but there had to be more. It couldn't go on like this forever. Eventually men met women, they married, they had children together. That was the world.

As he lay there, reveling in his fancies, he heard the soft

squeak of the door being pushed open. He didn't want to see Travis right now. It wasn't Travis. One of the Vassals, his name was Reginald Wexler, stood in the doorway, wearing a pair of boxer shorts. The black hair on his head glistened as if wet. The boy's almond skin stretched tight over his lightly muscled frame. An expression of sultry innocence played on his delicate features. Reggie was a firstborn. He helped keep the house clean. Ken knew the boy hated him. They had exchanged several frigid glances. So what the hell did he want? "Is something wrong?"

Reginald moved forward. He came within a few feet of the bed, and Ken saw the boy's erection pushing at the material of his shorts. The Vassal dropped his boxers and stood quietly naked as if waiting to be approved of.

"Does Travis know you're up here?" Ken asked, exasperated by the display.

"He sent me up," Wexler replied, climbing onto the bed. "He thought you needed..." Wexler moved in to kiss Ken's lips.

Ken rolled off the bed, rebounded off the nightstand, and spun into the center of the room. What was this? A joke? Some plot by the kid to foul his relationship with Travis? But no, Ken knew this wouldn't be the case. None of the Vassals would jeopardize their future.

So, Travis *had* sent the boy up. This was Travis's answer. He had no interest in fucking, so he'd have one of his Vassals do it for him. The insult to Ken's integrity disgusted and enraged him. Was this what Brugier honestly thought Ken had wanted?

He dressed quickly, oblivious to Reggie, who lay on the bed, looking confused. He left the room, ran down the stairs, and threw open the door of the library. Travis sat reading. He looked up in surprise.

"You son of a bitch!" Ken yelled.

"Baby," Travis placated, "what's wrong? Reggie not your flavor?"

He walked across the room and knocked the book from

Travis's hands. Travis's eyes, no longer powerful but immensely sad, stilled him.

"I thought…" Ken began, stifling the words in which he could not believe.

"You thought that I loved you." Travis finished softly. "Am I right?"

Ken could not answer. He preferred the anger; anger was easy.

"What do you know about love?" Travis asked. His voice grew serious and harsh. "You can't even say the fucking word. You're a child. Do you think that piece of meat between your legs measures love? You still cling too tightly to your religion, Baby. Breeding is not love. Animals breed. They rut and fuck and give birth, and life goes on. It's disgusting. It's degrading. And what of us? Two men. We can't even breed, so why waste the energy? All of this," Travis, infuriated, beat his breast. He reached up with a hand and gouged his own cheek, raking the flesh and drawing blood from the tanned skin. "All of this is nothing. It comes and goes. Beauty dies with the passion that defined it. Is that enough? Is it?" Travis grabbed Ken's shoulders, pulling the frightened boy closer. "Is that enough for you? A few years of passion? A handful of days to impale imperfect flesh with your cock for a few moments of pleasure or to create more like you?"

The oozing scratches on his face and his steely mien gave the man an otherworldly look. Ken wanted to run, but he remained frozen.

"That's why I sent Reginald to you. I wanted you to see how little it means, and how much more there is." Travis released Ken's shoulders. "You asked if I loved you. You have no idea what that means." Travis shook his head. "Go to bed," he said, turning his back.

Having been dismissed, Ken moved quietly out of the library.

20

Chuck sat in Paula Nicholson's living room, staring through the curtains. A cool place, he thought as he waited patiently for the woman's return. Heavy wooden furniture lay beneath plush cushions and comfortable armrests. And yeah, he knew it was the old broad's place, but he got the definite feeling that Nicholson had put it together, bought the furniture and the knickknack crap and everything.

He definitely liked the old guy's style. He pictured himself in twenty years, maybe twenty-five years with a mustache and gray hair. He felt certain the he would look as good, if not better, than Nicholson. And the rest was money. If you had enough money, nothing else mattered. Women, men, they could both be bought if the wad was big enough. Shit, even manners could be bought for a price.

Once Vicki came through with his fee, Chuck would be buying a whole new world.

He looked around the room, taking in the details of the furniture and the walls. The paint job was cool, almost white but with a hint of purple. The color contrasted surprisingly with the stark white of the moldings. The ceiling was painted the same color as the walls. Most of the rooms he'd seen during his short life were painted white. Just white, but this place was elegant like the old guy.

He decided to look around as he waited for the woman to get back. She'd left about thirty minutes ago. As he'd hidden behind a shrub across the street, she'd come out of the house and driven away. No one else had been in the car with her. That was good. He knew where the ugly little bitch was. Their mutual friend wouldn't be dropping her off for a couple of hours yet. So, Chuck had sidled across the street like he owned the entire neighborhood, slipped around back, and popped out a window pane to gain access to the door lock. Easy as pie. The alarm wasn't even set.

At first, he'd thought about sitting on the couch and just waiting, as if nothing were wrong. He would be sitting in the house when the old broad got back, and he'd talk at her all coollike until he was close enough to show his affection. He could tell her that he was waiting for the ugly little bitch. What was her name anyway? Janice or Jessica or something like that? What difference did it make? He wouldn't need a story.

But now, he wanted to see the place and really get a feel for the old guy. Nicholson had done pretty good for himself. He had that house in the Quarter and this place, neither of which was shabby, and the guy didn't even live in New Orleans. He probably had a house in Hawaii or Florida or something. Given time, Chuck might have met him on one of those Florida beaches. Who knew?

One thing was for sure, the old guy was loaded, and the woman told him that he'd had exactly what Chuck had when he was the boy's age: nothing. So, anything was possible.

He wandered through the dining room, stopping long enough to wonder at the plates on display in a huge glass-faced cabinet. They didn't look all that special to Chuck. Why the hell display them? Plates: just stack the fuckers up and deal them out when dinnertime came around. He stepped closer to get a better look at the blue borders. His eyes fought the shadows. His nose nearly to the glass, he followed the pattern around the plate. His eyes circled the border, making out the images depicted there. Guys on horses with dogs riding through a countryside painted the color of Smurfs.

Rich people were weird. Who wanted to watch something like that when they ate? He had expected more from the old guy. Gold trim, he could see. Chuck imagined drinking from silver goblets and eating off of golden platters. That's how the rich should live. That's how he'd do it when Vicki paid up.

He continued on through to the kitchen, and finding nothing special there, he invited himself upstairs. The first room he came across must have been the punk's. Trophies lined a low bookcase built into the wall. A jock, huh? Sure didn't act like one, Chuck thought. One good pop, and the guy was on the ground. The other blows had just been for fun.

He left the room and crossed the hall. This was where the old broad slept. On the nights he'd come to call, she always went to bed alone. But not tonight, he thought.

The walls in the bedroom were a deeper color than that of the room downstairs. It might have been some kind of blue, but it looked weird. Chuck shrugged. He moved to the woman's dresser and looked at the pictures on it. There were five of them. In the first, it was just the punk in a football uniform, looking like a jerk. The next picture was of a big grassy yard with trees around it. Two kids hugged each other. He assumed it was the punk and his sister. She wasn't really ugly in that picture though; too young to be really ugly. The third picture caught him. It was of the entire family, standing in front of this house. The old woman wore a lacy white dress that looked incredible on her. Of course the picture had been taken years before, and she was still young and not nearly so fat. In her arms a pudgy little brat chewed on its fingers. The punk as a little boy stood next to the woman, and next to him stood Nicholson.

Chuck lost his breath for a moment. It was almost like looking in a mirror. Sure the nose was different and the mouth wasn't quite so full, but the overall resemblance was startling. Chuck smiled.

He knew he'd look like the guy when he got older. And the proof was sitting right in front of him. He lifted the silver-plate frame and stared through the glass.

The guy was very cool. In the picture, he wore a pale blue suit. His hair, barely gray then, was short and neat. He looked like an actor, or a president or something. Chuck slid the picture into his jacket. He wanted to show Vicki when he got back. She said he didn't look like the guy at all, but now he had proof.

He ignored the other pictures, choosing to turn and check out the room. The bed was impressive. A thick blanket, the same color as the walls, covered the bed. They called those comforters, he remembered. White lace skirted the frame, which was made of a thick, dark wood. Two pillars rose up from behind the numerous pillows arranged at the far end, and at their head. Atop the tapering posts, headpieces were carved. They looked like nuts. He could not remember the kind of nuts that they reminded him of, but they did look like nuts.

As he moved from this room to see what else the place offered, he heard the door downstairs open. Chuck pulled the steel bar out of his jacket and turned for the stairs. He knew there'd be time to check the place out later. For now, it was party time.

Paula arrived home, parked in the drive at the side of the house, and hurried up the walk. In her arms she carried a thick wad of dry cleaning, the thin plastic coverings rustling like leaves against her body. Paula opened the front door and started for the stairs.

Every day the house seemed just a little quieter, and the silence needled her. She'd heard that when people lost a limb through accident or amputation, they had twinges of memory, feeling things in the extremities they had lost. Her family was like that now. Initially, it had only been Ken, the sound of him showering, the smell of him in the halls and on their bed. She missed these things, and her mind fed her tiny helpings of sense memory, which only served to aggravate her loneliness. Then, Bobby had gone off to college, and Paula imagined his rock and roll still playing too loudly in his room, sensed him running through the house when he was no longer there. And never would be again.

Paula refused to cry again. She stomped up the stairs, determined to maintain her composure. The last thing she wanted was another two-hour crying jag in the middle of the afternoon. That wasn't going to help anyone.

Soon, Jennifer would be grown and another limb would be lost, and Paula just wasn't sure what would be left. There would be memories of Jennifer playing her guitar behind the locked door of her room, strumming quietly as if trying to keep her music a secret, muffled phone calls between her daughter and friends, the memories of arguments and tantrums. Paula would continue to feel twinges, but they would be phantom pangs, resonating painfully on nerves scraped raw by silence.

At the top of the stairs, Paula took the corner quickly. In her room, she hung the plastic shrouded clothes in her closet. *Just unwrap them later*, she thought. But the responsible voice in her head wouldn't accept procrastination. She dropped her purse on the bed and then returned to the waiting chore. Paula scrunched the plastic into the smallest ball she could manage and shoved it under her left arm. Passing the bed, she lifted her purse as an afterthought.

In her haste with the laundry, Paula had not noticed that Robert's bedroom door stood open. Now, as she passed the opening, she caught a figure from the corner of her eye. She jumped. She saw a shadow standing in her son's room, and for a moment, she thought it might have been her son or the memory of him, but no, the figure was too small to be her son. And her son was dead.

She turned slowly to face the dark form. They stood there for what seemed to Paula like minutes, as the shadow in her son's room remained motionless. A tiny voice in her head told her to run for the stairs, told her to get out of the house and into the street. She heard the voice but could not move. She wanted to know who had the nerve to invade this particular room. As the form stepped forward, the details of the boy's face came clearer.

She knew him. He'd been at Jersey and Sam's party, and at the school before that. Of the thoughts that fought for her attention, the loudest was that this was the bastard that had killed her son. So violent was this realization that she acted before rational thought could stop her. Paula charged forward, dropping the plastic bags on the floor in the hallway. She didn't even notice the steel bar in Chuck's hand as she rushed forward and slammed her weight into the boy, sending him backward and down onto the carpet of Robert's room. Dazed from the concussion, Paula struck out blindly, hitting the floor and the boy's face in equal measure.

She kept the pepper spray in her purse. She also kept a small knife there. As she thought of these items, the boy swung his weapon, but Paula's flailing arm knocked the blow askew. Pain flared but she barely recognized it. She shifted her weight and found the boy's crotch with her knee. His eyes exploded from surprise to genuine fear. Grappling with his blond hair, Paula rolled off of the boy. Her nails raked his face, and then she knelt behind him. With a fistful of his hair in one hand, she clawed viciously at his cheek with the other.

"Bitch!" he screamed, tearing himself out of her grasp. He moved quickly, bending forward at the waist to free himself, and then jerking himself around like a striking serpent.

Paula was already digging through her purse for the spray. Finding it, she snapped the safety flap free and pointed the canister at the boy. The pipe bit into her shoulder, but this only caused her to depress the nozzle, spraying the boy's savaged cheeks and his eyes with the debilitating liquid.

His scream pierced her ears. Doubled over, the boy cried out again and again. He swung the pipe blindly from his kneeling position. His threats died beneath agonized wails.

Then, she was out of the room and running down the stairs. Only then did she hear her own screaming; only then did she realize she had screamed at all. She ran through the living room and lifted the phone. Quickly she pressed nine-one-one. When the operator came on she gave the woman her name and address. The operator repeated the information.

"S-s-someone j-just tried to attack m-me in my house," Paula sputtered. "He killed my son. He killed my son."

"All right," the operator said. "I want you to stay on the line while I send help."

Stay on the line? "If you want to come entertain this guy," Paula said, "that's fine. I'm getting the fuck out of here."

With that, she dropped the phone and ran to the front door. As she pulled it open, she heard the boy on the landing above her. He still cried, still swung the pipe. She turned in time to see him lose his footing and crash down the staircase toward her. Paula went through the door into the light of day and closed the door behind her.

⚜

Eyes burning, face scalding, his entire body aching, the boy rolled off of the last step. That bitch. He'd envisioned a hundred reactions but not this. As he waited in the punk's room, standing like a statue just inside the doorway, he envisioned the woman freezing in place; Chuck had imagined her screaming and running for the stairs; he had envisioned her softening, coming to him because of his resemblance to the man her husband had been. But no, she'd come for him in a different way.

You gotta feel your mistakes.

He stumbled forward, still blinded by that shit she'd put in his eyes. It ate at the open skin of his cheek; he could feel it working there like acid, as if the woman's assault weren't enough. His hip slammed a small table as he tried to navigate his way through the house. He wanted to hurt that bitch, wanted her crushed skull cradled in his lap as he stroked her beautiful hair.

He tried to open his eyes and nearly screamed again. Streaks of light cut through solid objects, their dismal colors blending into a hazy pool like oil floating on a puddle catching sunlight. Tears filled his eyes to wash away the chemical burn, but his vision wouldn't clear. He'd have to come back for the woman. By now, she was miles away, and that's where he needed to get.

A mind map of the house unfolded through his panic and suffering. The kitchen was off of the dining room. In order to get there, he would need to cross this room, and then it was a straight line to the backyard. Once there, he would take refuge in one of the neighbor's lawns or houses. It didn't matter; he had to get away, already he heard the sirens coming.

Hurrying through the house, knocking his shins and his hip into walls and furniture, he found the back door, threw it open, felt the sunlight hit his face. His barely opened eyes stung as he tried to assess the ground before him, but everything was one yellow-white smear. He rubbed at his eyes, but the pain only increased. And the sirens were getting so close.

That bitch. She fucked him up, fucked him up bad. Returning the favor would be his pleasure, he'd make that pretty face look like ground meat, make her fat body a…But he had to get away. If he didn't hurry, he'd never get his chance. They'd know he'd done the punk, they'd know.

Tires raced along the side of the house. The sirens were deafening. He spun and twisted, trying to make good an escape whose time had long passed. Already he heard the doors opening and the heavy clicking of weapons being released. "Freeze," someone called, and he almost laughed through his agony. Did they really say that? Still, he figured he'd better do what they said for now. Vicki would get him out.

Chuck stopped moving, stopped swiping the air with his pipe. When they told him to drop his weapon, he did it. When they told him to lay face down on the ground, he did it. When a heavy boot came to rest on the back of his neck, he let it. When they jerked his pained arms behind his back, grinding his chin into the concrete of the drive, he said nothing.

Whatever, he thought. He'd be back.

21

As Paula Nicholson was helped into an ambulance and a young man named Chuck Baxter was shoved into the back of a police car, Ken ventured through his memories. *Tell me a story, Baby.*

The magnificence of Wonderland wore on him. At night he read Travis stories from the large volume on the nightstand, but he wouldn't put feeling into the words as he once had. Now he merely recited the words before him, drawing no pleasure from them. Travis questioned him about this sudden disinterest, and he just complained of being tired.

He wanted out. Whether or not he ever found the life he dreamed became irrelevant; he wanted out of Brugier's life. The place was scaring him, as if the rest of the world no longer existed. Less and less they ventured out to shop or eat. Though not a prisoner—he was able to walk at his leisure through the Quarter—Ken felt captured.

One cool January day, he decided to visit Crow again. It had been nearly a month since he'd last seen his friend and that had been at The Parlor. The boy had been so drunk that he probably didn't even remember the evening. Ken wanted to make sure that Crow was sober. He had something to ask.

So, Ken crossed the quarter to the flat they had shared. Crow, predictably, lay on the bed, still sleeping though it was well past noon.

"Hey?" Ken said, laughing at his friend's laziness.

"Wha…?" Crowley tried. He coughed vigorously into his fist and sat up. "Hey!"

He crossed the room to give his friend a hug. "How's it going?"

"Cool," Crowley replied still trying to focus his eyes. "What brings you out here? Slumming?"

"Something like that," Ken said. "Haven't seen you in a while; thought I'd check up on you."

"Yeah well," his friend laughed, "as you can see I"m as productive as ever. I went out last night with this woman from Baton Rouge. You should have seen her. Damn child, she was a fine-looking thing. She had some of that acid shit. I don't even know where she went. I came out of it as the sun was coming up and shagged ass back here. Never even got to her. We just drank and laughed. God did we laugh. I wish I could remember what we laughed about, but hey, she was paying the bills."

"Sounds great," Ken said. A twinge of envy ran through him. He missed those late nights with Crow. He missed the action and the intoxication and the complete disregard for common decency. Most of all, he missed the freedom. "We should get together some night."

Crow didn't seem happy to hear this. "Sure," he said. He looked suspicious. "Thing's okay?"

"No," Ken said. He stood up and walked across the room. "I don't know. I mean, what have I got to bitch about? Everything I want, he gets me."

"Sounds good on this end."

"But it's not enough. I mean, the guy's acting like we're married or something. We spend all of the time together and…It's just not what I want."

"So tell him."

"I did, and he just brushed it off."

Crow slid out of the bed. His legs dangled over the edge as he looked at his friend. "I didn't tell you this," Crow said, moving his gaze around the apartment as if he expected to find spies. "Christ," he said, running a palm through his hair. "You didn't meet Brugier by accident, okay? He's had his eye on you for a long time now, long before I took you to see him."

The news settled about him like a cold mist.

"He came to me," Crow continued. "He'd seen us together on Bourbon and at the restaurant. The night that Gordon Lawless took me to The Parlor for the first time, Brugier introduced himself. We got to talking. He suggested I bring you by. Then he insisted."

"Shit," Ken whispered. If he had known how to identify his feeling at that moment, it would have been one of complete outrage. "What is this?"

"You don't get it," his friend said. His voice actually seemed pained, and Ken had never heard this tone from him before. "Darlin', you *are* married, like it or not. Lawless told me that Brugier never did shit like this. Never. Those other kids are different; they hang around hoping to meet someone rich. He doesn't give a shit about them, and they don't give a shit about him except for what he can get them. But Brugier wants you."

"No," Ken said. "I'm out of there."

"Ken, you're still not getting the picture. Brugier's a powerful man. He knows shit about everyone. Even the mob is afraid of this guy. Don't screw around. I mean it. You don't know what he's capable of. I don't think anyone does."

"So what am I supposed to do?" Ken asked. "Spend the rest of my life with him? Wait it out until he gets bored or I go insane? No. I'm leaving."

"Ken."

"Can I move back in?"

Crow looked up at him through his lashes. His bangs hung in

front of his beak nose, and something terrible played across his face. "No," Puritan Crowley said.

"Crow?"

"Fuck, Ken," Crowley spat. "This isn't like asking a cab to pull over because you're bored with the ride. Brugier has power. He *is* power. Do you have any idea who goes to that parlor? People who run this city, this fucking state. And everyone who goes there is breaking the law, Ken, but they still go. They go for *him*. They go to get a glimpse of him. Maybe they stay for those kids running around the place, but they're there for him. What do you imagine a guy does to get people like that to worship him? Hmm? He isn't famous, and he certainly isn't the richest guy around, though he probably could be. Nobody knows what he is, Ken. He's a mystery, but he's a mystery with power. And you are *his*."

Puritan Crowley's words sank in. Ken had met the man on a hot July night, sitting in a courtyard as he sipped a drink and observed the revelers who enjoyed his hospitality. What had Ken thought then? A good time? Fun and games? All part of the vacation he was enjoying before he started taking life seriously? Had he felt love for the man? Could he? And the plain answer was: no.

Even without his fancies of a normal life, even without the fantasy of a wife and a family, he did not feel love for Brugier. Awe. Compassion. But not love. That was the plainest fact. Perhaps with that emotion he might accept this unwelcome fate, but without it?

"I have to get out of there." Ken said. "I have to leave."

He turned from his friend and walked to the door. Crow called after him, but Ken stepped into the hall, with all of its odors and dismal paint, and walked out of the building. The heat of the day had increased. Sweat popped out on his collar, and by the time he reached Wonderland, his entire body was soaked.

Reginald passed him in the foyer, his eyes landing on Ken like an insult. "Go to hell," Ken said. He moved to the stairs and took them two at a time as he hurried toward the bedroom. He threw open the door, but Travis was not there. Downstairs he checked all of the chambers, but they were empty or occupied by the Vassals who cleaned or relaxed, depending on their status.

"Where is he?" Ken demanded of a young man who was reading a comic book while reclined on Brugier's favorite chaise lounge.

The boy shrugged and went back to the brightly colored rag in his hand.

He went to the balcony outside of the room he had shared with Travis. Standing there he looked out at the courtyard and the beautiful flowers. The garden always seemed to be in bloom here. Always. He neither saw nor heard Brugier come onto the terrace. When the man spoke, Ken felt chilled.

"You want to leave," Brugier said.

Ken turned. The man had not showered yet. His hair was a tousled bush, and his eyes looked bleary. The clothes he wore were wrinkled and uncharacteristically shabby. He looked like a drunk in the street, a bum; he looked sadder than Ken had ever seen another human being look.

Still, "yes" was his answer.

"Do you know how long I've been alone?" Brugier asked, staring over the courtyard and its lovely collection of flowers. His voice was ragged.

"Travis, it's not…"

"Of course you don't," Brugier interrupted. "The first time I saw you it was raining. You were at the restaurant on a break. I remember you were reading a book by Baldwin. You loved the book. The tragedy of Giovanni entranced you."

"I can't live like this."

"And what would you intend to do?"

"Move back in with Crow," he lied. "Then find a new job."

Brugier chuckled. "Then school and a wife and some little ones?"

"Maybe."

"Is that all?" Brugier questioned. "The mundane dream of the middle class? Is that the life you want? And what happens when the misery of truth creeps up on you? When the family is not enough and you realize that your dream has been nothing but an inexpensive entertainment diverting you from who you really are?"

"I don't know who I am. I need to find out."

"I can show you." Brugier turned and put a hand on Ken's shoulder. "You can have as many lives as you want with me. You can be anything you want, everything you want." His face looked miserable. The stubble of his beard showed thick gray trunks of hair. Brugier reached in the pocket of his wrinkled suit. He pulled out a chain with a small charm at the end. "Take this," he said. "I call it the Thorn. Keep this, and no matter what happens, we'll be together."

Ken accepted the charm and wrapped his arms around the man. He embraced Brugier and tears came to his eyes. For a while, Ken forgot about leaving.

❧

He stayed that night, wrapped in Brugier's arms. As the revelers celebrated another night of life in the Parlor, Ken barely slept. His eyes would close for a few moments and then pop open again, impelled by some new thought.

The fragile warmth, such an uncommon thing, had kept him in Wonderland with his mentor. Confusion guided him back into the bed, back into the terrible comfort of the fold, but its grasp was tenuous. Ken had not changed his mind. Perhaps he would give it a little time so that he could ease the man out of his life. The last thing he wanted was to hurt anyone. Especially this man who had been so generous to him. He touched the necklace and held it up so that it caught the light from the courtyard: an ugly little charm, granted, but obviously a precious piece.

Crow's words came back to him: *The man is power. A mystery with power.* But he was a man, and he hurt like any other. If only Ken could make Travis understand without hurting him.

But when the morning came, Travis again put on his wrinkled suit, buttoning his shirt wrong and cinching his belt loose so that his slacks hung low on his hips. He made no pretense of vanity; he ran no shower or brush through his hair. He didn't even spray himself with the sweet perfume he liked. Once he awoke, he put on the suit and went outside. He returned an hour later, after Ken had cleaned up and dressed himself.

Ken sat at the kitchen table and drank coffee while he read. The rain had just begun to tattoo the courtyard. A couple of the Vassals were taking their breakfast in the dining room while another puttered in the pantry, scrubbing the floor and organizing the shelves. As Ken skimmed the book in his hand, his thoughts returned to leaving the bizarre compound of Brugier's Wonderland.

If he could not stay with Crow, then he'd have to find a new roommate. Still, he thought Crow would let him come back. They were friends, after all. Ken knew that once he made an amicable split with Travis his friend would acquiesce.

Then someone slapped a newspaper on the table before him. Startled, he looked into the melancholy face of its conveyer. Travis appeared completely lost, his watery eyes unable to focus. "I'm sorry," Brugier said. "I know he was your friend."

Ken looked back at the newspaper and scanned the page. A small headline on the bottom of the right column announced:

YOUNG MAN KILLED IN TRAFFIC ACCIDENT.

Ken read the article. Puritan Crowley was dead. According to the paper, Crow had run into the street and was hit by a delivery truck. Witnesses described the young man's behavior as erratic, screaming and batting at the air as if warding off attack. The police would check for evidence of controlled substances during the autopsy. He was nineteen years old.

After reading the article, Ken stared into the courtyard. Rain and bright sunlight showered the stones simultaneously. Travis put a hand on his shoulder.

A mystery, Ken thought. *No one knows what he is. He's a mystery. A mystery with power. And you are his.*

&

He did not attend Crow's funeral. Travis insisted that he should, but Ken couldn't bring himself to do it. As those days passed, he marked the complete degeneration of Travis Brugier. Never shaving, never cleaning himself. Day after day, his hair remained in a nest on his head. The man's complete disregard for hygiene had become disgusting. He smelled, and his suit no longer looked fitted. Rather it looked like a crumpled rag taken off another man's back. He had lost weight, and his sallow cheeks were made more hideous by the bristling hairs of an unkempt beard.

Brugier's manner reflected his appearance. At times, he just sat quietly, in a melancholy haze or wandered through the house as if he were lost, his eyes seeing nothing of the treasures surrounding him. Other times he was volatile. Three of the Vassals had fled in those days, cowering under Brugier's harsh words and dashing out of Wonderland with nothing but the clothes on their backs.

Ken decided to leave four days after Crowley's death. If Brugier wanted to hurt him, then fine, but he was leaving. The man was a specter, a horrible ghost biding its time. Lying in the bed at night, Ken could barely sleep for the reek of him. Brugier's countenance became impossible to regard, and his temper was uncertain. Ken could feel the emotion building in the man, boiling, preparing to explode. He wanted to be long gone when that moment came.

The day of his departure, he went to the bedroom and found Travis in the chair occupying the slender track of wall between the French doors leading to the balcony. The light pouring in on either side made it all the more difficult to see the man. Dust floated in the columns of sunlight, and in the shadow between these pillars, sat Travis Brugier.

He appeared to be covered in dust himself. The gray cast of his beard had bled into the man's skin and his clothing and his eyes.

No longer did he look real. Rather he had taken on the quality of a charcoal drawing: light and shade, defining form but lacking the colors of reality.

"And now," Brugier said, "you leave me."

"Yes," Ken replied. He had not even seen the man's lips move. Trapped in the darkness, Travis might have been dead his form was so still. "I have to."

"I knew this would happen. Even though you stayed, I knew you'd never really stayed. The whole time you were making your plans to leave me."

"I didn't want to hurt you."

"How sweet," Brugier scoffed. The man leaned forward in the chair, knotting his fingers in his lap.

"Fine," Ken said. He shook his head and turned.

"Wait," Brugier called. "I'm sorry, Baby. I'm sorry. Please wait."

Ken stopped. He turned. "I hate this," he said.

"Yes." Travis stood. He walked forward and swung an arm toward the bed. "Sit down, please. I'm going to tell you something."

Hesitantly, Ken sat on the edge of the bed. He watched the shadow of Brugier move against the glowing curtains. More than ever he wanted to be away from this place. Like a panther Travis paced, his form dark and brooding.

"A long time ago, long before you were born, I decided to be alone. Someone I trusted, someone I loved, betrayed me. I offered her so much, but in the end she clung to the ignorance of her world, the foolish beliefs of her religion, and she cast me aside. I swore that would never happen again, but it did. With you."

"I just…"

"Shut up!" Brugier bellowed. The man stopped his pacing and inhaled deeply. "I'm sorry. You thought I loved you once." He fell silent and turned his head to look at the confused young man on his bed. "I do love you, Baby. There's a fire in you, and you feed it with experiences. You want to know more and do more than the rest of the world's sheep. Those flames attracted me, warmed me, and, yes, they made me love you. Perhaps, if you had been given some time to grow you'd have loved me too, but I acted from desperation. The thought of losing you confused me. It still does, honestly. But I realize your need. So, I want you to have the time you need to grow, to experience life, and when that's over, I want you to come back to me."

"I can't promise that," Ken said. *Never* was what he thought.

A bitter grin spread over Brugier's face before he whispered, "Never is a hopeless commitment. You jump to it far too quickly."

"You don't understand," Ken said.

"Oh, I assure you, I do. When time is a commodity of which you have little, you become quick to eliminate possibilities. You have to make choices. Do you see that? You only have so much time to spend, so you tell yourself. I can do this or I must do this, but I haven't got the time for everything, so I'll say never to this other. Passion and responsibility clash, because those things you desire steal time from the things you believe you need. So, the painter sets down his brushes and becomes a file clerk, and the man who wants to see the world puts away his duffle bag, so he can stay home to feed his children and wipe the shit from their asses. Every choice brings misery, because something must be killed to give space and sustenance for some other thing's life. And it's all because you know that one day the clock's ticking will stop."

As he spoke, Travis's voice rose. He was pacing and ranting, waving his hands in the air. Sweat covered his face, glistened in his unkempt hair.

"And you!" he continued. "You stupid, stupid prick. I'm telling you it doesn't have to be that way. If you'd just open your fucking ears and listen."

Ken had to get out of this place. The man was going mad before his eyes. And no matter how he felt, he could not watch this descent, could not witness the shattering of another human mind. He moved to leave the bed.

Brugier jumped forward and pushed him back. "You are not leaving."

Ken rolled off the bed. "The fuck I'm not. You think I'm one of those kids downstairs who needs you? I was here because I wanted to be here. And I'm leaving because I want to leave."

"You were here because I paid Crowley to bring you here. Your life has been mine for months now, and it will be mine for a long time to come."

"Bullshit."

"Is it?" Brugier said. "Let's find out. You go ahead and leave, Baby. You go live in this fantasy of yours. And do you know what you'll find? I do. I've done it all. It will drain you, suck you dry. You'll never know what life could be because you'll be too caught up in what it should be. But that will pass, and when it does and when you think you're happy, that's when you'll see me again. That's when I'll show you exactly how fragile all of this is. No one can give you what I can. *No one!*"

Ken walked to the door. He looked at Brugier for what he hoped was the last time, and then he turned and fled the house and the courtyard. He escaped back into the real world, leaving Wonderland behind, never imagining that he would return.

But Travis wasn't done with him. Not just yet.

22

David was torn. He'd spent his afternoon sifting through memos and newspaper articles, seeking documentation to support the strategic recommendations he would be presenting to his client. But his mind was not on the work, not fully. Ken was in there, messing things up, creating disarray with his face, his body, and his irrational and infuriating behavior. David couldn't even pretend to understand why he had allowed Ken to put him through such emotional turbulence. With no other logical explanation David had to believe that he was still in love, but the bitch of it was, he loved a man whom he hadn't seen in well over a year. Then, Ken had been charismatic, funny, and romantic, but David had seen nothing of these traits in the past few days; their time together had been colored by morbid drama and Ken's melancholy. So, why David expended so much thought on the man was incomprehensible. Maybe it was the idea that Ken actually needed him, or there was magnetism to Ken's vulnerability. David didn't know. Rationality insisted that he put an end to it, just walk away and return to the comfortable life he'd created for himself.

But rationality had a weak voice, rarely heard over the roar of emotion. So, when Ken called, asking if they could get together because he needed to talk, David had gathered all of his work into the appropriate files, logged off of his computer, and headed for his car.

Now, they walked along the river, saying little as the Mississippi gurgled and rolled to their left. The sky was clear except for wisps of cloud against the horizon. Ken wore a distracted expression, nothing new there, and he seemed to be struggling for something to say. David wanted to break the uncomfortable silence, wanted to lighten things up a bit. He threw a hip at Ken and nudged him along the path.

Ken didn't respond. He was lost in thought. When he finally spoke it had nothing to do with David's gesture.

"Sam died today," Ken said.

"Sam?" David asked. "Your friend Sam?"

"Yes. His lover, Jersey, started shooting at us. Sam panicked, tried to get away. A truck ran him down."

"There was shooting?" David asked with quiet incredulity.

"Jersey caught Sam in bed with someone. He snapped, went into a jealous rage. The thing is, I'm pretty sure the guy he caught Sam with was the same guy who killed Bobby."

"What? Are you sure?"

"No. But, yes."

"Less cryptic would be helpful."

"Then, I have to start at the beginning," Ken said without taking his eyes from the walk. "I told you why I left and how it had something to do with Travis Brugier?"

"Yes."

"I want to tell you the rest of it. It's important for you to understand what happened." Ken crossed the path and sat on an empty bench.

David joined him. Ken gazed over the water, lost in thought, and David waited for his friend to speak, anxious to get new perspective on an old story.

"I've been thinking about this all day, trying to get the pieces straight in my head," Ken said. "I remember most of it pretty clearly."

"Take your time."

Ken worked through his thoughts for several moments, and then said, "I met Travis Brugier on a summer's night back in seventy-four. I had this friend, Puritan Crowley, whom I called Crow. We used to…"

⚜

For thirty minutes David sat and listened to his friend's memory. He pictured Brugier's home and the Vassals maintaining the grounds and serving their master. This information was in keeping with what David had heard whispered in his youth. Then came the young Ken Nicholson, reading to the man in bed as the nights passed or the afternoons faded. When Ken began describing the deterioration of Brugier, David's nerves crackled and stung. He already knew how the story ended, but to imagine someone with such power losing his sanity was truly unnerving.

Ken stopped talking after describing his escape from Brugier's Wonderland. "Did I mention the necklace?" Ken asked.

"No," David said. "Is it important?"

Ken smiled bitterly. "Yeah. It's important. He called it the Thorn. You know how some people name their jewelry, particularly a piece that's valuable? Well, he'd done that with this necklace. It didn't look valuable. In fact, it was rather ugly. But he told me to keep it. He told me that it would bring him back to me one day."

"What did it look like?" David asked.

Ken fished in his open shirt collar for a moment and pulled a chain free. "Like this," he said.

A small charm in a golden setting that wrapped around the cap of the pendant like talons. The pendant itself was little more than the size of David's thumbnail. Shaped vaguely like a cross, with a thick vertical wedge that ended in a point and a horizontal beam that was ragged, the piece was hideous. Slightly gray like a rotting tooth, it might have been an old piece of polished ivory.

"It isn't the prettiest accessory I've ever seen."

Ken didn't reply. Instead he returned the charm beneath his shirt. Then he said, "After about a week, I thought I was safe from Brugier. I'd gotten a new job, and I was going to start the following day. Then, while I was wandering around the Quarter that afternoon, I saw them. Maybe they'd been following me all week, I don't know. But his Vassals were everywhere. I knew most of the faces from Wonderland, and I knew that if Travis had sent them out to do any damage, they would have been more than happy to do it.

"I went back to the apartment I'd shared with Crow. I threw my clothes in a paper sack and tried to get out of town. I didn't get anywhere. They found me, hiding in a bar. They took me back to Wonderland. I didn't know what to expect. Travis was so far gone by then. I thought he was capable of anything at that point. Still, I couldn't have imagined..."

Ken's voice trailed away. David looked out at the water. He placed a hand on Ken's thigh and rubbed lightly. The familiar touch seemed to bring the man back to himself.

"The courtyard was the same as it always had been, but I felt some sense of promise there, the promise that something horrible was going to happen. It smelled like a funeral. The flowers weren't pretty anymore. Their scent was nauseating. Travis stood on the balcony of the house, and he asked me to come up. I didn't really have any choice, so I went. We stood on the balcony, and he said something really odd to me, he said that even I would appreciate what was about to happen.

"By then, four of the Vassals were in the courtyard standing at attention like soldiers do with their arms at their sides and their backs straight, but they were paired off, two facing two. They were naked, but I didn't really look at them at first. I was too scared of Travis.

"When he clapped his hands, twice, like a sheik calling his wives, I looked at him and saw that his mind was gone. I saw that immediately. His eyes were too large, his smile too insane. Travis noticed me staring and jerked his head once, indicating that I should be looking in the courtyard. A terrible scream came up. It sounded like that of a woman, so shrill and panicked. I looked down into the courtyard, and one of the Vassals was backing away from the other three. His name was Reggie, the kid Travis had sent up to the bedroom that night. I didn't know what was wrong. I'm still not sure, but he kept screaming.

"One of the other boys, his name was Vern, I think. I only remember because he hadn't hated me like the others had. When he and I spoke, I always got the impression that he pitied me. Anyway, Vern stepped forward. He had his hands up in front of him, and he was stepping forward to comfort Reggie. I remember thinking that he shouldn't get too close because Reggie was out of his mind; he wasn't seeing Vern at all. Even from where I stood on the balcony, I could tell that whatever was scaring the kid was inside his head. I'm not sure how I knew—something about the eyes—but there they were, Vern and Reggie, kind of dancing with each other. One would step forward, and the other would step back.

"Finally, Vern got too close. I called to him, tried screaming for him to get back, but it was already too late. Reggie snapped and charged at him. He cut Vern's throat, and when he dropped, Reggie fell on him. The other two boys watched, wrapped in each other's arms, terrified.

"By the time he stood up, Reggie was covered in Vern's blood. His body was shaking madly, and his eyes still had that look in them. The other boys saw it too. Slowly, they separated. Reggie backed away, his head moving rapidly back and forth, following the movements of the other two, who were making wide circles to either side. I kept thinking that I had to do something, but I couldn't. When I looked at Travis, he had moved himself onto the railing, sitting there like a kid at a baseball game.

"I couldn't even say for sure what happened in those few seconds when I was looking at Travis. When I looked back at the courtyard, the three boys were tangled up with one another. I couldn't tell them apart; there was too much blood, too much movement.

"Then Reggie stood up again. The others were dead, like Vern. Reggie had torn them apart, and for a moment, he looked triumphant. He stood there in the courtyard, looking up at us like a surviving gladiator. I don't know what the boy expected, but Brugier was chuckling to himself. 'Watch this,' he whispered.

"Reggie screamed again. He was seeing something horrible, and it still came for him. 'Too late,' he cried. 'Too late.' Then he turned the knife on himself. He started cutting at his arms and body. Finally, at his own neck. I couldn't speak. I just stood there watching the blood pouring out of their bodies. Maybe I thought it was all an act. I don't remember.

"When it was over, Travis asked me if I liked his show. All I wanted to do was run. I wanted to get far away from Wonderland, but I couldn't; Travis wouldn't let me. Not yet. Travis and I spoke. I kept asking him what had happened and how he could just sit there, letting it happen.

"I was about to run when his face cleared. Suddenly he looked sane, like the man I had met all of those months before, and he told me that he loved me."

David reached out to touch Ken's shoulder. He squeezed it gently. "What happened?"

"He wrapped a wire around his neck. He told me that if I turned my back on him, I was choosing to kill him. He looked so calm then, even though he knew full well I'd already made my decision. He wanted to make me choose, maybe thinking I'd feel responsible for what was about to happen.

"But I turned and walked away, and didn't feel a moment's guilt over it."

❧

David breathed deeply, the horrible story affecting him like a long run: He was short of breath; his heart thundered; sweat chilled on his neck. He actually shivered, the hard bench digging into his back as he did so.

So, that had been the night that Wonderland fell. Everyone

assumed that Brugier had killed the boys and then taken his own life. It was the only thing that had made sense to the authorities. The papers had been vague as to the state of the remains, and no names were printed save for Brugier's.

David felt the story sinking in, filling in the gaps of the fable he had heard numerous times in so many different ways. Some of the less wholesome accounts of that night insisted that Brugier had sodomized the mutilated corpses and tasted of their blood and flesh. He remembered so many tellings of the story that it had become a grand fiction to him, like ghost stories told by boys around campfires: tales of the hook, tales of the swamp witch, tales of the babysitter who roasted babies in ovens, and tales of Travis Brugier. So intangible were the details of that final night, the fertile minds of his peers had expounded on the happenings as they saw fit. As a result, a brutal mythology had formed around Brugier.

"And you have no idea why that kid snapped?"

"I'm beginning to suspect," Ken said. "All I know for certain is that Travis made it happen."

"What did you do?" David asked.

"What do you mean?"

"After that night, what happened to you?"

"I ran," Ken said, still staring over the darkening river. "I hitchhiked out of the city. I went to Dallas, where I spent six months fighting nightmares. I pawned the necklace Travis had given me, and I think I got ten bucks or something for it. I worked sporadically, and then one day I called my parents. They told me that a man from New Orleans was looking for me. His name was Gordon Lawless."

"The lawyer?" David asked.

"Yeah. I always thought the name was ironic. Travis introduced me to him a few times at the house. He used to wear those summery dresses and camp it up in the Parlor until six in the morning, but a nice guy, I thought." Ken's voice drifted away for a moment. "Travis used to call him Goldie, even though his hair was carrot red. When I asked about the nickname, Travis just laughed.

Turns out that Travis had a quarter-horse ranch in Kentucky. Goldie was the name of his prime sire."

David Lane remembered Gordon Lawless well enough. He'd seen the man cruising along Rampart for years during David's early experimental phase. The guy was very popular. He was funny and rich, and word had it that he was exceptionally well endowed.

"What did he want?" David asked.

"I didn't call," Ken said. "I was afraid to call. He showed up in Dallas about a week later. My parents had given him the address of the house I was rooming in. When he came in, I knew something was wrong, or at least I thought something was wrong. I guess I thought he had come to take me back to New Orleans. Maybe the police had discovered my involvement with that last night in Wonderland.

"It turned out to be something very different. Lawless came with a check for fifty thousand dollars, a bequest from Travis. I was also to take possession of the house."

"Wonderland?" David asked.

"Yes. I told Lawless to sell the place, burn it down. Whatever the case, I didn't want it. There were stipulations in the will against me doing anything except residing in the place for thirty years. If after that I chose to sell, well…" His voice drifted away again, and Ken looked at David.

The gray of Ken's eyes, now deeper in the dim light of evening, traced over his face. What was he looking for? Belief? Disbelief? Though he didn't know what his expression might say, David believed him. There was only one thing that puzzled him.

"When did you get the necklace out of hock?"

"I didn't," Ken said. His eyes still burned into David's.

"I don't follow," David said. "When did you get it back?"

"A few days ago." Ken's voice grew rough with the words. "Vicki Bach gave it to Bobby, and then she killed him."

23

Ken's sense of unease increased as he rode with David toward Paula's house in the Garden District. He had to check on his ex-wife and daughter to make sure they were safe. Full dark had settled over the city and in Ken's thoughts. After a day of reflection, lost amid the diseased memories of Brugier and his boys, Ken had emerged with the certainty that his escape from Wonderland had been an illusion.

When you think you're happy, that's when you'll see me again. That's when I'll show you exactly how fragile all of this is.

And hadn't he been happy? Last year before he'd started seeing visions of David's death? He considered that the happiest time of his life. That's when all of this had started. His flight to Austin had only interrupted the cruelty, merely postponing his torment.

Brugier was still alive, or he had entertained such bitter foresight as to account for Ken's punishment before death. Neither of these choices seemed possible, but somehow Travis had made good on his promise to return for him, and Vicki Bach and her blond accomplice, Chuck, were his agents. Brugier could have used any number of incentives to recruit these violent children and more like them; his resources had always run as deep and dark as a mine shaft.

Ken needed to find out their connection to the master of Wonderland, find Vicki and Chuck and make this stop, because now Ken saw that the people he loved were being manipulated like dolls in a perverse puppet drama. None of them were safe, not Paula or Jen. Not David.

"Ken?" David asked.

"Yeah."

"You gotta say something," David said. "All of this quiet is messing with my head."

"I don't think you'd want to hear what I'm thinking."

"Then sing me a fucking show tune, because this brooding crap is wearing me down."

"I think the same kid that killed my son, killed Sam, and I don't think it's going to stop with them."

"I thought you said Sam's death was an accident."

"Only because Jersey didn't get the chance to shoot him."

"You're not making any sense."

"Look, David, the kid said some things to Sam. The description fits, and Paula saw this Chuck asshole at Sam's party, which is where Sam said he met the guy."

"So, you think there's a connection?" David asked, making it clear he saw no such thing. "Something between Bobby and Sam and this Chuck guy?"

"Yes, I do. I'm the connection," Ken said. He turned to see what David made of the statement, but David kept his eyes on the road. Ken detected a slight compression of the man's brow, but little else in the way of reaction. "It all goes back to Travis."

"Okay," David said evenly. "That's enough."

"It's not enough, because it's not over yet. He's not finished."

He watched David struggling with his comments. The man's hands tightened around the steering wheel, and he drew his upper lip between his teeth in an attempt to control the content of his response.

Finally, David breathed deeply and said in a very calm voice, "I thought you said you saw Brugier die."

"He could have faked it. I was in no state of mind that night to know exactly what I saw, not after what I'd already seen."

"Maybe," David said, "but the police identified the body. It was in every newspaper in the state. Besides, even if he were alive, he'd be eighty years old by now, wouldn't he? It makes no sense that he'd just wait around that long."

"I know," Ken admitted. "But…"

"No," David interrupted. He'd reached the end of his patience. "There is no *but*. You went through hell with Brugier. I get that. You're going through hell now. I understand that too, and I understand your fear. I even understand why you felt you had to leave last year. I think you really did have a breakdown. Furthermore, you're still having it. Bobby? Sam? Come on, you can't expect me to see a conspiracy behind your son's murder and a jealous spat that ended badly, especially a conspiracy that started thirty years ago. This shit is in your head, Ken. You can put it down to anything you like, grief or fear, but the fact is you're on your way to a complete emotional collapse. And honestly," David said, casting a serious look at Ken, "I can't watch that happen."

He understood the implication of David's words. He'd handled the conversation badly, had handled everything with David badly. He couldn't even pretend to be surprised that David was already fed up.

"I'm sorry," he said. "You're right. I'm just out of my mind right now."

"And with good reason," David said. "You've lost two people who were incredibly important to you. It's natural that you'd want to make sense of it, but Bobby's death wasn't your fault and neither was Sam's."

"I know," Ken said, though of course he knew no such thing. What he knew was that Brugier's threat was real, and anyone close to him was susceptible to that threat. He was just afraid of losing someone else, afraid of losing David, so he'd say what he had to.

David made a left off of St. Charles and shifted in his seat, apparently trying to get comfortable. The air in the car weighed heavy with his anxiety. With each breath, Ken felt it coiling in his belly and throat.

"So, am I just dropping you off?" David asked.

"No," Ken answered. "I mean, I hope not. I need to check in on Paula and Jen, but then I think you and I need to sit down and talk, work some of this out."

"It might be better if we hold off on that. I don't think you're in the best frame of mind right now. I know I'm not."

"Okay," Ken said, the tension in his chest tightening to an ache. "I know you've gone through more than enough because of me, and I'm really sorry, David. If I could wrap the last year up and toss it on the fire and burn it away completely, I would. When I saw you again, I thought I had the chance to do that."

Ken paused. He had much more to say, but he'd been watching David as he spoke, reading the vague changes in his expression for some sign that his words were getting through. David navigated a turn, the turn onto Paula's block, and his eyes grew wide. Only when David's hushed voice filled the car did Ken turn his attention to the windshield and the scene beyond.

"Oh my God," David whispered.

Police cars, their emergency lights cold and dark, lined the middle of the block in front of the Victorian Ken had bought for his wife as a wedding present. Men in blue uniforms wandered between the line of cars and the house. Seeing the activity sent a cold spike through Ken's chest.

He was too late.

"I think I owe you an apology," David said, speeding the Mercedes down the block.

Ken couldn't reply. His thoughts slid, made slick by desperation and a grief he prayed was premature. Paula? Jennifer? And in thinking about his daughter, she appeared in the glare of David's headlights.

Jennifer stood at the side of the road. She bent at the middle, hugging herself, making half circles back and forth. Tears streamed down her cheeks. Her lips twisted and trembled.

"Go on home," Ken told David.

"The hell I will."

"David, go. I don't have time to argue with you. I'll call you later."

"This is bullshit," David growled, slowing the car.

And he was right, Ken realized. "Okay. I'm sorry. Wait here."

Before the car came to a complete stop, Ken threw open the door and leapt onto the pavement, already running toward his daughter. Curious neighbors stood on porches or gazed out on the scene from slightly parted curtains. A police officer stood in Paula's drive and watched, jabbing his flashlight in Ken's direction.

When Ken reached Jennifer, she was bent at the middle as if punched. He grabbed his daughter and pulled her to his chest. Her body quaked violently as she sniffed back tears.

"Honey, what happened?" he asked. "Are you okay? Is your mother okay?"

Jennifer cried a low, mournful note and pulled away from him.

"Hey," someone called from his side, and Ken turned to see the police officer leaving his position in the drive to walk toward him. Behind the man, lights burned through every window of the house. Yellow strips of tape wrapped around the porch, announcing to the public that this was a crime scene.

The policeman's face was blubbery, thick, and moist. His eyes held concern yet behind this was a hard expression.

"Can I help you?" the officer asked, exhaling onions and garlic into Ken's face.

Ken swallowed hard against the offensive breath and said, "My wife...ex-wife..." and his voice died.

The officer nodded. "Mr. Nicholson calm down. She's fine. They've taken her to Mercy."

Why was she at the hospital if she was fine?

"What happened?" he asked.

"Earlier this evening she was attacked," the officer said. Jennifer moaned deeply and hugged herself. "But she's fine. She did a lot more damage to the creep than he did to her. We have him in custody, and your wife is being treated for minor injuries."

"You caught him?"

"We apprehended a man named Charles Baxter here at the scene. He's in our custody."

A wave of relief crashed over Ken, making his legs shake. He took a step toward Jennifer, and she backed away, still hugging herself. Her petulant display cut into him, but he had no choice but to accept it. He wasn't going to have a scene with her in the middle of the street.

"Thank you," Ken told the officer. He turned to Jennifer and reached his hand out for her. "We should go see your mother," he said.

His daughter looked at him as if he'd just called her something hateful. She cast a glance over his shoulder at David's car and then dropped her eyes to the road. With her arms still wrapped over her chest, Jennifer stepped forward, making a great show of avoiding Ken as she walked to David's car and climbed in the backseat.

The drive to the hospital was tense and quiet. When Ken introduced David to Jennifer, she mumbled a "hello" and looked out the window, curling her legs beneath her. Ken had always thought that introducing his family to one of his romantic interests would be uncomfortable, which is why he'd never done it. His theory seemed to have been proved. They all sat silently. None of them seemed to know what to say, and for the time being, Ken figured that was a good thing. The night had offered more than enough drama already.

At the hospital, he asked David to wait while he checked in on Paula. She was awake and in good spirits, and Jennifer's petulance went out the window as soon as she saw her mother's bruised face and slung arm. She hugged her mother and kissed her cheek.

"I was so scared," Jennifer said, laying her head across her mother's chest, just above the sling.

"How are you feeling?" Ken asked from the doorway, himself feeling awkward for interrupting the moment between mother and daughter, again sensing his outsider status among them.

"I'm good," Paula told him.

She looked happy to see him. Maybe he was imagining that, but he hoped not. "I'm glad," he said. "The police said you kicked the shit out of the guy."

"I hope I did," she said, wrapping her good arm around Jennifer's shoulders, wincing in pain as she did so. "It's all kind of a blur right now. Are you going to come in, or do you have to go?"

"No. I don't have to go," Ken said. "I've got one thing to take care of, and then I'll be right back."

He left the room and wandered down the hall to the visitor's lounge where he found David thumbing through an old issue of *People* magazine.

"She's okay?" David asked.

"Yes," Ken said. "She's going to be fine."

"Thank God. Do you need anything?"

"No," he said. "Thank you, though. We're good for now. You should go on home. We'll be here for a while, and then I'll have to take Jen back to my place for the night."

David nodded his head. "I'm sorry. About what I said in the car, I mean."

"It's okay. I've put you through a lot, and most of it was crazy."

"Give me a call in the morning," David said. He stepped forward, wrapped his arm around Ken's neck, and pulled him tight. "All of that's over. They caught the bastard. You can relax, now."

"Yes," Ken said. But he couldn't. Chuck wasn't responsible for the hallucinations Ken suffered, nor was he the sole villain in all that had happened.

Vicki was still out there. The police had caught Chuck, so maybe her plans—Travis's plans—needed to be revised, but Ken didn't believe that anything was over. Even if they caught Vicki he doubted things would change. In one way or another, Brugier was behind all off this. Until Ken understood exactly what influence he still had, how he was able to get into Ken's head or command and control people like Vicki and Chuck, and put an end to it, he didn't believe any of them would be safe. All he could do was try to protect the people he cared about until he figured it out.

24

Chuck sat in an interrogation room just like the ones he'd seen on television: It had dirty gray walls, a frosted window with bars over it, and one of those mirrors you weren't supposed to know people could see through, but everyone did. He thought it was pretty cool, imagining himself on one of those programs where the cops got all tough and stupid. What wasn't cool was wondering where in the fuck Vicki was. He could see again. They had rinsed his eyes to get that pepper shit out of them, and they had bandaged his cheek where the old bitch had scratched him, though he felt certain they should have stitched up a couple of the gashes; otherwise, they'd scar. Of course the assholes holding him didn't care what he looked like. They didn't know that in Florida, your face was your meal ticket. Even with all of the cash Vicki owed him, he'd have to make a living at some point. If his face didn't heal right, they'd have hell to pay.

And where was Vicki? She'd promised that if he were picked up, she'd get him out. She'd promised to take care of him. The way she threw money around, he knew she could make his bail, whatever it was. Besides, she wouldn't want him talking about her too much. Not only could he find her for them, he could explain the woman's intent down to the finest detail. She knew it. No way she'd just let him rot in this shit hole because it wouldn't be long before she joined him. She owed him, and damn if she wasn't going to pay.

Other than Vicki being a cunt, it wasn't so bad, though. It was just like TV. The detectives were hilarious, wanting to know why he did this and why he did that. They told him that a confession would make his life a lot easier. That was a total laugh. They had no idea how easy his life was going to be.

He'd faked them out, acting totally innocent and outraged, demanding a lawyer. He made it sound like the Nicholson woman had attacked him, which she had. He'd have scars for the rest of his fucking life because of her. When he got out, he'd pay the old bitch another visit before hitting the beach. He wanted to have a few words with her.

If only Vicki would show up and get him out. Christ, what was she waiting for?

Then a thought occurred to him, and he didn't like it one bit: What if she'd already skipped? What if she'd just bailed out on him, moved east herself, or back to Texas with her pretty face and fine automobile? Vicki Bach. That was the name she'd told him, but she could have lied. She could already be across the border with a new name and a new car, and they'd never even know she'd been there, leaving him to take the whole fucking rap. Then, all she had to do was wait it out until he was a number in the boys' club before coming back and finishing up with Nicholson.

No way, he thought. No way he was going to sit on his ass and let her ditch him. They'd be back soon. In a few minutes the detectives would come back through the door like they had done for the last three hours, and they'd ask him the same questions, hoping to find some hole in his story. Well, when they came back this time, he'd show them holes. He'd tear them open and fill in the name and the place and the fucking time.

Vicki should have known better than to fuck with him.

His head grew light with his decision. He hadn't eaten all day, and his stomach growled and rumbled, making him nauseous. They could have given him a sandwich or something. As it was, the dizziness grew worse, and his head began aching miserably. He felt like he might puke right on the table. His head spun, and his eyes clouded. Maybe they'd drugged him. They might have slipped a truth serum or something into the watered-down coffee. They never showed you that on television, but he knew it happened. Sweat broke out on his brow. What the hell was this? What had that old bitch done to him? What had the cops done to him?

Chuck rocked forward hoping it might ease his mutinous belly, and for a moment it did. He closed his eyes and tried to imagine something nicer than the dirty gray walls of the interrogation room. What he pictured was a long stretch of white sand and the crystal-blue ocean stretching all the way around the world. He was on the deck of a big glass house, staring out over the Florida coastline. That was cool. He liked that. He leaned forward and put his head on the desk, hoping the image would quit spinning and give him some sanctuary from the sickness rolling over him.

He pictured Nicholson at the house with him. Such a classy guy. He imagined the man walking through a pastel living room, wearing a thick terry robe and in his hands holding two silver goblets. The warm smile on Nicholson's face grew when he saw Chuck because he loved him. Like in a play, the images came to life, and he didn't even have to concentrate to see them. In fact, he felt certain that if he were to open his eyes, he would still be on that lovely beach with Ken Nicholson, sipping drinks from silver goblets as the sun warmed their skin.

Chuck relaxed into the image, and the sickness began to subside. He was just starting to feel better when Nicholson's face blew apart. The fantasy changed so quickly that he jerked his head off of the table. Opening his eyes, he was still in the brightly lit room with the empty Styrofoam cup on the table before him. His hands were cuffed behind his back.

The old guy's face had blown apart, and beneath it was the

face of Chuck's father, his head swollen and knotted from the work Chuck had done on him with a wrench.

You gotta feel your mistakes; it's the only way you'll learn.

Chuck knew the voice in his head wasn't real, besides it was bullshit. You didn't have to feel anything; in fact, everything worked much better if you just kept things cool and numb. But now that he'd thought of his father's sick claim, he couldn't get it out of his head. Chuck breathed deeply and looked up into the stark white lights.

Vicki. She was doing this to him. If that bitch wanted to play games, he'd give her games. When the detectives came back, Chuck was going to spill. He knew everything, and maybe he'd done some shit, but Vicki was the mastermind. She was the conspirator, and he'd seen enough television programs to know that they fell a lot harder than the jerks they got to do the work. She'd worked Bobby Nicholson to get up close to him and then told Chuck to whack him flat. She'd purposely found that Fleagle asshole. She could have used any real estate dork in the city, but she'd wanted Fleagle because he fucked Nicholson's buddy. Of course, so had Chuck.

Thinking about that Sam dude made him smile, not because of what they'd done together—that was just fucking—but because the guy had been a total chump. What a numb nuts. The guy's lying in bed, apologizing, and begging his boyfriend to "wait," while Chuck still had his dick buried in the guy's ass. Hilarious.

But none of that mattered. No. What mattered was making sure that Vicki didn't let him rot in the tank. He wasn't taking the fall for her shit.

You have to feel your mistakes.

She'd feel. Fuck yeah, she'd feel. He'd tell the cops her name, her address; he'd testify at the fucking trial; and when he got around to telling them about the epic mind fuck Vicki was planning for Nicholson, they'd be thanking him and treating him like a star, because what she was planning to do to that guy and his family made the Manson thing look like a church social.

All he had to do was get his story straight. They wouldn't believe him if he didn't make it very clear. They'd think he was lying, trying to take the heat off of himself. He had to get it right, but his father's fucking voice kept rolling around in his head, distracting him.

When the door finally opened and detectives Ogilvie and Reilly entered, Chuck thought the lights in the room dimmed. Neither of the men had touched the knob on the wall, but the place seemed suffused with a gloom it had not previously had. Probably another side effect of whatever they'd put in his coffee. He blinked his eyes and found it harder to focus on the men. Their faces were clear enough, but a vague light, like a halo, surrounded both of them. The thinner of the two cops, that was Ogilvie, he still looked pissed off, but the other one, the stubby one, he looked bored.

Chuck would change that soon enough.

"Your lawyer is on the way," Ogilvie said, walking across the room to stand beside Chuck. His buddy walked to the corner and stood with his hands crossed over his dick. "Now would be a good time to think about a few things."

"Sure thing," Chuck said, blinking again. The room spun for a second, just a quick drop to the right. He breathed deeply against the sickness the motion brought and closed his eyes to give his head a chance to adjust.

"You see, Chuck," Ogilvie said, "you gotta feel your mistakes. If you don't feel 'em, there's no way to learn from 'em."

His eyes flashed open, expecting to find his father, beaten and leaking as he'd been in Chuck's dream, in place of Ogilvie. But the thin detective remained, arms crossed over his chest, angry expression frozen on his face. Okay, Chuck thought, that's cool. Being locked up was just messing with his head, nothing to panic about. He checked on Reilly in the corner. The man had not moved. He still had his hands clasped over his crotch, his shoulders touching the walls. The right side of his face was purple and caved in from where Chuck had struck him with the metal bar. A clot of scalp dangled behind his ear like a chunk of roadkill.

"Shit," he yelped, sliding his chair back with an involuntary thrust of his hips. The chair legs screeched over the floor. His heart tripped in his chest. "What the fuck is going on?" Chuck asked, nodding toward the corpse of the Nicholson kid, propped in the corner like a damaged mannequin.

"What's wrong with you?" his father asked, leaning forward to grab Chuck's shoulders. His old man's shattered jaw hung open, barely moving with the words. The lumps covering his face and scalp were open and leaking blood over the lacerated brow and onto the tabletop.

This wasn't real, Chuck told himself. It was like in his dream when Ken Nicholson's face had come apart to reveal his father's brutally beaten head. Except, he knew the difference between a dream and reality. His dream had been flat and stark. What he saw now occupied space, cast shadows, gripped his shoulders painfully. His father's face was less than a foot from his own. Chuck saw every welt and dent in the skull. The foul, whiskey breath filled his nose.

In the corner, the corpse of Bobby Nicholson looked on, the body motionless, the face blue-gray with death. Only his eyes moved, racing back and forth in the sockets like living creatures caged in a dead shell.

The detectives were doing this to him, something in his coffee. Vicki was doing it. Someone had to be doing this to him, and he wanted him to stop now.

"Please," he whimpered. *Please make it stop.*

"You gotta feel your mistakes," his father said, the voice infuriatingly calm. "It's the only way you'll ever learn."

Trapped in the interrogation room with the two dead men, Chuck screamed. He fought against the cuffs at his wrists. His body convulsed and trembled in revulsion and fear, trying to break the aching grip of his father.

I've learned, Chuck thought. I've learned. Please stop.

That was the last coherent thought Chuck had. He didn't even hear his own screams as he sank down and away into a dark void where emotion and thought and physical need would never touch him again.

III

THE DUST OF
WONDERLAND

25

Morning.

Word of Chuck Baxter's meltdown while in custody reached Ken via a call from Detective Ogilvie. He'd just gotten home from dropping Jennifer off at school when the call came, and what little hope he'd maintained evaporated. The kid's capture had solved nothing. Ogilvie suggested they were likely to find Bach based on what they knew about the boy, but Ken doubted it. Vicki was ahead of this game. Her skills were intellectual, and she wasn't likely to sit back and let herself get caught. She was still out there, still plotting. How long would it take her to find a new vassal, some other disturbed punk to finish what Chuck had started? Not long, he knew.

Brugier had wanted to get Ken back to the beginning, but Ken had only gone back so far. If he intended to finish this, there was only one place left to go. There, he might find Vicki Bach or a clue that would lead him to her. If nothing else, he felt certain he would find all that remained of Travis Brugier.

He needed the keys to Wonderland.

⚜

Ken stood in the offices of Barclay and Lawless, facing the ghost of Travis Brugier's lawyer. He had entered the large, dark room to find himself surrounded by intricately molded mahogany paneling and rich, burgundy leather furniture. Hundreds of law volumes lined a wall of bookcases to his left, and before him a wall of tall paned windows provided a view to the river beyond. A long mahogany desk separated him from the windows. A high-backed leather chair sat regally behind the desk. The lawyer who led him into the room seemed far too whimsical for such dark surroundings. Despite a very well-tailored charcoal-gray suit, the man positively radiated joy and energy.

Andrew Lawless had his father's blue eyes and his carrot-red hair. Already in his sixties, this younger Lawless was not quite as gaunt as his father, but the resemblance was startling. When Andy smiled, it lit up the room just as his father's happiness had. Ken wondered if the son also wore summery dresses and cruised little boys through the Quarter. He decided that it wouldn't be hard to believe.

Lawless seemed to know the reason for Ken's visit before he was asked. They'd had the file sitting around for thirty years, shuffling it from one cabinet to another as they'd waited for the house's owner to reappear. Lawless also knew Ken.

"My father spoke very highly of you," Andrew informed.

The pleasant—though, in view of Ken's haste, tedious—conversation was similarly complimentary except for the lawyer's disdain that the house had been left unoccupied and untended for so many years. "Shame to let such a historic piece of property crumble like that."

But Ken could think of nothing he'd like more than to see that house fall to the ground, decimated by termites and rot.

"I go by there a lot," the lawyer said. "I keep wondering what's inside. The place has probably been stripped clean by thieves and destroyed by vandals, but I hope not. A grand old mansion like that shouldn't go untended."

They spoke for much longer than Ken had intended. The conversation turned to Andrew's father and his "curious fascination" with Travis Brugier. And then Andrew gossiped for nearly thirty minutes about Brugier himself, carefully avoiding any comment that might offend the man's heir. Finally, as the morning was nearly half gone, Ken excused himself. He retrieved the keys from the mammoth mahogany desk, then shook Andrew Lawless's hand. "Thank you, Andrew," Ken said.

"Any time," Lawless replied. "I'll send father your regards."

The comment stopped Ken as he reached for the doorknob. He turned slowly. "Excuse me?" he asked, certain he had heard incorrectly.

"I'll say hello to father for you," Andrew replied.

"Andrew," Ken said, "I thought your father passed away."

The old lawyer laughed dryly. "He shoulda' a couple of times, but he's still hanging in there."

Gordon Lawless had been Travis Brugier's best friend, and to Ken's knowledge, his only confidant. If anyone knew the connection between Wonderland's master and Vicki Bach, it would be Lawless. Maybe Ken wouldn't have to return to that house after all.

"Andrew," Ken said, "would your father see me?"

"I'm sure he'd be tickled," Andrew said happily. "Let me just call Peg and have her get the old boy cleaned up."

⚜

Thirty minutes later, Ken stood in a larger room that seemed to be the parent of the law office he had recently left. Another broad wall of glass allowed wedges of sunlight to cut into the room, but they stopped inches from the foot of the four-poster bed containing the flesh and bones of Gordon Lawless. The room was alive with dust hovering over the tiny, drawn form of the lawyer who reclined on half a dozen fluffy down pillows. Most of Lawless's hair had deserted him, leaving a pale orange froth above each ear and a dozen wisps above the arch of his forehead. His once gaunt face now appeared skeletal, but his eyes were clear and brilliant, and his smile upon seeing Ken was nearly as charming as it had been three decades before.

"Mr. Nicholson," Lawless said. Age and illness had drained the resonance from the man's voice, leaving him with a hoarse whisper. "I was hoping we might meet again one day. I can see that time has been far kinder to you than it has been to me. But then, you've just begun to taste time. Perhaps once you've gorged on it, you will have faired little better than myself, but let's hope not. You have always been a gorgeous morsel."

This last sentence, uttered breathlessly, brought with it an odd sense of déjà vu for Ken. Memories of a dozen such comments layered in his head, making this unlikely reunion feel familiar. Ken recalled that the lawyer often associated people and events with food. Everything had a flavor, a texture, and a scent. Ken could find no indication of Lawless's mood from his voice, though. The rasping hiss of the words carried no inflection. "How are you, Gordon?"

"Two steps from death," Lawless replied. "Fortunately, they don't allow me to walk anymore, so I'm able to hoard those and carry on a bit longer. I imagine if I weren't on three different painkillers, I'd be far more upset, but as it is, I'm rather content, or at least I allow myself to believe I am. And I suppose as long as I believe I am, then I must be, don't you think?"

"Yes," Ken agreed.

Lawless tried to laugh but managed only a slight cough that made the hovering dust dance frantically. "Look what they've done to my study," the withered man hissed. "This was my sanctuary…Well, this and Travis's Parlor. I used to love this room. Now they've buried me alive in it. I'm almost looking forward to dying, if only for the change of scenery."

"Don't talk like that," Ken said as he sat on the thick paisley-print comforter covering the bed.

"You were always such a sweet boy. Delicious. That's what you are," Lawless said. "But I'm not afraid of death. I beat death my entire life. I lived the way I wanted to live every moment of it. Death didn't stand a chance with me."

Ken tried to smile, but he did not have a clue to what the old lawyer was talking about. He said as much.

"Death only wins when you invite it to join your life," Gordon said. "It's one thing to cross the finish line and get a stitch in your side. It's something wholly different to carry that stitch with you through the whole race. Now, when death gets me, he gets me for a few seconds. Life had me for eighty-seven grand years. I'm happy enough with that. I just wish they hadn't put me here in my old study. I loved the view from my bedroom, but the stairs were too hard on old Peg: all the climbing and carrying. I told Andy to hire a younger nurse, but she's been with us for a long time, and I guess I was just being a selfish old goat. It just doesn't seem right that I should dry up in this room where I had some of my most stimulating conversations and liveliest thoughts. Do you know that Travis and I created The Parlor right here. Right in this room?"

Ken shook his head. "No. I didn't know that."

"Yessireeeee," Lawless cackled dryly. The effort brought on another spasm of coughs. Once the fit passed, the old lawyer pushed himself deep into the pillows and fixed Ken with an intelligent and serious gaze. "You did come to talk about Travis didn't you? After all, while I always enjoyed your company and the sight of you made my mouth water like a coon-ass at a crawfish boil, we weren't exactly close. I don't think I have even laid eyes on you in two decades, but Travis said you'd be coming by one of these days, and I was to answer any question you asked as honestly as I was able."

"Travis said I'd be coming by?" Ken asked nervously. The old lawyer nodded his head slowly with ominous deliberation. "Then he's still alive?"

Gordon Lawless fixed him with a curious look that fell somewhere between exasperation and exhaustion. "Anything is possible. Personally, I have neither seen nor heard from him since his death, but he knew you would have questions. I expected you many years ago, but this is as good a time as any what with us both still breathing and all."

"Do you know a woman by the name of Vicki Bach?" Ken asked.

The old lawyer wriggled against his pillows and stared down at the paisley comforter. He tried to clear his throat, but the sound was little more than a sigh. "I do know Ms. Bach," the lawyer said dryly, "but as she is a client of my firm, I cannot discuss her with you. I'm afraid it would be inappropriate."

"Can you tell me her connection to Travis Brugier?" Ken asked.

"Well, Delicious, tell me why you think there is a connection, and I'll see what help I can be."

"She had my son murdered, and someone else was killed. She sent her Vassal to kill my wife."

The lawyer's lips curled into a hungry smile and his eyes observed some far-off splendor. "Vassal," Lawless whispered dreamily, remaining absorbed for several moments by the memories that expression evoked. When he finally spoke, his voice still dreamlike, he said, "Despite Travis's many peccadilloes, he always had a fine taste in boys. Do you remember a savory selection by the name of Maurice?"

"Gordon," Ken said sternly, trying to get the conversation back to Vicki Bach.

"Of course, you wouldn't," Lawless said. "Maurice was one of the first children on Travis's buffet. Such a treat, he was. I can still smell that child, all salt and leather like he'd just been pulled out of the ocean. Oh, I do miss him."

"Vicki Bach," Ken said.

The lawyer nodded his frail head, which seemed like it might roll of his slender neck at any moment. "She wants to destroy your life," Lawless said, "What makes you think this has anything to do with Travis?"

"They are connected," Ken said evenly. "You tell me how."

"I'll tell you this," Lawless offered. "Travis had a very difficult will. In fact, if he had had any living relatives, I'm quite sure they would have contested his wishes and would have walked away with a fortune. As an orphan, Travis had nobody, and as with all things pertaining to Travis, there was a story." The lawyer paused for a moment and reached out a pencil-thin arm for the tumbler of water beside the bed. After taking a sip he returned the glass. "Tell me a story," Lawless said. "Do you remember Travis saying that?"

"Yes," Ken replied. The phrase had the ability to freeze the blood in his veins.

"Well Travis's will was another story," Lawless continued. "You see, he didn't name an heir in his will. Oh, he left a pittance here and there, like the bequest I brought you in Dallas, but the bulk of his assets were to remain invested. They were to remain invested until someone came to me and told me a story. He didn't say whether it would be a boy or girl, man or woman. He simply said that one day someone would approach me and tell me the story of a young Indian couple. I remembered the story vividly because of the way that Travis told it. White Dog and Passing Cloud were their names. A tragic story. His entire estate, except for the bequests and the house, of course, was to pass into the hands of the person who came to me with that story."

"And Vicki told you the story?" Ken asked.

"I can't answer that," the old lawyer rasped. "Which should answer your question sufficiently. Though apprehensive, I had no choice. The client reminded me a lot of Travis. Her mannerisms and sense of humor were exactly like his, except the client in question was so much colder than Travis. She didn't possess an ounce of his depth. When she called me Goldie, it wasn't the way Travis said it. He always seemed to use the name as a term of endearment, but not this client of mine. She used the word as a cold defamation." The old lawyer stopped speaking for a moment. "I wonder how she knew that Travis called me that?" he pondered aloud. "He certainly couldn't have told her."

"Did Travis have any siblings, any children?" Ken asked, sensing he had suddenly found his connection. His face fell when the old lawyer rolled his head on the pillows.

"You should know better than anyone how Travis felt about fucking. He had splendid taste *in* flesh but absolutely no taste *for* it. Delicious child, do you have any idea what The Parlor was?" The lawyer again fixed Ken with weary exasperation. Ken shook his head. "The Parlor was Travis's experiment. Or maybe the proper word would be *joke.* The only people who got into The Parlor were the people who had the most to lose by being *in* The Parlor: politicians, clergy members, prominent citizens such as myself and anyone else who kept a thick veneer of morality. Travis stocked his experiment with tasties to draw out the hungry, and then he sat back and watched them sink into the fantasy of his parlor. He'd often say, 'Do you see the power of flesh?' And how could you not see it? Sodomy laws, drug laws, statutory rape laws—all were being broken night after night by the most self-righteous members of our society, and Travis just sat back and laughed because while he acknowledged the power of flesh, he held power over all of them because the flesh meant nothing to him. The entire place was a giant practical joke. Even the name was a joke."

"Said the spider to the fly," Ken said, his voice hushed.

"Precisely. It wasn't until a year or two before you met Travis that people started calling the place Wonderland. At first, he hated the nickname, as it took away from the amusing title he had given his experiment, but after a while he found the title fitting, and he allowed his guests to use the slang."

"And what did Travis get out of his experiment?"

"Amusement," Lawless said. A fit of coughs followed the word and the lawyer again reached for his tumbler of water. He stifled the fit with a long draw from the glass. A thin stream of moisture fell down either side of his mouth to his stubbled chin. "Amusement," he repeated, "information, and control."

"He blackmailed these men?"

The lawyer's head rolled on the pillows. "No," Lawless said. "Travis didn't need to blackmail anyone. He had given these men what they wanted, and in return they gave Travis anything he wanted. A simple arrangement. Quite amicable. Then you came along, and things began to change." The lawyer closed his eyes and fell silent for many seconds. Ken thought Lawless had drifted off to sleep, but soon the lawyer was speaking again, and his eyes sought out Ken's. "You think you killed him, don't you?" Lawless asked. "Don't bother denying it. I know you were a part of it. I also know that if Travis Brugier died that night, it was because he had other plans."

Now the old man was rambling. "He was insane," Ken said.

"Delicious child," Lawless said, "if you believe that, then you never understood a thing about that man, and you *are* doomed." The lawyer rolled his head slowly across the pillow again. "How could you have been so close to Travis and have remained so naïve? Perhaps it was your youth, or Travis might have shielded you from some of his talents."

"Gordon, what are you talking about? What talents?"

"Travis's talents were the glue that held The Parlor together. Oh, he never made those boys do much they wouldn't have done on their own, but he certainly nudged them in the right direction on occasion."

"Are you talking about hypnosis?" Ken asked. He had often thought that Travis possessed the ability to force his will on others through the act of suggestion.

The old lawyer leaned forward and let out a long rasping hack, which was meant to be a laugh. "Hypnosis," he mused. "My God, you are naïve. Travis didn't ask permission to get into people's heads; he just got in there. Your friend Crowley knew it, or rather he found out."

"Crow never said anything to me," Ken whispered.

"He knew better. As mercenaries went, Puritan Crowley was among the best." The lawyer sighed raggedly. "Don't get me wrong; I adored that boy. We had many splendid evenings and afternoons together. He was as tasty as a pecan pie, but Crowley knew the value of silence and the value of compliance. When Travis wanted you, Crowley brought you to him and was duly compensated. I'm not sure where Crowley fouled himself with Travis.

"I paid my respects at his services. I noticed you didn't attend. Perhaps that was best. It was a dreadful little service: a plain pine box in an unmarked crypt. Only three or four people actually showed up. I felt bad for the boy."

"Gordon, you still haven't answered my question about Vicki Bach. Did she know Travis? Are they related? What is their connection?"

"She wasn't even born when Travis died, and to the best of my knowledge, you and I are the only living people who had any real connection to Travis at all."

"Then, was there some contract in his will, some agreement that bound her to him? Certain steps she had to take to inherit his money?"

"She had to tell me the story. There was nothing else."

"Then, he's still alive." There was no other possibility.

The old lawyer fixed him one last time with the angry exasperated look. "I highly doubt that." His head seemed to weigh too much for his neck, and his chin drooped to his boney chest. "Besides, it hardly matters whether he is or isn't."

"How can you say that?" Ken asked.

"Because, Delicious," Gordon Lawless said, "Travis Brugier's death would end nothing."

26

How long he stood in front of the gate to Wonderland Ken couldn't say, but he found himself terrified by the place. Like a wasp's nest, this structure and its grounds had served as a shelter for vicious and poisonous things. History and the disease of memory emanated from the decimated structure. Windows, filthy and dark, played the films of history; they showed a magnificent courtyard and a bubbling fountain, and they harbored a unique master with incomprehensible power. Ken remembered numerous wonders, numerous pleasures and a single atrocity in which four children had battled for their lives. A soft bed spoke words of confused sensuality. Hallways led visitors through priceless ornamentation. Wandering these halls were the ghosts of children who were lost in their pursuit of happiness as they served their benefactor. All was brilliant light. All was unfathomable darkness. All was fractured reality. All was a story.

But he'd escaped this place once before.

Maybe you never escaped at all.

Ken unlocked the gate and pushed it open. He walked down the shadowed alley, between a stone wall and the exterior of what had been Brugier's Parlor. When he entered the courtyard, Ken came to a stop. Death surrounded him. The four boys still lay on the flagstones in a muddied heap. Ken blinked, and they were gone. Weeds, long dried and ragged, reached for him like dead fingers. The fountain no longer spat its plume into the air; foul green sludge filled its basin. The façade was equally soiled, the paint having flaked away to expose wood nearly black with rot.

Inside, he found Andrew Lawless's miscalculation. Ken walked through the filthy rooms, enormous and stiflingly hot, observing the treasures contained within. No thieves had ransacked Travis's home. The precious furnishings had suffered only from dust and infestation. As a young man he'd had no concept of their value beyond the way the antiques seemed perfectly suited for the large Quarter house. The paintings on the wall were pretty, and that was as far as he had been able to go in their appraisal. Now, he recognized many of the artists whose work hung beneath layers of dust and filth. The furniture he once had treated indifferently now took on meaning as he realized its rare and precious qualities.

Ken rubbed his palm along a filthy frame holding a painting by George Bernard O'Neil. Ken had seen a similar piece auctioned in New York for nearly sixty thousand dollars, and he recognized the painting as the least precious in the home by far.

And where was the collector now? What had Travis become? In light of his conversation with Gordon Lawless, Ken felt certain that Travis, like himself, had survived that last night in Wonderland. Death could be faked. Authorities could be bribed, particularly in this city. Ken had not waited long on that balcony. Travis could have woken and struggled his way back to life, patched the tear in his throat. For all Ken knew, he'd hallucinated the entire thing, the way he had repeatedly hallucinated David's death. Perhaps that pattern had been set then. Whatever the case, Travis was certainly capable of such a dramatic feat. The rest would be lies and money, lots of money. For Travis, this would be the easy part.

And Vicki Bach? What was her reward?

Ken ran his fingers over a Lord Leighton bust, wiping the

grime on his pants as he passed. So beautiful these objects were, and some incredibly valuable. How did a monster find appreciation for such things?

Upstairs, Ken entered the bedroom he had shared with Travis Brugier. So much filth covered the place that Ken could barely make out the Persian rug at his feet. It was indistinguishable from the floor as both lay beneath a thick frosting of dust. He pulled the thin quilt off of the bed and coughed through the cloud that rose high into the room. He tossed the pillows on the floor. Though thinking it a useless gesture, Ken crossed to the light switch and toggled it up. When the light above the bed burst on, Ken's heart leapt as if witnessing some conjured magic, but Travis had accounted for a lot of things before his death. Obviously, keeping the power pulsing through Wonderland was one of them.

Ken crossed the room to a bookcase lined with hundreds of dust-frosted volumes. He was searching for a specific book, a leather-bound text from which he'd read countless times. He found it resting at the end of a shelf, next to a row of small journals of varied binding. Dragging the book from its nest, he brushed the dust from the covers, front and back. It had no title, no inscription. He leafed to a random page. The typeface, stark and precise, without a hint of a publisher's elegance, brought back pangs of fear and wonder and longing.

Book in hand, Ken returned to the bed and reclined against the headboard, resting the large leather-bound volume in his lap. Once comfortable, Ken opened the book. It had no table of contents or preface. On the first page was the first story. Each chapter was marked by a name. He thumbed through, remembering fragments of narrative, sometimes so clearly that entire tales unwound in his mind from the prompt of a single sentence. But the story he most wanted to read, the first story he would read, told of a young Native American couple. This story connected Travis to Vicki Bach, or so Gordon Lawless had suggested.

Tell me a story.

The disease of memory returned with virulence, and Ken began to read.

⚜

The Fathers looked upon the children as sacred. They would be the gold amongst the dirt. In the boy, White Dog, and the girl, Passing Cloud, they saw their future a prosperous place.

Wind made the grasses bow to the children. Rain showered them with glory, and their families gazed on with pride as boy and girl moved as a single being. No question was ever spoken of their marriage. It was as certain as the moon's rise and the brightening of dawn.

But all was not well.

The day before their union was to be celebrated, Passing Cloud ran into the village. She cried, wailing from grief and fear. She showed the elders her hand, and they counted only four fingers. White Dog had taken her finger, she explained. He was making a pact with evil spirits. The elders found the girl's words difficult. They had no evil spirits in the village. The ground had been cleansed, and no omens had arisen to tell of an approaching manitou.

The elders scoffed at the girl. They made her wait in the long house until her man returned from his wanderings. But Passing Cloud's mother, Lame Bull, insisted that she be allowed to speak with her child. She was admitted an audience with her daughter, who lay curled in a corner of the great building.

To her worried mother, Passing Cloud explained that White Dog was not one of them but rather a spirit traveler born into the tribe by accident. He spoke of powers. She had seen manifestations of his powers in the meadow by the river, where Passing Cloud said she saw a man with a bear's head rise up from the rushing water, and he danced there for her. At first, she had found the vision greatly humorous, but then she realized it was an omen.

White Dog told her that she too could travel as he had.

They could become the parents of a new powerful tribe. They could wipe out any who opposed them for in their children would be the power of the spirits.

And that morning, the morning before the morning of their wedding, White Dog made her take a spirit into her body. He called it up, and it glimmered like iron dust. She felt it come into her, working through her skin like blowing sand. Then White Dog took her finger.

Even now, he remained in the meadow, making charms from the finger. The charms were for the spirit. They guided the spirit once the body went to the Earth. With the charm, the Spirit could find its way back into the world of the living. Then Passing Cloud cried, not because the wound ached but because it did not, and she knew it was a sign of a true curse.

Lame Bull was terrified for her daughter. Never would the horse come to guide her to her people's souls if she had bargained with the evil ones. She would remain in the ground, her spirit lost without its guide. Mother spoke to daughter, telling her to pretend. White Dog, the spirit traveler, must not know of this betrayal until the spirit could be taken from Passing Cloud's body.

But White Dog already knew. As he entered the village carrying two rings and a necklace in his hand, the elders converged on him, and told him that his woman was taken with fever. She spoke craziness, spoke of demons and evil, and said that White Dog was not truly of them. Had he really taken Passing Cloud's finger?

The accusations enraged White Dog. Clutching the jewelry tightly in his fist, he went to the longhouse. He cast Lame Bull out, cursing her.

In the shadowed shelter, he pleaded with Passing Cloud. Again he told her of the new tribe. He showed her the beautiful rings he'd made from the bones of her finger, showed her the necklace on which the largest bone hung like a bear tooth, filed and polished into a sharp point. But Passing Cloud begged to be released from him, from the spirit that threatened her soul.

White Dog beat his woman, screaming like the hawk. His fists fell upon her. The elders, hearing this disturbance, came into the longhouse and watched as White Dog expelled his rage. Then, the betrayed lover began screaming in a foreign tongue. Like the white men who traded with the tribe, White Dog's voice came. The Elders grew frightened.

Passing Cloud's mother drew her skinning knife and ran for White Dog, but as Lame Bull approached, she began to scream, cutting at the air as if attacked herself. Moments later she fell dead on the hard dirt floor.

Then, White Dog pulled his own knife and slid it into Passing Cloud's belly. He pushed his hand deep into the wound, leaving the charms he'd made from her lost finger inside the warm cavity. Tears burned along his cheeks as his bride crumbled to the ground. A cry of agony filled the longhouse, the village, and the sky surrounding them.

The Elders backed away as White Dog left the longhouse wearing Passing Cloud's blood on his hands and her death in his eyes. He walked out of the village, and the spirit traveler was never seen again.

⚜

Ken closed the book, placed it on the musty sheet, and stood from the bed. On edge, he took to pacing the room as he considered the story. He grasped the Thorn at his neck and thought of the charms the man had made of his intended's finger. Likely, the necklace at his throat was made of similar material, not ivory at all, but a piece of human bone. Disgusted, Ken released the bauble and walked to the doors leading to the balcony. He pulled them open and stepped outside.

The air was gray with rain but still sauna hot. A startling dislocation greeted him when he looked over the railing. The last time he'd looked down from this vantage, four boys had destroyed one another on the stones below. Like Passing Cloud's mother, Reggie had tried to defend himself against a nightmare no one else could see. But where Lame Bull's knife had found only air, Reggie's had found skin and bone and blood. Puritan Crowley had run into a busy street, fleeing some invisible danger, and his behavior had been attributed to insanity or drugs, but it was Travis.

He didn't ask for permission to get into people's heads; he just got in there.

Gordon Lawless's words found new relevance for Ken. This was the talent the lawyer had spoken of. Like White Dog, Travis could paint nightmares and display them in the minds of his victims. How many of these dreams had Ken endured, all the while telling himself it was the product of his own wasting sanity?

He imagined David hanging from a ceiling, from a balcony, from the eaves of a house. Brugier's talent hadn't died with him.

The story of the Native American couple might have been nothing more than legend, but Travis had seen himself in White Dog, and as such, he'd included the tale in his storybook.

What else might Ken find between its covers?

Ken returned to the bed, to the book. On the first page, he read the name *Alice*, and then he read her story.

27

David spent his afternoon in the offices of Laray Pharmaceuticals arguing with the legal department and the in-house public relations officers. The sky spat rain against the long paned window, beyond which the sky looked nearly black. His eyes roamed periodically to the darkness as he had struggled to make the men and women in the room realize the delicacy of their situation.

Laray and its parent company, Aldine-West, were facing serious litigation in the form of a class action suit as a result of questionable ethical practices. The action group, a collection of distraught parents, claimed that Laray had released the shipment of a blood product without having screened it properly. Worse yet, they possessed a memo from Laray's president, Hank Lafayette, that stated that the shipment was to go out regardless of purity to meet their sales demand.

David hated corporate work. Fighting with legal departments and *suits* all day frustrated him. Laray was screwed. If they didn't want to protect themselves, that was their business. Besides he had other things on his mind. He was worried about Ken.

He hadn't heard from him all day, though he imagined Paula's injury had probably been such that her care was occupying his time. That or he really was looking for Vicki Bach, and David had to admit this possibility made him uncomfortable.

After driving home from the meeting, David opened his front door and felt a wave of light-headedness. He leaned on the jamb for support and saw a small black shape scurry over the threshold. The creature bumped his shoe and then rushed off toward his baseboard.

Flesh Eater.

His skin pimpled and a shudder ran up his body.

As a child he'd hated these creatures, thanks in great part to an uncle who had stayed with David's family one summer. His mother's only sibling, Uncle Joe was a big, classless man with all of the grace and charm of an armadillo. And Uncle Joe called roaches *Flesh Eaters*.

Even before hearing Uncle Joe's dissertation on the vermin, the things had terrified David. Their sleek little shells, like some hell-made defensive armor, harbored the ragged and bristling form of their bodies. The things looked evil, and with a child's imagination the very sight of such an unwholesome-looking creature attested to the presence of monsters on Earth.

Once, when he was seven, he'd been helping his mother cook breakfast for the family. He loved getting up early and helping her in the kitchen. Sometimes she had him stir the hot cake batter or she'd have him make toast while she fried eggs and boiled grits. Just being with her, assisting her, had made him happy, and she always gave him an extra slice of bacon or a few extra berries as payment for his services. Uncle Joe had been in the kitchen that morning, picking at the calluses on his feet and making lewd comments about their neighbor, Mrs. Dillon. His mother decided on oatmeal, and she asked him to get the box of Quaker oats out of the cupboard. This request had always pleased him because when the box was empty, he could take it to school and make a new drum out of it by pasting bright paper and golden trim on the cardboard cylinder.

When David pried off the top of the oat box and found a fat roach burrowing through their breakfast, he'd cried out and dropped the entire box of oats on the floor. His Uncle Joe laughed spastically, but David stood horrified. Several roaches moved in the spray of pale oats, their shells hiding the hideous nature of the bodies beneath. They began to scramble, having survived the shock of the crashing box, seeking dark places beneath the cabinet and under the stove. His mother asked him to sweep up the mess and get another box out of the cupboard as if nothing had happened, but his uncle had something to say on the matter.

"Them's Flesh Eaters, boy," his uncle teased. "Once they shove you in a box, the Flesh Eaters start making dinner plans. You just best hope you're really dead in there. They'll take you quiet or screaming."

For weeks after, David barely ate, picking through the food on his plate to see if any of the monsters had returned to invade their meals. And now the Flesh Eaters had returned.

Upstairs, David changed out of his suit and checked his voice mail, but he'd received no calls. He stretched out on the bed, letting his muscles unwind as he gazed at the ceiling. He considered calling Ken and asking the man out to dinner. Then, decided it might not be the best idea. Likely, he was with his family. After all of the terrible things that had happened to them recently, he imagined Ken would be spending a lot more time with Paula and Jennifer.

David thought that was a fine thing. They needed Ken right now, and quite frankly he didn't mind the idea of having an evening of peace and quiet. He'd had a lousy day and unless his mood made a sharp one-eighty, he wouldn't be very good company for anyone, especially Ken.

Worn out, David closed his eyes and relaxed into the mattress. He really didn't know what to make of Ken's situation. A kid named Chuck had murdered his son and tried to murder his ex-wife. David was even willing to believe that the kid had succeeded in orchestrating the ruin of Sam Martin's relationship and might have predicted the jealous and violent aftermath. David had no idea why, but it didn't take much to get a lunatic's notice these days. For all he knew, Chuck was simply obsessed with Ken and wanted to get his attention with extreme displays of brutality.

Ken's implication of Vicki Bach struck David as being within the realm of possibility, though far less likely. The stuff about Travis Brugier was just crazy.

Don't let Ken drag you into this, David told himself.

He wanted to be supportive. He wanted to be there for Ken, hoping that once the man's paranoia blew away, something good would remain. Maybe they could get back to where they'd been before all of this insanity had begun. If not, David needed to know that he could walk away, because right now, that seemed the most likely outcome.

These thoughts ran in loops through his head as he drifted into a light doze. They broke apart and frayed at the edges, becoming fuzzy and indistinct as he sank deeper into sleep.

"They'll take you quiet or screaming."

His uncle's voice woke him with a start. Heart racing, David searched the room but found it empty. He whispered a curse into the air, closed his eyes, and went back to sleep.

Ken woke, uncertain of his location. He blinked several times, wiped the blur from his eyes, and looked around the dusty room, now gloomy with the fading day. When had he fallen asleep? He couldn't remember exactly. The day had passed while Ken read the storybook. Some of the stories he'd read twice, sensing that he had missed something important in the text.

Throughout, he noted common elements in the tales, subtle threads of observation that linked the seemingly disparate characters from one story to the next. But such filaments of perception were vague in the stories. What stood out were specifics that reappeared sporadically throughout the text. The name "Goldie" (the nickname of Travis Brugier's lawyer), for instance, showed up in four of the stories.

Even more startling were the references to a piece of jewelry. In one form or another, under a handful of varied descriptions, the Thorn that Ken carried around his neck appeared in every single story.

After his day's reading, Ken no longer believed that Travis had filled his storybook with tales that happened to appeal to him. Rather, Travis had written or dictated stories about himself, camouflaging his identity with fiction. Hiding behind different genders, different races, and placed in a variety of historic times, Travis's storybook was really a single story, telling of a man who had become disenchanted with the world and had grown bitter. Though the transformation took place subtly throughout the volume, the end result was a man who held the people sharing his world in such low regard that they amounted to little more than toys. He'd had the book printed and bound and kept it near, just so he could have his life read back to him in an act of unbelievable ego.

Ken stood from the bed, leaving the book resting on the sheets. He returned to the bookcase and the line of journals that formed a neat row, ending at a gap where the storybook had been. He pulled one of the small volumes free, opened it, and read the precise, evenly spaced words, written with a florid yet controlled penmanship: *But Passing Cloud begged to be released from him, from the spirit that threatened her soul.*

Ken closed the book and reached for another, much older journal with a frayed silk-wrapped cover. The writing in this book was faded, almost illegible. The pages were yellow-gray and warped in pronounced waves. Pages were torn, some missing entirely.

It told the tale of a young woman who had been stolen from her land and sold into slavery, a woman who came to be known as Alice. This story too had appeared in Travis's book. The book Ken held had been written in the same hand as the journal with White Dog's tale, but it was at least a century older.

He checked another book and another. All of the stories had

been re-created word for word in Travis's storybook, and all were written in the same florid hand. The clear supposition was that one person had written all of the journals, but Ken struggled with this idea. The journals spanned hundreds of years. His gaze ran over the wall of books as a dark notion took root in his mind. If once, if Brugier were back now, then why not before? What if Travis hadn't hidden behind the lives in his books but, rather, had lived them?

He backed away from the bookcase, shaking his head. It wasn't possible, Ken knew. People lived and died in a simple and inescapable cycle of life. Even Travis, with his power and financial resources, couldn't change such a fundamental element of humanity. Yet, it seemed he had found a way to alter this sequence. Was that what he'd been talking about in the days leading up to Ken's flight from Wonderland?

In the last two weeks, he'd witnessed a number of impossible things. Though many of these—David's hanged corpse, Puritan Crowley's torn visage—could be written off as the delusions of a lunatic, Bobby was dead. Sam was dead. These were truths.

Ken pulled three small journals from the bookcase and returned to the dusty bed he had shared with Travis Brugier. He stacked the volumes on the sheet. He retrieved Travis's storybook and set it down next to them.

If what Ken believed was true, this being, whatever it might be called, had lived for generations. It had experienced the worst of mankind and very little of the good as it had attempted to find its place among them. Perhaps it had gravitated to darker, unwholesome things, but there could be no doubt that its perceptions had been stained by the least flattering traits of man: greed, perversion, lust, ambition, jealousy, and spite. Not only had it endured these qualities, but it had done so alone.

Ken understood, with absolute clarity, how the monster had been made, and he believed he understood what it was capable of. No one close to him was safe.

So, where are you? Ken wondered.

I'm right here.

Ken had spent the day amid the memories and the dusty orna-mentation of Wonderland, thinking he might draw Brugier out. Travis's penchant for the dramatic would be perfectly served by a confrontation here, where so much misery had been born. Yet while there, Ken had been visited by the disease of memory, made all the more virulent between these walls, and had encountered stories, leg-ends, and myths written by a single hand, suggesting an aberrant be-ing unfettered by the restrictions of mortality, and should he accept the unnatural presence of such a being, then Ken had been reintro-duced to his sanity. Travis, however, remained absent.

Gathering the books in his arms, Ken turned for the door, then paused.

A slender woman stood in silhouette halfway down the corri-dor. From her posture, she appeared to be gazing at the floor.

"Can I help you?" Ken asked, not recognizing his guest.

"I thought you came to see me," the woman said, walking down the hall toward the bedroom threshold. Framed by the doorjamb, she appeared small, but her eyes glittered with confi-dence.

Power, Ken thought. Those were the eyes of a woman who worried about nothing because nothing was beyond her control.

"Welcome home, Baby," Vicki Bach said and stepped into the room.

❧

Ken trembled. The books in his arms seemed to double in weight, so he put them down on the bed, never taking his eyes off of the round, baby-doll face of Vicki Bach. His chest grew heavy, his lungs aching as if the room's dust had accumulated and clotted in them.

With slow gliding steps, Vicki walked to Ken, gazing into his eyes with a playful smirk on her lips. "I've missed you, Baby. You don't know how much."

He said nothing. The woman's breath touched his cheeks. A gentle scent of flowery perfume came into his nose.

"Can't you talk to me anymore?"

"What do you want?"

Vicki stepped around him and into the bedroom. "You let it fall apart," she said with mocking sadness. "I spent a lifetime creating this place, gathering its treasures, and designing it to be the most wonderful home in this city. Do you know I imported the fabric for those drapes from Italy? The bed came from an old hotel in Vienna. You can't imagine how difficult it was for me to acquire. Everything had to be perfect. Everything was perfect. How could you let it all disintegrate like this?"

"It wasn't mine," Ken said.

"I gave it to you."

"You gave me a lot of things I didn't want."

"I told you I could give you anything you ever dreamed of, but you always doubted my sincerity. Can you see it now?"

"All I see is that you murdered my son," Ken said.

"Flesh rots, Baby. In time, the cells give up, and the cycle closes down. Bobby would die one day with or without me. Everything around you is going to be dead, destroyed in just a few years. Everything except me."

As soon as the words left her lips, bodies appeared at her feet—Bobby, Sam, Jennifer, Paula—all except for David, who hung at her back. The battered and torn bodies shook, convulsed, and leaked blood onto the floor. Their dead eyes looked up at Ken, pleading.

"On that night," she said, "our last night together. I understood your youth. When you deserted me, I let it happen so you'd have the time you needed to grow. And when I came back, nothing had changed. I gave you so many years, and you still hadn't changed. You knew more about the world, but you understood nothing about life."

"So, you started murdering people to make your point?"

"You have only yourself to blame, Baby. You didn't listen. I told you there would be choices to make. The first was turning your back and letting me die."

"That was your decision."

"It's not that simple," Vicki replied. She kicked out at the form of Paula, squirming like a bound lunatic on the floor. The toe of Vicki's shoe sank into a wound at her crushed temple. "Do you think Paula decided to have her life stop the minute you walked out on her? Do you think she looks forward to a cold empty bed every night, fingering herself to your memory? You didn't tell her to wait for you, but does that make it her decision?"

Ken ground his teeth. Vicki's needle-sharp accusation jabbed, stung.

"And, Bobby," Vicki continued, "trying so hard to please you, wanting to bring Daddy home by being the perfect son. He couldn't even enjoy his accomplishments, because they all failed to get your attention. The smallest mistake sent him into a self-loathing panic, and day by day he learned to hate himself because you didn't care enough to be there. You couldn't be bothered with such a failure."

"He wasn't a failure," Ken said.

"Well, he did have excellent taste in women."

The bodies at Vicki's feet writhed and bucked. Their eyes grew wide. Their wounds pulsed fresh gouts of blood onto the grimy floor, pooling and graying with the filth. Ken looked at the battered ghost of his son, whose mouth ratcheted open to a gaping hole. A ragged roar rose from Bobby's mouth, then from all of the mouths. A chorus of hollow, warbled guffaws filled the room. The dead laughed at him.

"And Sam thought that he'd be next, thought that once you left Paula, you'd run to him, and his love would finally be reciprocated. Oh, how he hated you when that didn't happen. He carried that hate like a tumor in his chest but kept smiling, hoping."

"Stop it," Ken said, tears filling his eyes.

"Don't you want to hear about Jennifer? In some ways she's the best of all. The things she wants to tell you, the things she wants to share. I think even you would appreciate the irony of it."

"Stop it!" Ken closed his eyes, blocking out the grotesque shapes at Vicki's feet.

"One decision, Baby, and so much damage. I told you that passion and responsibility would try to murder one another as the clock ticked and tocked. There's only room for so much in a single life. It's the nature of all of man's stories, a perfect conflict over the great mortal question: What will I be before the ticking stops?

"I could have spared you that," Vicki continued. "If you'd accepted my proposal, such decisions would have been irrelevant because the clock would have had no power over you. You could have been anything and everything, a different path with each birth, but you refused. You spit in my face and turned your back."

Ken opened his eyes. The bodies of his loved ones remained in a heap before him, distracting him with their glassy stares, their twitching limbs. "But *they* haven't done anything to you."

"And they mean nothing to me," she said.

Vicki walked toward Ken, and the bodies on the floor flickered out as if nothing but refracted light. "I was here a year ago. I showed you what I intended for David, but I didn't have to be so subtle. I could have taken them all at once: Bobby, Sam, Paula, Jennifer, and handsome David. Every one of them. Believe me, they'd have opened their wrists before facing what I could show them."

"Then why didn't you?"

"You really shouldn't tempt me, Baby," Vicki said, walking past him, touching his cheek lightly.

Ken shot his arms out and grabbed Vicki's shoulders. He forced her around to face him. His left hand slid behind her head and grabbed a handful of silken hair close to her scalp. He jerked viciously until her eyes were locked on his. His body shook. His only thought was to keep pulling the hair until the woman's neck snapped.

"You're going to kill me?" Bach said. "That's your answer? Go ahead Ken. Do it. Do it a dozen times, and every time I'll come back. And every time, I'll take another piece of you with me! This time Bobby and Sam. Next time David. You'll watch your pretty little man rot in a snake pit, if I let him live. And do you know what he'll see? You want a little glimpse of what I've got for him?"

Ken didn't reply. He pulled hard against the knot of hair in his palm.

Vicki Bach's face began to melt before his eyes. The skin rippled and puffed. Behind her, the doorway and wall disappeared. A sheet of tiny black bodies bubbled from floor to ceiling. The insects—roaches, beetles, millipedes and maggots—blanketed the portal, and the dusty walls came alive with the tiny forms. The face before him continued its slow disintegration, and the entomological blockade fell forward, covering Vicki's head, just as her face split apart, revealing the creatures burrowing beneath her skin.

Ken jumped back, repulsed by the touch of a thousand mandibles on his wrists. He cried out, recoiling. His ankle caught a hitch in the tattered rug, and he went to his knees. The climbing tide of creatures crested near the ceiling, and then the curling wall came down on him.

He threw an arm over his face as the bugs rained down. Their sheer volume pushed him to the floor. They burrowed under his collar as he writhed to dislodge or crush his attackers. His skin itched ferociously as the insects clamored over him. A fat cockroach pushed its head into his nostril. Its antennae tickled the membranes of his sinuses as it climbed into his nose.

Then silence. The terrible itching disappeared. Ken opened his eyes. He sneezed repeatedly, certain that the roach still bore its way into his skull. He frantically slapped at his neck and shoulders, but the creatures had receded back into his head. Distantly he heard the front door open and slam.

Ken stood. He scanned the room with hurried sweeps of his head, but Vicki Bach was gone. And so was Travis Brugier's storybook.

⚜

Ken staggered along Royal Street until he was able to flag down a taxi. He gave the driver David's address and collapsed against the backseat.

Once he got to David's, he had to call Paula to make sure she and Jen were all right. He would have had the driver take him there first, but Vicki had aimed her threat at David, and Ken didn't want the man to be left alone and unaware.

After Vicki left him in the filthy room, Ken had searched for the storybook, but it was gone, along with several of the smaller journals. As a result, he suspected that there was information in those books she didn't want him to have. In fact, he felt certain everything he needed to know was in the account of the Native American couple, but as Ken tried to recall the tale of White Dog, he found the story broke apart. He remembered Passing Cloud's panic and fear and the ritual involving her finger, but when he tried to follow the story to its conclusion, his memory of it shattered.

He was just exhausted, worn from too many painful revelations and burdened by Vicki's ongoing threat. He would have to try piecing it together later.

At David's house, he asked the taxi to wait for him while he checked to see if David was in. He jogged to the porch and rang the bell. After several minutes, David opened the door, blinking and rubbing his eyes as if he'd just woken up. When he saw Ken his eyebrows arched.

"What the hell happened to you?" David asked.

Only then did Ken consider how he must have looked. His clothes were rumpled and covered in filth; he'd spent the entire day in a room with no air conditioning so a good layer of grit had formed around his neck. Perspiration stains circled the fabric under his arms and across his chest. He was a mess, but David looked disheveled as well.

"Am I interrupting anything?" Ken asked.

"You look like you just got done wrestling a mummy."

"Can I come in?" Ken asked. "I mean, is everything okay? Are you busy?"

David yawned widely, covering his mouth with a fist. When it passed, he said, "Why don't we see if we can't have the same conversation? You are not interrupting. You can come in, and what the hell happened to you?"

"I'll tell you in a minute," Ken said. He jogged back to the cab and paid the driver.

Once he was inside David's house, the door closed and locked behind them, Ken asked for a glass of water. Now that his tension was eased, seeing David unharmed, he was becoming aware of his body's needs. Not only was he parched, he was starving, but for now, the water would do. He followed David to the kitchen and caught a plastic bottle David tossed at him while standing beside the open refrigerator.

"So," David said, making a squiggle line in the air with his finger. "What happened here?"

"I was at Travis's today."

"Alone? Are you nuts?"

"No," Ken said. "As it turns out, I'm not."

David scrunched his face, apparently trying to make sense of what Ken had just said. Having failed this, he settled for "You used to be a lot easier to talk to."

"I thought I might be able to figure some of this out if I went back there. And I did."

David leaned against the refrigerator, wearing an expression of cautious interest. He crossed his arms over his chest. "What did you find?"

"I was right," Ken said. "Travis is behind what's been happening."

David's eyes lit up. "He's alive?"

"No."

"I don't follow."

Ken didn't know what else to say. He was at a loss to explain the being that was both Travis Brugier and Vicki Bach. Even if he had managed to bring the diaries, he doubted that he would have been able to convince David of something so strange. He knew he couldn't finesse this kind of information. The truth was his only option, but even before he spoke he realized how ridiculous his explanation would sound.

"Travis died that night in Wonderland. He didn't fake his death, but he didn't have to. He knew he could come back."

"Okay," David said. He rubbed his eyes again. "I'm going to beg you to not do this to me tonight. I have had a shit day, after a shit night, after a shit week. Now, they caught that kid. He's in jail. So, for tonight, give it a rest. Tomorrow, we can wake up to a banquet of crazy if you want, but right now, I'm stuffed."

"David, there are some things you need to know."

"I'm sure that's true," David said, his tone sharp and sarcastic. "But tonight that's not an option. The options tonight are pizza, television, martinis, conversation about anything except Travis Brugier, and fucking. You mix and match those any way you see fit, or we can call that cab back here right now."

"I'm serious."

"So, am I," David replied, his voice a barely audible growl. "And I'm sick of you making me miserable."

The kitchen closed in on Ken. Fresh sweat popped up on his neck.

"Look, I'm sorry," David said. "But I need a break from all the Edgar Allen Poe crap. Everything has been too dark since you got back, and I'm tired of it. If we can't have a quiet evening together and enjoy each other's company, then you have to leave. And I'm not just talking about tonight."

Ken knew David well enough. He wasn't making a hollow threat. In fact, he was surprised David didn't just throw him out, because at the moment, he looked angry enough to chew nails. So Ken had to back off. At least if he was there, David wouldn't be alone. Maybe that would be enough.

"Whatever you want," Ken said.

"That is a phrase I need to hear a hell of a lot more often."

"You will," Ken said.

"Thank you." David crossed the kitchen and wrapped his

arms around Ken's neck. He kissed him lightly and pulled away. "I care a lot about you. You know that. You just have to quit making it so difficult."

Instead of replying, Ken leaned forward and kissed David hard on the mouth, pulling him tight. Familiar emotions—comfort and desire and so much love—welled in his chest. He clutched David tighter and let the taste of the man settle on his tongue.

After a minute, David stepped back and put a hand on Ken's chest. "Slow down, Buddy. Let's get some drinks and a little supper."

"I could use a shower."

"And brushing your teeth would be a bonus," David said with a smile. "I've got some work to clear up. It won't take long. You know where everything is."

Ken nodded, already unbuttoning his shirt. As he pulled it open, he noticed the Thorn around his neck, the chain catching light, the charm all but glowing. Opalescent and perverse, the bauble dangled teasingly.

Lifting the chain over his head, Ken crossed the room to the credenza. He dropped the Thorn amid the tangle of keys and paperclips on its surface.

Upstairs he called Paula while the water ran. He was grateful to hear her voice, though a pang of guilt, sharpened by Vicki's recent accusation accompanied it. Vicki had wanted to hurt him, and she'd succeeded, but only because her attack had become part of an ongoing battle: Ken versus his guilt. He'd often thought that Paula was holding on to an unrealistic hope of reconciliation. She'd never admit to it, of course, but the certainty had been with Ken for years.

Feeling awkward but trying to disguise it, Ken attempted a casual, even pleasant conversation with Paula. They'd released her from the hospital that morning as they'd planned, and her friend Esther, a perky and overly flirtatious woman, if Ken remembered correctly, had spent the day with her.

"She'll be here tonight," Paula said. "Burt is in Biloxi at a meeting, so we're having a girl's night."

"Is Jen there?"

"Yes. In her room, pouting again."

"What now?"

"She wanted to go out, and I thought it better if she stayed in. I'm feeling a little paranoid just now, and I want her where I can see her."

"That's a good idea," Ken said. "I'm going to want to talk to you both in the morning, if that's all right? Can I swing by?"

"I can't see why not. What's this about?"

"Vicki," Ken said. Again, he was faced with the fact that he'd never be able to explain, with any clarity or to any real effect what he'd discovered in Wonderland. "She's as involved as we thought."

"You're sure?"

"Yes," Ken said.

"What happened?" Paula asked.

"I can't explain right now." *You have to see my face and know I'm serious. Then, I can answer your questions, maybe make you believe.* "I'll tell you all about it tomorrow, but she is dangerous. So, be careful."

"We're not leaving the house."

He was surprised that Paula didn't demand more information, but she seemed to be in the same state of mind as David: She needed a night of relative peace. So, Ken said good night and hung up the phone.

Ken walked into the bathroom, which was thick with steam and stepped under the shower's spray to let it wash away the day's sweat and filth. He worked the soap into his skin and combed it through the hairs on his body, working up a thick lather while the hot water massaged his back.

One decision, Baby. And so much damage.

The voice filled his head, clear and crisp like the rapping of the water on the shower's tiles. The scent of the soap became sharp and pungent as if its floral perfume had been distilled from a rotted bouquet. Ken returned the soap to its holder and rested his head against the tiled wall.

How much of what Vicki had told him was true? He might never know. She'd needled his guilt, burdened him with mistakes he could no longer make right, but was it all just another layer to her cruelty, or had there been truth there? Despite the accuracy of what she'd said about Paula, Ken wasn't so easily convinced of her other charges. Had Bobby excelled for Ken's benefit, driven by a misguided sense of inadequacy? Had all of his boy's accomplishments been invalidated by Ken's absence? No. That was ridiculous. Bobby was a smart and talented kid. He would have been exceptional under any circumstances. She'd told him that Sam had expected a romance from him. When it went unrequited, he had fashioned a hatred for Ken, but there was no evidence to suggest this. They had always been close friends. Hadn't they?

The doubts Vicki raised made Ken furious. Wasn't it bad enough that he'd lost two remarkable people from his life? He already wore the guilt of their deaths like stones on his shoulders. Did he have to believe he'd failed them at every turn as well?

He scrubbed his face harshly, bringing a sting to his cheeks. He lathered his jaw with shaving cream and then reached for the razor David kept in the shower caddie. Changing the blades and setting the old head on the shelf, Ken gazed into the small round mirror attached to the wall by the showerhead. In the reflection, he saw David's body swinging behind him in the tiny shower stall. Ken spun, nearly losing his balance, barely catching himself with a palm against the tiled wall, but no corpse dangled at his back.

He pushed the image away and set to shaving, but the longer he stayed in the shower, the stronger his fears grew. He dragged the blade over his chin with a shaking hand. *David is standing on a ladder, attaching that wire to his ceiling.* He scraped the whiskers from his neck and rinsed his face hurriedly, ignoring the rough places. *David is slipping that glimmering cord around his neck. He'd do anything to stop them. Anything.* Ken reached for the knob with quaking hands to turn off the shower's spray. He had to stop this, had to stop…

David kicks away the small ladder. See how his weight crashes downward and the garrote tears through his throat. Blood splashes the room. Those beautiful eyes are fading, darkening, dying. His body is shaking. His bloated tongue pushes against dead lips. Remember how those lips tasted? How would they taste now?

Frantic, Ken pulled aside the shower curtain.

David's gone. And there's nothing you can do. Nothing.

"I thought I'd come up," David said, pulling his shirt over his head and draping it on the doorknob. "Dinner can wait a while."

His panic disappeared as if caught beyond a slamming door. So powerful was Ken's relief that he found himself leaning against the wall for support.

David's chest flexed as he unbuttoned his slacks and let them fall to the damp floor. His muscular legs, covered in a fine brush of hair, stepped free of the garment at his feet. White jockey shorts gleamed against his dark skin. Already erect, his cock made a significant ridge in the fabric. David stepped forward and removed a towel from the rod by the shower. He ran the cloth over Ken's shoulders, chest, and belly and then dropped it on the floor. A moment later, his lips followed the same path, over the pectorals and to the stomach and then upward. He caught a nipple in his mouth and teased it gently with his teeth and his tongue, wrapping his arms tightly around Ken's back.

Ken returned the embrace and coaxed David upward so they could kiss and Ken could feel the weight of his body, alive and undamaged, against him. Ken stepped forward, guiding the man toward the vanity. He slid the underwear from David's hips and pushed forward, pinning David against the sink. The hair on the man's chest padded Ken as he leaned in to taste David's tongue, his hands sliding along the muscled back. He pulled David away from the counter and cupped his ass as his tongue explored the panting mouth.

When they reached the bedroom, they fell on the bed. Ken pinned David, rubbing his erection along the man's belly and burying his face in the warmth of David's neck. Strong legs wrapped around his hips, and Ken pushed David's head back into the pillows for another chance to kiss him.

In no hurry for release, they held each other, tasted and teased each other's skin. Every shifting of their torsos and reaching of their arms was anticipated and exciting. Ken became wholly lost in the familiar shape and tone and texture of David's body, the scent of fresh perspiration on the man's skin, the low groans of pleasure rumbling in his throat.

When he entered David, David's eyes closed. Ken pressed forward and kissed him again. His lips were met with a gasp, and Ken remained perfectly still until David's eyes opened and the man's hands pulled strongly against his back. Ken began a slow rhythm with his hips, and together they eased their way toward climax.

Afterward, he held David. Neither man moved, hoping that the moment wouldn't be driven away by motion.

⚜

They sat on the sofa. David had cleared away the empty pizza box and the plates, refreshed their drinks, and now reclined against Ken's chest.

For Ken, it was a warm and long-missed intimacy. Sitting there with David's comforting weight against him, he could almost convince himself that their past had been mended. It wasn't, of course; it couldn't be that simple. They were on the right track, though, and Ken thought they might actually have a chance.

"I'm not going to leave again," he said.

"I don't remember inviting you to move in," David replied.

"Don't be a smart-ass. You know what I mean."

David didn't answer immediately. When he did, he measured his words carefully. "Take it slow, Kenny," he said, rubbing his palm over Ken's stomach. "You've got a lot of things to work out, and who your next boyfriend is going to be should be pretty low on that list."

Maybe David was just being flip; Ken didn't know for certain. He hoped that he wasn't alone in the way he felt.

"I love you, David."

"I love you too." David patted Ken's stomach. "And right now, alone, that's easy to hold on to. Tomorrow, when everything else comes rushing back, it might not be. We'll see. Just take it slow. There's plenty of time. I'm not going anywhere."

28

Vicki hated the end of things. After so many years, the passing of people and events still had its melancholy sting. She was nearly through with Ken. By this same time tomorrow night, she'd have finished his lesson, and then it would be time to move on. He might hunt her, try to exact some pitiful revenge, but she doubted he'd make the effort. He'd be too busy pitying his lot and burying his loved ones.

She walked through the dark and quiet streets of the Bywater, a district of Orleans Parish that didn't benefit from tourist dollars. She looked over the crumbling façades of homes and felt the river moving very near. A light breeze shook the treetops but stayed too high above to cool her neck. Two men walked behind her. They were trying to look casual but were clumsy and obvious. They'd do just fine.

In thinking about Ken and the end of things, she was reminded of a woman named Charity (a trait that was so lacking from the woman's countenance it was laughable). This was long ago, before this country was even a country. Vicki had been a man then, named John, like all around him had been named John.

Charity was his wife, and her cruelty had often confused John, even when it was directed at others.

The woman, a plump hag, found no greater joy than spreading mischief and misery. Being Charity's husband, John knew this all too well as his pain had amused her on innumerable occasions, from her insults about his manhood to her disdain at his meager landholdings.

Late in their relationship, John had forged a brittle truce with his wife by showing her his talent for thought pictures. He'd toyed with the gift for years, for lives in fact, but had never quite managed its subtleties. Still, in order to direct his wife's energy away from persecution, he had taken to entertaining Charity with fanciful scenes.

He'd conjure for her flights of pink birds, swirling and dancing in the rafters of their house or make a field of daisies sprout from its floor. He enjoyed these simple images, but Charity's predilections ran to darker subjects. She demanded perverse amusements like seeing Minister John sobbing on his hands and knees, being raped by the biggest, ugliest men in the village. Charity wanted to see Frances Goode bleed out from her privates and crumple on the floor, at which time Charity would stand and cross the room to kick the illusion's head, laughing and demeaning the figment with each cruel stomp of her foot.

Were this the extent of Charity's unwholesome behavior John could have endured it, but his wife was never satisfied. She insisted he paint thought pictures, terrible and nightmarish images, for their neighbors. At first, he refused, offering instead to manufacture their torment in the confines of their home whenever Charity requested. The bargain had no validity, of course, because he was already doing this very thing for her.

In the end, he relented. At her direction, he sent madness to the village in the form of grotesque beasts, devil's spawn, and rampaging animals. Men saw their wives dancing naked under moonlight, and children saw their parents coupling with demons.

When the trials began, Charity was the fourth woman to be

charged as a witch. On a night of God's wrath storm, with the trails and roads already flooding, the court came for John's wife. He did not fight them, nor did he say any farewell to Charity. She tried to put the guilt on him, where in fact it belonged, but the court was deaf to her words, lest she cast them under a spell.

John hid in the shadows beside the blacksmith shop, saturated to the bone by beating rain. The court stripped Charity and bound her to a post, foregoing a courtroom façade for her. They whipped her unconscious, lacerating her breasts and belly, feeding the storm with her blood. They passed their sentence then. Amid flashes of angry lightning, they cut her from the post and dragged her out of the square, toward the hanging tree in the wood. John followed.

Charity regained consciousness when her binds fell and cried out, scratching at her captors and begging for her husband to use his magic to lay them low. But John had had enough of his wife. He turned his back on her, and returned home to spend the remainder of his life in peace.

Vicki paused on the sidewalk. The men behind her were getting braver, less cautious about the volume of their voices and the rapping of their footsteps; they intended to rape her. How amusing.

Resuming her stride, she made a right at the intersection, knowing it would take her to a vacant plot of land separating the neighborhood from the Mississippi River. No streetlights here. No interruptions. A black stretch of ground rose up to become a low hillock.

As she led the young men away from the street, grass *shush*ing beneath her shoes, Vicki wondered what had brought Charity to mind. She'd been thinking about Ken, and without warning Charity had been there. Odd. The two were near opposites in every way: gender, social status, aesthetics, temperament. In fact the only trait they seemed to share was a covetous nature. Maybe that was what linked them in Vicki's mind: Charity coveting the comfort and happiness of her neighbors; Ken coveting a pristine duality in which he sought the best of both worlds, while proving himself worthy of neither.

Vicki wanted to explore this thought further, but the boys at her back were moving toward her rapidly. It would have to wait.

She turned to face them. The boys were obviously college students from good homes, out for a wild night and a bit of felony to make them feel alive. They wore expensive shirts with horse logos and khaki shorts—clothes that were more appropriate for a clambake than a night of violence—but Vicki knew that they'd been out drinking. She also knew that they'd reached a point of harmonic malevolence. Neither boy left to his own devices would have presented the slightest threat, but when brought together, something dark catalyzed and engulfed them. This union spawned a dangerous creature with a single mind focused on base and destructive ambitions.

As she'd suspected, they'd do just fine.

"Can I help you boys?" Vicki asked, running her eyes up and down their bodies. First she checked the taller boy, the one with the brown hair and the white-as-snow smile. The other boy, not nearly as attractive but made more ambitious for it, licked his lips.

The taller boy spoke first. "We want to get our dicks wet," he said.

"Charming," Vicki replied.

The other boy, the unfortunate one with the porcine features and kinky, rust-colored hair, snorted a laugh. "And we chose you for the honor."

"I'm flattered, Gentlemen," Vicki said, "but this isn't about getting your tiny little rocks off, is it? This is about showing off, challenging your entitled existence with a shot of mischief. Just angry little boys trying to prove they're men, trying to show who's the boss."

"Fine," the taller boy said, losing his smile. His hands reached down to the button of his shorts. "You want me to show you?"

"Oh, no," Vicki said, stepping forward. "Me first."

29

David drank his coffee hoping the caffeine would charge his exhausted system. He heard the water forcing itself through the pipes in his wall upstairs where Ken was showering. His second meeting with Laray had been postponed until two that afternoon, so he had the morning to kill, and he might even be able to grab a quick nap around noon if his fatigued mind required it.

Though Ken had kept his word and had made no reference to Wonderland or its owner, David's dreams had been filled with the place. He pictured himself in Brugier's Parlor, dismal and reeking, and walking through the infested remains of Brugier's home, avoiding the roaches and beetles that scurried at his feet. When he'd awakened in a panic for the third time around four thirty, he'd felt the tiny creatures dancing over his skin. They had gotten caught in the hair on his chest and pubis. He'd brushed himself frantically, but a quick survey of his body revealed no hungry insects. He was only touched by remnants of dream.

The water stopped moaning through the pipes. David stood and poured himself a second cup of coffee. He filled a mug for

Ken and dropped in two heaping spoonfuls of sugar. He sat the mug across from him at the dinette table and waited.

A few minutes later, Ken came into the kitchen dressed in a pair of blue jeans and a black Polo knit, clothes he'd left at David's over two years ago. He kissed David and looked around the kitchen as if someone had just called his name. His eyes settled on the table. "This mine," he asked indicating the mug.

"I'm not expecting anyone else."

A heavy silence hung between them then. The two made eye contact and broke it quickly as neither seemed able to find a suitable topic of conversation. Finally, Ken grasped his mug with both hands and caught David's eye. "What's your morning like?"

"Wide open," he said as he tried to decipher the strange look in Ken's eyes. "I've got a meeting in the CBD at two. Beyond that, I'm free. What's going on?"

"I have to see Paula this morning. I spoke to her last night." Ken seemed uncomfortable with the words. He looked back into his mug and then tapped a finger rhythmically against its side. "I'd like you to come with me."

"Are you sure?" David asked.

"Yes," Ken told him. "You said you'd be ready for a banquet of crazy today, and I've got one for you. More importantly, I've got to stop trying to juggle everything. If I don't, something terrible is going to happen, again."

⚜

David turned the Mercedes into the drive of Paula Nicholson's house and parked in front of the garage. His stomach crept into his throat as he killed the engine. Ken hurried from the car and met David at the bottom of the stairs leading to the back porch.

"Are you okay with this?" David asked. "I can come back and pick you up later if you'd rather."

"You don't want to come in?" Ken cocked his head to the side. He squinted as if trying to see David through some sudden mist.

"I just want to make sure you're comfortable with this."

"Well, David, I'm not comfortable." He delivered the information with a calm resolve in his voice. "If this were a comfortable prospect, I would have done it a long time ago, but you were right the day of Bobby's funeral: My life is in pieces, and I'm the one who's kept it broken. That's stopping today."

David nodded his head and followed Ken up the back porch. Paula Nicholson came out of the kitchen. Her right arm was in a sling, and she looked tired, but beyond that she didn't seem too badly hurt. When David came into sight, Paula slowed. A thin smile flashed over her lips as a precursor to the confusion that quickly replaced it. David wondered what mask covered his own face? He felt himself smiling, but did the expression appear silly, kind, or just awkward?

"Paula," Ken said, "this is David Lane."

"David," Paula said. Her eyes ran back and forth between the two men almost as if waiting for them to attack. "Pleased to meet you."

As for himself, David felt a weight drop into his stomach. He'd often wondered what this moment might be like. Now that the event had come to pass, it proved just as awkward as he'd always imagined.

Ken hugged Paula gently, accommodating the slung arm. "You okay?" he asked.

"Fine," she said. "You just missed Esther, but I've got coffee on. Let's go into the kitchen."

They passed through a small mudroom and into a slightly larger laundry room that opened into the brightly lit, well-maintained kitchen. Black and white tiles checkered the floor and disappeared beneath gleaming modern appliances and sleek white cabinets. David took in as much of the room as he could without appearing to pry.

"Where's Jen'?" Ken asked, leaning over the threshold to peer into the dining room.

"Still in her room," Paula told him. "Apparently, the world

sucks, and I'm its queen. I hope you don't mind, but it's serve yourself today."

"What?" Ken asked.

"The coffee."

"I'll get it," David said locating the pot on the counter. He found mugs in the cupboard above and reached for the small sugar bowl next to the coffee maker.

"At least she's home," Ken said. "I don't like the idea of her roaming the streets with Vicki out there. In fact, when we get done here, I'm going to make some calls. If the police won't take this seriously, I'm going to hire a couple of off-duty cops or find a personal protection agency to keep an eye on your two until this passes."

"Do you really think Vicki is going to try anything else?" David asked. "I'd think she'd be running to the hills now that her accomplice is in custody."

"She'll try something," Ken said without hesitation. "The police don't scare her, and she isn't done with us."

"Why?" Paula asked. "What did we do to her? What does she want?"

"To get to me," Ken said. David watched him stand and circle the dinette so that he faced both Paula and himself. "Do you believe in reincarnation?"

"What?" Paula asked, shooting a curious glance at David as if relinquishing her answer to him.

"Not really," David replied.

"Can you accept the idea of reincarnation for argument's sake?"

"I suppose. But what's this all about?"

"In a minute. Let's say reincarnation exists, and let's say that every time you come back, you remember your previous lives, not in a New Agey kind of way, where you get impressions or memory flashes, but complete and total conscious recollection. Just like you never died at all but rather went to sleep one night and when you woke, you were a baby, newborn, with a completely different body."

"So basically, you could live forever," David said. "Not immortal in body, but still immortal."

"Exactly."

"Having assumed this, then what?" Paula asked.

"I know who Vicki Bach is. I knew her years ago, and I know what she wants."

"You knew her?" Paula asked. "And you never said anything?"

"It didn't make any sense at the time," Ken said. "Travis Brugier killed himself thirty years ago, and now he's back as Vicki Bach."

"Insane," Paula replied, her voice thick with derision.

"Absolutely," Ken said. "But it's also true. Everything that's happened to Bobby and Sam and you is part of Brugier's plan, a plan he's been committed to carrying out for over thirty years.'

"Impossible."

David listened to the exchange but added nothing to it. Ken had promised a banquet of crazy and was certainly delivering on his word, but David wasn't ready to write him off just yet. He'd scoffed at Ken's conspiracy theory before, only to arrive in front of this very house and see that, indeed, something dangerous was at work.

"It's not impossible," Ken said. "It should be, but it isn't. I thought Brugier was insane when he told me about all of this years ago. And don't get me wrong, Travis is insane, but he's also powerful. He killed himself because it meant nothing. He knew he'd come back, knew that he could find me. He'd made enough arrangements to assure finding me, but he didn't count on me moving to Austin. So, Vicki Bach dated Bobby, even accepted his marriage proposal. Then, she had Chuck Baxter attack him so I would have to come back."

"Why?" Paula asked. "Why not just track you down to Austin, finish things there?"

"Because I don't care about anything in Austin."

"And this doesn't strike you as the least bit nuts?"

"Fuck," Ken said, exasperated and growing angry. "When I was eighteen years old, I offended this thing. I left it at the altar, so to speak. Now it's paying me back."

David shook his head and finally joined the conversation. "Okay, why now? Why you? After so much time, wouldn't he have found someone before if he had wanted to?"

"He did," Ken said. "I found a book, and I think that it tells the story of his first attempt to change someone. I think it might also tell us how to stop him. But there's more. He's able to do things, to make you see things. He can get inside your head. It's a game to him."

"Him?" Paula asked. "I thought we were talking about Vicki?"

"We are but..." he let the sentence drift off. "But we're also talking about Travis Brugier."

Ken's conviction needled at David. He could see how easily Ken's fantasy had formed, particularly in light of his earlier relationship with Brugier. It took only a simple twist of the facts to arrive at Ken's conclusions. Still, impossible was impossible.

"Let's take Brugier out of this," David said. "For now, let's just stay focused on Vicki Bach. You're telling us that she's dangerous. Fine. I think we can accept that."

"Okay," Ken said, sounding dejected. "Ignore everything else. Vicki is dangerous, and she isn't likely to be alone."

Paula made a small throaty sound next to him. Ken and David both looked at her.

"Will you accept that?" Ken asked of her. "Put the rest of this out of your mind. Will you at least believe Bach is capable of serious harm?"

"She's already proven that to me," Paula said coolly.

"So," David said, "what are we going to do now?"

"I'm going to find her."

Jennifer's voice startled them. They'd all been so focused on each other, they hadn't noticed her enter the room.

"Why can't you leave her alone?" she cried.

David's heart jumped into his throat, and he turned to see a rather plain girl, her features twisted with rage, standing in the archway between the kitchen and the dining room. Ken spilled coffee down the front of his shirt as he spun, and Paula jumped to her feet next to him.

"She didn't do anything," Jennifer continued. "She loved Bobby. She loved him a lot more than you two ever did." Jennifer's face burned red. "You two think you know so much, but you don't. She was as afraid of Chuck as anyone. He threatened her! Said he'd kill her. Maybe she just wants to be left alone. Did you ever think of that? Just leave her alone."

"How do you know this?" Ken asked.

"None of your business!"

"Jennifer," Ken's voice rose. "Do you know where she is?"

"Fuck off," Jennifer screeched.

Then the girl spun around and ran through the dining room, tearing a path across the house to the front door, which opened and slammed behind her before any of the adults in the room could move.

Ken's paralysis broke first, and he set off after his daughter. Paula, turned to David, "I'm so sorry you had to hear that." But David was already on his feet and chasing Ken out of the kitchen. He followed Ken through the living room and forced himself to run faster. In a full sprint by the time he reached the front door, David came to a stumbling halt as he tried to understand the scene before his eyes.

A thunderstorm raged beyond the porch, but it wasn't like any storm David had seen before. The raindrops pelting the ground were silver cast and dangerous looking, like shards of metal. These silver drops played against a screen of charcoal-gray mist that climbed through the storm toward pitch-black skies. Dark forms, men in black coats and broad-brimmed hats, trudged down the center of the street, which was already flooding, the metallic water running like a river of mercury. Lightning flashed over the house across the street, and its electricity rode the rain, spreading out in a brilliant aurora that covered the houses, the yards, and the road in blue-white light. The thunderclap that followed exploded in David's ear, and he leapt back, a sharp curse flying from his lips. The air crackled with static and sizzled, raising all of the hairs on David's body.

"David!"

He snapped his head around and saw Ken at his side, wearing an angry expression and a sweat-beaded brow.

The next bolt of lightning zagged into an oak farther down the road, exploding the tree into a thousand burning twigs, which were quickly extinguished by the downpour. But in its flash, David saw the figures in the road. Six hard-faced men, dressed in the black of puritans, dragged a stout woman through the silvery river. She was naked, exposing her ample breasts and belly, which were torn with the deep gashes of a lash. Her tangled white hair fell over her face like a tattered cowl. She kicked at the rising tide and clawed at the men hunched over her. Her screeching protests rode the crackling air before the second bolt of thunder deafened David to her pleas.

Strong hands came to his shoulders, and Ken shook him. "David?"

"You were right, weren't you?" David muttered. Even without the pilgrims and their witch, he couldn't believe what he was seeing. The skies had been blue and clear when they'd entered the house less than twenty minutes ago. A storm, regardless of its peculiar and disturbing elements, just wasn't possible.

"Yes, this is his doing," Ken said. "We need the car, now, before Jennifer gets too far away. Where are the keys?"

"How are you going to drive through this?"

"Just give me the keys."

He dug in his pocket absently until his fingers wrapped around the key chain. He pulled it free and handed the keys over to Ken. The awesome and violent storm continued to draw his attention.

"Oh, my Lord," Paula cried from the door. "Ken, where the hell do you think you're going?"

David caught movement from the corner of his eye, turned,

and saw Ken running back into the house. *He's going to get the car,* David wanted to say but couldn't force himself to speak. With her face full of frantic expectation and questions, Paula looked at him. *She really is an incredibly beautiful woman,* David thought. He had no answers for her, so he turned back to the pelting mercury, the gloom, and the dark figures moving within.

The six puritans and their captive were far down the road, now barely visible, merely smudges against the gloom. The gush of water and the rapping of the drops feeding it filled his ears so he could no longer hear the panicked woman. He smelled the moist air, tinged with the fecund odor of a forest and the scent of salt as if they were near the ocean.

David walked across the porch, reached out from under its shelter and felt water tapping his fingers, his palm, and his wrist. The cuff of his shirt turned dark with absorbed liquid.

"It came up so fast," Paula said, standing close to him. "And Jennifer ran right into it. My God, she's going to be soaked."

"Sure," David said, seeing no benefit in challenging the woman's denial. She might not have seen the pilgrims and their witch. She could have attributed the metallic tinge of the rain to any number of meteorological anomalies, but David suspected it was fear that drove Paula to rationalization. "We'll go find her."

"Thank you," Paula said quietly. "She couldn't have gotten too far in this."

"I'm sure you're right."

His Mercedes rolled into view from the side of the house, and Ken honked the horn. David said good-bye to Paula, hunched low against the brutal weather, and ran down the porch stairs toward the car.

⚜

Ken stared out the windshield searching the neighborhood but could see little through the thick storm. A car rode his bumper, the horn bleating in rapid bursts. Of course, the driver of that car was not caught in the same squall as Ken. He reached across the seat and touched David's shoulder. David jerked slightly at the touch and then sighed deeply.

"What's happening here?" David asked.

"Travis," Ken said simply.

"So, it's not really raining?"

"No," Ken told him. "I told you, it's one of his talents. He can get in your head. This is what he was doing to me a year ago. He made me watch you die more than once. Since I've been back, he's done a lot worse."

"But I felt the rain."

"I know, but it isn't there."

"He can create any fucking nightmare he wants, and it's all real to whoever goes through it?" David sounded beaten and tired.

"Yes."

"So," David said, "I might not even be sitting here. I could still be at home in bed, and the whole morning has just been a little skit your friend is running through my head. Or, you're still in Austin, and everything that's happened in the last week has all been a mind fuck, a virtual reality game without an Off switch. Is that what you're telling me?"

"David, don't," Ken said, hearing the panic in David's voice. "He can't alter things indefinitely; there'd be no way for him to sustain it."

But did Ken believe that? Even he had begun to wonder how much of his life, how many of his thoughts, were actually his own. That morning, he'd woken up and seen David, and his first thought had been how completely fortunate he was that something so unlikely as their reconciliation should happen. From that wonderful thought, nagging doubts began to grow, but he had quelled them, put them away. He had to have some control over his life, or else nothing he did mattered.

"Any chance you feel like taking the family on a vacation, really far from here?" David asked.

Ken shook his head. "Not now. Not with Jennifer gone. But you can leave, David. You can get away from here until this is settled. Go to my house in Austin, go to London or Florence, just name the place, and I'll send you."

"He wouldn't let me leave if I wanted to," David said. "Besides I don't want to."

"Look around, David," said Ken as he twisted the wheel to pull the car to the curb so the anxious driver behind him could pass. "Do you really think there's anything you can do? I'm not sure there's anything I can do at this point, but I have to stay. You don't."

"Shut up and drive," David told him.

The beating rain stopped. The mist and gloom, the river they'd been driving through dried up and faded. The sun burst bright on the hood of the car, illuminating the yards and homes of the Garden District. The street before them was dry, and the spatters on the windshield vanished.

"Thank God," David said with a sigh.

Ken pulled away from the curb. He wasn't as pleased about the sudden cessation of the weather. If it had come to an end, it meant that Vicki saw no need to continue with its distraction. Though the idea made him nauseous, Ken couldn't help but believe that Jennifer was already with Vicki, somewhere that Ken was unlikely to find them.

Ten minutes later, they drove into the Quarter, and fifteen minutes after that, they wandered through the musty atmosphere of Brugier's Wonderland.

In the upstairs hall, David paused in front of a painting, squinting to make sense of the image beneath the dust. "Is that a Gauguin?"

"Yes," Ken said, keeping an eye on the door at the end of the hall.

"And it's just been hanging here for thirty years?"

"David, come on."

Their footsteps *shush*ed along the carpet runner on the landing. Next to him, David wore an expression of awe as he took in Brugier's treasures. Every few steps, though, David would pause, look down, and search the floor.

"How does he do it?" David asked.

"Do what?" Ken asked, poking his head into the master bedroom. The chamber was empty, just as he'd left it the previous evening.

"Get into your head?"

"I don't know," Ken admitted. The tales he'd read in Travis's storybook only referenced the growth of this skill, not its mechanics. "He used to call them thought pictures. A long time ago, that may have been all they were."

"Did you ever wonder why he chose you?" David asked.

Ken let the question roll over him. He stood across the room at the doors to the balcony, holding the handles. Unsure of his response, he whispered, "All the time," and pulled open the French doors to reveal the balcony and courtyard below.

The concrete fountain, its cracked basin filled with scum the color of cooked spinach stood in the center of the flagstones. Overgrowth crept along the stones. Across the court, the smaller building, Travis's Parlor, stood dark and ominous.

David walked to his side and leaned forward on the wrought-iron rail. When he spoke, his tone was matter-of-fact, without a hint of false consolation. "You can't blame yourself for what's happening. No matter what Vicki does, it's not your fault. There's nothing you could have done to deserve this."

Ken wanted to believe that but couldn't. Travis had to have seen something—ambition, hunger, hubris—that had set Ken apart. There had to have been some element, perhaps deep and dark, that had drawn Travis to him.

"Hey," David said, snaking his arm around Ken's waist. "You didn't ask for this."

Unable to agree, Ken said, "We should keep looking."

With heavy concern in his eyes, David nodded and stepped back from the rail. He patted Ken's back with three light raps and returned to the bedroom.

They searched the remaining rooms speaking little. Ken's thoughts drew him inward, away from David and his consolation.

Each new room, abandoned and empty, layered in filth, reminded Ken of a decision, a failure. His life was filled with such rooms. Once occupied by friends, family, David, and a host of forgotten romantic partners, the house Ken had built for himself looked hardly different from Travis's dilapidated estate.

By the time they ended their search back in the foyer, despair had ensnared him. His daughter was missing, and he could spend days searching for her. Who knew what manner of horror she'd endure as he wandered impotently through this house, this city? A lifetime of faults accumulated on his neck and shoulders, driving shivs into his back to pierce his lungs and heart. The search was futile.

"Where to?" David asked.

"I don't know," Ken admitted. Vicki could hold up in any hotel, or she might have bought a new house. The possible locations were overwhelming. "She could be anywhere by now."

Something he said triggered a look of surprise from David. He jerked his left arm up to read his watch. His face relaxed immediately.

"Forgot about my meeting," he said. "But I've got a couple of hours yet. I'll get you back to Paula's before I head home."

⚜

For the second time in three days, the sight of a police car greeted David as he made the turn onto Paula's street. It sat, lights dead, in the drive of her house. He pulled to the curb and left the engine idling.

Next to him, Ken said, "She called the police." He stated this information as a banal fact, like driving directions.

He doesn't think they can help, David thought, making his own sense of unease tingle and spark.

Despair had hung over Ken since they'd stepped onto the grounds of Wonderland and had intensified with every step they'd taken through the filthy place. Ken felt guilty for bringing Travis Brugier into the lives of his family, and though David considered this guilt misplaced, he understood, but there was more at work. David sensed that Ken had given up, had finally crumbled; this sense covered him like a magnetic field, drawing his own hopelessness to the surface.

"I'm going to head out," he said. "I don't have time to talk to those guys, and I really don't have anything to tell them."

"That's fine," Ken said.

"Jennifer is going to be okay."

"Thank you," Ken told him, wrapping a warm hand around David's wrist. "I hate you running off like this. Can you cancel the meeting?"

"I could, but I won't. Once this is over, I'll still need to make a living. I'll call you as soon as I'm done. After that, I don't have anything else scheduled for the week."

"Be careful," Ken told him.

"Consider it done."

Back at his house, David showered and changed into his favorite gray Armani suit. He ran a brush through his hair and left the bedroom. Downstairs he searched the living room until he came across his briefcase. He set this on the credenza and noticed the strange necklace Travis Brugier had given Ken. David lifted the ornament and dangled it in the air. He'd have to get this back to Ken, he thought. David shoved the Thorn into his pocket and returned to the contents of his briefcase. Having all of the papers he needed for his meeting, David closed the case.

A thick roach ran across his hand, rushing for the shadows at the back of the credenza. David slammed his fist down painfully on the smooth surface, but he'd missed the creature.

"Gonna have to spray," he whispered to himself.

They'll take you alive or screamin'. Thanks Uncle Joe.

David lifted the case off of the furniture and walked into his kitchen. He retrieved some cold cuts and a jar of mustard from the refrigerator. He slapped some salami on a slice of wheat bread, gave it a thick frosting of mustard, and squished the top slice of bread onto the meat. He poured himself a glass of cranberry juice and sat at the dinette table. He'd have to clean the crumbs off of the counter before he left. He didn't need to be feeding any unwanted houseguests. David lifted the sandwich to his mouth and stopped before taking a bite.

How many Flesh Eaters you think fall into a commercial sausage press?

He considered the texture of his sandwich meat. God only knew what those little specks were. They were supposed to be pork and spices, but what else might have slipped in?

"Marvelous," he hissed and dropped the sandwich on the plate. He finished his cranberry juice and stared at his unappealing lunch. "Screw it," he said. He lifted the sandwich and carried it to the disposal. After grinding away the questionable meal, he sprayed his counter and the tabletop with disinfectant and wiped up all sign of crumbs with a wad of paper towel.

David hoisted his briefcase from the table and left the house.

30

Ken found Paula pacing in the living room. She was speaking with the two detectives who had handled Paula's and Bobby's attacks while a uniformed officer looked on from beside the television set. His arms were crossed, his face blank. The slender detective—Ogilvie, Ken remembered—stood behind the sofa, and his partner, the stockier Reilly, took notes beside him. They all looked up, startled, when Ken entered the room.

Ken nodded to the men and raised his hand in a low wave.

Paula turned on her heels and rushed to him. Her skin, always pale, was now white. Trails of tears stained her cheeks beneath pink eyes.

"You didn't find her?"

"Not yet," Ken said. "Did you try her cell phone?"

"About fifty times; it goes directly into voice mail."

"Mr. Nicholson," Ogilvie said, breaking away from his partner to round the sofa. "Can you tell us which direction your daughter was headed when you last saw her?"

"I didn't see her once she left the house," he said. He reached out an arm and wrapped it around Paula's back, giving her a tight hug and feeling the tremble of her body beneath his hand. "David and I searched the blocks around here, and we drove into the Quarter, but we didn't find anything."

"Why did you go to the Quarter?" Ogilvie asked.

Ken hesitated. He didn't know how much Paula had already told the men. Had she told them that he knew Vicki Bach? Worse still, had she told them Ken's improbable story about Travis Brugier?

Before a functional lie formed in his head, Paula rescued him by saying, "She always goes there when she's upset."

Ogilvie nodded, and Reilly scribbled on his notepad.

"Does your daughter have friends there, anyone we can speak to?" Ogilvie asked.

"Not that I'm aware of," Ken said.

"Mrs. Nicholson," Ogilvie said, "you called this in as a kidnapping. Isn't that correct?"

"Yes."

"But there's no real proof of a crime. Your daughter ran away after a family dispute."

Paula tensed against Ken. He felt her prickling energy course through his body like a charge.

"That's correct," Paula said, using the measured voice she reserved for her family when she was furious. "But Detective Ogilvie, Jennifer has been in contact with Vicki for weeks, maybe months. Somehow, Vicki was able to convince Jennifer that she had nothing to do with Chuck, that she was just an innocent bystander who happened to know a psycho with a lead pipe. I don't know what lies Vicki told her, but Jennifer believed them. That makes my daughter naïve and foolish. She's a child, so she has that right. You do *not*. You have known about this woman since my son was attacked, and you haven't done one damned thing about it."

"Mrs. Nicholson," Ogilvie said with a tone meant to soothe.

"I am not finished," Paula said, pulling away from Ken and marching toward the detective. She was crying again, but the tears made her seem no less imposing. "You haven't done anything, and now I have a second child at the mercy of that woman. So, don't read me passages from your rulebook. Jennifer is with Vicki Bach. Now, you go find that bitch and bring my daughter home!"

Both Ogilvie and his partner flinched. Ken looked at the uniformed officer by the television, but his expression had not changed.

Reilly, who Ken imagined was rarely given the chance to speak during such interviews walked around the sofa, approaching Paula. "I'm sorry," he said. "I know this is impossible for you."

"Do you?" Paula snapped.

Reilly dropped his arm so that his notebook hung at his side. "I lost my daughter four years ago."

The detective's eyes weighed with compassion, but it wasn't a performance meant to comfort hysterical loved ones. It was warm and sincere. Ken was touched to see it.

"I'm sorry," Paula said.

"Thank you," Reilly replied. "What we know about Vicki Bach is that she's using her real name. She's twenty-nine years old and originally from Phoenix. Her father was a prominent banker in the Southwest, and her mother was a physician. Both parents were killed in an automobile accident ten years ago. Since then, Victoria Bach has held no employment outside of heading a philanthropic organization she created called The Wonderland Foundation..."

Ken's focus on the stout detective intensified when he heard those words.

"The foundation provides food, shelter, and counseling to runaways and homeless children. She has no criminal record, yet. Her last known address was here in New Orleans, where she rented a house on Burgundy Street. She let the lease expire eleven months ago, and her whereabouts since then have been unknown." Reilly paused and tapped the notebook against his leg. "I'm sorry we didn't tell you all of this before, but considering the nature of our investigation we thought it best."

The information seemed to calm Paula. Though not at ease, she appeared more controlled with the knowledge that the police were not sitting idle.

"We have two problems here," Reilly continued. "The first is that Victoria Bach, up until now, has been a model citizen. Her foundation has donated over a million dollars and helped a lot of kids."

"That doesn't mean anything," Paula said.

"Maybe not. But outside of you and your husband's statements, we have no evidence linking Vicki Bach to Chuck Baxter. I'm not saying they weren't working together; we just can't find anything to prove it. We're doing what we can to track her down, but it's going to take some time."

"You can't expect us to sit around and wait," Paula said.

"No," Reilly told her, his voice warm and measured. "I can ask you to let us do our job, and I can suggest you try to stay calm until we find something. But I don't expect you to take that advice. I know I wouldn't."

"Hey," Ogilvie said, disturbed by an obvious breach of procedure.

"Give it a rest, Mort," Reilly said. He turned back to Paula and clasped the notebook in both hands so that it hung just below his belt. "I believe Vicki Bach is dangerous. I don't want anyone else to get hurt. So, I have to trust that neither of you is going to do anything rash."

Ken watched this exchange. He saw the expression on the burly detective's face flicker from concern to earnest warning and back to compassion in a matter of seconds. The man was showing Paula that he took this seriously, even personally. The approach was not only kind, it was effective.

Paula's posture eased. She nodded her head and wiped her eyes with two graceful sweeps of a finger.

"We're going to go," Reilly said. "You have my card, and I want you to use it if you hear anything. We'll check back with you later this afternoon."

Ken met Paula on the porch. She appeared calmer. She sat on the padded bench beneath the window, a mug of coffee clutched in her good hand. The front door stood wide open, and Ken imagined it was so Paula could hear the phone should it ring.

"She'll be all right. At least, for a while," Ken said. He wasn't attempting to ease Paula's mind, though he hoped he might. He really believed that in the short term their daughter would not be harmed. If he understood the gist of Jennifer's tirade, then Vicki had had numerous opportunities to hurt his daughter over the last few weeks, and yet Jen remained certain that Vicki was her friend. Jennifer was obviously more valuable to the woman as an ally. "Travis— I'm sorry. I mean Vicki is using her to manipulate me. I don't know how yet, but it won't be too long before we find out."

Paula leaned back against the windowsill and cocked her head at him. Ken squirmed under her appraisal. She was reading his face again. "Why didn't you ever tell me that you lived in the Quarter before you started school in Texas?"

"Because I couldn't handle what happened here. I wanted to bury it."

"So why did you move us back here?"

"You know why," Ken said. "I was recruited by..."

"You were approached by a lot of companies Ken. And only one of them was in New Orleans. Why'd you come back, and why did we stay? You could have put your company together anywhere. In fact, Texas was a much better place for it from a business standpoint. You could have gone anywhere in the country, but you came back here."

"What are you trying to say? That I planned all of this?"

"No," Paula said. "I was just thinking about everything that's happened and the story you told me about Travis Brugier. I'm wondering if maybe he planned this."

"What?"

"Did it ever occur to you that maybe Brugier accounted for your future? They offered you far more than even you were worth."

"No," Ken said. This much he couldn't believe, and yet he did; the truth of it sank in like a doctor's prognosis of malignancy. Brugier had done his best to ensure that Ken came back, back to the beginning. He had wanted finding his betrayer to be an easy task. A few choice requests of Gordon Lawless, and the rest was simply money.

"I'll bet if you look back in the records that name is going to show up. He might have had someone else arrange it, who knows? But if he's capable of everything else you've described, then…"

"So you believe me?" Ken asked.

"I'll believe what I have to right now. Jennifer's gone, and that's all I care about. I've already lost my son, and I'm not going to lose anyone else. If this is what I have to believe, then I'll believe it. So, I'm asking you again, What do we do?"

And the truth was Ken had no idea. That depended on Bach and Jennifer. It depended on a lot of things that he had no control over.

"Why don't you stay here?" Paula asked. "I don't like the idea of you being alone."

"We're not the only ones in danger," he said.

"You mean David?"

"Yes," Ken replied.

"How come you never mentioned him before?" Paula asked.

"I don't know."

"He knew about us though, didn't he?"

"Yes."

Paula sat her coffee mug on the arm of the bench, rubbed her injured shoulder and kept her hand over it as if she were cold. "I don't understand. Two years, Ken? You spent two years with this man, and you never once mentioned his name."

"At the time, I honestly believed that you didn't want to know."

"That's ridiculous."

"No, Paula. It isn't. You were wonderful and practical, but you weren't being realistic. I know you tried to be, but you weren't.

Somewhere in your head, you thought we'd get back together. You were holding on to a piece of me that wasn't there anymore, and I didn't do a very good job of giving you anything else to hold on to. I saw how much my life was hurting you and the kids, and as a result I felt like shit for putting you through it. That's why I stopped talking about all of this. That's why I never mentioned David."

"I didn't realize."

"I know," he said. "I know you didn't, and I'm not blaming you for anything. We both know that the problems here were mine. You said you wanted to understand, and I'm trying to help you understand."

"We probably should have talked about this a long time ago," Paula said. "And David's welcome to stay if he'll be comfortable here. We've got plenty of room."

"Okay," Ken told her. "Thank you. I'll ask him."

They sat quietly then. Paula sipped her coffee. Ken looked over the neighborhood, his thoughts with his daughter and Travis Brugier. Ken knew that Travis was taking his misguided revenge slowly; he could have easily killed them all in a matter of days or hours or minutes. He was giving Ken the time to think and suffer, because hurting Ken wasn't enough. No. Travis wanted more. He wanted Ken to discover the moral of this fable.

While in Wonderland, reading Travis's stories, Ken had followed the descent of this being, from a soul with hope and innocence to a monster of abject hatred. The most dramatic change occurred after the story of White Dog. It was then, having been forsaken by a lover, that this being had turned completely dark. Ken tried to recall that tale; it had relevance, but he could only recall a few minor events that befell the young lovers. His mind wouldn't allow him to access its details. But there was something important in that story, something he couldn't quite grasp.

Despite his cloudy remembrance of the Native American legend, all of the other stories came clear to him. They all contained tragedy and disappointment. Many contained revenge. *We're just characters in a new tale for Travis's storybook*, Ken thought. He'd accounted for so much of Ken's life, even during the years he'd been incapable of manipulating it. Travis had seen to it that Ken returned to this city more than once. His first job. Bobby. Who knew what other, subtler, plot points Travis had sketched for Ken over the years?

Wonderland's lunatic master was writing their lives. Everything that had happened to Ken, to his family, to David: another tale to be written down and perhaps, one day, spoken back to the aberration that had penned it.

Just a story.

And Ken knew, Travis didn't believe in happy endings.

31

David parked in the lot beneath Laray's offices. By now, Jennifer might have returned home. He found himself wanting to call, but he was already late for his meeting, so he gave a quick prayer for Ken and boarded the elevator.

While checking his watch, he saw a roach out of the corner of his eye. It crouched in the corner of the car beside a gum wrapper and a few grains of dirt. The creature's little legs worked furiously, and David noticed that it was emerging from a hole in the bottom of the car.

They'll take you quiet or screaming.

He grew cold and nervous as the fat bug pulled its way out of the hole.

The elevator opened, and David nearly leapt into Laray Pharmaceutical's lobby. The receptionist, a pretty woman with platinum-bleached hair and a black body-tight dress, asked what he wanted. After he told her, she pointed him down the hallway toward the meeting room he'd sat in only the day before. As he set off down the hall, he heard her announcing him over the telephone.

When he entered the room, the first face he saw was Antoine d'Aquin's. d'Aquin was the vice president in charge of corporate communications, so his presence was mandatory. Beside him was a blonde woman with candy-apple lipstick. Four other people, three men and a woman, David immediately recognized as lawyers.

"David Lane," d'Aquin said, already commencing the introductions. "These folks are from our legal department. They'll be joining us this afternoon."

Lovely, David thought. Another three hours wasted.

⚜

Two hours passed, and they were still haggling over what could and what could not be disclosed. Still, the clock was running, and Laray would be receiving a bill whether they took his advice or not, so he sat in the comfortable chair and argued his points, which had not changed. Full disclosure, he'd told them, was the only way to salvage the company's reputation. Apologize and map out a course of action that clearly reflected the company's concern for the families of the victims. Then pay up and don't fuck around with people's lives in the future.

Honestly, David didn't know why Laray had called him back. His dislike for corporate public relations showed vividly in his work history. He knew the processes from his early days in the corporate structure, and he kept up on the current literature, but he certainly didn't have a reputation in the field.

So, he sat there and fought a losing battle, haggling over the use of words like *guilt* and *sorry*.

Antoine d'Aquin, the heavy man with the perpetual sheen of perspiration, eyed him cautiously. David raised his eyebrows quickly for the fat man's benefit. Like a shrug, the gesture was meant to say: *I've told you what I think. If you don't like it, then we're wasting time.* The lawyer's voice droned on, and David pretended to pay attention.

He shot a glance at d'Aquin and noticed something moving in his shirt. At first it might have been the flutter of a passing draft, but the movement came from beneath the cotton material. David lifted his pen to his lips and cast his eyes down, so the sweaty man wouldn't notice him staring. The shirt bubbled near the right breast, and the movement unnerved David. What was the man hiding in there? The bump moved, and when a large roach appeared through the opening between two buttons, a shiver ran through David's body.

Quickly, the insect dashed into the shadow beneath d'Aquin's jacket.

"Mr. Lane?" The blond woman was speaking.

"Yes?"

"Are you with us?" she asked, her lips wrinkled and pinched.

Even now the insect might be crawling through the swamp of d'Aquin's armpit. David's throat tightened. He wanted to check himself out, brush through his own clothes.

"Mr. Lane?"

"I'm trying to find a middle ground, but none seems plausible," he said. "I realize your concern with the lawsuit, and I've heard the bullshit before: 'If we say we're sorry, then we're admitting guilt.' But the facts remain: You have guilt; there is sufficient evidence of that guilt, and even if there were not, people rarely side with a corporation in these things. Having said that, it isn't my job to pass judgment one way or the other. I'm not suggesting that you disclose to look guilty. I'm suggesting you do it so you look concerned. Whether you are or not is your own moral dilemma, but from a media standpoint, your only chance at shutting this thing down is to get it out of the papers and off the networks as quickly as possible. That means an apology and a sincere effort to make restitution to the families. If there's no conflict, then there's no news."

"And we've told you, Mr. Lane," the youngest lawyer said, "that isn't possible."

Such a shame, David thought. The lawyer could have been quite attractive were it not for blatant ambition and cold eyes.

"Then," David said, standing up from the table, "I guess I'll see you on *Sixty Minutes*. It's been a pleasure."

David packed his papers back into his briefcase. He shook the hands of the lawyers and the blond with bright red lips and met Antoine d'Aquin at the door. The heavy man followed him into the hall.

"I know you're right," d'Aquin said. "We're up to our asses in this one."

David just wanted to leave. The building gave him the creeps. God only knew how many insects crept through the man's clothing, hid beneath the water cooler, and fed in the corners of the break room.

"This isn't going away," David said.

"That's what I've been telling them. I thought if I got an outside source to confirm my position, they might take it more seriously."

"Well," David said, "this is the Big Easy. If it ain't gonna make you flower food, then it ain't a problem. It'll keep."

"Thanks for your time," d'Aquin said, extending a moist, meaty palm.

"You're welcome. You're screwed, but you're welcome." David replied, tentatively shaking the hand, keeping his eye on the jacket cuff so that no unwelcome visitor crossed onto him from d'Aquin's body.

When he looked back up, a plump roach was pushing its way along the flab of the executive's second chin, fighting and bumping the wave of fat as it struggled to emerge from the man's collar. David closed his eyes as a wave of nausea rolled up his throat. He turned and hurried down the hall. In the elevator, he brushed his clothes and scanned the floor.

Quiet or screaming.

Back in the Mercedes, David wiped the film of sweat from his brow, thankful that he would be away from the building in moments.

Once he was on the road, he called Ken, who picked up after one ring.

"Any word?"

"No," Ken said. "Nothing yet. The police were here. They know a lot about Vicki, but they still can't find her. Paula and I went back out, checked some of her friends' houses, the River-walk, anyplace we thought she was likely to go, but nothing. How was your meeting?"

"Fine," David lied. "Look, I'm on my way home to change clothes. Is there anything I can do?"

When Ken suggested that David pack up a few belongings, his initial response was to refuse, imagining that, again, Ken was asking him to leave town, but instead, he wanted David to spend the night with him at Paula's house. David didn't like the idea. Not one bit. He'd just met Ken's ex-wife and hardly considered it appropriate being her houseguest. But Ken insisted and delivered a compelling argument for them to stay together, made all the more profound by the thunderstorm-that-never-was he'd witnessed earlier in the day. So, despite misgivings and considerable unease, David agreed.

"Good," Ken said. "Then, I'll need a ride into the Quarter to pick up some things from the house. Once we're all settled back here, we'll figure out what to do."

David agreed and ended the call.

32

At the house in the Quarter, Ken led David through the dining room to the kitchen. He checked his voice mail, but no one had called. Why he'd held any hope that Jennifer might try to reach him, he couldn't say. That was simply the nature of hope. If his daughter was with Vicki, it was unlikely he'd have any news that Vicki didn't want him to have.

So far, her only failure had been with Chuck. He'd been dispatched to kill Paula and had, instead, been captured, which afforded Ken some minor relief. Vicki wasn't omnipotent; she could fail. But could she be stopped?

Ken didn't know. The answer was in the storybook, specifically the legend of White Dog. He was sure of it. Reading that story, he had experienced an epiphany, which had quickly dulled and died. Every time he thought about that tale, his mind grew cloudy. He could not remember its ending. More and more he believed that he couldn't remember it because Vicki didn't want him to remember it.

"Have you got anything to eat?" David asked.

Ken was startled by such a practical request. He turned away from the phone. David leaned on the counter, looking around the kitchen floor as if he'd lost something.

"Sorry," David said. "I haven't eaten all day, and my gut is rumbling. It's actually making me kind of light headed. Just some crackers or something until we can get dinner."

"I'll see." Ken searched the cupboards. He found a box of shortbread cookies. He'd kept the box in a Ziploc bag to deter pests, but the cookies had to be over a year old. "They're probably stale, but it's about all I've got."

"Fine," David said, taking the plastic shrouded box. "You better grab your things. We shouldn't leave Paula alone."

Ken was watching David tear open the bag and reach in for the cardboard box when the phone rang. The sound startled them both, and David nearly dropped the package of cookies on the floor but hastily snatched at it, retrieving the box in midair.

"Ken, it's Paula."

"Any news?"

"I've got her," Paula said, sounding frustrated. "She called right after you left. Turns out, she decided to spend her afternoon at the movies."

"The movies?"

"Apparently so," Paula said.

"Okay," Ken said. "She's with you?"

"Yes, we're on our way back to the house now."

A wave of elation crested in him and then crashed.

"Good. David and I will be along shortly, but Paula…" Ken said, suddenly unsure of how good this news was. "Are you sure it's her?"

"What?" Paula asked. It took her a moment to realize exactly what Ken was saying. "Of course it's her. I picked her up at the theater not ten minutes ago. Now, do you think I should call Detective Reilly and have him meet us?"

"Maybe I should talk to her first," Ken said. "As long as she's safe."

"Well, I'm not too happy with her, but she's fine."

"See you soon."

Ken hung up the phone, relieved, but it didn't last.

He turned back to David, intending to tell him the good news, and saw him trembling, staring at a morsel of cookie, pinched between his fingers. David's eyes were wide with revulsion. He threw the box of cookies away from himself, and it clattered across the floor. A shudder ran through his body, and he flicked away the half-eaten cookie as if it had come to life and bitten him.

"God," he said, his voice garbled.

"David?" Ken asked.

But David didn't reply. His body hitched with sickness. Covering his mouth, David fled the kitchen.

⚜

David ran, trying to beat the sickness rising from his belly. He'd been listening to Ken on the phone, absently devouring the stale cookies, which didn't taste as bad as he'd imagined they would. He'd been so hungry, ravenous to the point of aching. The hunger was so great that he kept pulling the snacks out of the box and crunching them down to quell the pangs.

After Ken hung up the phone, David reached into the box for another of the shortbreads. He crunched it in half and waited to hear the news. Then, he'd felt the tickle on his fingers.

Looking at his hand, David grew hot with disgust. Between his index finger and his thumb, the lower half of a roach squirmed, its remaining legs kicking for purchase against his fingertips. He slammed the bathroom door open and leaned over the toilet as his nearly empty stomach convulsed and expelled. His body shook with nausea, sweat popped out on his neck and face. Again he heaved and again, his eyes squeezed shut from the violent sickness.

When his stomach refused any further exodus, David opened his eyes. Strands of meat hung from the lid and floated in the stained water of the toilet. Hundreds of tiny creatures filled the bowl. Beetles, worms, roaches—the Flesh Eaters had already come for him. Their bodies, shiny from his bile and the water in the bowl, writhed and fought for the pink morsels. Their numbers increased as they foraged. Bubbling and growing, the ravenous creatures pushed at the rim. They covered the porcelain, cascaded toward the ground, and flowed over the shiny tiled floor. David backed away. Suddenly he was covered with ice, and he trembled, swiping at his mouth and chin to make sure none of the creatures remained on him.

David turned to the mirror running over Ken's sink. Nothing wrong. His face, untouched, stared back at him. A sheen of sweat over the pale skin glimmered in the harsh white lights, but he was okay. Alive, he thought. Still alive.

⚜

Ken sped onto Canal Street. He tried to blink the strange fog from his eyes, he rubbed them viciously with his fingers, but everything they touched fell under the haze.

"He got into my head," David told Ken.

"It's not real. It's like a movie you can't turn off."

"I felt them inside of me," David said. "I tasted the goddamned things."

Ken's chest tightened as he felt the man's fear and anger creep over the seat. David shuddered visibly and pushed deeper into the leather upholstery as if he could become part of it and hide from whatever horrors came for him. Ken's fingers strangled the steering wheel. Their anxiety increased by twos with every second that passed.

The strange haze grew thicker as he drove along St. Charles Avenue. The streetlights cast no illumination but rather glowed like weak candles in the night air. The headlights of approaching vehicles came at him as if from under water. All of the homes oozed a ghostly aura fed by table lamps and porch lights.

"You said you thought Brugier's storybook might give clues to his weakness," David said. He twitched and slapped at his arm before a pained smile spread over his lips and shame filled his eyes. "Have you thought about that anymore?"

Of course he had. He thought about it endlessly, but there seemed to be a wall that kept him from seeing the answer. He knew it had something to do with Travis's first attempt at creating a lover. White Dog had taken Passing Cloud's finger to perform a terrible ceremony, but, as Ken thought about the story, even though he'd freshly read the piece only a couple of days ago, the details were gone.

"Is there any chance we can find that book?" David asked.

"We don't need the whole thing. It's that damned Native American legend. I'm sure of it," Ken said, "but none of it's clear. I think Travis knows I can use the information, and he's keeping it from me."

"Do you really think he can do that?"

"Considering everything else he's capable of, yes."

"Okay," David said. "So, let's go over what you know. We'll piece it together."

"I don't see the point. I only remember the beginning."

"Ken," David said, stern now, "tell me the story."

Ken's wet palms throttled the wheel as the words came from David's mouth, but there was no story to tell. He could not remember the ending. No matter how he tried to see through the haze, he could only make out a few vague images. "All I remember is," Ken began. He licked his suddenly dry lips and loosened his grip on the wheel. "There are these two kids: White Dog and Passing Cloud. They were very much in love and were about to be married. White Dog took the girl into the woods and cut off her little finger to use in a ritual that was meant to fuse her being with a spirit's so that she could be with him always. Life after life, they would be together." Ken bent his head forward to break some of the tension out of his neck.

"And what happens?" David asked. "Do they get married?"

"No," Ken told him. "Passing Cloud believed that she was possessed, and she returned to her village in a panic." This is where the story always ended in Ken's mind. He could almost see the poor child frantically begging her people for help against this outsider, but they did not know White Dog was an outsider. They couldn't know. He'd been born into their tribe. He had grown up with them. None knew what lived within him.

"Does she have family?" David asked. "Does she try to get help from her family?"

Ken was about to remind David that he couldn't remember when part of the haze broke, and he remembered Passing Cloud's mother. She had joined her daughter in the longhouse. "And she told Passing Cloud to pretend to the elders and to White Dog himself that nothing was wrong, but it was too late. White Dog had returned, and the elders warned him that his wife-to-be had gone mad. And then..." The haze grew thick again. Ken fought to keep the window of recall open, to keep the mist at bay, but it rolled in to obscure the mental landscape.

"Did White Dog play along? Did he laugh it off or seem concerned?"

"No," Ken said. "He got angry." Another curtain of mist pulled away. White Dog burst into the longhouse. Lame Bull, Passing Cloud's mother, charged him with a knife but fell victim to one of the being's hallucinations. "He killed Passing Cloud's mother. He got into her head, and she died instantly."

"Did he try to reason with Passing Cloud?"

Ken shook his head as the mist thinned and became transparent. He watched White Dog run his knife into Passing Cloud's belly. "He murdered her. He stabbed her with a hunting knife and then pushed his fist into the wound."

"Why?" David asked.

"I don't know," Ken replied as the fog settled heavily over the memory.

"Was he trying to take something out of her? You mentioned a ceremony. Did she have to eat or drink something?"

Ken shook his head. "The only aspect of the ceremony he wrote about was the taking of the finger to make the charms. The rest followed Passing Cloud as she witnesses a vision from the river: a man with a bear's head. There's nothing in there about incantations or..." Ken stopped himself. What had he just said? Something about the charms. White Dog had made a necklace and two rings from the severed finger. And... "Christ he was putting them back."

"What?"

"He didn't cut Passing Cloud open to take anything out. He was putting something in. He pushed the charms he'd made from her finger into her stomach."

"Making her whole again?" David asked.

That was it, Ken realized. The fog had pulled away and left the perverse image of White Dog's fist lodged in his lover's belly. "He made her whole again, yes."

"Were these charms like Brugier's Thorn?"

"Yes. They were exactly like that."

"Did Vicki make one? Is there any chance we'd even find it?"

"No," Ken said. "We don't have to. You're seeing Vicki and Travis as separate beings. They aren't. Vicki wouldn't need to make a new charm. Travis hadn't needed to. The Thorn came from this thing's first incarnation, a woman named Alice. A part of her essence or soul is held within the Thorn along with a piece of the spirit that possessed her. I think if it's with Vicki when she dies the cycle ends."

"So, we can use the Thorn to stop her?"

"We can use it to stop her from coming back."

"You left it at my house," David said. "I picked it up this morning but forgot to give it to you."

"Okay," Ken said. "We'll make sure that Paula and Jen are safe, then I'll go back to pick it up."

❧

The lights on the first two floors of the painted lady burned. Ken pulled into the drive, relieved when he saw Paula passing the dining room window. For the first time since Bobby's attack, Ken had a sense of control. Brugier had been in his life and in the world for too long, but with his new understanding of the Thorn and its role in Brugier's resurrection, Ken found hope and a swelling sense of determination. He could stop this thing. He could salvage what remained of his life. All he had to do was keep his family and David safe for a little while longer.

"They're okay," David muttered.

"For now," Ken told him. He unfastened the safety belt and opened his door. "Let's try and keep it that way."

Inside, Ken made a beeline for the kitchen, which was where Paula had been headed, and David made his way to the sofa in the living room, where he took a seat and stared at the floor.

Ken found his ex-wife leaning on the kitchen counter and shaking her head.

"Are you okay?"

"Fine," Paula replied tersely. "I swear to God, I am two seconds from shipping that kid to Switzerland. Running off that way and then having the gall to call me for a ride."

"What happened?"

"I don't know, Ken. She won't talk to me, as usual. I sent her to her room, and right now, I'm thinking she can stay there for the next two years until it's time for her to move out."

"She knows how to find Vicki," he said. "If she won't talk to us we'll have to call the police back here. In fact, you'd better call them anyway."

"That'll cause quite a conniption," Paula said.

"I don't give a shit," Ken said. "We've tiptoed around her feelings for the last eight years, tried so damned hard not to wound her, and it's done more damage than good. She walks all over us, and we flatten out hoping she's good and comfortable with the stroll. But after today's stunt? Running off and looking for Vicki after what that woman's done to this family?"

"Well, we don't know she went looking for Vicki. She told me she'd been at the movies all day. I know that doesn't mean much. She might have tried to find her. I'm just glad she didn't."

Only because Vicki didn't want to be found, Ken thought. The storm she'd created, the diversion that had allowed Jen to escape in the first place, proved she'd been nearby. Why she didn't take the opportunity to ensnare Jennifer, Ken didn't know. Maybe having Jen gone was enough. Another petty torment before her real plan was set into motion.

"I still think you should call Reilly," he said.

"And tell him to bring a rubber hose?" Paula asked.

"If that's what it takes," Ken said earnestly. "I have to run to David's for a few minutes. When I get back, we all need to sit down and talk this through. And I need to know where to find Vicki. I may have a way to stop her."

Paula pushed away from the counter. Her face scrunched inquisitively. "You actually think you can stop this?"

The surprise in her voice was not flattering. In fact, little she could have done, short of laughing in his face, would have hurt more.

Wounded and mystified by what he took as cruelty, Ken stepped back into the doorway of the kitchen. "We'll talk about it when I get back."

"Fine."

In the living room, he leaned over the back of the sofa and put his arm around David's shoulders. "Are you feeling any better?"

David looked up, dazed, as if he'd just been woken from a deep sleep. "Yeah. I'm just..." he let the sentence die. "Are we ready to go?"

"I need you to stay here and keep an eye on Paula and Jen. I don't know what Vicki's planning, but I don't want any of you alone until we've taken care of this. I'll only be a few minutes."

"Okay," David said, a great distance in his voice.

He's falling apart, Ken thought. "I'll need your house keys," he said.

Once he had them in his hand, Ken leaned over the sofa and kissed David's neck. The man jerked away and threw a hand to his collar, rubbing fiercely at the skin Ken's lips had just touched.

David's face went red, and he looked up at Ken with an expression so hopeless that it cut.

"I'll fix this," Ken said around a knot of emotion lodged high in his throat.

"You better hurry," David said.

33

Ken had just left, and David sat on the sofa thinking about sunsets, not that he pictured brilliantly colored skies or held the notions with a single ounce of romance. Sunsets were an end, the death of a day, and at the death of this day, David saw nothing but darkness. The future was a ridiculous thing to consider with everything going on, but he couldn't help himself. His priest, Harv, had been right. There won't be any riding off into the sunset.

Something moved along his arm, tiny legs scurrying through the hairs there. David slapped the place and the sensation stopped, only to reappear on his shin. He breathed deeply and exhaled a trembling sigh. He knew that nothing crawled on him, knew that it was just a trick being played with his mind, but the deception was maddening and immune to any balm of logic. He told himself again and again that there were no Flesh Eaters, but they were everywhere.

The sound of his car backing out of the drive snapped him from his reverie. He gazed at the television screen sitting across the room like a black window looking out on a motionless void.

David's reflection hovered at the center of this void. Then, the darkness surrounding his reflection began to move, to separate and crawl.

For one lunatic moment, he felt a thousand tiny legs, covering every inch of his body. They tickled his face, his neck, his back. They squirmed against the fabric of his pants and shorts, scratched at his legs, his buttocks, and the warmth between his scrotum and anus. He bolted from the sofa with a muffled cry, slapping and wiping at his arms and legs, spinning in a frantic circle.

Paula Nicholson stared at him from the arch of the dining room. Embarrassed, David managed to regain his composure, but when he looked up at the woman, the ex-wife of his lover, he felt it slip again. Her face was as blank and cold as a corpse's. Her eyes were icy pits without a bit of humanity in them.

"Paula?" he asked.

"Not even close, Darlin'."

An illusion, David thought. They'd been so caught up in the vile, obvious mind games, that neither he nor Ken had considered Brugier could easily re-create the mundane as well. Paula was a figment, but what about her daughter?

"Jennifer!" David called, backing away from the sofa, working his way toward the front door.

"Not home," Paula said. "Hasn't been for a while now."

"Where is she?" David asked, stumbling over his own feet.

"With me," the apparition said. "Where she's always been."

David turned and bolted for the front door. Behind him, the illusion of Paula Nicholson's voice roared, "Do you really think he loves you?"

David yanked on the front door, pulling it back with enough force to send it crashing against the wall. What waited for him on the porch sent him back a step.

Two young men in polo shirts and khaki shorts, arms crossed, faces stern, blocked the threshold. David threw a glance over his shoulder to see where Paula had gone, but the room behind him was empty. Desperate and half mad, David made a fist and buried it in the pig-snout nose of the boy on the right, throwing his body forward with the motion, propelling himself out of the house. A third man stood on the porch, he noticed, but whoever it was stood far back out of the light spilling from the doorway. Strong hands locked on David's shoulders and spun him around, while the man he'd hit rolled on the porch, cupping his injured face. David swung again, landing a glancing blow on the second man's jaw, but the guy had moved fast, and David's punch had done no harm. The boy responded by burying a fist in David's stomach, doubling him over and forcing the air out of his lungs. Then, he shoved David backward into the house. He lost his footing and crashed to the floor.

"Da' fugger broke my node," the man on the porch cried.

"Well," his companion said, "that ought to make this next part a lot more fun."

❧

Paula stood on the corner, impatient and growing angry with detectives Ogilvie and Reilly. Jennifer had called to demand a ride home in an infuriatingly casual tone before giving Paula an address in the French Quarter. Though her daughter insisted that Vicki wasn't with her, claimed to not know where Vicki was, Paula was taking no chances. She called Detective Reilly the second she'd hung up on her daughter.

The street lamp on the far sidewalk lit, then another ignited a block down. It was getting late, and Paula felt ridiculous standing on the corner half a block from where her daughter was. She'd been waiting for twenty minutes, because Reilly had insisted she not approach the building until they arrived. Well, where the hell were they?

Frustration drove her to dig the cell phone out of her purse. She flipped it open and then searched its memory for Detective Reilly's number. Once she had it, she hit the SEND button and put the phone to her ear. A piercing siren tore from the earpiece, startling Paula into dropping the cellular on the sidewalk. After the surprise passed, she reached down for the device as if it had teeth, with great caution and unease. Lifting the phone, she hit the END button and tried calling again but with the same result. She searched the memory for Ken's number. This time she held the phone well away from her ear in case the shrill interference was a defect in her phone or service.

She waited for a few seconds, anticipating the sharp tone, but it didn't come. Relieved, she rested the earpiece against her head.

At first, she couldn't be certain what it was she heard. It sounded like little more than static. Then a sharp hiccup broke the hiss, followed by a sniffle.

"It hurts," her daughter cried through the phone.

"Jennifer?" Paula said, her heart thrown into a rapid beat.

"You never came," the pained voice said.

"Jennifer, I'm right here, Honey."

"Why didn't you come, Mommy? Why didn't you…"

A high scream cut the line, slicing into Paula like a lash, setting her skin alight, forcing her to move. She ran up the block toward the address Jennifer had read off, her head full of panicked cries. Paula's frayed nerves made her clumsy. She stumbled, then righted herself. "Mommy!" Desperate, her gaze darted into every doorway, through every wrought-iron gate, hoping to catch a glimpse of her child.

"Why didn't you come?" Jennifer pleaded in her ear.

The phone went dead. Paula threw it on the sidewalk in frustration. She charged forward until she arrived at the house Jennifer had described. Peering through the wrought-iron bars and down an alley between the fence and the slave quarters, the house beyond the courtyard loomed. It looked miserable in the late evening gloom. Dilapidated, filthy, and deserted. Worse still, it looked dangerous. But her daughter was in there. Something terrible was happening to her little girl in that house. Paula gripped the metal gate and pushed it open.

34

Ken opened the door to David's house and hurried across the living room. He went immediately to the credenza where he'd left the Thorn, but the smooth surface was bare. He opened each of the drawers in turn but they held only papers and the odd household gadget. Then he remembered that David had said something about bringing him the Thorn. He'd taken it that morning and then forgotten about it.It could be anywhere in the house.

He walked to the kitchen and scoured the countertops. Nothing. Ken ran upstairs and pushed open the door to David's bedroom. The sight of the bed chilled him. Cold moisture came up on his neck.

Never again, a thin voice teased.

David had thrown his suit on the bed, probably to rush over to Paula's that afternoon once his meeting had ended. Ken went to the nightstand on the near side of the bed and rifled through the papers and packages of condoms he found within. Nothing. He went around to David's side. Nothing.

Ken checked his watch. He'd already been in the house ten minutes.

Noticing David's suit on the bed, he yanked the jacket into his hands and checked the inner pockets but came up empty. He tossed the garment back on the bed and went for the pants. He dug into the left-hand pocket and pulled the lining out with his fist as he hurriedly searched the clothing. He flipped the trousers around and shoved his hand deeply into the opening of the other pocket.

A sharp pain stabbed his index finger. Ken's hand recoiled. A thin bubble of blood welled over the fingertip. He shoved the digit in his mouth and then retrieved the Thorn from David's pocket. Looping the charm around his neck, he dropped the pants on the floor and raced out of the bedroom.

Paula's house was dark when he returned. No lights burned inside or out. Amid the other houses on the block, all lit with chandeliers and televisions, the place looked deserted. Spiders of anxiety scrabbled in his stomach. This wasn't right. They wouldn't have left, not on their own. The place wouldn't be this dark unless someone had cut the power.

Ken's dread intensified. He ran to the porch, and then forced himself to approach the door with caution, twisting the knob gently and easing it inward. He slid his hand along the wall, found the switch, and toggled it up. The foyer fell under a bath of light. Ken crossed to the living room and slid the rheostat up, bringing illumination to this room as well. No one had cut the power, but he could already feel the emptiness of the place.

What had happened? They'd all been here less than thirty minutes ago.

Ken searched through the first floor, calling, "David? Paula? Jen?" On the second floor, he listened for any sounds of life and called Paula's name again. Bobby's room was empty, and so was

Jen's. Ken stopped before the master suite, the only closed door on this floor.

When he pushed it open, he saw a familiar shadow in the gloom. Another of Brugier's hanging men dangled over Paula's bed. Ken flipped on the light, barely taking the time to look at the body.

"Is this the best you can do?" he whispered. He crossed the room and stood at the edge of the bed. The legs dangled beside him. Where the hell had everyone gone?

"You still think you can stop this, Baby?" the corpse said.

"You need a new act, Travis," Ken said, swinging his arm to break through the latest illusion.

His arm cracked against the shin of the hanging man, sending him spinning on his wire, and though he knew Brugier could easily create the sensation of contact for him, he also felt certain that this time, he was not in the presence of a trick. Ken stumbled back, forcing himself to look at the one thing he had hoped to never see again.

David Lane, his eyes vacant and stained with broken blood vessels peered down at him. Still swaying and turning from Ken's blow, the blood that had accumulated on his shoes spattered the violet duvet of Paula's bed. Gristle or vertebrae snapped under the constricting wire, and Ken's stomach rose, threatening to expel its contents on the floor.

"They were never here, Ken. They never came back because no one comes back from Wonderland. You left me alone…again."

"I'm sorry."

Ken backed away, tears filling his eyes, spilling over his cheeks. The pain in his chest sent him to his knees. This couldn't be real. Not David. Not like this. He'd thought Paula's tone suspicious, but he'd still left. He hadn't gone upstairs to check on his daughter, and even if he had, Travis would have provided another illusion. They'd never come back, *because no one comes back from Wonderland*. He'd been so arrogant, thinking it would all end to his favor.

"Oh, I'm not going to make it that easy for you." This time

the voice was Travis Brugier's. His thick honeyed tone, as clear and calm as the night they'd met, rolled over Ken's shoulder. He didn't look up, instead he continued to mourn and pray against his palms. "You've always been torn, Baby, between who you are and what you think you should be. Now, look what that's gotten you. You lied and hid and played all manner of games because you thought you'd keep the folks you claim to care about from getting hurt. And that just didn't work out worth a shit."

"Shut up, Travis."

"So, here's my deal. You get to choose. How's that? Do you keep Paula and Jennifer, or do you keep David? It's a fun and simple game, Baby."

"David's dead," Ken said.

"Look again."

Ken did as he was told. Wiping the tears from his eyes, clearing the scene before him, he looked up at the hanged man and saw Jersey Fleagle's weathered, gaunt face staring back at him.

"He was going to eat a bullet after poor Sam got his head split against that curb," Travis said. "That would have been a damned shame. A complete waste. I think this worked out much better for everyone."

"Jesus," Ken hissed.

"Now, you come on and see me. You know where I'm at. We'll have us a nice old-fashioned reunion."

35

Ken raced David's car dangerously through traffic. The horns of the other drivers blared their discontent, but he didn't care. On Decatur Street, a mule-drawn carriage pulled out in front of him. He slammed on the brakes and flew forward against the wheel. The driver waved a gloved hand in the air as Ken watched the worn wagon with its cheap brass fixtures and sconces of desiccated flowers pull away. Jackson Square stood to his left just past a row of a dozen similar carriages. The river rushed beyond the embankment to his right. A true fog had come up in the thick, hot air. The strange haze he had experienced all evening had left him, but now nature had stepped in to blur the night.

Throngs of tourists still roamed the street despite the late hour. They wanted to suck as much enjoyment as they could from the city to feed disbelieving neighbors when they returned from vacation.

Ken gave the carriage in front of him a few more feet of space and then punched the gas. The traffic was maddening: one lane in, one lane out. Just as he passed Dumaine Street, not six blocks from his home, the traffic came to a dead halt. He climbed out of the Mercedes and looked over the row of motionless cars. Up ahead, near Ursulines a silver Ford Explorer had crossed the line and smashed into a delivery van.

He fell back into the car and shifted into reverse. The car behind him blared its horn, but Ken swung the Mercedes sharply and retreated down the wrong lane. No cars approached because of the accident. He slid past Dumaine, then cranked the wheel to make the turn. Halfway through the turn he slowed and brought the car to another agonizing stop.

Brilliant lamps and the open tails of massive cargo trucks informed Ken that the film they had been shooting near his home had moved further down the street. Everything between Chartres and Royal on Dumaine had been barricaded. He looked back at the street he had just left, and a line of cars stretched back as far as he could see. Ten yards away, a shadow peeled itself away from the deeper shadows behind it. A policeman moved across one of the blinding lights as he waved for Ken to back up.

He couldn't waste any more time. Ken got out of the Mercedes and threw the keys at the startled officer, who caught them against his chest as Ken sprinted toward the barricade. The policeman yelled something, but Ken was already jumping over the wooden beam, which was meant to keep the curious at bay. The scene around him seemed little more than a blur as he raced along the sidewalk. Characters moved under the false daylight of the set. Shouts came up as he passed, but then just as quickly he was consumed by shadows, the sounds receding beneath his insistent heartbeat.

He turned right on Royal Street and slowed his pace only because he could not seem to catch his breath. The fog came on thick past Ursulines Street. The few lights on the distant block were worn and exhausted. The street before him was empty. He could still hear the traffic and frivolity on Decatur, but the noise came as if it were a memory to offset the utter silence of this stretch of road. His side kicking with pain, he slowed to a fast walk. Sweat slathered his face, dripped into his eyes, and blurred the already fuzzy scene. His heart tripped manically in his chest as he gasped the hot night air that burned along his tongue and throat. Ken reached for the bauble around his neck and felt the cruel point of the charm.

He gazed back over his shoulder. He'd passed St. Phillips Street, but he still had a long way to go. He forced himself to stop for a moment to regain his breath. All he needed was a moment, a moment to breathe.

Ken pushed away from the wall and settled into a slow jog. After a blind series of turns he stopped a block from Wonderland and again forced his aging system to catch up. He tried to imagine Travis's home and where this final confrontation might occur. Travis's flare for the dramatic almost assured Ken that they would meet on the balcony as they had all of those years ago, only instead of the pretty Vassals putting on a show in the courtyard, it would be Ken's family, Ken's lover.

Would Travis have them tear each other apart? A shudder, like a rivulet of ice water, ran down his spine.

He resumed his slow jog and crossed the intersection. Wonderland came up on his left. He noticed the sentries at its gate only as he stepped onto the far curb. They were both well-groomed young men with casual attire and angry expressions. The taller man stepped away from the gate. The shorter man with the stained white shirt and swollen nose waited a moment before following.

And look at you, right back where you started.

He pushed the voice away. The boys moved quickly to meet Ken in the middle of the foggy street. The taller man with the blue knit shirt reached for his arm. He twisted away from the grasp. "I know the way," Ken growled.

After a deep breath, Ken walked through the gate and back into Wonderland. In the distance he heard the clicking of hooves on the pavement: a carriage being drawn toward the noise on Bourbon Street.

The long alley beside Travis's parlor engulfed him. Even the fog had not seeped into this murky corridor. As he entered the courtyard, Ken noticed the reek of burning oil. No blossoms this time. No electric bath of illumination. Just the dancing flames and the dead foliage. The house before him was carved from the darkness. His eyes immediately lifted to the balcony, but he saw nothing there. His escorts moved to either side of him. "Travis," he called, his voice echoing back.

A light came on in the upstairs room. The doors opened, and two figures walked onto the balcony.

"What is this," he heard Jennifer say. "Vicki?"

"Come on up," Bach called. "The view's better."

He started across the courtyard, and for a moment there were blossoms. For the tiniest of seconds, flowers bloomed around him and a fountain sparkled, its plume glittering amid colored lights. The rich perfume tingled in his nose. The house before him, monstrous and beautiful, had not yet fallen to indifference and time. But the image passed, and Ken once again walked toward the worn wood of Brugier's house.

Inside, he went directly to the stairs, climbing them quickly to the landing above. The dusty atmosphere caught in his throat, and he coughed the accumulation free. There was no going back now.

And what have you decided? David? Paula? Jennifer?

Ken walked along the corridor, stopping at the master suite's door. He pushed the door open and stepped into the chamber. The mattress had been thrown from the bed, and the room was in complete disarray. Wallpaper had been shredded on the far wall and now dangled in strips to the floor. Dust danced in the gloom. A large document had been torn to scraps and the pieces littered every surface of the lifeless room.

Ken crossed the dismal chamber and stopped in front of the French doors. He pulled the curtains aside, and a sharp ray of light burned into his eyes. Shadows moved within shadows, and a dull haze held them all together. Only the searing beam of the spotlight cut the fog. Ken grasped the silver handles tightly and twisted them to free the latch. Slowly he pulled the doors open. As if his action had kindled a fire, Ken found himself awash in light.

Floodlights bathed the stagnant fountain and the overgrown courtyard walls.

He stepped onto the terrace. Jennifer ran to him and threw her arms around his back. "I want to go home," she cried. "Can we go home?"

"Soon," Ken said, patting her hair.

Over his daughter's shoulder, Vicki Bach leaned against one of the wrought-iron posts. Then he saw David, and his throat clenched.

"Yes," Bach said, "he's nearly gone. Not nearly as far as Chuck, but it won't take long at this point."

David crouched in the corner of the balcony. His handsome face was twisted. Curled up as tightly as physically possible, the man whimpered and cried as he tried to keep Vicki Bach's horror at bay. He stamped his foot and rubbed an invisible bug into the flaking wood. His eyes darted back and forth.

Dangling from the eaves across the rail from him, a wire noose shimmered.

"Have you made a decision?" Vicki asked. "Take your time. I've got plenty of it." The woman laughed lightly and ran a hand over Ken's cheek. "Gentlemen," Vicki called, "would you please escort our other guest into the courtyard?"

Ken couldn't take his eyes off of David's twitching figure. He held his daughter tightly, stroking her hair, but his eyes were with the man in the corner.

"I'm sorry, Daddy," Jennifer said. "I thought…"

"*Shhh,*" he said.

Vicki said, "How wonderful."

"Shut up," Ken warned.

"Be nice, Baby," Vicki said. "I have them all here, and promises were made to be broken. But I'm feeling generous, so you go ahead and pick."

"You know I can't make a decision like that."

"Then they all die," Bach said easily as she paced along the balcony. "Poor, poor Ken. You still want to have it all, don't you? You want your happy family, and you want to suck dick, and you want the whole world to revolve around *you*. And even when it does, you're miserable. A clean slate is what you need to put yourself together."

"Damn it, Travis," he said. "It's not that simple."

"Of course it is. Just turn your back, and let one die. Like when you turned your back on me. That decision came easily enough. So, here we are again. You've lived two lives, Baby, and now you've got to decide between them."

"And how many have you lived?" Ken asked. He pushed Jennifer aside lightly. "You've lived a dozen lives. More. And what have you accomplished? After all of this time, you're still a bitter and angry child, wasting your lives and the lives of those around you, creating meaningless fables."

Bach turned her back on him. She walked to the shivering heap at the end of the balcony and pointed at David. "Him?" she asked. "Or them?" Vicki turned and pointed into the courtyard.

Paula stood next to the fountain, looking around in confusion. Her hands were tied behind her back, and a thick strip of black tape wrapped around her head. The last Vassals stood by the exit, blocking escape. Next to him Jennifer made a sound deep in her throat.

"You lied to me," Jennifer said. "We were friends."

"In time," Vicki said, "you'll grow accustomed to the lies." She faced Jennifer and rubbed the girl's cheek lightly. "Whether you have that time is in your father's hands. It's his choice now."

In the courtyard below, Paula spun rapidly, trying to keep her eyes on the men guarding her escape and the scene playing out on the balcony above. The thick black tape covering her mouth played in counterpoint to the bright white of her perfect skin and large terrified eyes. He looked at Jennifer, who was crying, struggling with something of her own. David had grown motionless on the balcony.

"David?" Ken shouted.

Vicki stepped forward. One hand traced along the rotting iron and the other went to the lapel of Ken's shirt. "Decide," she whispered.

Before he could stop them, Ken's hands flew up and wrapped around Vicki Bach's slender throat. In his mind, he saw himself plunging over the balcony, his arms securing the body of the creature that had manipulated and destroyed his life.But that didn't happen.

Seconds after he decided to carry them both over the balcony, Ken's mind erupted in color. Nausea rose in him so quickly that he pulled his hands back. Reflex brought his palms to his mouth as his head swam for a cohesive thought. Lightning flashes of orange and purple blinded him. The balcony was gone. Vicki Bach was gone. David and Jennifer and Paula—all were gone. In their place were the bolts of color and the pain.

And then he was alone on the balcony. The pain vanished so quickly that it left him swooning. A cool breeze blew over his face, filling his nose with the scent of jasmine. The quiet, so intense, so soothing. He gazed over the courtyard at the magnificent blossoms: reds and whites and greens blended into a tapestry of floral perfection. The fountain gurgled; a plume of water sparkled, lit by the numerous bulbs, shining from the ground.

How beautiful it was again…

Again?

⚜

"Lovely night," Travis called from the bedroom.

Ken couldn't answer; he still reeled from the strange dislocation he'd just experienced, and everything felt different. He was staring out at the courtyard, expecting to see something there beside flowers, stones, and the fountain. The mellow notes of a rag played in the building across the way. Men moved past the windows of The Parlor, drinks in hand, smiles on faces. Looking down, he saw that he wore only pajama bottoms, but it was too early to go to bed. Confused, he ran his gaze over the railing of the balcony to where it met the side of the house and then down to the shadowed boards.

Hadn't he left something there?

"I told you it might be difficult," Travis called. "Come back to bed, Baby."

Ken did as he was asked. He turned away from the balcony. Travis lay naked on the bed, looking as handsome as he always did, but he also looked concerned, his deeply tanned face twisted with fret.

"You wanted to see what it would be like," Travis said, sounding ashamed. "I know it wasn't easy for you, but at least you know now."

Names and faces, the ghosts of dreams, floated in his head. Someone named David and a woman named Paula. He couldn't get it all straight. He'd been married. He had had two children, but one of the children had died. The only thing he could remember with any clarity was the constant feelings of dread and a pervasive misery, extending year after year.

At eighteen years old, Ken had the history of a much older man. But how?

"You'll need a second to let it all sink in," Travis said. He ran a hand over his belly, upward to scratch his chest.

"I made you a monster," Ken whispered.

"No, Baby," Travis said. "I made me a monster. There was so much to show you that I wanted to make sure you understood, so I made it a bit of a haunt."

"Understood what?"

"Where shame would lead you."

"I'm not ashamed." Ken sat on the soft, silk duvet. He reached out and grasped Travis's hand where it lay on his chest. The skin beneath his touch was warm and familiar.

"But you want to leave," Travis said. "You have everything you could ever need or want, you have love, but you refuse it. Why would an intelligent man run toward misery? Why would someone so exceptional choose the mundane? You don't have to answer. We both know the answer. He wouldn't. He would not run toward those things. He would, however, run away from something. So, you have to ask yourself what is here that you are so eager to escape? Is it me?"

Ken tried to respond but was interrupted by Travis's thick chuckle.

"Did I suddenly get too ugly, too old?"

"No," Ken said. He leaned forward and put his head on Travis's chest, listened to the soft beating of his heart while his ear warmed on the skin. "Not even close."

"So what else is there? The food isn't good enough? The company is dull? Again, we both know the answers. That's why I created Vicki for you. You wanted a second life, so I gave you a villain that had lived two and three and a dozen lives and as you, perhaps naïvely, pointed out, wasted them. Because that is what you can expect, Baby. That's where shame will take you. It will break your life into unmanageable shards that cut every time you try to juggle them."

"But it's not that simple," Ken said.

A soft tearful voice drifted in from the balcony. Crying. No words. Just sorrow.

Ken pushed away from Travis's chest to get a better sense of the noise. "What's that?"

"One of the Vassals, I'm sure. Likely, he found a less-than-kind suitor for the evening. It's nothing."

Ken nodded his head. Now that his mind was settling, details began to emerge from his muddled thoughts. He'd woken that morning in a kind of panic to be away from Wonderland and Travis. He couldn't say exactly what had sparked this desperate emotion. Maybe it was Crow's death. Puritan was just a kid, Ken's best friend. For him to die so arbitrarily in the middle of the street was just too much to fathom. Sam had died nearly the same way, but Ken didn't know any Sam except for the one he had imagined.

That morning, when he'd told Travis about his sudden urge to leave, the man had tried to console him. "I understand," Travis said, embracing Ken. "But before you go, there's one last story you need to hear."

Ken had made to protest, but Travis *shush*ed him and walked to the bookcase against the wall of the bedroom. Lifting the leather volume down, Travis said, "Do you want to read or should I?"

Confused and feeling anxious, needing to move, to go, to put distance between himself and Wonderland, Ken had told Travis that he was done with stories. He didn't want anymore of those haunted tales in his head.

"I need something real," Ken had said.

"Just one more," Travis had said evenly. "One last story and then you can gather your things and go." The man had walked to the bed, stacked pillows against the carved headboard and lay down. He opened the book, thumbed through its pages. "Now, shall I read or would you rather?"

Ken had been in no mood to sit. He couldn't concentrate on anything but the needling desire to leave.

"Tell me a story," he'd whispered.

So Travis had. Even hours later, late in the evening Ken remembered how startled he'd been by the first line of the tale, how quickly it had woven into his thoughts and pulled him down and into himself.

"Kenneth Nicholson stood at the window of his home and watched the sky darken as he struggled with the news that his son might not live through the night," Travis began. "Like the evening light, his son's life was fading and perhaps would soon flicker out..."

Another sharp sob from the balcony pulled Ken back into the present. Who was out there? Travis smiled up at him from the bed.

"Must'a been quite a heartbreak," he said with amusement, nodding his head toward the open balcony doors.

"Maybe I should check on him," Ken said.

"Oh, he'll be fine. Don't bother yourself. Young hearts break easy, but they heal fast enough."

Something about the voice was familiar, and the more Ken heard it, the less it sounded like a boy. It had the timbre of a girl's voice. He thought about the daughter he'd had in the story Travis had told him. Jennifer.

"I'm going to go check," he said and rose from the bed.

"Always so concerned," Travis said.

"Sounds really upset," Ken said, withholding the pronoun because he was not sure which gender to identify. The cries were decidedly feminine, and they sounded more frightened than sorrowful.

As he crossed the room peering into the night beyond the threshold, Travis said, "Tell me who you would have chosen."

Ken paused and looked over his shoulder. "What do you mean?"

"If you had to decide between David and your family, who would you have chosen?"

"I guess we'll never know."

"Oh, but I have to know how the story ends," Travis said, his voice teasing.

The girl sobbed a final time. Her voice faded from a guttural hiccup to silence.

Ken continued to the doorway. He crossed the threshold onto the balcony and said, "I suppose I would have chosen…" But his declaration was interrupted by a shriek so sharp and feral that it made his skin pimple and his muscles turn to ice.

"Decide!" Travis roared from the bed.

The piercing cry blended with Travis's baritone command. They wove and knotted. The night air wrung with their clashing.

On the balcony to his right, a plain girl of no more than sixteen screamed, holding her hands to her ears in a pose of unqualified hysteria.

Jennifer?

⚜

"Decide!" Bach commanded.

Ken stepped forward out of reflex, turning in time to see his daughter charging forward. Arms outstretched, Jennifer hit Vicki Bach in the chest, her momentum throwing the woman backward.

Vicki's hand fumbled over the fabric of Ken's shirt. Nails tore at his chest seeking purchase. Finally a fist locked around the Thorn.

Vicki Bach teetered on the balcony rail. The banister caught her just behind the knees. Only the pillar and the Thorn grasped in her hands kept Bach from toppling back. Arms wide and legs kicking, she looked like a child on a swing. The Vassals at the gate stepped forward and then froze. They were also curious about this new development, and without instructions, they waited for resolution. The necklace's chain dug into Ken's neck. He stared at Vicki Bach, who closed her eyes. Farther down the balcony, David Lane moaned.

When Vicki opened her eyes, she looked at Ken. "Forever," she said.

With one hand, he grasped the slender golden chain at his neck; with the other, he clutched the back of Vicki Bach's head. Ken broke the chain to which Vicki clutched. He pushed The Thorn forward as he pulled Vicki toward him, burying its pointed stem deep in her throat.

"No," he said, releasing the woman from his grasp.

Vicki Bach emitted a wet gargle as she fell. The support of the pillar was no longer sufficient to maintain her balance, and she toppled backward. Her form almost ceased moving. The body seemed to hover endlessly in the air. Her eyes never left his. Ken had expected to witness a different expression on the coldly beautiful face—rage, maybe even relief—but what he saw was nothing less than absolute terror. Then the legs pulled up, sending the body into a headlong dive. Vicki Bach's face crushed on the flagstones below, her torso and legs slapping the pavement in turn.

Ken stepped away from the railing. Jennifer, sobbing wildly next to him, eased up to his side and wrapped her arms around his waist, burying her head in his chest. Below, Paula spun on the two boys by the corridor, but they'd had enough sport, and their meal ticket lay broken on the ground before them. The last Vassals backed away into the corridor and were gone.

David?

Ken looked over his shoulder, into the shadow at the end of the terrace. David lay propped against the siding, staring at the floor of the balcony. His features were difficult to read amid the shadows, but he didn't move. That was clear enough.

With great care, Ken separated himself from his sobbing daughter. Still charged with prickling adrenaline, he approached David quickly and knelt down at the man's side. He spoke his name and reached out a hand to touch the handsome face. His fingertips were met with moist, cool skin.

David continued to stare at the boards, not responding to the voice or the touch.

"David?" he whispered.

Still, no answer.

EPILOGUE: TOMORROW

One morning, Ken woke to the familiar décor of his bedroom in Austin. He didn't want to get out of bed yet. The light filtering through the shades was gray and weak, the sun again obscured by clouds. It was the third such overcast day in a row. Hardly the kind of weather one wanted on his birthday.

He slid his palm over the sheets. The fabric was still warm, and he rolled over into the recently vacated space. He lay on his back, looking at the ceiling.

Fifty-two, he thought. Today, he was fifty-two years old.

Usually, his birthdays came and went, marked by a celebration or a fine meal, some gifts, but he never felt any sense of change. They were days fundamentally like any other, made important by the space they occupied on the calendar, not by any identifiable change in him. Just coins to be collected in a jar, eventually adding up to whatever sum he was owed.

Today was different. He was different. In a few hours, he'd be getting on a plane, flying back to New Orleans. Paula had apologized a dozen times for her oversight, scheduling her wedding so that he'd have to fly on his birthday, but her husband-to-be had to accommodate the itineraries of a large family. Apparently, the Reilly clan was enormous.

Ken didn't mind the trip at all. He was happy for Paula, glad she'd found someone to share her life with after all of these years. Detective Reilly was a good man, and since he'd retired from the police force to write a crime thriller, Paula wouldn't have to spend her days driving herself crazy with worry about the well-being of her second husband. When she spoke about Dan Reilly, she sounded happy, and Ken was grateful for it.

Jennifer would be at the wedding. She had flown in from Spain last week.

After that last night in Wonderland, she'd gone to see her grandparents in El Paso, and she'd never really come back. These days she preferred the vistas of foreign cities to home, but she called and wrote long e-mails. He'd spoken to her the night before. Jennifer wished him a "Happy, happy birthday." She gushed about the cottage she was renting in Madrid. Her partner, Leslie, a young woman she'd met in Austria, was still with her. Leslie also wished him well and told him that she couldn't wait to finally meet "my beautiful J's father."

Finally, unable to excuse any further laziness, Ken swung his legs out of bed. He pulled on his robe and walked downstairs to the kitchen, where he was met by the scent of coffee. He poured himself a cup and read the note, sitting next to the pot: *Back in a minute. Birthdays demand donuts.*

Ken smiled and replaced the sheet of paper on the counter. He walked through the living room and down the hall to his study. He set his mug on the desk, booted up his computer, then turned away. He crossed to the bookcase and lifted a silver frame from the shelf, his gaze drawn, as it always was to the handsome face and the crystal-green eyes. Ken looked at this picture every day, knowing that things could have ended so differently.

The paramedics had gotten David's heart beating again; they'd brought life back to his eyes before taking him out of Brugier's damnable estate. The relief that flooded Ken had sent him to his knees, weeping. They lived together. They were happy. They made love like teenagers, frequently and passionately. They traveled and invited friends over for dinner parties, but most nights, they lay curled up in each other's arms on the sofa, watching television or chatting or reading. Just being together. That was enough. Or, rather, that would have been enough.

It didn't happen. That was just a story Ken told himself whenever he looked at the photograph.

David died that night. Neither Ken's initial attempt at resuscitation, nor the more professional efforts of the paramedics had gotten his heart beating again. So, Ken had held him tightly to his chest, stroked his hair.

Even then, on that balcony, with Jennifer sobbing at his back and policemen shouting in the courtyard below, Ken had begun to write this happy ending. Devastation gnawed at his chest, sickened him with its scrabbling claws. To escape this beast, he'd retreated into his mind, where he could imagine David's arms returning his embrace.

This tale and others like it, stayed with him for the months following his last night in Wonderland. Ken drank. He slept. When awake, he looked for answers and told himself stories about what might have been. The hours and days stretched before him, blank pages needing to be filled. Alone in the Austin house, secluded and aching, he let questions and fictions distract him, committing them to the empty leaves of his life.

What if? Maybe... If only I'd... We might...

So many white sheets requiring something, anything, because the pages never stopped turning.

Four months after his son's death, Ken found a gold money clip Bobby had given him as a Christmas present. He'd stared at it for three hours before passing out in a chair. When he woke, the clip was gone.

Its disappearance panicked him. After all that he'd witnessed, Ken couldn't be sure that he'd ever held the clip at all.

The cleaning woman found it two days later. The gold trinket had fallen out of his hand during the night and bounced under the chair. When it was returned to him, Ken felt foolish but oddly better. He wrapped the gift in a tissue and placed it in the bottom drawer of the cabinet he kept in his study's closet. It rested there still, undisturbed, for over a year.

Now, holding the picture of himself and David, Ken walked toward the closet. The pang this picture brought to his chest was vague now. Present but not powerful as it once had been. Opening the door, he looked at the cabinet standing against the back wall amid the closet's gloom.

Three months ago, he'd met a man named Ed Schroff at a cocktail party held in celebration of Ken's retirement. Schroff, a bull of a man with a square face and a deep, resonant voice, had come as the guest of Ken's former assistant Donna. They'd chatted and laughed and ended up in bed together a week later.

They hadn't spent a night apart since.

Ken knelt down and opened the bottom drawer of the cabinet. His gaze landed on a white tuft of tissue sitting atop a small gold-leafed box. The money clip—the gift from his son. He looked at the picture again and knew he would never see it the same way. From this point forward it would be a token of memory, a bit of pleasant history. The story it told belonged to another time.

Tell me a story.

In the photograph, he and David stood arm in arm on a grassy hill outside a small village twenty minutes from Florence. Behind them, the sunset painted the sky, casting oranges and reds onto their shoulders as the two men smiled into the lens.

From the front of the house, Ed's voice boomed, reaching for him. They'd have breakfast, then pack for the trip to New Orleans, where Paula was getting married. He'd be introduced to his daughter's girlfriend, whom he already liked. Ed would fuss over his bow tie and crack jokes about Paula's father.

Ken put the photograph in the drawer and slowly slid it closed.

The time for stories was done.

« THE END »

ACKNOWLEDGMENTS

This is, at best, an abbreviated list of those whose knowledge, support, and kindness made this book possible. Through encouragement and inspiration, these folks kept the wheels turning—Linda Addison, P. D. Cacek, Ellen Datlow, Kristine Dikeman, Gerard Houarner, Jack Ketchum, David Thomas Lord, Mark McLaughlin, James A. Moore, Jane Osnovich, Lori Perkins, Joseph Pittman, Michael Rowe, Sarah Self, and Amy Stout.

For their friendship and critical acumen—Daniel Braum, Nicholas Kaufmann, Sarah Langan, K. Z. Perry, and Stefan Petrucha. They all get cake.

A special thank you to L. William "Bill" Jones for telling me a story.